D0961300

Golden Years

Also by Andrew M. Greeley

from Tom Doherty Associates

All About Women

Angel Fire

Angel Light

Contract with an Angel

Faithful Attraction

The Final Planet

Furthermore!: Memories of a Parish Priest

God Game

The Priestly Sins

Star Bright!

Summer at the Lake

White Smoke

Emerald Magic (editor)

Sacred Visions (editor with Michael Cassutt)

The Book of Love (editor with Mary G. Durkin)

Bishop Blackie Ryan Mysteries

The Bishop and the Missing L Train

The Bishop and the Beggar Girl of St. Germain

The Bishop in the West Wing

The Bishop Goes to The *University*

Nuala Anne McGrail Novels

Irish Gold

Irish Lace

Irish Whiskey

Irish Mist

Irish Eyes

Irish Love

Irish Stew!

The O'Malleys in the Twentieth Century

A Midwinter's Tale

Younger Than Springtime

A Christmas Wedding

September Song

Second Spring

ANDREW M. GREELEY

The Sixth Chronicle of the O'Malley Family in the Twentieth Century

A TOM DOHERTY ASSOCIATES BOOK

New York

This is a work of fiction. All the characters and events portrayed in this novel are either fictitious or are used fictitiously.

GOLDEN YEARS

This book is printed on acid-free paper.

A Forge Book
Published by Tom Doherty Associates, LLC
175 Fifth Avenue
New York, NY 10010

www.tor.com

Forge® is a registered trademark of Tom Doherty Associates, LLC.

Library of Congress Cataloging-in-Publication Data

Greeley, Andrew M., 1928–
Golden years : the sixth chronicle of the O'Malley family in the twentieth century
Andrew M. Greeley.—1st ed.
p. cm.
ISBN 0-765-30338-8
EAN 978-0765-30338-7
1. O'Malley, Chucky (Fictitious character)—Fiction. 2. Irish American families—Fiction. 3. Mentally ill women—Fiction. 4. Fathers—Death—Fiction. 5. Missing persons—Fiction. 6. Irish Americans—Fiction. 7. Middle aged men—Fiction. 8. Married people—Fiction. I. Title.

PS3557.R358G65 2004
813'.54—dc22

2004047175

First Edition: November 2004

Printed in the United States of America

0 9 8 7 6 5 4 3 2 1

In memory of Monsignor John M. Hayes,
the counterpart of John Raven in this story
and indeed a man of gold and silver,
on my own golden year in the priesthood
to which he first attracted me

Descendants of

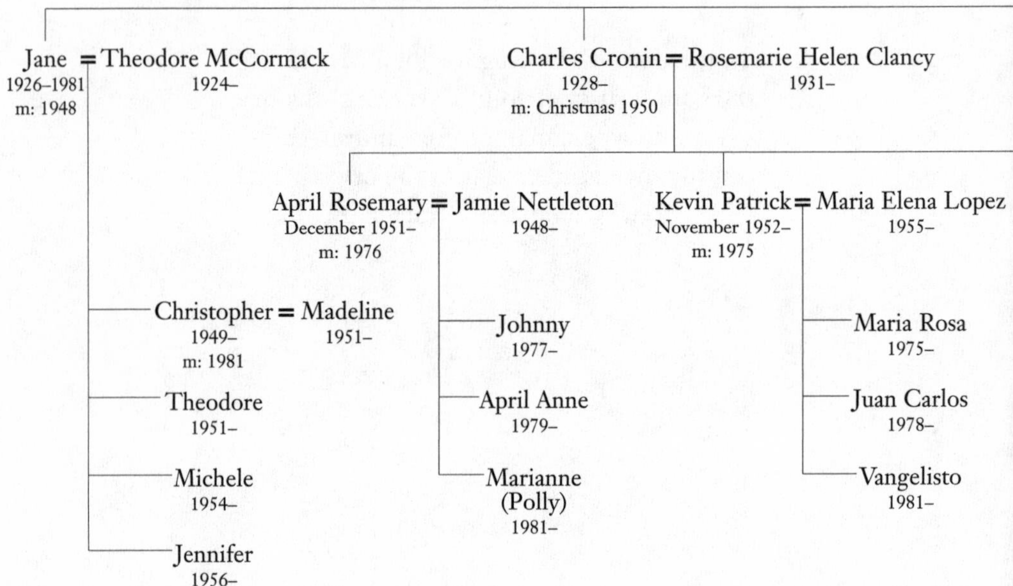

JOHN E. O'MALLEY

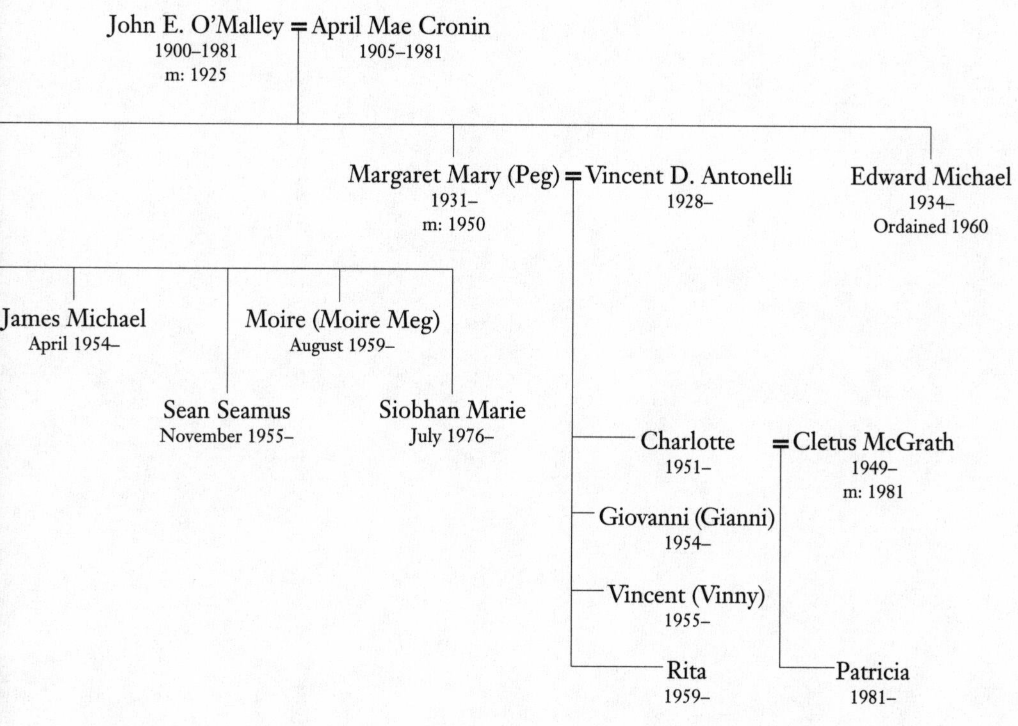

Chuck O'Malley's prediction in the early 1980s is not fiction. To read the original prediction, see *The Book of Predictions* by David Wallechinsky, Amy Wallace, and Irving Wallace (Morrow, 1980). See also the comments by Willard Mathias of the Office of National Estimates, which Chuck quotes to President Reagan. The comments are cited on page 374 of Robert Dallek's *An Unfinished Life: John F. Kennedy 1917–1963* (Little, Brown, 2003).

Chapter One

Rosemarie

"This country," the ambassador said in his most ambassadorial tone, "will implode in ten years."

"On what grounds do you make that prediction, sir?"

The lean, hungry man with thin black hair who had been introduced to us as the second secretary of the US embassy in Moscow was obviously the CIA resident.

At that very moment we would soon learn, back home in Chicago where we should have been, tragedy was stalking our family.

"It should be obvious to all of you," Ambassador O'Malley said, with serene confidence. "It's falling apart. When it does collapse, most—probably all—of the constituent republics will depart quickly. The satellite countries—which our presently gloriously reigning president has deigned to characterize as an 'evil empire' will also leave. After six decades the Bolshevik revolution will reside in the ash can of history."

My husband is a man of many different personae. He can slide back and forth among them with considerable ease, not to say delight. Usually he is Chucky Ducky, my adorable and funny little redhead lover, about whom I write an occasional story for *The New Yorker.* However, tonight at the formal embassy dinner (myself the only woman present), he had become Charles Cronin O'Malley, ambassador of the United States of America with all the rights, privileges, and solemnity pertaining thereto. In fact, his term as ambassador to the Federal Republic of Germany had ended in 1964, seventeen years ago. Yet, as he explained to me, "once an ambassador, always an ambassador, just like being West Side Irish."

He was also known as one of the "wise men" who had advised a hapless Lyndon Johnson to withdraw from Vietnam in 1968. In the world of the Foreign Service he was therefore by definition wise, even if he doesn't look like it. He was treated with enormous respect, the kind of which the family never accorded him. So when a young member of the embassy staff encountered us on the Moscow subway the day after we returned from Siberia, it became mandatory that the embassy invite us to dinner.

They were disappointed and a little miffed that we had not announced our arrival at the beginning of the trip. They could have given us some warnings. Surely the KGB knew who we were and would shadow us during our month of wandering the Soviet outback. They did not trust people with cameras. They were not eager to have the impoverishment of the Soviet Union revealed to the media of the world.

Chucky replied with ambassadorial aplomb that the secret police agents who were our guides had been very friendly and offered no objections to the pictures of ordinary Soviet people that he had snapped. "Snapped" was his word. My husband's persona as a photographer required that he create the image of a little kid with a Kodak box camera, such as the one he had used to take my picture when I was ten years old, a photograph which still shocks me. He saw too much.

"The Russians," he said, "are a friendly, gregarious people. They love to have their pictures taken."

This was much less than the truth. However, the Russians were as likely as anyone else to succumb to West Side Irish charm. Our guides could see no harm to the Soviet image in what we were doing. All we did was "snap" pictures of families, and kids, and elderly people. We put the camera away when we were near factories or military installations. Only if the secret police had a chance to see all our pictures or to read the notes I had taken would they realize what an indictment of Soviet society our work really was.

We arrived at the embassy with all my notebooks and nearly a hundred rolls of film Chucky had used, the latter in three X-ray-proof bags. The ambassador, a handsome WASP with silver hair and a red face, was only too willing to agree to put them in the diplomatic pouch.

"You may have trouble at the airport," he said. "They'll want to know where all your photos are."

"I'll tell them that they went home in the diplomatic pouch."

He nodded.

"They won't like it but that's just too bad."

Everyone around the dinner table seemed hostile to the Soviet Union. The Cold War was still on. They didn't quite call it the "evil empire," yet their attitude was that the struggle with the Kremlin could go on for decades. Then my dear husband dropped his bomb. He was telling them in effect that all the intelligence on Russia the State Department and the CIA had labored so diligently to assemble was dead wrong.

"I don't quite see it that way, Mr. Ambassador," the DCM (Deputy Chief of Mission) replied after a couple of moments of awkward silence. "I admit that nothing is very efficient here, but I can't imagine people turning out in the streets as they did in 1917."

"They won't have to, Tony." Chuck smiled serenely. "The revolution will come from within the party, some of the middle-level apparatchiks will come into power in the next ten years and replace such senile Neanderthals as Brezhnev, Chernenko, and Andropov. They'll try to change the system to solve some immediate problems, and it will all fall apart."

"The party won't let that happen," the resident said dismissively.

"The party has made the same mistake that the Catholic Church made. It educated its technicians and middle management. They have begun to think for themselves. Such people become revolutionaries."

"I have never met any revolutionaries in the *nomenklatura*," the DCM said sternly. "They don't promote men with any tendency to think for themselves."

"How much of their gold reserve do they spend each year to buy foreign grain?" Chuck fired back.

"Billions."

"In a country which has some of the best farmland in the world?"

"They keep trying," a younger staff member observed. "When they succeed in making their agriculture work, they'll become a forbidding adversary."

"We've been threatening ourselves with that possibility for a couple of decades . . . And when they run out of gold reserves?"

More silence around the table.

"Socialism doesn't work," my husband continued. "Never has. Never will. The workers have no motivation to work. Stalin is no longer around to put a gun to their heads. So they don't work. The regime is both incompetent and corrupt. Male life expectancy is down to fifty-seven years, less than many third world countries. A quarter of the men are chronic alcoholics. Highway deaths are higher than in the United States, and they have a tenth of the cars. They make the best ice cream in the world, however."

"Many countries are both corrupt and incompetent," the ambassador, all diplomatic charm, said. "All of Africa, for example."

"The African countries have not promised their people a dream of the good life for seven decades and they are not industrial giants with an educated population. The evidence is all around: one of the great industrial powers in the world is grinding to a halt, good ice cream or not."

"We don't quite see it that way, sir," the resident said. "And our experience is much longer and has more depth than your month of wandering about with a camera."

"The lens of a camera has no ideological filters," Chuck replied. "It sees the results of a collapsing social structure which you don't see."

That was an insult. My husband was arguing that he was more of an expert on the Soviet Union than men who had spent much of their lives studying it, precisely because he was free of their Cold War ideological blinders.

I had warned him as the embassy limousine had delivered us to the door that he should not start a fight and insult our hosts.

"We both agree about what we saw, Chuck," I said. "But we look at this country from the perspective of the West Side of Chicago. The people we saw out there in Sverdlovsk might see it differently."

"They all call it Yekaterinburg," he replied and kissed me gently. "They know that this regime is only temporary, even if it has lasted seventy years."

I knew then we were in for a fight.

The ambassador deftly intervened to change the subject. Chuck, knowing that he had made his point, just as deftly backed off.

"Well, you creamed them," I said as the limo took us back to the Cosmos Hotel.

"Yeah, I won't say the same thing to the president when I take his picture next week."

"The heck you won't!"

There is a tradition dating back to Ike that my husband "take a picture" as he calls his work of every president. He was not looking forward to the trip to the White House to "snap" a man he called "a washed-up actor."

"Idiots who try to build a Hilton and end up with a dump like this," he said as we climbed out of the limo, "can't stay in power much longer."

The tile was peeling off the tub in our bathroom, the curtains hung at half-mast, the TV worked intermittently. The staff were indifferent, but not unfriendly, especially when Chuck tipped them with Yankee dollars.

He had slept most of the way to the hotel. My husband travels very badly. I was astonished that he had survived the Trans-Siberian Railway, the endless rides on very bad roads, and the crazy pilots on Aeroflot's domestic routes who seem to feel that they had to prove they were totally unafraid of death. Indeed he kept muttering that we were pushing our respective guardian angels too far. It would take him a couple of weeks to recoup once we were home. My role on these trips, besides that of a film provider and an occasional lover, was to take care of him. This time I was worn-out too. We were a long way from home.

It is probably clear already that I love him deeply, passionately, permanently. He is not much to look at, unless you happen to like pint-size altar boys with red hair like a wire brush, gentle blue eyes, and a grin that would melt your heart. His exact height is classified information but at five-eight I tower over him, even when I don't wear heels, which I usually do. He doesn't mind that because he is slow to anger except when pushed. Then it's not Clancy who lowers the boom as in the song which I say is about my ancestors, it's Chucky lowers the boom.

His strongest appeal is that he is a sweet, gentle, passionate man. The first time he kissed me at Lake Geneva when I was, I think, ten years old, he persuaded me that a man might love me someday, which had always seemed impossible. Then the first time he held me in his arms, the day I tried to drown myself after a Fenwick prom, the whole world seemed kind and good. Neither of us knew much about sexual love when we were married, but he was a confident and tender partner and I learned from him.

I have never made love with another man and never will, so I don't have any comparative data. But from listening to conversations among women—at which I usually remain silent—I think he's a pretty spectacular lover. He knows me completely. I cannot hide from him. His tenderness and sweetness completely overwhelm me. All he has to do is to look at me with desire, much less touch me, and I surrender. Indeed I abandon myself completely to him.

I shivered and not from the cold when we left the limo after our trip to the embassy.

"It already feels like winter," I said. "And it's only September."

"I'm glad we took the film over to the embassy today," he said sleepily. "Doubtless they've searched our hotel room while we were gone, since they know we're leaving tomorrow."

"Shouldn't they have done it last night?"

"Like I said, they're incompetent."

Back in our room, Chuck noted that the search of our clothes had been inept.

"Clumsy oafs. James Bond wouldn't have left any traces at all. Now they're trying to figure out what we did with the film."

"They'll search us at the airport."

"But they won't try to prevent us from leaving. They don't need an incident just now."

"I hope you're right."

I wanted to be flying over Lake Michigan on our way home, more than my husband did.

I found a plain envelope in one corner of the room. Inside was a cable.

"Chucky, listen to this: 'Joe Raftery wants to talk to you. Urgent. Vince.' "

Vincent Antonelli, attorney-at-law, was married to our sister Peg. He was, as they say in Chicago, clout heavy.

"Joe Raftery, you remember him of course, Rosemarie?"

"Fenwick football team?"

"He was the unfortunate end to whom Vince's pass was intended when the evil Ed Murray blocked it and the equally evil Mount Carmel went to the city championships."

Ed and his wife Delia, one of Chuck's sometime sweethearts, lived just down the street from us. They are anything but evil.

"Chucky Ducky," I said with some impatience, "you know damn well that's not the way the game ended. You caught the blocked pass and stumbled into the end zone. We beat Carmel."

"Pure legend."

"Then you saved my life when I tried to drown myself in Lake Geneva after the prom."

"I have no recollection of that event either. Perhaps you tricked me into pulling off your prom dress."

He was hopeless. He was also a mystery. I had yet to understand him completely and never would. He knew damn well that he had beaten Carmel and saved my life. Why did he deny these events? Part of the game no doubt, a game in which I was a player, but I didn't know the rules.

I grew warm at the thought of our subsequent embrace that afternoon. So I changed the subject back to Joe Raftery.

"Wasn't he a tall, slender boy with sad brown eyes and the mystical glow?"

"He was quiet, perhaps because he didn't have anything to say."

"What happened to him?"

"He ignored the blandishments of the Golden Dome and went off to Leland Stanford, Junior, Memorial University where he was an all-conference end. Then he played for the Los Angeles Rams, even though he failed to catch Vince's pass. I believe he married a starlet, then passed into the obscurity of La La Land twilight."

"What do you think he wants?"

"What we all want at one time or another—help."

"Will we help him?"

"I fear, Rosemarie my darling, now that we are in our golden years, we are too long in the tooth for these adventures."

"Speak for yourself, Chucky Ducky, I'm not in my golden years yet."

"In another month . . ."

"The world might come to an end first."

"Speaking of removing gowns." His fingers touched the zipper of my dress. I knew I was doomed. He played idly with the top of the zipper, knowing that such actions turn me on. After forty years or so of watching me closely, my husband senses my every mood, my every need, my every reaction. I'm putty in his hands, so to speak, not that I mind it.

"Chucky!" I protested for the record. I am not quite his sex slave, not exactly.

"Hero has routed bad knights," he whispered as he kissed my neck, "now he must ravish the defenseless matron."

I sighed, again in insincere protest. It is by no means a bad thing to have a husband who understands you so completely.

He undressed me slowly and delicately, sweeping aside the remnants of my womanly modesty. I shivered in momentary embarrassment as I always do. Then I felt my body and soul swell with great longing. He played with me gently, teased me with his fingers and his lips, nibbled on me with his teeth and then, after I had begged repeatedly that I could no longer endure his depredations, he entered me and carried me off into a firestorm of ecstasy.

"Not all that long in the tooth," I laughed weakly when my breath returned. We both laughed together and gathered each other in our arms and fell into satisfied sleep.

The phone rang from a great distance. I ignored it. Where was I anyway? Why was I sleeping in a sloping bed? What was wrong? Why didn't Chuck answer the phone? Anyway it was a dream, wasn't it?

Finally, to shut it up, I picked up the receiver and turned on the almost useless bed lamp.

"Rosemarie Clancy," I said hoarsely.

"Hi, Rosie, it's your intermediate daughter."

Bad connection. Dammit, we were still in Russia where all connections are bad.

"What's wrong!" I screamed.

"Gramps died this afternoon. Massive heart attack. Grams said that there are worse ways to die."

I covered my breasts with the sheet. You shouldn't talk to your daughter naked, especially on a bad connection.

"Moire Meg, he can't be dead!"

She had metamorphosed recently into "Mary Margaret," her baptismal name because she liked the "Catholic sound of it." Now was no time for that stuff.

"Grams found him reading in his favorite chair. She thought he'd fallen asleep."

"How is she!"

"You know Grams, Rosie," my totally gorgeous red-haired child's voice was calm and even. It would be. "She's Irish like the rest of us. No hysteria. Quiet tears. The usual kind of comment."

"Which was?"

"I'm not going to pray for the repose of his soul. Fifty-six years married to me is enough purgatory for the poor man. Then everyone laughed. Still the Crazy O'Malleys."

I laughed too.

"Who's in charge?"

I knew it was all a dream. People die, but not my foster father.

"Aunt Peg is still numb. Everyone is. So I guess I'm in charge."

Naturally. People said that she had Chuck's red hair and my figure and her grandfather's cool. But he had died the first time in 1918 so he could afford to be cool.

"Rosie, are you still there?"

"I guess I'm numb too, dear."

"That's all right, Rosie . . . are you coming home tomorrow?"

"Today . . . No, yesterday your time . . . No, that's wrong . . . Wednesday afternoon on Aer Lingus if we can make the change in Shannon . . ."

"Uncle Vince and I will meet you."

"Is the wake tonight?"

"Thursday and Friday, funeral at St. Ursula, of course, on Saturday. Father Ed will say the Mass, Father Raven will preach, Father Keenan will concelebrate, and Jimmy will be the deacon. One eulogy. Chuck will give it."

"You decided all of these things?"

"Someone had to. So I was Ms. Take Charge again . . . Father Ed is a totally cool priest. More quiet than the rest of you, but a wonderful priest."

"How's Shovie?"

Siobhan Marie, my youngest daughter.

"Like the rest of us . . . You know Grandpa doted on her . . . She wants you to come home right now."

"Tell her we're on our way."

"It will be good to see you again, Rosie."

"We've been away too long."

"I didn't say that."

I couldn't cope with her. Never could. She could, however, cope with me, so it was all right.

"Hug everyone for me, especially the Good April."

"I will . . . You'll tell Chucky?"

"Of course, I don't know how he'll react."

"He's Irish, Rosie, like the rest of us."

"Yes."

The tears were unaccountably falling down my cheeks.

"Rosie . . ."

"Yes, dear?"

"I love you very much, both of you."

"Now I'm really going to cry."

"Me too."

Mary Margaret O'Malley at twenty-one was cool and self-possessed, the woman who would take charge when "Rosie" was away and Aunt Peg was out of action, and "Chuck" was sleeping off a sexual romp in a broken bed in Moscow. Yet beneath the cool were the combined fires of her two passionate parents.

I must say something about Peg, my sister-in-law, sister, confidante, mother confessor, and best friend for almost all of my life. We're so close that the Good April claimed that we had our first periods on the same day. Actually mine was the day before hers.

I will always remember the day in first grade, feeling lonely because no one seemed to want to talk to me and I was afraid to talk to them. I was walking home on Menard Avenue and this little girl, pretty with brown hair and intense brown eyes caught up with me.

"I'm Peg," she said.

"I'm Rosemarie."

"What a pretty name . . . Can we be friends?"

"I'd like that very much."

Later, I can't remember exactly how old we were, she took me over to her house, a small, disorderly second story of a two flat near Menard and Augusta. It was a house full of love and laughter and I wished I could stay because there was none of either in my house. We had bonded, as the kids say now, instantly. Slowly and without quite realizing it I became part of the Crazy O'Malleys. My shrink says that relationship has been my salvation.

She had this funny big brother with red hair and kind eyes and a smile which was also a grin that lighted the whole room and I fell in love with him too because he was so nice. I had to fight with him and he with me, because that's what little kids do when they fall in love. Peg and I have seen one another through good times and bad and always talk to each other on the phone every day, except when I'm in some dumb place like Russia. We push each other about exercise and diet and that sort of stuff and are very competitive in a good way. I'd be dead if it were not for Peg.

When the O'Malleys made a lot of money after the war—he was a successful architect—and moved into their big home on New England Avenue in north Oak Park—there was a bedroom that was permanently designated as "Rosie's room."

When we were teens, Chucky compared us to two jungle cats, lithe, handsome, and extremely dangerous. I think he said tiger and leopard, but he insists that he did not because tigers and leopards don't live in the same places. We pretended to be deeply offended, but in fact we were flattered. Brats!

I would have to wake Chuck, now the titular head of the clan, as if that mattered with all the Irishwomen who surrounded him.

I shook him gently. He grumbled and turned away, burying his head in a thin pillow, the best the Russians could do.

"Chucky," I shook him, "wake up!"

He rolled over and glared at me. Then seeing my tears, he sat up.

"Who's dead, Rosemarie?"

I had known and worshipped the man for more than forty years, slept with him for thirty years, and bossed him all the time, except when he saved me from alcoholism. Yet he was a mystery to me. How many men would have reveled in his role as the funny little redhead in my stories? There were depths beneath depths in him, fascinating depths indeed, but so far in our lives impenetrable.

"Your dad. April found him asleep in his reading chair, his last afternoon nap. Massive heart attack."

He lay back in the bed, folded his hands behind his head, and closed his eyes.

"There are worse ways to die."

"That's what the Good April said."

He smiled.

"She would . . . Who called?"

"Ms. Take Charge, who else?"

He smiled again.

"What are her plans?"

"Wake Thursday and Friday. Mass at St. Ursula. Father Ed says it. John Raven preaches. . . ."

"And I give the eulogy?"

He opened his eyes. Tears had appeared in the deep blue depths. They broke my heart. I touched his bare chest gently.

"Titular head of the family."

"Emphasis on the first word."

"Naturally!"

"Mary Margaret and Siobhan send their love."

I moved my fingers across his chest.

"I knew that this would happen, sooner indeed rather than later. Yet parents are not supposed to die, especially when one is in Moscow."

More tears, quiet tears.

"Rips you apart?" I said as I continued to caress him. He knew what I was up to. His eyes shifted to my breasts after which, I had often told him, he had lusted even before I grew them.

"The door slams shut, Rosemarie. I'm alone, an orphan."

"April is still alive."

"Not for long. Without him she won't want to stay here on earth."

My parents had died long ago, my mother in a drunken fall down the basement stairs, my father in a Mafia explosion. Neither had loved me very much, not that they were to blame for that. Yet I still missed them. In my dreams I often imagined them still alive (the preconscious, Maggie Ward, my shrink, had told me rejects death) and begging that I help them, which of course I could not do. What would Chuck's dreams be like? What would the regrets be in his dreams?

"Now we're the parents about whose death our children will look forward to in denial and fear," I said.

"The cycle of life . . ."

Chapter Two

Our escape from Moscow was a nightmare. We were tired from the trip, heavy with grief, drugged from our romps of love, and desperate to get home. We had a roll and a cup of tea that the staff of the coffee shop seemed reluctant to provide. It took forty minutes to collect our passports and check out. No porters were willing to bring down our luggage. I stopped our limo to Sheremetyevo just as the driver tried to abandon us. Twenty American dollars was enough to persuade him to wait a little longer. I smelled conspiracy. The secret police wanted us to miss our plane so they could question us further about our film. My good wife insisted that as someone who had preached to the embassy staff about the inefficiency of Russia I should recognize incompetence and indifference when I saw them. I was not convinced.

Because we had made the terrible mistake of flying Aeroflot, we had to leave on our return ticket if we wanted to get out of Moscow. Hence we had to depart from Sheremetyevo, a depressing barn, instead of the new international airport Domodedovo, which was supposed to be more efficient. Ms. Take Charge had arranged with Aer Lingus that when we arrived at Shannon, they would rescue us from the Ruskies and put us on their plane to Chicago. The layover was an hour and a half. If we missed the connection, we would have to take a flight to Boston in late afternoon or wait till the next day.

Rosemarie had convinced me that we should take Aeroflot because we would have the opportunity to take snapshots of our fellow passengers. However, they were mostly drunk when the plane took off from Chicago. We had huddled in our broken seats save for occasional cautious trips to the bathroom. The "fasten seat belt" signs were apparently only advisory, perhaps because they were in Russian as was the pilot's advice that we should return to our seats. The cabin attendants were rude and bossy. The food was terrible. One could obtain a vodka quickly enough, but a cup of tea did not seem possible. The flight over was rough. We bounced around all the way to Shannon and our Tupelov shook like it might tear itself apart. Our singing, drinking fellow passengers did not seem worried about the turbulence. However, they were too drunk to notice the rough ride. I wanted to get off at Shannon and take pictures of the Irish instead of the Russians. My wife, however, insisted that we had a commitment to visit Russia and we had to honor it. As always I agreed with her.

"Besides, she said, these people are so wiped out that they will sleep all the way to Sheremetyevo."

"What's that?"

"The Moscow airport."

"Do they have a gulag there?"

How can I describe my Rosemarie? The most notable quality is her enormous willpower. She was an alcoholic in her early teens. Yet when I threatened to end our marriage, she stopped drinking—with the help of a couple of first-class psychiatrists. She had a terrible childhood—an abusive father and a drunk mother. Yet she determined to be a good mother and manages our large brood with great skill and affection. Though she was raped by her father, she decided that she would be good in bed and surely is—a languorous and creative lover. Despite six pregnancies she ruled that she was not about to lose her glorious figure and by rigorous exercise and dieting, she has not. She wanted to be a writer and now she writes for *The New Yorker,* mostly about an inept little redhead who in the end is always maddeningly right about the big things in life. She is Ms. Take Charge. When she enters a room, she radiates authority and competence, a trait she has passed on to Mary Margaret. In our ordinary public relationship she certainly runs the show. Yet privately and especially in the bedroom she is helpless and vulnerable, though sometimes very aggressive in a vulnerable way. When we walk into a restaurant, every eye turns to her, and herself a few weeks short of fifty. I won't tell you what she looks like with her clothes off. It's none of your business.

She is, in short, a whole lot of wife. Mind you, I'm not complaining.

She was right about the Moscow airport when we had first arrived, as she usually was about such things. Moreover, the smiling teenager who glanced at our passports and waved us through immigration did not seem like a gatekeeper at the entrance to a police state. One smile from the pretty lady with whom I sleep seemed to have melted his socialist heart. The battered taxi which was our "limo" to the Cosmos Hotel was waiting for us in the dark and, save for a detour to fill up his gas tank, the cabbie took us directly to the Cosmos. Eventually, after many delays at registration, apparently over our passports and visas, we finally stumbled into our room, which occasioned a scream of horror from my fastidious wife.

We had studied Russian before the trip. I knew a few words which caused many of the people we met to laugh when I tried to pronounce them. Rosemarie, however, is a good mimic and a quick study at languages. She was hardly a fluent Russian speaker but her mature beauty went a long way. People smiled at her and laughed at me. So it always has been.

However, she agreed with me that we would try to dump Aeroflot at Shannon and hitch a ride back to Chicago on Aer Lingus. Enough of Russia already, all right.

On the ride back to Sheremetyevo when we were going home, I despaired of our ever leaving Russia. There were traffic jams all along the dubious superhighway. Our driver probably had a couple of drinks before he picked us up. We would miss the plane, the secret police would arrest us slam us into the jail. Rosemarie on the other hand chatted with our driver in broken English and Russian and admitted that she had never met his sister who lived in Detroit.

She gave him an exorbitant tip but we had to drag our luggage into the vast barn by ourselves. We stumbled around seeking the check-in for our flight. Finally, we found what looked like the right desk. Scores of shouting, pushing Russians were crowded around it. We would never fight our way through them. We'd miss the plane but so would most of them.

Rosemarie, who wonders why our intermediate daughter is Ms. Take Charge, always takes care of getting me on and off planes. She waved down a young Russian woman, blond hair, round face, in an Aeroflot uniform, who was wandering about looking both officious and useless.

The woman, Tanya it turned out, smiled brightly in response to the pretty lady in the dark blue business suit with a short skirt. She must have felt sorry for her when she looked at the ridiculous little guy in jeans and a University of Chicago sweatshirt who bumbled after her. She looked at our tickets, our luggage, and the useless little redhead the pretty lady had in tow. She conducted us to a vacant check-in counter, gave us boarding passes, ticketed our luggage for Shannon, and conducted us to passport control. I tagged along between the two women now jabbering like old friends in pigeon English and pigeon Russian. Clearly worthless little redhead was good only for hauling luggage.

The woman proudly displayed a blurred picture of a solemn infant, also blond and round-faced. My wife produced a picture of our brood, children and grandchildren who disproportionately display the hair color of the luggage toter. Tanya threw up her hands in astonishment and hugged my wife. They parted with tears. Typical Russian scene—rude people and friendly people randomly juxtaposed.

"I still don't think we'll make it," I said. "They'll never get our luggage on the plane."

"Hush, Chucky dear. We're in Russia. Nothing ever happens on time."

"Are we there yet, Mommy?" I whined, earning a small chuckle for my efforts.

The rude took over again during the agonizingly long wait in passport control. If they were going to search for our film, this would seem to be the ideal place, especially since the virtuous Tanya had cleared our luggage without examining it. The man who paged through our tickets and our documents was, I thought, big enough to wrestle bears. Probably he dispatched an ursine every evening before consuming a bottle of vodka. He frowned at us, fingered our documents suspiciously, permitted himself an astonished glare when he saw the diplomatic stamp on the passport and pointed at me dubiously. Patently I was too insignificant to be a CIA agent. I nodded, confessing that the idiotically grinning redhead was indeed me. He shook his head in dismay. Finally, five minutes by my watch before departure time, he wielded his stamp like it was a dangerous weapon and imposed large red stars on everything. Then with a jerk of his head, he waved us on to security.

This last hurdle before we got to our Tupelov was perfunctory. They did not even examine Rosemarie's purse or my bruised and easily lost briefcase. Did they not know that we were American spies?

Then as we began the long walk to the boarding gate, the giant from passport control came after us, not running exactly but moving with ponderous speed, a linebacker exiting the field. We were in deep trouble. The KGB or whatever was on to us.

"Here comes trouble," I whispered to my wife.

The bear killer caught up to us, bowed solemnly to me, handed me our passports, and shook his finger as if to warn me that we should not leave without them. Rosemarie said appropriate words of deep gratitude while I stood there staring at the passports like a useless little child.

Which, of course, was what I was.

Rosemarie has long since given up reprimanding me for my sorry performance as a traveler.

"You should have reminded me," I grumbled.

She merely laughed.

We found two seats together on the Tupelov. I ignored the swarm of already intoxicated comrades, even when they were still standing as the plane took off. Let them kill themselves if they want.

"Take a nap, Chucky dear," she said in the maternal tone usually reserved for Siobhan Marie, our five-year-old. "We'll be in Shannon soon and that's the next neighborhood over."

I withdrew into myself and pretended that the routine chaos of an Aeroflot flight didn't exist. Inside myself I found intolerable grief. I sighed deeply with the pain of it. My wife took my hand. She knew that I was suffering from more than my usual travel ennui.

There had been moments of grief previously in my life. I had thought I would lose Rosemarie when I ordered her to seek psychiatric help for her alcoholism. Our two elder children were missing in action during the Vietnam era. Yet, as I knew in my heart of hearts, Rosemarie Clancy was merely waiting for me to, as the song says, lower the boom. I also knew that Kevin Patrick and April Rosemary would reappear, even if at times my faith wavered. The pain was different this time. My loss was permanent, definitive. I would never see my father again, not in this world. I felt like someone had hit me over the head with a hammer, kicked me in the stomach, and stabbed me in the back. All at the same time. My organism, body and soul, had been savaged, violated, crushed. Grief pressed me down, impeded my breathing, tore at my intestines. How long would it last? Probably forever. Even at eighty my father had mourned for his father.

Guilt tormented me. I should have been home for my father's death. I should have been kinder to him during his life. I thought that because I saved him from death in New Guinea when the army was about to ship him there, I had done enough. My whole career was an oedipal rival with his. He was a Cubs fan. I was a Sox fan. He was a Bears fan. I was a Cardinals fan. He was a painter who earned his living as an architect. I became an internationally known photographer who earned his living by taking pictures. All right, at the end of his life his paintings became fashionable. The Worcester Gallery had mounted an exhibit of his work, built around his brilliant *Rom Women.* The retrospective had toured the country, appearing even at the Art Institute and the catalogue, turned coffee-table book, was a great success. *John E. O'Malley: Artist of His Times.* I'm sure he knew that I was behind the scenes, just as I was when I visited the home of the local congressman in our parish at Christmastime in 1941 and explained why it would be a grave mistake to send him to New Guinea. He knew that I had orchestrated his artistic success and that must have dimmed his joy. His son had done again something that he could not do.

Except such thoughts were an injustice to him. I may have been his rival, but he was never mine. He bragged to his friends that Chucky did a wonderful job on the art exhibit. And his wife, the Good April, would protest, "Chucky should never have let them use that picture of me."

The painting was a chaste, mildly erotic, and appealing portrait entitled *Nude Flapper.* The Good April insisted that he had painted it "after we were married . . . Well, almost."

I laughed. The pas de deux of the genders is different in every marriage. My parents' dance was light comedy, the Charleston from their era.

"Do you think Vangie resented my success?" I whispered to Rosemarie.

"What?" she asked.

The rattling of the Tupelov and the drunken carousing of its passengers had drowned out my voice. I asked the question again.

"Go back to sleep, Chucky dear, and don't torment yourself with silly ideas."

We were the Crazy O'Malleys in those distant days of the Great Depression, mostly because we did not take the Depression or anything else all that seriously. We were poor but we always had the best roast beef and the best sherry in our house. And the best music. Neither "Vangie" (short for his middle name "Evangelist") nor April seemed to mind their fall from upper-middle-class prosperity into penury. They had each other, they had their kids, Dad had a job (architect for the Chicago Sanitary District) and life was good. They viewed poverty as a passing phase in their life. "Our ship will come in" was their mantra. I dismissed this easy optimism as foolish.

Only the ship did come in, a very big ship. I went off to Europe in the Army of Occupation in 1946 because I figured that the family didn't have enough money to pay college tuition. When I came home in 1948, we were rich, though Vangie and April (now driving a "cute little white Olds convertible) no more thought of themselves as "rich" than they had as "poor" ten years before.

Unlike my father, I resented our poverty and their, as I saw it, shiftless living. I feared the return of the Great Depression long after my economics training had taught that my fear was absurd. Only at my fiftieth birthday celebration did I officially admit that the Great Depression would probably not return.

I admired Vangie enormously. As the years passed I had come to respect his talent. I realized that his "laid-back" approach to life was the way we all should live. *Admirandus sed non imitandus* as one of the Dominican Fathers at Fenwick High School taught us when discussing the great penances of the saints. I was ambitious, pushy, determined to succeed—as an accountant, of course, not as picture taker. That was too easy. I would become a commodity trader, the king of the corn pit, a calling at which I was a flop. Then when I had tasted success as a picture taker, I pushed that new role into which the women in my life had pushed me with fanatic determination, even if the work was in fact mostly effortless. Dad must have smiled at my frantic efforts.

I used to say that I was the white sheep of the Crazy O'Malleys. The only one who took life seriously.

"You try to be serious, Chucky dear," my mother once said, "and you almost do it, but then you become your adorable madcap self. That's why poor, dear little Rosie is so good for you."

I insist that I'm neither adorable nor madcap. Rosemarie (as I insist that she be called, in vain) is certainly good for me, delicious in fact, but our marriage is a good deal more complex than April thought it would be.

The memories were all happy, yet it was a torment to remember them. They had passed so quickly. I had wasted them. My youth was gone before I knew it and my father was now gone too. I had lost him before I had ever told him how much he meant to me.

Maybe he had always known. Yet how could I be sure?

"Remembering the old days, Chucky?" Rosemarie whispered in my ear.

I nodded.

"All gone."

"You know better than that . . . You were such a nasty little boy I don't know why I started to love you when I was ten and loved you ever since."

"I was in love then too, so of course we had to fight. That's the way of it."

"You looked at me so intensely. You just wanted to take my clothes off."

"Some things haven't changed."

"Well, you're getting better at it!"

I remembered that when my parents discussed whether we would permit Rosemarie to adopt our family, April had some doubts. Would it be good for our children? Would she be as unstable as her mother? They were scruples for the record, not doubts which would change her mind. Dad had laughed. "What difference does one more make?"

Now he was gone and I had yet to learn the lesson of his nonchalant cheerfulness. I never would. That contentious, obnoxious little girl spent only nighttime in her palatial house (or so it seemed) a half block away. She wormed her way into our lives and assumed direction and control of mine. Were there any other fathers in the parish who would have tolerated the daughter of a drunk and a crook?

Not very likely.

Then my anguished mind returned to the delights of the night before. The month-long haul through rural Russia would not have been conducive to sex even if were not deep into my travel-lag slump. Passion returned quickly enough when I beheld my wife in the (kind of) modest dinner gown she had worn to the embassy dinner. Thirty years together and she could still melt me. She was a good enough lay, as I always told her. In fact, I would concede grudgingly that she had improved through the years.

I had absorbed from my father an attitude toward women

that had helped me through the ups and downs of marriage and the cycles of lovemaking. He had always treated the Good April with the reverence and respect that was appropriate for an archduchess. I knew no other way of dealing with women. If as Rosemarie occasionally said, I treated her like a subject of delicate delight, the reason was that I was merely imitating my father.

"How does the wise man eat a big dish of chocolate ice cream?" I would ask my sons when I began to discuss the subject of women with them. "Does not one gobble it down as if there would never again be such a dish?"

Each of them, separately of course, was sensible enough to reply with some version. "That's no way you gulp down ice cream, Dad. You destroy it. Our generation is more civilized. We eat it very slowly, savoring every taste, enjoying every moment."

"So it must be," I would say, "when you make love with a woman."

"A woman is like chocolate ice cream?"

"Only sweeter and more fun."

That would stop them.

And now the man who had initiated me (implicitly and doubtless unconsciously) into the pleasures of married love was gone. Forever. Or at least till we met again somewhere else. Wherever that might be.

My imagination returned to the body of my wife in the heat of sexual arousal. We had exorcised death for a few precious moments the night before. Was death or sexual ecstasy—not unrelated events—the stronger promise? A question of some import. I squeezed my wife's hand. She put her arm around me. No matter how mired in grief and exhaustion I might be we would defy death in our own bed tonight.

I banished my erotic fantasies and returned to the serious business of grief. April, whose health was dubious, would soon follow her husband home, if it is to home that the dead go. Her blood pressure had been high for years. She took her medication regularly only because Dad reminded her. Someone from the family would have to move into the house. Ms. Take Charge, who had a year left at Rosary? How would we keep her out? She was something of an archduchess too.

My mother had her music and her grandchildren and her great-grandchildren. Yet Vangie had been her life since her flapper days at Twin Lakes in the 1920s. She would want to be with him again. More grief.

Would she be a beautiful flapper again in the world to come? Would she and Vangie be young lovers again? Would he no longer be bald?

I figured that if God couldn't work out something like that then he wasn't really God.

"You were wonderful last night," I said to my wife.

"You were fun too, Chucky Ducky. It was a very unromantic trip."

"Sorry. I should never travel any farther than Grand Beach."

"Not even to Notre Dame games?"

I had been thrown out of Notre Dame on a setup thirty years before. I had no love for the school. However, blood tells and I still wanted them to win.

"Only with an overnight at Grand Beach."

We both laughed and snuggled closer, though the seats on an Aeroflot Tupelov were not conducive to such behavior. We both knew that I would travel again. It went with my job. After my disastrous trip (both motion sickness and jet lag) with Ike to Korea in 1952, I swore that I would never travel again and repeated the oath after each trip. I had violated it every time.

"Is sex or death a better symbol of the meaning of human life?" I asked her.

"What do you think?"

"If death is, God doesn't know what He's doing."

We laughed again. Both of us presumed that God knew what He was doing.

I began to sneeze.

"Not *another* cold, Chuck?" A mother impatient with an unruly child who had once again succumbed to a virus which would make her life difficult because the child was a very poor patient.

"No way," I pleaded. "Anyway, it's what results from flying Aeroflot."

"The incubation period is twenty-four hours as you know very well, Chucky. You probably picked it up at the embassy last night."

Guilty as charged.

"We'll never make it to Shannon in time," I groaned, glancing at my watch. "We'll be marooned in a peat bog in West Clare when we should be home organizing things."

A cloud layer covered Europe. Aeroflot pilots never tell you where the flight is or how long it will take. You know that they're about to land only when they put the plane into a steep dive.

"I'm sure Ms. Take Charge will have everything organized when we get there."

This was a routine exchange on our travels. I would express a worry and Rosemarie would smother it with a curt response. Naturally she was usually right. Not always.

Why does the Soviet national airline land at an Irish airport? Their airline industry had proved incapable of producing a plane that could fly nonstop to the Western Hemisphere. So Aeroflot had to touch down at the outer edge of Europe to refuel for flights to the United State and to Cuba. The Irish, who have a wonderful indifference to where any money comes from, were only too willing to sell them landing rights and fuel and to permit them to rampage through the duty-free store—under the watchful eyes of a large group of Garda.

It was alleged by Uncle Vince (husband of my sister Peg, a lifelong ally of Rosemarie in all ventures to keep me in my place and my friend for the same period of time) that passenger agents of Aer Lingus would meet us at disembarkation and transfer us with the magic of the Irish fairie to their flight to Chicago. I didn't believe a word of it. The real Irish, I had always argued, are a people genetically programmed to hospitality, but not necessarily to efficiency. To escape to our nighttime rest in the Clare peat bog we would have to overcome many bureaucrat obstacles. We might end up barred from Ireland, Russia, and the United States.

And meself, as the Irish would say, with a diplomatic passport.

As we tried foolishly to push ourselves off the plane ahead of the Russians, who were world champs at shoving on airplanes, I repeated my concern to Rosemarie, "We might end up barred from Ireland, Russia, and the United States."

"Our own people wouldn't do that to us," she replied firmly, without specifying which country was ours.

In the noisy anarchy of the lounge, a phalanx of green-clad Aer Lingus agents labored to channel the pushing Russians into an orderly line to the duty-free store and passed out brochures in Russian, which many of the potential customers simply crumpled up and threw away. None of the green folk seemed interested in us.

Finally, two young men appeared on the scene, glanced around for a minute, caught our eye, and smiled.

" 'Tis easy to recognize two of our own," the youngster with the curly hair informed us.

"And himself a leprechaun with red hair."

"Welcome to Ireland, Ambassador and Mrs. O'Malley."

"Would you ever have your baggage tickets?"

"Ah very, good. The Ruskies are supposed to off-load them here. Seamus would you ever make sure they do."

"Righto, Sean."

"We have a son," my wife informed them, "named Sean Seamus."

They both laughed as if that were the greatest joke they ever heard.

Sean unlocked a door outside of the lounge, led us down a stairway and up another one. At the head of the stairs was a broadly grinning official of the US Immigration Service.

"Do you have your customs declaration and your passport, Ambassador?" He asked.

"Huh?"

"Here they are, officer." Rosemarie handed over the documents. "My husband doesn't travel very well."

" 'Tis true," I admitted, putting on my Irish face.

He stamped the documents and gave them back to me wife.

"You won't have to clear immigration at O'Hare, ma'am. I don't imagine customs will trouble you."

"Just down here, ma'am." Sean led us down another stairway and out on the tarmac, where a Volkswagen, painted green of course, waited for us.

"Get in the back, Chucky," I was told.

I crawled in. A woman as exquisitely dressed as Rosemarie should not risk rumpling her clothes in the backseat. In the distance, halfway to Galway I estimated, was a green 747.

"Is that our plane?" I grumbled.

" 'Tis," Sean said over the whine of the VW engine. "It won't leave for another half hour. We should have no trouble at all, at all, in claiming your luggage."

The Irish, I had learned, were not bound to tell the absolute truth. There was a tendency to tell you what they think you wanted to hear. I abandoned hope of recovering our luggage.

"You'd think, Mrs. O'Malley," I said, "that the national color of Ireland was green, wouldn't you?"

"Isn't it?" she said, having long ago learned to play the straight person for me when I was showing off.

"What color is it, Ambassador?" Sean asked as we careened toward the 747.

"The national colors of Ireland," I proclaimed, in a tone that the Supreme Pontiff might use in making an infallible statement, "are saffron and blue."

"Not many of your Yanks know that," Sean admitted.

"Irish-Americans," I corrected him. "A Yank is either a player on a hated New York baseball team or a Protestant American."

Sean and my wife favored me with a laugh.

We were led upstairs into the plane and into the deserted first-class section.

"Come back soon," Sean said in farewell.

"We certainly will," Rosemarie agreed.

" 'Tis a more efficient country than Russia," I admitted.

A blond cabin attendant asked whether we'd like something to drink before we took off. Rosemarie settled for a cup of tea.

"Would you ever have a drop of Jameson's?"

"Special reserve, is it, sir?" she grinned.

" 'Tis very dear these days, is it not?"

" 'Tis complimentary in first class."

"Beats vodka." I sighed, as the Irish do. "A double please."

"On the rocks?"

"Would you be thinking I'm an ignorant Yank and meself one of the Tipperary Ryans."

"And yourself not looking like a rogue at all, at all!"

We were alluding to the Irish saying that in the County Tip all the Ryans were rogues, but not all the rogues were Ryans.

"Have a good nap on the way home, Chuck," Rosemarie instructed me. "It will be a busy time."

"Organizing things."

She had the good grace not to tell me that Mary Margaret already had them organized.

I sipped at the Jameson's Special Reserve, then remembered Seamus.

"Ma'am!"

The young woman who had only us to worry about on the trip across came quickly.

"Yes, Ambassador?"

"Where's Seamus?"

"Coming up the steps, sir. I am Kathleen, by the way."

"Your bags are loaded, Ambassador. Here's the checks."

I almost asked him if he were sure. Rosemarie, however, would be upset if I did that.

"Thank you much, Seamus," she said.

"Come back!"

"Count on it!"

I returned to my Jameson's, much of which seemed to have evaporated.

"I've got all their names, Chuck. "We'll write nice letters about them on the way back."

"And send them copies of the book."

"Autographed."

The woman thought of everything.

"I'm afraid I'll have to take your drink, Ambassador," Kathleen said to me.

" 'Tis no problem"—I emptied the tumbler—"at all, at all."

" 'Tis yourself that has the strong stomach."

"Don't count on it," my wife warned her.

Chapter Three

Rosemarie

The second tumbler of a double Jameson's, straight up, because he wasn't an ignorant Yank, went far beyond my husband's usual quota. However, he needed a long nap to prepare for what we'd encounter when we arrived at the Georgian house on New England Avenue. Mary Margaret had certainly imposed some order on the chaos, but Chuck would be expected to whip everything into final shape, no matter how tired he was. And all the while his poor heart was breaking, just like everyone else's, of course, but his relationship with his father was special in a way that no one could quite describe.

I knew for sure that his skills as a lover were absorbed from Vangie, not that anything had ever been said. Chuck had grasped the passion between his mother and father in the ordinary matters of life and modeled himself after his father's style. My sons, tall black Irish—who looked like Union raiders riding under Phil Sheridan (as had one of their ancestors) had told me separately about the chocolate ice cream metaphor.

"Do you like being chocolate ice cream?" each asked.

"Well, it's only a metaphor and I'm a lot more than chocolate ice cream, but, it's not a bad metaphor."

"What kind of ice cream is Dad?" Kevin Patrick had asked.

"An endless malted milk with whipped cream," I replied promptly. Only later did I realize the possible oral connotations the metaphor implied. Well it was good for young men to realize that their parents had an active sex life.

The myth that Chucky was a hapless little urchin protected

by a beautiful mother was part of the game he played when we were traveling. It was true that he was a poor traveler. It was also true that I was more efficient and quick-thinking when we were on the road. Finally, it was true that I didn't trust him not to lose himself on a trip, or so I said. He argued that I was afraid that he would be unfaithful. I laughed and said he wouldn't dare. He admitted that. The real reason I went along on the trip and took care of him was that I missed him when he was gone. Also he was fun even when he could barely keep his eyes open. Witness his performance at the US embassy. Chucky was a great act. I loved him, even when he was exhausted.

Both Tanya and Kathleen whispered that he was adorable, which of course he was, but he was mine and the bitches shouldn't have sized him up. Well, they were nice young women actually and I should feel flattered that they admire my cute little husband.

Also when I traveled with him there was more romance than I would have experienced if I had stayed home while he wandered about the world. Sometimes, like the night before in the Cosmos Hotel, it was quite spectacular. Malted milk with whipped cream—and two butter cookies.

Sometimes even dark chocolate as I described (to myself) the pleasure when he brought me orgasm by highly creative play with my boobs.

I chased away erotic fantasies and thought about his father, poor dear man, as the Good April called him—and everyone else. My own father was a psychopath who had molested me. I hated him with all my heart and soul, though now I think I finally have the grace of forgiveness. Usually. So John the Evangelist O'Malley had become my foster father and delighted in me as much as he did in my inseparable friend, his real daughter Peg, née Margaret Mary.

"I don't want to take your father away from you, Peg."

"You know me well enough, Rosie, to know that I'm not the jealous kind."

"Sure?

"Sure!"

So, however belatedly, I had a paternal role model. Maggie Ward, my permanent shrink, had told me early on that he was the most important one in the family, more than Peg and more even than Chucky. "You needed a father figure and you moved in with a family that had the most attractive father on the block, a good and gentle and tender man, a man of whom you'd never be afraid. That was your salvation."

"No accident that I married his son?"

"What do you think?"

I had never thought of it that way, but I told her that she was probably right.

I had never thanked him properly. Or the Good April either. I just moved in. Indeed when after the war they bought the big old house on New England Avenue in Oak Park, there was a room designated as "Rosie's room" where I could stay all night if I wanted. I had wanted very often. My father had learned by then not to try to control my life.

"It's too bad a night, Rosie dear," April would say, "for you to drive home." It mattered not in the least that it be a lovely early June or mid-October evening.

I would pretend to myself that it made no difference that when Chuck came home from Bamberg, he slept in the same house. He was at the far end of the corridor and we hardly ever ran into each other. At that time I loved him, but I did not want to sleep with him or anyone else. Or so I said to myself. By that time my hormones were active enough that I should have been thinking of sleeping with someone.

Well, one night after a dance at the parish sponsored by the Catholic war vets, Chuck actually came into my room after only a token knock. I was wearing the black corset with which I had punished myself at the dance (as we did in those long-forgotten days). I was brushing my hair and trying to make up my mind whether I really was in love with Charles Cronin O'Malley. Was it only an adolescent crush? Or . . .

He came in, kissed me, touched my bare shoulder gently, assured me that everything would be all right, and departed. Talk about marriage and then an engagement ring would come much later. But that night I knew I would belong to him forever.

So far so good.

Maggie Ward insists that I was almost preternaturally wise to choose the O'Malleys, indeed the Crazy O'Malleys.

"I certainly didn't do it consciously," I said.

"We know that doesn't matter, don't we?"

Good taste in a foster father, good taste in a lover? Or just plain dumb luck? Didn't matter.

Yet when I had all these insights I was a married woman with children. How could I explain to Vangie and April what I had done? They had known it all for a long time. So I had never really thanked them. And now it was too late to thank them both.

I put down my copy of *Confederacy of Dunces* and wept. Silently and calmly for a long time.

And prayed.

Dear God, I don't know why You've ever bothered with me. I was a spoiled, obnoxious brat, the kind of young woman who was barred from the eighth-grade May Crowning, until April went to see Monsignor Branigan. I was a troublemaker then and probably still am. Maggie Ward, bless her please, says I chose the Crazy O'Malleys. But You chose them for me too. I didn't deserve them. I still don't. They saved my life as You well know. I could say "thank you" every minute for however many years You still intend for me and still not adequately express my gratitude. I am sorry I never really told John the Evangelist O'Malley how much I loved him. Now it is too late. I hope You give me a chance in whatever world awaits us. Forgive me for my negligence.

This will be a difficult time for my husband and the whole clan. The joy with which they have lived meant that they didn't think about death very much. They knew it would happen. They knew they wouldn't be ready for it and they're not. These will be tough days for them. Please help them all. Please help me too. Help me even to see them all through their terrible grief, especially this mysterious and wonderful little guy to whom You have entrusted me.

Have I covered everything? If I haven't, please forgive me.

The O'Malleys even taught me how to forgive when they forgave me for being the fall-down drunk I had become. So right now and permanently I forgive my mother and father. You forgave them, I know. It's my job to forgive too, so that I can reflect Your forgiveness.

Excuse me. I have to cry some more before I can keep praying.

I'm back now.

The odd thing is that my parents and the O'Malleys were great friends in the days before they were married and when John E. O'Malley was helping to design the lower level of Wacker Drive in downtown Chicago and riding in silver armor with the Black Horse Troop, there were scores of pictures of them wearing old-fashioned swimsuits at the Commodore Barry "country club" at Twin Lakes. They were so young and happy, their whole lives stretching out in front of them with a future promising peace and happiness. Even my father, even then a little guy losing his hair, seemed happy. I could not see him as the same evil man who almost ruined my life.

My mother and April were younger than Mary Margaret is now, both of them knockouts. April really did look like a flapper, though I wasn't sure what a flapper was. A harmless hairstyle mostly. I wondered why Helen, my mom, had ever married my father. Maybe her home life, a subject about which April would never go into detail, was hellish. I pray for them all, the three dead and the one still clinging to life. When we went through Vangie's paintings in the basement, neatly organized and cataloged by my husband, we were astonished at how many of them were of Helen and April. They were luminous canvases, copied from pictures with colors filled in, the same sort of work that he had done in his famous *Rom Women.*

Vangie had far more talent than he had realized then—or even than he realized at the end of his life. It was too bad he had to wait so long for recognition. Better late than never, I guess.

"Poor dear man," his wife had said when the catalogue of his retrospective appeared. "He was really obsessed with the bodies of girls when he was young."

"Fortunately," my husband commented, "the subsequent generation did not inherit that flaw."

There will be hard days ahead. The O'Malleys will bury their dead, dry their tears, and go on with life. That's the Irish Catholic thing to do. However, the mourning will go on, more painfully perhaps because it is suppressed. They'll need help. Especially April and Peg and my beloved Chucky. They've taken care of me all my life. Now I must take care of them. And gently. Not easy. Please help me.

I looked at my peacefully sleeping husband. Poor dear man.

I nodded over, closed *Confederacy of Dunces*, removed my reading glasses, and slipped into sleep. My last thought was to wonder what Joe Raftery wanted, poor dear man.

I woke up over Ontario as the 747 glided toward Chicago. Clear sky, bright autumn sun, trees changing color beneath us. Nature was dying too.

"Would you ever like a drop of tea and a bun and maybe a sweet?"

She pronounced "bun" the Irish way as in "boon."

"Thank you, Kathleen. Give my sweet to himself."

She was so young and fresh and I was groggy and bleary-eyed. And almost fifty.

I leaned over Chuck and shook him. He turned his back to me and grumbled, "Go 'way."

"Time to wake up!" I said brightly.

He opened his eyes and glared at me.

"Are we there yet, Mommy?"

"Half hour out of Chicago. Have a nice nap?"

"Drunken dreams." He closed his eyes firmly.

"Your friend Kathleen is preparing a snack for us. You can have my sweet."

"What kind of sweet?"

"We'll have to wait and see. I told her that she should give mine to you."

He sat up and rubbed his eyes.

"I'm a wreck, Rosemarie."

"So am I."

"I dread the days ahead of us."

He sneezed. Bad sign.

The "bun" was an English muffin slathered with strawberry jam and clotted cream.

"Is this the sweet?" Chucky demanded as if he were the victim of a shell game.

"No," Kathleen said. "It's the bun. But you have to eat it first before I bring on the sweet."

I ate half of my bun and sipped my tea while Chucky wolfed down his. Then Kathleen produced a chocolate sundae with whipped cream and nuts. Chucky not so much ate it as inhaled it.

"A dish of ice cream," I remarked, "should be consumed with the same delicacy as the body of a woman."

He stopped and glared at me.

"I should have sworn those bozos to secrecy. Besides, I was talking about *chocolate* ice cream. Besides a second time, as you well know, there are other and more vehement ways of consuming a woman."

"Besides a third time there's another one coming."

"Another woman?"

"Another chocolate sundae."

"Be thankful for small favors."

"One voracious woman is more than enough."

The plane slipped over Lake Michigan and the Chicago skyline, pastel in the sunlight, materialized on the horizon. Even though Chicago wasn't its home, the plane seemed happy to be home just as we were.

"Most beautiful city in the world," Chucky murmured as we crossed the shoreline. "Somehow I don't want to come back to it just now."

"It's not going to be easy, especially April and Peg."

"Sad times, Rosemarie, sad times."

"I'll be with you, Chuck."

"Thank God for that," he said, leaning over to kiss me and smearing my lips with chocolate sauce.

Our luggage appeared immediately and we dragged it through the doors of the arrival lounge. A girl child of five years with curly red hair jumped up and down and screamed, "Mommy! Daddy!"

Behind her a dazzling young Celtic goddess in a fawn-colored autumn shift waited, a half smile on her face. I caught my breath as I always did when I saw my "intermediate" daughter.

Chucky picked up Shovie, spun her around, and kissed her.

"Don't ever go away again, Daddy!"

I hugged Mary Margaret.

"You look wonderful, Rosie," she said. "Chucky looks like someone the cat wouldn't drag in."

"He has one of his colds!"

"Oh, that!"

"And you, Mary Margaret, look like a luminous Celtic goddess."

"That's what Joe Moran says."

"He still hanging around?"

"Now and then."

Joey Moran was a nice Fenwick boy whom Mary Margaret described as her "occasional beau." Chuck and I both approved of him. Noisily so.

Then Shovie embraced me and warned me that I was never to leave home again. "Momeg was so lonesome for you."

Shovie was the only one in the family who could still use her sister's teenage name.

Chuck embraced Mary Margaret.

"Chucky, you look like something the cat refused to drag in. Rosie wear you out?"

"She's an absolutely ruthless tour guide. No respect for a worn-out old man."

"That's because she's not fifty yet."

"She tells me that."

Mary Margaret lifted one of her mother's heavy bags.

"Uncle Vince is driving around outside and will pick us up."

Ms. Take Charge was still in charge, even if the big tuna had come home. I gave Shovie my purse so she could help.

In Mary Margaret's world, everyone was assigned a proper title—Uncle Vince, Grandpa, Grandma, Father Ed—but with us she was on a first-name basis. Her big sister, April Rosemary had once protested this in her days of righteousness.

"That's all right when you're a little kid, but you should show more respect now."

"She uses our names respectfully, dear. Don't we call April and Vangie by their names?"

"That's different."

Our two older daughters were reconciled now, more or less. Yet Mary Margaret thought her sister had been a creep for slipping away into the drug-and-rock-music underground and causing so much worry. April Rosemary in her heart thought that her sister was a selfish brat.

"How's Aunt Peg?" I asked as we walked out into soft September sunset.

"Pretty numb, worst of them all. She just sits next to Grandma, like she's clinging to her. That's the way daughters are when their fathers die. Which means, Chucky, that you must get over your cold and not die for another fifty years."

"Yes, ma'am."

"You too, Rosie. I don't like it that parents have to die."

"Even kids have to die sometime," I said. "They get old too."

"I know," my daughter said solemnly.

Uncle Vince's Cadillac rolled up as we dodged taxis that seemed bent on running us over and crossed the street. Vince is a great big, dark lineman, all-American from Notre Dame who by enormous effort and under orders from Peg has just managed to stay in condition. He was a behind-the-scenes operative in the late Mayor's government and now that Jane Byrne is the mayor, a successful LaSalle Street lawyer. The papers describe him as "clout heavy" even though his wing of the party is currently out of office. He is in fact a sweetheart, though it has taken some effort from Peg to persuade him that she didn't think him inferior because he was a Sicilian.

And a few tough words from myself.

Chuck sat in the front with Vince, the three womenfolk in the back. Mary Margaret warned both of us to put on our seat belts.

"Rosie," Mary Margaret said as we pulled out of the airport, "they want you to sing the *Ave Maria* at the Communion of Mass."

"Sure, Schubert or Gounod?"

"Father McNally doesn't want either. He says they're too operatic."

"Uncle Father Ed," Siobhan Marie announced, "says that Father McNally is an asshole!"

My intermediate daughter and I both blew up.

"Siobhan Marie O'Malley! You shouldn't use that word, not ever!"

"Uncle Father Ed did!"

"He's a grown-up!" I insisted.

"But he's a priest!"

Clever little witch.

"And you're a little girl!"

"Yes, Ma."

She would use it often again, I was sure. If parents don't want you to speak a certain word, you will certainly do it, right?

"We had a lot of trouble with him," Mary Margaret said. "He told me that he would be the principal concelebrant and he would preach and there would be no eulogy and that his singers would provide the music, not the deacons that Jimmy is bringing in from the seminary! These were all rules for his parish and he could not change them."

I decided Father Ed was absolutely right.

"So you said?"

"I said that the laity who paid the bills in the parish would not accept those rules and we would appeal. I was a real brat!"

"Poor dear man." Chuck sighed.

"So when she told me," Vince said, "I made a few calls to some friends downtown. The good father was told to keep his mouth shut and not to interfere. He was also told that he could not impose himself as concelebrant."

"We're going to have more trouble with him," Mary Margaret warned. "He's a narcissist."

"Is that a bad word, Mommy?"

"Ask your father."

"Is that a bad word, Daddy?"

"No, dear, it isn't. But it's not a good idea to use it."

"Unless you're angry like Momeg was? She never uses bad words."

"Well, hardly ever," I said.

Like her mother, Mary Margaret has an extensive vocabulary of obscenity and scatology, which she can on rare occasion use with considerable skill.

"Rosemarie," Chuck said, "don't you still have that multipart arrangement of the Gregorian *Ave Maria* you and April put together for Kevin and Maria Elena's wedding?"

"Sure, it's in the files you make me keep."

The accountant in Chuck makes him a paper saver. He has files for everything. I tend to pile things up. He insists that I be orderly and for the sake of marital bliss I go along with him. I'm not as obsessive as he is.

"After we receive Communion, why don't we all walk over to the Blessed Mother's altar and sing it, April conducting of course. You could practice it tomorrow and Friday."

"He might try to stop us," Mary Margaret said.

"He won't try a second time," my Chucky said firmly. "Besides, practicing it will give us something to do. Aunt Peg can accompany us on the violin."

We stopped at our house to unload our baggage and to pick up the score for the multipart Gregorian chant *Ave Maria.* Vince, Chuck, and Mary Margaret carried in the bags and Shovie took charge of my purse.

The arrangement was in the cabinet in my office where Chuck insisted that it would be. The file was neatly labeled in his small, precise writing, Ave Maria, underlined to indicate that the words were Latin.

"It was where I said it would be?" he said as he sneezed again.

"NO! I had to search for it!"

He laughed because he knew I was fibbing.

A long line of cars were parked outside of the house of the elder O'Malleys, the big old home into which they had moved after the war thirty-five years ago. It had been an empty nest for a long time, even more empty after Vangie had finally sold his architecture business and Chuck converted the workrooms in the back to a studio where his father could paint the watercolors that finally brought him the fame as an artist to which he was entitled. They refused bluntly to sell the house and move downtown or even to a new condo over on South Boulevard near the L tracks. Too many memorable events had happened; weddings, Baptism, a first Mass, family recitals, the birth of the jazz orchestra in the third generation with my three boys, Gianni Antonelli, a young Latina named Maria Elena Lopez (now my beloved daughter-in-law) and the Good April on the piano. It would be a *very* empty nest until Mary Margaret moved in.

"It's kind of unstable in there," Vince said. "Like the Mayor's family when he died. I don't quite understand the Irish . . . I kind of wish you'd go a little bit hysterical instead of holding it all in."

"You tell Peg that?" I asked.

"Yeah. She laughed and said I was probably right, but the Irish have been around too long to change . . . By the way, Chuck, the obituary editor of *The New York Times* wants you to call him right away."

He handed Chuck a note which I took while my poor husband struggled with a sneezing fit.

The big parlor of the home of the elder O'Malleys was a bubbling cauldron of kinetic energy—tension, laugher, grief, anger, all mixed together in random patterns. Nerves were frayed, emotions raw—an Irish prewake wake. With a lot of little kids, mostly with red hair, hence my grandchildren, running around frantically. Someone had to take charge. Only my sniffling, hacking husband would do.

There was a moment of silence as we stood at the door of the room. "It's about time," someone said.

April Mae Cronin O'Malley rushed to her son.

"Chucky, darling, I'm so sorry for your sadness. I know how much he meant to you and how much you will miss him."

This was quintessential Crazy O'Malley—the widow consoling her son.

All my weary, mourning, sick husband could do was to return her embrace.

Peg, who had been sitting with April, hugged me silently.

Peg, my best friend for more than forty years, sleek, vibrant, dazzling, now seemed worn and, God forbid, old. She was two weeks younger than I was and suddenly she was an old woman. She would recover surely, yet . . . Was I old too?

My daughter-in-law, Maria Elena, hugged me after Peg. She was pregnant with the third child, probably another red-haired Latino, like the two who were running around.

"I too have lost a father," she murmured.

"Chucky," said Jane McCormack, the oldest of the O'Malley children, "tell Edward that it is all right for Mother to come home with me after the funeral. It won't be good for her to stay in this old house and this dull neighborhood."

Jane is and has always been clueless. A bubbling enthusiast, she was behind the door when sensitivity was passed out. Ted McCormack, a navy pilot whom she married after the war despite the objections of his family, is a successful psychiatrist up on the North Shore. They moved up there after their honeymoon because "Doctor" as his surgeon father was always called, wanted him near his family. Poor Jane went native and became almost a stereotype of a North Shore matron and also put on a lot of pounds, so that she was just barely under the obesity level, poor woman.

She kind of passed out of the family then. The ride from Kenilworth down to Oak Park was just too much for her, she told us often. She praised the wonders of the Country Day School, New Trier High School, Faith, Hope parish (as in SS Faith, Hope, and Charity AKA Faith, Hope, and Cadillac), and the civilized lifestyle of Kenilworth. She urged all of us to move up there before Oak Park "went completely black." Her siblings were not impressed, but charitably didn't argue because they knew it would be a waste of time. None of her four children were with her, the only grandchildren who hadn't been interested in Grandpa's death. They were all products of the Day School, New Trier, DePaw, and Kendal College. "Creeps," the usually charitable Mary Margaret had dismissed them. "No fire, no hormones, no nothing."

Jane was happy up there, what the hell. Father Ed, however, social activist priest that he was, sometimes lost his temper with her.

"Jane," he fired back at her, "April is not a snob. She couldn't stand living up there. And Oak Park is a fascinating neighborhood, even more now that it's racially integrated."

My sons were hugging me as though I had been on Mars instead of only in Siberia and never expected to see me again, Kevin Patrick who was finishing his doctorate in musicology at THE University (as one must call my own alma mater) and was Maria Elena's husband; Jimmy, who will become a priest in the spring; and Sean Seamus, a commodity trader whose love for a young Jewish woman was shattered when she married an officer in the Israeli Air Force.

"Ed! Jane!" My husband did finally take charge. "Chill out!

"But . . ." Jane began.

"I said chill out. The matter doesn't have to be settled now . . ."

He was interrupted by another spasm of sneezing.

"It can wait a couple of weeks till things settle down. In the meantime April will want to stay here."

"Well, yes," his mother said, still holding him. "That's a good idea, Chucky dear. I'd like to stay here till things settle down."

Her tone suggested that the idea had just occurred to her.

April Rosemary Nettleton, my oldest child, was last in the hugging line. Chuck had wanted to call her "Rosemary" after me and I wanted to call her "April" after her grandmother. We compromised on the combination, but I won because "April" was her first name. That's what we call an Irishwoman's compromise.

"As if," April Rosemary, whispered to me, "you could get April out of here with a forklift."

"Especially," her grandmother and namesake continued, "if poor sweet little Mary Margaret will come visit me some of the time."

Poor sweet little Mary Margaret leaped into action.

"Grandma, I'll move into Rosie's old bedroom and commute back and forth between Rosie and Chucky's house."

A commute of all of two blocks.

She gently eased her dad away from Grandma and embraced her.

"Only on one condition, Grams, you totally gotta teach me how to do the jazz piano."

Over in the background at the edge of the group, Joe Moran grinned proudly.

"Well, dear, I'm sure you don't need much teaching."

"I'll move in tonight."

That settled that and that settled the group down.

"She is really something," April Rosemary murmured.

Mary Margaret turned and winked. April Rosemary gave the pointing sign with which black basketball players praise one another. Mary Margaret winked again. Had those two finally made peace?

I glanced at Peg back on the couch next to April. She looked so tired.

April Rosemary was pregnant again, her third child. She was becoming a successful photographer of children. Both her toddlers, Johnny and April Anne had been afflicted by the red hair gene. I could see myself confusing the redheads as they grew older. Peg's oldest, Charley (Charlotte named after my husband) McGrath was also expecting. Life was asserting its latest victory in the ongoing battle with death. Poor dear Charley—I'm sounding like April—a lawyer like her father and a dark shapely Mediterranean beauty, thought she would never marry until she met Cletus McGrath.

"Now listen up," Chucky ordered. "I hear that the pastor over at our church won't let my wife sing either the Bach-Gounod or the Schubert *Ave Maria.* So I propose that she sing the Gregorian chant version. Then we reprise with the arrangement we did at Charley's wedding!"

"Great idea!" that Mediterranean mother-to-be shouted.

"It just so happens," Chuck continued, "that I have here a stack of the arrangement, though I doubt that this crowd will need it. The church will be filled, so we must do it perfectly, which means the Good April will have to direct."

A bright smile lit up the face of April Mae Cronin O'Malley.

"That is very sweet of you, Chucky dear."

"Peg can accompany on the violin."

"Whatever you say, Chucky Ducky!"

The extra twenty years on Peg's face vanished.

"Now here's the drill: after we receive Communion and the priests are distributing Communion to the rest of the church—and it will be filled—I'll click my fingers like the nuns used to do and we'll go to the Blessed Mother's altar. Ed, if the pastor tries to move in our way, block him."

"With the greatest of pleasure!"

"Now I suggest we practice it tonight, then tomorrow and Friday too. April Mae? I have to return a call from the *New York Times* newspaper."

More coughing spasms.

The O'Malley chorus fell into place as it often had. There were more of us than there had been before.

Chuck went off to talk to the *Times*.

We went through the piece a couple of times. It was ragged, in part because the small fry were a bit too enthusiastic. Still everyone in the church, with the possible exception of the pastor, would love it.

People began to drift away. Jane and Ted went off to the paradisal North Shore. I wondered if their kids would show up for the wake. By the time Chuck came back from the phone only Peg and Vince were still there. I was ready to sleep till the day after the last judgment. Poor dear Chucky could hardly breathe. Ms. Take Charge took charge.

"Aunt Peg, I'll drive Chuck and Rosie home, grab some clothes, and come back to stay with Grams."

"Thank you, Mary Margaret," Peg said.

We kissed April good-bye. When I first elbowed my way into the O'Malleys in 1939, she was in her middle thirties. I imagined that with her height, her lovely face, her graceful movements, and her long skirts, she was some kind of princess. Chucky later said grand duchess. She still looked and acted like a grand duchess. Tears stung at my eyes again.

"Now," my intermediate daughter said, as we pulled up to our house, "you guys will wake up early, so I'll come by about a quarter to eight and pick you up for the eight o'clock Mass. Naturally I'll bring Grams along too."

I did not want to get up and get dressed for Mass. Yet I'd better do it.

"Mary Margaret," my husband said as we entered the house, "I will doubtless be in the intensive care unit at Oak Park Hospital tomorrow. So I want you to call Kevin Patrick and ask him if he thinks we can reassemble the jazz group to perform 'When the Saints Go Marching In' at Queen of Heaven."

"Good idea, Chuck. We'll want to practice it, won't we?"

"Certainly."

Chuck and I stumbled into our bedroom. I gave him several different kinds of medicine, none of which would do any good.

"Did you notice anything about Jane?" he asked.

"No, not really. A little hyper maybe."

"I'd say a lot hyper . . . That crazy stuff about moving April to the North Shore."

"You know Jane."

"Yeah, I know her, Rosemarie my love. I think we'd better watch her."

"If you say so."

Then, changing the subject, I said, "Jazz at the cemetery, Charles Cronin O'Malley?"

"Why not?"

"You are the craziest of all the Crazy O'Malleys."

"I have had to work at it."

We both collapsed into bed, far too tired to think about sex. Some other time, I promised myself.

Chapter Four

Chuck

Architect and Artist —for the Second Time

John E. O'Malley, nationally known architect and artist died at his home in Oak Park, Illinois—a Chicago suburb—on Wednesday. The cause of death according to his son, Charles C. O'Malley, was a massive heart attack. It was, Charles O'Malley said, his father's second death. The first was on the parade ground at Fort Leavenworth, Kansas, on November 11, 1918. The O'Malley family still has the telegram from the War Department reporting John E. O'Malley's death from influenza. Charles O'Malley said that his father's body was in a casket when he began to pound on it. Mr. O'Malley declined to speculate on whether it was a classic near-death experience, but said that after that experience his father never worried about anything, Depression, war, children, the acceptance of his work, taxes.

John E. O'Malley was born in 1900, son of a prominent Republican politician and an Irish immigrant, Jane Curtin. He attended St. Ignatius College and Armour Institute of Technology (now Illinois Institute of Technology) and worked on the design of the Wacker Drive expressway in Chicago. He also designed many churches, including St. Ursula in Chicago, for which he won a national architectural award. During the Great Depression he was Architect for the Metropolitan Sanitary District and served in the Black Horse Troop, a reconnaissance unit of the Illinois National Guard. After Pearl Harbor the Troop was mobilized into the regular army. John O'Malley served as an architect for the US Army Signal Corps at Fort Sheridan and designed several different buildings for Signal Corps use.

After the war he designed many suburban developments in Chicago and elsewhere which he described as "suburbs for human beings." These projects earned him more than a dozen architectural awards and a citation of "Special Merit" from the Association of American Architects.

Throughout his life he also painted, both in oils and watercolor; however, this work was not well-known. Charles O'Malley said that his father always defined himself as an artist. In the last ten years his work has received considerable attention. The Worcester Gallery created a retrospective around his painting *Rom Women* which hung in its American Artists Gallery. *The New York Times* review of that exhibit said that *Rom Women* must be recognized "as perhaps the most solid example of American Realism in the first half of the twentieth century." It also said that his painting *Nude Flapper* is "a delightful insight into the chaste eroticism of the 1920s." The exhibit traveled to many museums, including Chicago's Art Institute and the published catalogue "John E. O'Malley—an Artist for His Time" was a success. Mr. O'Malley continued to paint during his retirement, especially in watercolors.

He is survived by his wife of fifty-five years, April Mae Cronin, four children, in addition to Charles: Jane McCormack, Margaret Mary Antonelli, and the Rev. Edward Michael, fourteen grandchildren and four great-grandchildren, all of Chicago.

A funeral Eucharist will be celebrated at St. Ursula Church in Chicago on Saturday morning.

I passed the *Times* over to my good wife. We were riding over to St. Agedius Church for the eight o'clock Mass in Mary Margaret's Chevy Impala, which did not look at all like an African antelope. My daughter and my mother were in the front seat.

The aforementioned good wife had awakened me not fifteen minutes earlier to inform me that Mary Margaret would soon arrive to pick us up for the eight o'clock Mass.

I felt like a 747 had rolled over me. I opened my eyes to see my wife climbing into jeans and pulling on a red sweatshirt with a drawing of St. Basil's Cathedral in Cyrillic script. It was always pleasant to watch her dress.

"Your child is a religious fanatic," I complained and closed my eyes.

"Her red hair suggests she is your child too."

"Maybe you had a lover with red hair."

My comment earned a derisive snort.

"Mary Margaret is an enthusiastic Catholic, as you well know . . . Now get up and get dressed. Your mother will be with us. Don't disappoint her."

"She's a religious fanatic too."

I struggled out of bed and kissed the back of her neck.

"Chucky! Take a quick shower and brush your teeth! Now hurry up! If Father Keenan sees us coming in late, it will embarrass your mother."

Hardly likely. However, as someone who did not expect to live the rest of the day, I was in no shape to consider lovemaking even as a theoretical possibility. The shower didn't help.

"Where's the kid?"

"Erin has already brought her over to school."

Erin was our shy, pretty Irish babysitter, close to being even a foster child.

I was dragged downstairs and out the door just as the Impala pulled up. I grabbed the *Times* on the run.

"Good obit," Rosemarie said. "I notice that this Charles O'Malley person receives considerable attention."

"They don't talk about any of my awards."

"Would you ever read it to me, Rosie dear?"

"Well, it doesn't say that he claimed to see my face when he was dead," Mom said. "I'm thankful for that."

"That would have been too spooky for *The New York Times*," I replied. "But we all know it was true."

" 'Chaste eroticism,' " Rosemarie said.

"Well, I suppose that's one way of describing that awful painting. Thank goodness no one thinks it was me. I was never a flapper."

She knew that everyone said it was she.

"It was just the way everyone wore their hair in those days, wasn't it?" Mary Margaret said.

"That's right, dear."

Phonies all of them.

I decided to stir the pot, just a little.

"I don't know how chaste it is. The woman seems to enjoy modeling with most of her clothes off."

"You've never been a woman, Chucky darling."

I was saved from responding because we had pulled up to St. Agedius. Msgr. Packy Keenan, a fellow warrior in the birth control commission and a contemporary from the neighborhood was waiting for us.

We live inside the boundaries of St. Agedius, but St. Ursula was always our parish because we had grown up there and Dad had designed the church. However, when Packy became pastor of St. Agedius we yielded to canon law.

He embraced all of us and congratulated me on the obit in the *NYT.*

"I didn't write it," I pleaded.

"No one will believe it."

Probably not. In fact, I had merely suggested a few additions. Including the lead. That would be my response: all I was responsible for was the lead. The headline was a grabber all right. All the anti-Catholic bigots who read *The New York Times* every morning would be furious at the suggestion of near-death experiences. That delightful thought made me forget about my cold for perhaps thirty seconds.

Packy said a few nice words about Dad in his homily after the Gospel. He asked the congregation to pray for him, though he was sure that whatever purgatory Dad might have deserved was long since expiated by putting up with his son the photographer. The congregation sniggered and look around at me. I waved a weak hand in acknowledgment of the attention.

"I get no respect," I complained to Packy after Mass.

"More than you will on Saturday from that idiot over at Ursula."

"He seems to have been warned."

"By the new archbishop . . . Yet he's pretty much a cement head. I'll be there to take care of him if he misbehaves."

"You will have to beat me to it."

"That's a nasty cold you have, Chucky."

"My wife dragged me around Russia for a month, small wonder that I'm sick."

"And I'm going to drag you over to Oak Park Hospital to have your chest x-rayed."

"No, you're not!"

"Yes, I am. I'm not going to have you laid up with pneumonia again."

I knew that I was suffering from an allergy picked up in Russia and not a cold, because a person of some importance and influence had assured me that I would never suffer a cold or pneumonia again. The promise had been kept, as one might expect that it would.

Anyway, before my wife permitted me any breakfast save for a cup of tea, I was forced into the confines of Oak Park Hospital where I had come into the world and whence I had expected not long ago to depart from it. The chest X-ray was negative of course.

"Just a minor allergy," the doctor told Rosemarie.

Doctors never communicate with me.

"Are you sure?" she demanded.

"The allergy medicine will clear it up in a couple of days or a frost will take care of it."

I had never told the good Rosemarie about the woman who

had visited me in my hospital room and given me instructions about the rest of my life. I sensed that it was a personal exchange and one I should not share with others. Moreover, better an occasional unnecessary chest X-ray than facing off with one of her psychiatric friends.

We stopped at the bakery on the way home and bought a dozen sweet rolls. In my weakened condition I was able to consume only three of them.

"I'm going back to bed," I insisted.

"You're on jet lag. You won't be able to sleep."

"Just watch me."

"We have practice at April's with the family choir at two-thirty and the jazz group at three-thirty."

"Who ever had those crazy ideas?"

"I'll wake you up."

"I'll count on it."

I tumbled into bed. I should have eaten two more sweet rolls.

Then I thought about my dad and felt a stab of pain in my gut. Tears rolled down my cheeks. No sobs, just restrained mourning, which is what we Irish tend to do.

I remembered the story of his life as he had written it out. He was fond of bragging that he was conceived out of wedlock in a rectory bedroom on a hot summer afternoon. Whether his father, a very proper Republican politician on the make, had seduced the immigrant Irish maid or she had seduced him was not clear. Mostly, I have observed, people seduce one another. They were both in their thirties and, if one is to judge by their wedding pictures, quite handsome. Hormones may abate a little between the age of fifteen and the age of thirty-five—though that has not been my experience. Nonetheless, you put a lonely young woman and a lonely young man, both of them with what we could call today sex appeal, in a hot rectory on a hot afternoon with the pastor (uncle of the young man) away and something is likely to happen.

It was a happy union, my father said, and they certainly looked happy in subsequent pictures. He was their only child and he had remembered them fondly. The woman, I should remark, had red hair. My mother had also been fond of them, which meant that they liked the outspoken little flapper.

"Well, you have him back with you finally," I said to the couple who I assumed would be listening closely to my comments. "I hope you're as pleased with him as we are. Help us to learn to live with losing him. And, you redhead woman, look kindly on those who have the same gene. I mean me especially. And all the little kids too. I wish I had a chance to know both of you. April said you were 'cool.' Well, she said 'swell.' "

Then my incoherent prayer faded away into incoherent dreams.

Then I was awakened by a phone call from Vince. Would I please have lunch with Joe Raftery at Filander's on Marion Street at twelve-thirty. It was kind of urgent.

I said that I would and went into a spasm of sneezing.

Joe Raftery seemed perfectly sane and normal across the table from me at the restaurant. The same easy smile, the same glittering blue eyes, the same curly hair parted in the middle, now silver instead of black, the same almost preternatural calm. He hadn't changed much, tall, slender, dreamy brown eyes, a man you've known very well.

Joe and I ate our spaghetti Bolognese with gusto and reflected on the good old days and the changes.

"No trouble recognizing the neighborhood," he said. "Your wife is a permanent beauty as is your sister Peg."

"They conspire," I said, slurping down some of the pasta. "What's happening in your life? I know you played safety at Stanford and made all-American . . ."

"Fourth string . . . then like Vince and most of our cohort I went to Korea. I was a supply clerk in Seoul for a year, then came home. Nothing like what Vince went through . . . Is he over it?"

"Pretty much, still some bad dreams; but he's tough, as is my sister Peg."

"Lots of clout in Cook County, I hear."

"So they tell me."

"The Niners had drafted me in the sixth round, so I decided to give it a try. I was free safety for nine years till 1961, about when you were one of the PT boat boys over in Germany. Sounded like interesting duty."

"It was till JFK died, then the whole world fell apart. No one has put it back together since."

"I went native, became a real La La Land cowboy. I married a young actress, beautiful but not very bright. She went on to bigger things."

I nodded, as if I understood, but I didn't.

"When I retired from the Niners I went to work for a real estate developer over in the East Bay. We made a lot of money, some of it honest. I fell in love again with another real estate person, younger than I was, but like me she read books. Irish-born, thick brogue. We had a daughter."

He showed me the picture of a lovely young woman with soft brown hair and a baby that looked like she might become a clone.

"I quit the big company and opened my own winery, would you believe. It was a lot of fun. Then one day two years ago I drove back to our vineyard and they were both gone. There was no sign that they had left. Bride and Samantha had disappeared. Her car was still there, Sam's toys, everything."

Tears formed in the deep blue wells of his eyes.

"How awful," I said.

"At first I couldn't believe it . . . I still can't as far as that goes. I was confident that they would turn up or that the police would find them. Nothing. They went on a missing persons list and are still there. The cops aren't looking anymore. I can't blame them."

"No credit card traces, no bank accounts?"

"She had her own account and we had a joint account. No money taken from either."

"I'm sure that the cops asked you all these questions. No known enemies?"

"Not to my knowledge. I didn't know much about her background. As I said, she was from Ireland, Cork I think. If she had relatives over there, she never mentioned them. The people she had worked with didn't know anything either. That's California. Not like this neighborhood, where everyone knows everyone else and everyone else's relatives. I've had private investigators searching for two years. They haven't found a trace. No one saw them leave the house or the winery. They simply vanished from the face of the earth."

"So there's no closure?"

He shook his head sadly.

"The cops found lots of bodies. None of them match her dental records. Realistically I have to assume they're dead, but I still have hope. I guess I always will."

"Was she involved in Irish politics?"

"She was totally uninterested. Said they were all a bunch of phonies. She didn't want to go back to Ireland either. I had offered to take her there, but she wouldn't hear of it."

That was a little strange. Most Micks always wanted to return to the Holy Ground if only to be thankful that they had migrated. I nodded, though I didn't see what this had to do with me.

"Did you travel much?"

"Hardly at all. Over to San Francisco for the opera and concerts—she was a great one, as she herself had said, for classical music. Sometimes up and down the wine country to learn tricks of the trade. She seemed utterly happy with our life and our daughter . . . I'm still rocked by it, Chuck. I guess I always will be."

"Let's suppose she's still alive. Would you not expect her in some fashion to contact you, if she possibly could?"

"Unless for one reason or another she does not want to."

"What would that reason be?"

"Perhaps it might put my life in danger—or Sam's."

"I'm not clear on the ages. How old would they be now?"

"Bride was thirty when I married her. She'd be forty now. Sam was born when her mother was thirty-three. She'd be seven now."

I finished up my pasta and ordered iced tea and a dish of chocolate ice cream.

"Same old Chucky, eats ice cream and doesn't put on weight."

"A special grace from God which I will not reject."

"Chuck, I know they're both dead. I will never find out why they died or who killed them. I feel foolish bothering you at this difficult time in your life. Yet Bride keeps telling me to see you."

"She does!"

A chill started at the base of my spine and crept up into my head. I did not like the uncanny because it made me feel uncanny.

"How did she know I exist!"

"I bragged about my famous classmate who was a photographer. She likes photography herself. So I bought her a bunch of your books. She was very impressed."

"And she's been in contact with you?"

I thought of my own wife on whose breasts at that moment I wanted to bury my head in search of protection from ghosts and fairie and creatures that go bump in the night.

"In dreams and sometimes in waking hours I hear her voice. She always says, 'See Charles O'Malley.' I ask her why and she simply repeats the instructions."

When she had hugged me before I left for lunch, Rosemarie, in a black silk robe and not much else, had pressed herself fervently against me. One woman haunting my imagination was more than enough.

"This has been going on for a long time?"

"Actually, it has not. I had plenty of dreams after they disappeared, but they tapered off. About five months ago these very vivid dreams returned. At first she smiled and told me that she still loved me and always would. Sometimes Sam was with her, a big girl now. She looked just like her mother. Then the words came, especially for the last month or two."

" 'See Charles O'Malley'?"

My hands were clammy.

"Yeah . . . You must think I'm crazy, Chuck. I told my shrink about these dreams. He said they were wish fulfillment. I guess maybe they are. Still your books keep falling off the shelves . . ."

I shivered. Joe didn't seem to notice.

"What did the shrink say about that?"

"He thought it was some kind of telekinesis that I had unleashed."

Rosemarie! Come hold my hand! I'm scared!

"How did the worthy doctor explain her choice of me?"

"He asked me about you. I told him about the Carmel game.

He said you had become a symbol of someone who wins against impossible odds. It was natural that I think of you . . . Maybe he's right."

"Patron saint of lost causes," I said.

"St. Anthony of Padua."

I did not believe in St. Anthony of Padua, even if Rosemarie's prayers to him almost always found us a parking place.

"You've talked to a priest?"

"Sure. An old Irish fellow who is pastor of our tiny parish. He says I should pray for the grace of peace for myself and for Bride and Sam. He offered to say Mass in the house, a kind of exorcism."

"It didn't work?"

"No way."

"She shows up now outside of dreams?"

He hesitated.

"You'll think I'm out of my mind."

"I don't think that at all."

In fact, I did suspect that, yet Joe was so calm and reasonable that I wasn't ready to write him off as a kook. Not just yet.

"I think I hear her voice when I'm working around the winery, advising me what to do with our different vintages, like she used to do. Then she says something like 'Are you ever going to see Charles O'Malley?' It's always a sweet, pleasant voice, the way she used to talk. It's urgent that I see you, yet she seems patient too."

"And you ask her what I'm supposed to do?"

"Sure. She doesn't answer that."

"They never do."

"You don't see her physically?"

"Sometimes I think I catch a glimpse of her—like in a blink of an eye. I'm not sure. To tell you the truth, Chuck, I'm not sure of anything anymore. I won't blame you if you tell me the same things that my priest and my shrink did."

"We patrons of lost causes never do that. We're afraid we might be wrong."

I shivered again. What if, living or dead, Bride was trying to tell her husband something? I'd not want to meet her in the world to come and have to explain why I hadn't listened.

"Would you like an after-lunch drink?" I asked.

"I stay away from the stuff these days, Chuck. I don't trust myself much anymore."

The poor man, devastated by the loss of his family and tormented by voices surging up from his unconscious. I had to offer to help. If I didn't, Rosemarie would be unhappy with me.

I was the one who needed a drink, but I'd better not.

"What do you want me to do, Joe?" I asked.

"I don't know . . . Her instructions are always vague. Perhaps I should say that she doesn't seem tormented so much as insistent."

I was supposed to find a woman and child who were probably dead or who had disappeared into a misty world between life and death. All because people believed that I had actually won that game against Mount Carmel.

"I brought along a file for you to look at," Joe continued. "I don't know why. I had to do something . . ."

He removed a bulging accordion file from a large case, the kind of sample case that many men carry around and that make me glad that all I have to carry is rolls of film.

"I asked a security analyst from the Rand Corporation to collect all the reports that we had and try to put them together in a single narrative. This contains his narrative and some of the supporting materials."

"Did she have any relationships before you?"

"She was thirty and we lived in La La land. She lived with one man, another immigrant, for several years in her twenties. He didn't want anything 'permanent' so she dropped him. We checked him out. Harmless intellectual. There were one or two others. Nothing serious, though as I've learned there is no such thing as sex which is not serious . . . It's all in here."

He lifted the file tentatively. No way I could refuse.

"I'll read every word of it, Joe. So will Rosemarie. She's much better at this kind of thing than I am."

Joe sighed with relief.

"I can't tell you how grateful I am, Chuck. This will be a tremendous burden off my shoulders. I won't worry anymore that I'm not doing what Bride wants me to do. I don't expect you will find her and Sam. Deep down I know they're dead, as I guess I've said before. I hope I can find some peace and get on with my life."

"Any prospects?" I asked cautiously.

"If there are, I haven't been able to see them."

A curious way of putting it.

As I drove up Harlem Avenue, the steady beat of rain warned that summer was taking her leave. I had never minded winter in Chicago till my parents had bought the house in Tucson. One did not have to shiver between Thanksgiving and Easter. Yet I was a Chicagoan, even if my son Jimmy called me a suburban parasite, and a few weeks away from it were more than enough.

The gray chill day fit my mood. Too much death. Joe's wife and daughter were certainly dead, probably brutalized and raped by California hippies. I didn't want to study their death right after my father's. Yet I had promised Joe.

The truth is that I did score that touchdown against Carmel in the mud of Hansen Park Stadium on Central Avenue in 1945. It was a mistake, or pure dumb luck, as much of the rest of my life was. I don't remember spearing Ed Murray on the following kickoff, however. Well, Ed has made the charge so often that I kind of remember it.

So I had to study his files. But only after my father was buried.

Chapter Five

Chuck

The rehearsal of the *Ave Maria* was a success even if little April Anne Nettleton had a bit of a hard time staying on key. It began with Madame my wife singing the old Gregorian hymn a cappella. Then Peg struck a key on her violin and the whole group sang it through, then repeated it all in three-part harmony—men, women, and kids. The last were the two Nettletons, Johnny and April Anne and the two O'Malley-Lopezes, Maria Rosa and Juan Carlos. Our own Siobhan Marie, technically the aunt of these rug rats, added volume and the perfect pitch Rosemarie and I expect in our offspring. Rosemarie ended it.

We did it several times and the Good April nodded her approval.

"The little kids make the choir even better," she said, perhaps with more love than accuracy.

"There'll still be people coming up to Communion." Rosemarie glanced at her watch. Then we'll try to sing *Salve Regina* as an encore. In Gregorian. The kids don't know it, so they don't have to sing."

The final *Salve* is, I think, the most poignant and beautiful prayer in the whole Catholic tradition.

"Now," Grandma said, "I yield to my grandson, soon-to-be Dr. Kevin Patrick O'Malley."

Back when they were preteens, "the boys," as we called them collectively because they all seemed to have been stamped out of the same genetic mold, purchased secondhand horns, a sax, a trombone, and a trumpet. I had introduced them to Vangie's old friend Louis Armstrong in Cologne when we were there for Jack Kennedy and, after listening to him, they became jazz enthusiasts. They signed up "Little Gianni" Antonelli, and later a teenage Latina vocalist called Maria Elena Lopez. Sometimes Rosemarie and I did background vocalizing with them and April accompanied them on the piano. The kids had taught themselves more or less and purchased slightly better instruments with Christmas and birthday presents. Kevin Patrick's career as a musicologist began with the horn blowing (which drove our neighbors on Euclid Avenue and in Grand Beach crazy). The group folded when Kevin lost his foot to a land mine in Korea. However, they had "reunions" at our various family festivals. They weren't good enough to go on the road, but they were good enough to have a lot of fun.

"Now," Father Edward said, "as I understand, Chuck, the idea is that we do this after the final obsequies at Queen of Heaven Cemetery. Monsignor Keenan says the last prayer and we begin to sing 'When the Saints Go Marching In.' Does Packy know we're going to do this?"

"Certainly," Mary Margaret said. "I told him."

Of course she had.

"Then we all gather and march around the tomb three times, singing about the saints like the ancient Celts did, then back to the cars?"

"Right! . . . Kevin, you do the opening bars on your trumpet, then bring us all in?"

"With great pleasure!"

"And Gianni, you pound the drums with your usual vigor?"

"Absolutely! Uncle Chuck!"

Gianni, at twenty-five, was no longer "Little Gianni." He was bigger than his father and had also been a linebacker at the Golden Dome. His brother Vinny had joined the group with a very loud tuba.

"Kids too, Chuck?" Maria Elena asked.

At least I was no longer "Mr. O'Malley."

"Only those who are redheads."

So we gathered around in a circle, Kevin blew the first bars on his trumpet, Rosemarie and I came in immediately on key, then the whole crowd exulted about what would happen when the saints went marching in.

"I wonder what the other people in the cemetery will think?" Edward asked, somewhat dubiously.

"They'll think the saints are marching in," Peg said happily, "and Dad with them."

My sister looked a lot better than she had yesterday. The distractions were helping.

"And everyone will know," I added, "that it's the Crazy O'Malleys."

"Hooray for the Crazy O'Malleys," Rita Antonelli, Mary Margaret's age peer, shouted, "and all their relatives too."

Afterward, as people were leaving the house to drive over to the wake, Peg and Rosemarie and I huddled.

"Wonderful, Chuck! Pure genius! You don't make the mourning go away, but you distract us from it and point to what our faith tells us death means. The saints really go marching in."

"Saturday morning," I said, "is about grief and healing. The music in the cemetery will defy death and begin healing."

That was a little pompous, but neither of the women, companions of my youth, seemed to notice.

"She didn't come," Peg sighed, meaning our sister Jane.

"And she'll show up at the wake without her kids at suppertime and drive back to Kenilworth about eight-thirty," my wife added.

"It's not Ted's fault," I said. "He loves her and he's never been able to tell her how clueless she is—if he even notices."

"It's hard to be oldest daughter and to be followed by two like us," Peg said. "You'd feel you're not in the same ballpark."

"Not even the same league," Rosemarie added.

"Its not the fault of either of you," I said quickly.

"We know that Chucky Ducky," Rosemarie replied. "Yet you can't help but wonder if she really wanted to leave the neighborhood to get away from us. She was pretty and would still be if she'd shed twenty pounds, and the life of the party, but . . ."

"How do you compete with the tiger and the leopard?"

"Chuck!" they both protested.

I was right, however. In the middle 1940s how would a bright young woman without a whole lot of depth cope with the Peg/Rosemarie. She might have become part of the crowd. They would not have excluded her . . . No, no, that would never have worked. What was, was.

I remember April telling Vangie one night in our tiny apartment on Menard Avenue that Peg and Rosemarie had managed to have their first periods on the same day.

Witches can do that sort of thing.

Mums are beautiful flowers, white at weddings, gold on Halloween and All Saints, white again at Easter. Yet I hate their scent because they remind me of funeral parlors, the most melancholy places in the world. I used to hate wakes; but I now understand that they rally the community around to close ranks and rededicate themselves to the life that continues, for the deceased hopefully in the world to come, and for the rest of us temporarily in this life. They also keep the minds and the emotions of the immediate relatives active so they won't slip into deep gloom.

Yet the challenges on both sides of the receiving line, even at Irish wakes with their odd mix of sorrow and celebration, are almost intolerable. The immediate mourners have to combine pain, resignation, and hope in a blend that will enable the rest to say that they are bearing up well. The rest of the mourners have to offer consolation for what just then is inconsolable. There are few readily available phrases with which this can be done. "Sorry for your troubles," was at one time perhaps an adequate comment, though I kind of doubt it. But most people who come to Irish wakes are incapable of saying it so that it doesn't sound trite. It is, however, much better than the intolerably fatuous question, "Don't he look natural?"

I hope—which is what one does at a wake.

I stood on one side of my mother, Peg on the other, Ed next to Peg, and Rosemarie and Vince in order. Then the children and the grandchildren filled up the line. Mary Margaret and Rita and Erin took turns watching the small fry in a room off the lobby, including Shovie, who wasn't exactly sure where she belonged.

All my womenfolk, from the Good April to Mary Margaret, looked sharp, simple black dresses, no jewelry, just the right amount of makeup. What a shame they had to stand next to an insignificant little redhead who provided no contrast at all for their elegance.

I glanced sideways often at my wife. I was falling in love with her again. Why at a wake? Perhaps because she stood for life, perhaps because she was so lovely, perhaps because I was so lonely for my lost father. To be dizzy in love with her suddenly and all over again was, all things considered a sensible response to the situation.

Or maybe it was only the allergy medicine and the jet lag.

John E. O'Malley was an important man in Chicago. Crowds came to pay their respect—the new mayor with her large entourage of guards, the new archbishop, a quiet, gentle man who asked who was the daughter that called him about the Mass.

News to me.

"Joey," I said to Joey Moran, who was lingering on the edges of the crowd, "would you get herself?"

And then to the archbishop, "She'll be the redhead at the end of the line. She's watching the little children."

"She is an intelligent and direct young woman."

"Tell me about it."

Later Mary Margaret reported that he had thanked her for calling and promised that we would have no trouble at Mass.

"He's a nice quiet man," she said. "Better than the last one."

Father Ed had worked for the "last one," who drove him into a mental health center.

My sister Jane, accompanied by her husband but not by her children appeared about 7:30. She was wearing a navy blue dress which would have been attractive had she lost the twenty pounds of which Peg and Rosemarie had spoken. She was bedecked with several pounds of gold jewelry and her short skirt revealed not too much leg but legs which were, alas, too thick. I winced. She had once been a very pretty girl with impeccable taste. I heard gasps from farther down the line.

She embraced the Good April and began to sob piteously—and loudly.

"We will all miss him so much!"

Another series of gasps down the line. The noises from Peg and my wife indicated their opinion that Jane did not miss him much when he was alive because she rarely came to our house for family celebrations. The McCormacks usually went off to gated developments in Florida with their rich friends from Kenilworth. I would have a hard time calming down the troops.

Then she flopped on the kneeler in front of the casket and said, with perhaps better grammar, "Doesn't he look natural, Chuck?" I said nothing in return. He didn't look natural at all. He didn't look a bit like my father. My faith, however tremulous it often is, forces me to insist that my father's corpse is not my father at all, though it will be again one day when body and spirit are reunited.

Then, dabbing her ruined makeup, she rose from the kneeler and elbowed her way between Peg and April. She also dragged poor Ted. He looked as if he felt foolish, but he had apparently long since given up trying to restrain his wife.

I leaned behind Mom and found the eyes of Rosemarie and Peg already waiting for mine. The lionesses were ready to strike. I pointed at them with both hands and forbade them to do or say anything. They turned away, clearly displeased with my warning.

Jane made herself the center of attention at the wake. She interceded between visitors and the Good April, intercepted people who wanted to shake hands with me, and blubbered often. She was, after all, the oldest in the family and she should be in charge.

I was angry too, as angry as Peg and Rosemarie. Jane's routine was tasteless and narcissistic. It was also unfair. She had opted out of the intimate family circle a long time ago. It was inappropriate that she should suddenly reinsert herself into it.

However, what if you're the first child, attractive indeed, but without any particular talent and you are followed by dangerously colorful characters like me and Peg and then Rosemarie. Then a jet pilot comes along and carries you off into a new and better world. You experience the turning point of the late forties and early fifties in a different context than the rest of the family. Your brother achieves some, arguably illusory, fame for his pictures, your sister directs the West Suburban Symphony, your foster sister writes occasional stories for *The New Yorker*, and your little brother becomes a priest who marches with Martin Luther King. It's a world in which you feel distinctly out of place.

Charles C. O'Malley, when did you begin to think like a Christian?

This sudden conversation was aborted by the appearance of the pastor of St. Ursula. The custom at Catholic wakes is for a priest to do a "wake service" each night, if a priest is available. Ed said a few prayers when we arrived. Msgr. Raven would come about 8:00 tonight and Msgr. Keenan the next night. The presider at the wake would recite some preliminary prayers, read a passage from scripture, then preach a brief homily. John Raven, our family priest back in the thirties and forties when Monsignor Mugsy Branigan presided over St. Ursula was a man, as my father once said, of silver and gold. He had helped Rosemarie when she was agonizing about her father's abuse and me when I was not sure it was wise to marry her. We both owed him a lot. So did all of the family.

However, the new pastor at St. U's beat him to it. He swept into the funeral home—in cassock, biretta, and black cape though it was a warm and humid evening—bounded up to the front of the line, turned to the crowd, and announced, "I am Father James Francis McNally, pastor of St. Ursula parish where the requiem Mass will be celebrated tomorrow. I will now lead in the recitation of the Rosary."

A plump man with a round face and a thick neck, he knelt heavily at the casket and recited all five mysteries of the Rosary in a nasal singsong voice, interrupted only by Jane's loud sighs. His manner as he assaulted the deity with his prayers was officious and demanding. He controlled the whole funeral parlor. He was indeed, as Mary Margaret had said, a narcissist. Ed left the room so his temper, still on the hair trigger after his ordeal with the late cardinal, would not explode.

When he had drained the last bit of boredom and torment from the phony piety of his prayers, he lumbered to his feet and quickly worked his way down the line of mourners, clasping each of our hands in a clammy grasp and muttering, with no eye contact, "Sorry for your trouble."

As he turned to leave, I decided to have my revenge.

"Father McNally, the new archbishop was just here!"

He wheeled on surprise, glared, then stomped out.

"Chucky," Peg said to me, "you're absolutely incorrigible!"

Yeah, and I was a Christian just a few minutes ago.

"I think it was nice of Chuck to tell that poor priest that the archbishop was here."

"Chucky," Jane protested, as she struggled off her knees. "why didn't you get rid of that obnoxious priest? We would never tolerate a man like that in Faith, Hope."

"Alas, I'm not God."

Vince brought a comfortable chair for the Good April to relax on.

"Thank you, Vincent dear, I am just a little tired."

The new cliché among the mourners was, "Isn't it a great turnout?"

To which I would reply, "The people from the rest of the country will be here tomorrow."

Jane persisted in her act. I wondered if she had fortified herself for the ordeal with some of the drink taken. Her perfume was too strong for me to be sure. That accusation would certainly be made by Peg and Rosemarie. Fortunately for me, I was a Christian (intermittently) and I would not indulge in rash suspicions.

John Raven arrived, quiet and diffident as he always was, a gentleness which did not quite hide his intense integrity and compassion.

"I gather that there was a priest here before," he said, with his typical little smile. "I promise I won't keep you for more than a few moments."

The crowd became silent as they fell under the spell of John's charm and holiness.

"I think tonight of the passage in St. Paul, 'O death, where is thy victory, O grave, where is thy sting.' At first it seems that the sting of death is everywhere in this room. A good and wonderful man is no longer with us. A life in which he did many good works for so many people, in which he raised with his lovely wife this fine-looking brood of children, is now ended at least for the moment and the wife and children must struggle on without him. That looks like a lot of sting, doesn't it, a lot of victory for death? Yet all we have to do is to look at this handsome, confident group up here and know that they simply deny death any sting, any victory. They see with the keen eyes of faith that John O'Malley's life has just begun and that we will all someday laugh at death together with him. There are good days ahead."

The mourners were mesmerized by his simple words. For a moment after he had finished, there was total silence, then the buzz began again, slowly and carefully, as if people did not want to violate the magical moment that Father Raven had created for us.

It was a nice touch to point at the principal mourners as a sign, a metaphor for the defeat of death. I'd have to use that metaphor sometime.

He moved along the line of the O'Malleys saying something personal to each of them. Everyone of us, save for Jane, laughed when he talked to us.

"Well, Chuck," he said to me, "I suppose everyone is telling you that you're the head of the family now."

"I've heard that once or twice."

"And you don't respond that you've been in charge since 1941 at the latest."

"More like 1939."

"You've done a good job."

"I try."

"Still married to that beautiful woman?"

"She hasn't thrown me out yet."

"A good sign."

I managed to catch his conversation with my wife.

"It's been a long time, Rosemarie, hasn't it? And yourself more beautiful than ever. Apparently that redhead galoot shaped up pretty well?"

"He's making progress, Father Raven."

"He's not at all like his father, yet just like him, isn't he?"

"You got it!"

"Well, he'll continue to progress, I suspect. Take good care of him Rosemarie."

"I will."

For the first time at the wake, tears poured down my face. Father Raven knew that the original design was that the galoot was supposed to take care of Rosemarie. So did she.

At nine people were pouring in. My womenfolk, despite their rage toward Jane, were still gracious, charming, elegant. I was slumped, weary, about to collapse. My smile was frozen on my face, perhaps so it would never go away. I was sweating, my hands were moist, my head ached, my eyes hurt, my legs were sore, and my memory was failing me. I belonged in a comfortable hospital bed.

Jane prevented Joe Raftery from shaking hands with me.

He returned to me after he had spoken to Mom.

"Of course, Joseph. You didn't catch the pass Vincent threw, but Chucky did. He's never quite got over it. Did you see Edward Murray? He was the Mount Carmel player Chucky knocked out. They live right across the street now."

"Would you please move on, sir?" Jane said to him. "There are other people waiting."

I almost warned her never to say that again to anyone. I resolved that if it did happen again, I would.

Fortunately for me, she ran out of steam.

"Teddy, it's almost ten and they're still coming. I'm ready to drop. This wake hasn't been well organized. Take me home please. It's a long ride back to Kenilworth."

Poor Ted did not argue. Rather he took her arm. She slobbered over the Good April and left. Peg now was on the other side. I could see the optical daggers following Jane out of the funeral home. Things might get very difficult when the wake ended. If it ever did end.

At a quarter to eleven, I found myself in the office of the

funeral parlor, surrounded by my wife and sister. Outside the office, Delia Murray was taking care of Mom, and Mary Margaret held a sleeping Siobhan in her arms.

"Chuck," Peg began, ominously I thought, "you really ought to have stopped her."

"Am I God!"

"She's a coarse, vulgar woman," Rosemarie, with whom I was still falling in love, joined the fight. "You must not permit her to come back tomorrow night."

"The last time I checked things she's Dad's daughter, indeed his firstborn child."

I thought of the joy with which young April and Vangie must have welcomed her coming.

"Did you see that dress?" Peg demanded. "It might have fit her ten years ago. And twenty pounds of jewelry? Is that stylish on the North Shore?"

"I'm sure people up there think she's coarse and vulgar too. They tolerate her because she's Ted's wife."

A woman he had dreamed about when he was chasing Japanese Zeros in the Philippines.

"She stole the show!" Rosemarie shouted. "Did you see the way she slobbered over poor April? Why didn't you tell her to get her drunken fat ass out of the funeral parlor?"

My good wife rarely shouted at me in anger.

"No one could steal the show with you two up there in front of the casket."

"You're full of shit, Charles Cronin O'Malley!"

My wife was truly angry, though I was not the proper target for her rage.

"She spoiled everything!" Peg argued. "For everyone!"

"No, she didn't," I replied.

"Yes, she did," Rosemarie shot back. "She's a crude bitch!"

"Will both of you please shut up," I said.

"What?" Peg shouted.

"How dare you talk to us like that?" my wife's beautiful face contorted in icy rage.

"She ruined everything for poor April and you didn't stop her."

"I said shut up and give me a chance to talk."

I must have sounded pretty fierce because the two jungle felines backed up.

"You have every reason to be angry . . ." I began, then collapsed into an easy chair. I wanted merely to go to sleep. "Jane was indeed a disgrace. However, she did not spoil anything but her own image and reputation. Everyone thought how sad it was she should come to her father's wake and act like a vulgar drunk . . ."

"And you let her do it! You're a coward when it comes to fighting with women, Chucky Ducky!"

"I cite the present confrontation as evidence to the contrary. Now dear wife, if you could manage your mouth for a moment or two, I'll make my important point."

"Which is?"

"The important person in our discussion is the Good April . . ."

They opened their mouths.

"Let me finish, damn it all."

I became aware of Mary Margaret standing in the doorway, listening to the fight.

"Jane didn't fool April. She saw her becoming what she is long before we did. Yet it would truly break her heart if we tried to ban Jane from the wake, or, even worse, if there was a huge family fight up there in front of Dad's casket. Jane can't ruin anything for Mom, but you two could if you lose your tempers."

Silence.

"Chuck's right," Mary Margaret announced.

"Who asked your opinion, young woman!"

"Chill out, Rosie. Both of you are being unfair to poor Chucky."

Thereupon she put her charge in my arms

"I have to take Grandma home to her house."

She departed the room with all the serenity of a seraph who had made her case.

The five-year-old curled up on my lap. She was, I noted, getting heavier.

"What we have to do, all of us," I continued, "is keep our anger under control. For Dad's sake, for April's sake, and even for our own sakes. I hope that's clear to both of you. I won't tolerate any fighting in front of Dad's dead body."

No argument from either of them.

"We'd better take poor little Shovie home . . . Do you want to drive, Chuck?"

"You better drive. I'll hold the kid in my arms."

I had carried the day, just barely perhaps, but I had won. I didn't feel very good about it. None of us were ourselves. Rosemarie and I were on jet lag. Peg was doubtless remembering the sibling rivalries between herself and Jane which I had been too insensitive to notice. Didn't little girls always fight with one another?

"Did you take your medicine?" Rosemarie asked as she started the old Mercedes which was "her car."

"No more till three."

That was our only exchange.

"Mommy," Shovie said as she stirred in my arms.

"Mommy is driving the car because Daddy is too sleepy. We're almost home."

Daddy is also too sleepy to make love with Mommy though we should really defy death tonight. This is not the time to suggest it anyway because Mommy is angry.

"I'll put her to bed. You'd better turn in before you collapse."

I struggled up the stairs, took off my clothes, hung them up because even if I were dead, which I might have been, I would still hang up my clothes, and fell into bed.

Sometime later, a woman crawled into bed and kissed my forehead.

"Mary Margaret was right, Chuck. I'm terribly sorry."

"It wouldn't be an Irish funeral if there weren't a few fights." I whispered.

A gracious loser, my wife. No wonder I was falling in love with her again.

Later in the night I woke up with a start. It was late morning in Moscow. I should be awake.

On the bed table at my side of the bed, I felt a glass of water and my two allergy pills. I swallowed the pills, spilling only half the glass of water. I plunged back into sleep. My dreams, I think, were about Jane and Dad.

Chapter Six

Rosemarie

We were sitting silently at the breakfast table after Mass. Shovie, over her strong protests, was at school. Mary Margaret had brought the Good April home from Mass. April was in a good mood. Everyone had been so nice last night. Not a word about Jane, not even as "poor dear Jane."

I had consumed my orange juice and fruit salad. He was listlessly stirring his raisin bran and bananas. He would also polish off some of the remaining sweet rolls from yesterday. The so-and-so never put on weight.

"Chucky," I began uncertainly, "I owe you an apology . . ."

"You apologized last night," he said glumly. "There is a general amnesty for all fights in the present situation."

"I can't believe how terrible I was."

"You and Peg, but it's okay, I understand."

"I can't remember when I have been worse."

"Even at your worst, Rosemarie Helen, you're not very bad."

His eyes were bleary and bloodshot, poor dear man.

"I thought I'd say that it's not easy being the head of the family, but you were the head of this family when you were ten."

He grinned, his old Chucky Ducky leprechaun grin.

"You noticed that?"

"The last time you were so angry at me was when I got drunk in Stuttgart."

He pondered that, not enjoying the discussion.

"No way," he said, slurping up the remnants of his cereal. "Last night I knew I was just a substitute target for Jane. It was all right. You had something to be angry about. If I'm a useful target, be my guest."

"Poor Chucky Ducky, an inkblot for all the Crazy O'Malleys. Except Mary Margaret."

"She was right, of course . . . I hope you apologized to her."

"Certainly!"

"Jane," he went on, "is in a bad way. Tough to be a first child when the next three were what they were."

"I never understood that till last night . . . Ted has to do something about her."

"I wonder if he can."

"You're not angry at me anymore?"

"No way."

"Wonderful! Now finish your sweet roll. We have work to do."

"Sweet rolls," he said. "I need my energy."

In the afternoon we went through the *Ave Maria* again and "When the Saints." Neither effort had the professional polish that I would have liked, but given the circumstances they would be fine. Chuck and I had a cool vocalization around "Go marching in."

After the practice, he summoned Peg and Ed and me to a conference.

"We are dealing, gentle souls," he said, "with two challenges and two imponderables. The challenges are the musical pieces we just practiced. They are unorthodox. There'll be a lot of priests at St. Ursula's. They may be shocked at our *Ave*, we must be prepared for their disapproval."

"Many of them will love it," Ed interjected, "We are the Crazy O'Malleys after all. There are separate rules for us. Everyone knows that."

"Precisely." Chuck nodded sagely. "What we propose to do at the cemetery will be discussed far and wide . . . I don't know who the kook was who thought it up. I don't care what anyone says. It's for Mom and Dad, both of whom will love it, each in their own reality."

"We Crazy O'Malleys have a reputation to live up to," Peg said.

She had called me earlier.

"Did you apologize?"

"Over breakfast."

"What was he like?"

"Sweet."

"I'd better call before he changes his mood."

"Fine," Chuck continued. "I always like unanimous consent in this family. The imponderables are Jane and Father McNally. We cannot anticipate what either will do, especially when we sing the *Ave* during Communion at St. U's. I would not imagine that either will be at the cemetery, but again we must be aware of the potential for mayhem. I think we must all concentrate on keeping cool at all times."

"Chill out," I said.

"Precisely. Jimmy has been instructed to head Father McNally off at the pass if he tries to disrupt our prayer at Mary's altar. I think, by the way, that we should do our best to make it a prayer and not just a performance."

We all laughed, because we knew it was true.

On the way over to the wake, he whispered in my ear.

"A funny thing is happening to me, Rosemarie."

"Oh?"

"I think I'm falling in love with you again."

I felt my face flush.

"I am forewarned. I'll have to remember to lock the doors."

"It won't do any good."

A reversion to teenage is not an unusual phenomenon for men. It is not merely that they want more sex, they also want to lavish more attention, more affection, more admiration on their spouses. A lot more of what we called in the old days petting and necking. Chucky seems to be unique in that he solemnly announces that it is happening, which is good strategy I suppose. Some women find these reversions disgusting, others think it is silly; yet others, like me, find it amusing and even delightful. I adore being adored. Yet Chuck had certainly picked an odd time and place for this reversion to adolescence.

"You want to be a teenager again?" I asked him skeptically.

"Why not?"

"And I'm supposed to regress too?"

"That would be nice."

"Why now?"

"What better time?"

"I was a terrible bitch last night."

"Only for a few moments."

I pulled the car into the parking lot on North Avenue for the second night of the wake. Before I could slide out, he kissed me, a very provocative and lingering kiss, and rested his hand on one of my breasts.

"Teenage behavior," I commented as I got out of car, my face flushed and my body warm.

"What else? . . . You're beautiful!"

"Blarney!"

I was in for a lot of touching and caressing. What better time than when we are denouncing death. I was not beautiful anymore. Presentable, yes. Attractive, yes. But beautiful, no, not for a long time. Yet the look in Chuck's eyes said that he saw me as beautiful. So maybe I was.

Vince and Peg were waiting for us at the wake. Peg and Chuck embraced, celebrating their reconciliation on the phone in the morning.

"How did your talk with Joe Raftery go yesterday?"

"Yeah . . . He was a little strange."

"How so?"

"He lost his wife a couple of years ago, second wife, young, married her in church."

"Poor guy," I said.

"What's strange about that?" Vince asked. "Tragic maybe, but it happens."

"He's not sure she's dead."

"Oh . . . Did he seem to be crazy?"

"Not at all. Same old Joe."

Then April and Mary Margaret arrived. I was so proud of my daughter and my mother. They both looked smashing in their black dresses. The Good April seemed quite perky.

"Well, I think we're all doing just fine! I'll be glad when this is over, but it's all going nicely, isn't it, dears?"

Chuck sometimes calls his mother Dr. Panglossa, the sort of thing a University of Chicago graduate would say.

"Except for poor Janie," she went on. "Dad's death has really hit her hard. You've all been very nice to her, even Father Ed. I'm sure that up in heaven, Dad is proud of you."

Mary Margaret and Shovie joined us. The former glanced from me to her father and back and approved of us with a slight smile.

Little witch.

We walked up to the front of the funeral parlor. Father Ed was waiting for us, brooding over the casket. We said a few prayers and stood up to greet our fellow mourners. Our kids—mine and Peg's—joined us. The great-grandchildren had been left at home. One night was more than enough for them. Shovie and Mary Margaret were at the end of the line, where they could make quick exits if necessary.

"I AM going to Grandpa's wake," Shovie had informed me earlier with determination. "He EXPECTS me to be there."

Family stubbornness, from my side of the family doubtless.

I turned on all my charm as we greeted our fellow mourners. If Chuck said I was beautiful, then I was. So I should act like I was. I don't know that it made any difference, however, though a lot of women complimented me on, "how wonderful you look tonight, dear."

My poor husband, however, looked absolutely awful. He was fading quickly. His body clock was a mess, still on Moscow time. The allergy medicine limited his sneezing and coughing but made him drowsy. He should have been in bed sleeping.

As afternoon turned into evening, the procession of mourners became a blur. You smiled at them, hopefully greeted them by name, took their hand, gratefully acknowledged their sympathy, smiled again, and thanked them for their prayers. If you did not know them, you tried to remember their name from the introduction and thanked them by name at the end. They deserved the best of your attention and grace. I tried to provide both.

Occasionally, someone would say that the tribute in *The New York Times* was wonderful and asked whether my husband had anything to do with it. I would say with a grin that he might have.

A few would comment on how tired Chuck looked. His father's death has been a great strain on him, hasn't it?

"On all of us. Chuck and I just returned from a month of photo shoots in Russia. He's still on Moscow time and allergy medicine."

"It's lucky for him that you travel with him."

"That's what he married me for, someone to take care of him on trips."

Jane appeared about seven in a gray pantsuit and lots of diamonds. I didn't think she'd been drinking this time. But the rest of the act was the same, sobbing over Mom, elbowing her way into line, assuming control of access to Mom, cutting Chucky out of the picture. She was more embarrassing than obnoxious I decided. Most people would have no trouble reading her act. Poor woman. We should do something to help her, though that would be very difficult because her sad, apologetic husband ("Sorry, a lot of bad traffic on the way") had taken on the role of protecting her.

I was angry because her brat children had not come to the wake either night. Chris, Ted, Micky, and Jenny had always seemed to me to be self-satisfied prigs, complacent slugs, hollow phonies. I didn't like them much either. Yet Vangie was their grandfather too. One shouldn't compare one's own children with other people's children. But everyone does. Peg's kids were wonderful, genial and handsome cousins. No comparisons permitted there, though I was sure that, if there were comparisons, mine would win. But Jane's kids never seemed to be alive. Well, it was none of my business.

Not much.

Vince brought a chair for Mom.

"Thank you, Vincent. You're so thoughtful."

Vince had progressed through the years. Peg did not have to remind him of such thoughtfulness nearly as often anymore.

"Chucky looks like he needs a chair too," he whispered to me.

"More likely a bed . . . But you know Chuck. He'd be much happier if he passed out."

We both laughed softly. Chuck would never pass out.

Father Packy Keenan arrived with his brother Jerry and the latter's wife, the notorious Maggie Ward, my shrink. I would have to be on my very best behavior.

"These are very difficult experiences, Rosie," she said, her gentle gray eyes carefully examining my face for signs of strain. "And a troubled woman like your foster sister don't help."

Witch!

"She needs a Maggie Ward in her life," I said gracefully.

Maggie, a lovely little woman with gray hair and a warm soul, smiled.

"You look exceptionally beautiful tonight, Rosie."

"We Irish defy death," I said.

"So I understand."

Maggie's past, before she married Jerry Keenan, was a mystery. She had apparently married very young and had lost both a husband and a child. In her office there was a small frame with a picture of a very young sailor and a very little child. Somehow one knew that one did not ask about them.

Packy Keenan began the wake service with a reading about the daughter of Jairus.

"You've surely noticed the gracefulness of Jesus in this scene. He lets the little girl play. In the middle of all the celebration the important thing for the child is to get back to her play. She doesn't know that she's been dead. She does understand that it is the role of kids to play, so she plays. New life is not a big deal unless you can play. I suspect that this is a hint of what the life of the resurrection is like. We will wake up as little kids and begin to play because that's what we're supposed to do. We'll be children like Siobhan Marie here looking forward to life, or teens like Mary Margaret and Rita here were a couple years ago eager for the next surprise, the next excitement, the next joy in our rapidly expanding lives. We who have the faith know that whatever else might be ahead of us, there'll be lots of fun. And wherever there's fun that's where the Crazy O'Malleys will be with their music and song."

Laughter and applause from the congregation.

"What's he talking about?" Jane said in an angry stage whisper. "No priest at Faith, Hope would say anything that stupid."

I felt a charge of rage leap through our receiving line. I wanted to brain the little fool.

It takes a lot more than a stupid woman like Janie to shake Packy's cool. Like John Raven the night before, he went along the line with words of hope and healing for all of us after the brief wake service. Except Jane, who turned to talk to Ted as Packy left April.

"Rosie," he said to me, "I hear you're going to do your music in the church and the cemetery?"

"Who told you that?"

"Your husband, who else?"

"He never could keep a secret."

"He wanted me to promise to prevent McNally from disrupting it. I promised that I would."

Packy, a big, burly man like his brother, could certainly do that.

"He's not likely to go to the cemetery," Packy continued, "It would disrupt his schedule . . . The jazz group is going to do 'Saints'?"

"Yep."

"I wouldn't miss that for the world . . . By the way, Rosie, you look stunning tonight."

When he had left, Jane spoke up again, "Mom, you certainly have strange priests here on the West Side . . ."

"Janie, dear, you shouldn't say things like that. Father Keenan has been a good friend to the family for a long time. We all love him dearly. That's why we've asked him to preach tomorrow."

"No one talked to me about it."

I was now convinced she had been drinking.

The crowds continued to pour in. I was astonished to learn how many people Vangie had helped, especially GIs coming home from the War and priests in poor parishes who needed a design to repair their churches. He had not only designed them for free, but sometimes paid for the construction work. Many people who lived in the suburban developments for which he'd won prizes told us that they had to come to the wake to express their thanks for the wonderful homes he'd built.

"I feel I never really knew him," Peg spoke softly in my ear. "He certainly hid his generosity. That's the way it should be."

"There was more of Chuck in him than I realized."

Peg laughed. She knew what I meant. My husband is obsessively generous, not bad for a man who only at his fiftieth birthday party admitted that the Great Depression probably would not return.

Jane was growing more restless. Her show had worn her out. She turned to her husband, "Ted, I can't stand any more of this. Please take me home."

Ted McCormack calmly nodded, doubtless glad that it was almost over.

"I have to go home now, darling," she said as she drooled over the Good April. "My kiddies are expecting me. I'll be at the Mass tomorrow of course, but I won't be able to go to the cemetery. You know I can't stand cemeteries."

"I understand, Janie dear. Give my love to your children."

Mom seemed to be relieved to be rid of her.

She left the funeral parlor with a noisy display of distress and weariness, as though it all was too much to bear. Jennifer, her youngest "kiddie," was three years older than Mary Margaret and was allegedly working in an "alternative" record store at Old Orchard.

That was a nasty thought. I should be ashamed of myself. I glanced at my husband. He had been looking at me. He rolled his eyes and seemed to sway. He might still pass out. Then what would we do with him?

He might be falling in love with me, but there would be no sex tonight, even if we didn't have to drag him down to Oak Park Hospital. How would he ever give his eulogy tomorrow morning?

Suddenly I was very tired too. My feet hurt, my back was sore, my mouth was dry. Would this ever end? Shovie and Mary

Margaret had disappeared. Big sister was doubtless hovering over sleeping little sister. I was thankful that Jane would not be at the cemetery.

Then a good-looking, slender man with white hair was shaking hands with me.

"You're holding up a lot better than Chuck, Rosie," he said with a slow smile, "but I bet you'd love to sit down and kick off your shoes."

"It would be great, Joe Raftery."

"I was very happy to hear that you and Chuck had married. It seemed a perfect match. If I'd any sense in those days, I would have sent you a note. Unless I'm mistaken, it's been a happy marriage."

"Chuck will do until someone better comes along," I said with a laugh.

He seemed to be a normal, intelligent man, with more grace and courtesy than most. Looking for a dead wife? Chucky knew how to attract some weird stuff.

Finally, it was over. A quarter to eleven. Only the Good April was sprightly.

"It was an evening I'll always treasure, wasn't it, Peg dear?"

"A little hard on the feet, Mom, but a night to remember. Dad was truly a remarkable man."

"Is . . ." she replied. "Poor Janie took it harder than anyone else, didn't she? Ted really ought to see that she gets some help."

Panglossa, as usual, spoke harsh truth under the guise of sweetness. No, that was not right—she mixed sweetness with harsh truth.

My husband was slumped in a chair, his eyes closed, his shoulders sagging, his mouth hanging open.

"Are you all right, Chucky Ducky?"

"Mommy, I wanna go home."

"Daddy sounds just like me!" Shovie, who had just joined us, exclaimed. "Better take him home, Mommy."

"Right away, dear."

"Don't let him go to Russia ever again."

"Good idea, hon."

So I took them both home, put Siobhan to bed, and discovered my husband sound asleep.

Falling in love again, indeed!

He descended to breakfast at seven the next morning in a charcoal gray suit with a black tie, scrubbed, shaved, polished. It was the first time in a major event in our years of marriage that he had accomplished these or similar tasks on his own initiative. His eyes were clear and focused, his back and shoulders in almost military posture. We were back in Bamberg in 1946.

"Take your allergy medicine?"

"Not till after the eulogy . . . no, just a cup of tea . . . Afterward I will."

"Your manuscript ready?"

"Charles Cronin O'Malley should need a manuscript? Come, dear wife, you jest?"

His eyes sparkled. He had put on his fun mask.

"Pardon me, sir husband. I assume you know what you're going to say."

"More or less." He waved off my concern, in a gesture that I have often occasioned. "I am obviously no match for John Raven. So I will be brief and simple."

"And I'm the queen of Sheba."

"Woman, you are not. You are my wife Rosemarie with whom I am falling in love again."

"Big talk," I scoffed.

The soft late-September weather of the previous days was followed that morning by a cloud cover that might be described as "preominous." It fit the mood of the day. The battered family, which assembled at the funeral parlor, seemed eager to get the day over with, something like a necessary but painful physical exam. We worried, as Chuck said we should, about Father McNally and Jane, the latter not present at the funeral parlor. She would surely make another demonstration at the funeral against the rest of us. I did not expect that I would be the target.

Pulling up to the church Vangie had built and for which he had won a prize was a depressing experience. Our marriage was the first one in it. Other marriages, Baptisms, First Communions, confirmations, concerts made it one of the important monuments of our lives. This was the first funeral in the family.

The air was heavy as Chuck and Vince got out of the limo, as were our hearts. April, Peg, and I, all in deep black and with veils (April's idea) waited till the mourners lined up on the sidewalk and the casket was lifted onto the dolly, which would bring it into the church. We were signaled to line up and lead the procession behind the casket.

The pallbearers lifted the casket, carried it up the steps, and placed it again on the dolly. The three of us paused at the bottom of the steps.

Then Jane, in a black dress which was too tight, shoved me out of the way.

"You don't belong here," she snarled. "You're an interloper in our family. You're not one of the family. I belong with Mom. I will walk with her."

I was astonished though I should not have been. Jane must have believed for a long time that I had taken her rightful place in the family. I was the cause of her unhappy life. I had never noticed the rivalry. Neither had anyone else.

I backed away silently. April and Peg stumbled forward, not wanting to create more of a scene. What do I do now?

Mary Margaret and Shovie eased me into line with them, at the very end of the immediate family. They too were wearing veils. The three of us slowly climbed the stairs. Inside, Jimmy's seminarians were singing beautiful Latin chant, sad, but hopeful, which is what the Catholic liturgy is supposed to be about. Either way life is a toss-up. Catholics opt for hope, though sometimes just barely.

I was in another world, not far in the distance, only two blocks away on Menard Avenue, but light-years in time. I had barged my way into the family because I knew that my life depended on finding a family of my own. Heedlessly, I had elbowed another child away, as surely as she had elbowed me aside a few moments before. I had never realized what I had done. Vangie and April, always sensitive to their kids' emotions, had not even considered the possibility that Jane would feel that they had abandoned her. Yet the wound must have festered for forty years.

Dear God, why did You let this happen?

My reverie was interrupted by a loud tapping sound. The choir stopped in midverse. The funeral procession came to a dead stop. I looked up. Father McNally, in cassock, surplice, and long cape was at the pulpit, impatiently tapping at the microphone to gain attention.

"I am Father James Francis McNally, the pastor of this parish. I wish to make it clear that this liturgy is in explicit violation of the normal rules of my parish. Ordinarily I preside over all the funeral liturgies in this parish. Ordinarily I prescribe the music for the liturgy. Ordinarily we have funeral liturgies only for registered members of the parish. However, this is a special situation and I have acceded to a temporary suspension of the rules.

"I wish to make it clear that in no sense should this liturgy be considered an invitation to receive the Holy Eucharist when it is distributed. Only Catholics in good standing and in the state of grace should approach the altar."

He turned and walked back into the sacristy.

For a moment there was total silence in the church, Vangie's church, I thought. Then the choir resumed its interrupted hymn and the procession moved slowly forward. Next to me, my sainted Mary Margaret was stiff with rage.

The liturgy moved forward with stately grace, marred only by Jane's bubbling tears. What do Peg and April think? Their emotions are probably a mix of anger and pity, with the latter stronger. Poor April, she had lost the love of her life and her first-born was adding to her grief. She must have wondered where they had gone wrong with Jane. Naturally she would blame herself.

In the back of my head or maybe down in one of the sub-basements of my consciousness a story was taking shape that I might send off to *The New Yorker.* I asked God to forgive me for the distraction, but I assume that God knows how powerful the imagination is when it has fixated on a story.

It was time for the Gospel and the homily. Jesus raised from the dead the little brother of Martha and Mary, silly little teens. He told them that he was the Resurrection and the Life. A very Catholic story.

John Raven walked down to the edge of the sanctuary to deliver the homily on Jesus as the Resurrection and the Life. He spoke as the great men of gold and silver always speak, in a calm, matter-of-fact, reassuring voice. Like priests of his generation, he quoted many of the Catholic writers he had read in the seminary. He began with G. K. Chesterton's story about the 'bus that ran out of control and raced madly toward the Thames. Faced with sudden death, G. K. realized that life was too important to ever be anything but life. With that as his theme he pointed out all the instances of resurrection in our lives—the baby must die to become an infant, the child must die to become a grammar school kid, the eighth-grader must die to be reborn in high school, the teenager must die to rise as a young adult, the young adult must die to become a spouse, and the spouse must rise to become a parent. Life and death are patterns of life. John O'Malley was now experiencing another death and rebirth, one in which we all would eventually join him.

> There is nothing dies but something lives
> Till skies be fugitives,
> Till Time, the hidden root of change, updries,
> Are Birth and Death inseparable on earth;
> For they are twain yet one, And Death is Birth.

"Francis Thompson," Mary Margaret whispered.

" 'Ode to the Setting Sun,' " I whispered back.

And then felt guilty for showing off.

The congregation was quiet and motionless as Father Raven returned to his chair in the sanctuary.

The little kids, including my Siobhan Marie, brought up the

bread and wine. She was in charge of course, gently and protectively guiding the smaller ones. Where did she ever learn to do that?

As if I didn't know.

Then I began to wonder about my own death. I would surely die long before Chuck, who would live to be at least as old as his father. What would he do without me for perhaps twenty years? He would have to marry again. I would insist on that.

Yet what if he died first, as Vangie did? I would not be the graceful grand duchess with a straight back and firm posture. I'd probably be a contentious, senile old fool, a great burden to my children and grandchildren.

Neither alternative seemed all that attractive.

Our best years were behind us. "Golden years" is a euphemism for "old age." I never wanted to get old, but I had done it without even noticing.

I could live to ninety like my ancestor, another Rosemarie. Chuck might live that long too, out of meanness. We'd both be doddering old fools—cranky, crabby, crusty, cantankerous curmudgeons. We'd really drive the kids crazy. Serve the little brats right.

Suddenly it was Communion time.

"We will deny no one the Eucharist," Packy Keenan said with gentle authority.

My priesteen, Jimmy, put the host on my tongue and grinned, I grinned back. I was terribly proud of him. Any young man who wanted to be a priest these days was very brave. He would not be a dead serious cleric like his uncle Ed, who didn't know how to relax. He'd be a fun priest.

I would have returned to the pew if Mary Margaret had not stopped me.

Oh, yes, we had to sing the *Ave Maria.* Suddenly I lost my nerve. This was a Crazy O'Malley caper. We ought not to do it. Jane would misbehave. How should we sing it? The rest would follow my lead. Softly quietly, like a monastic choir from long ago, but with deep faith and joy.

We were all there at the Blessed Mother's altar. My throat was dry. My stomach was churning. This was a terrible mistake. We faced toward the altar. The Good April caught my eye and enveloped me in the most wonderful smile. Chuck was holding my hand. April hummed the key, and, almost unbidden, the enchanted words flowed from my lips.

Ave Maria, gratia plena, Dominus tecum;
Benedicta tua in mulieribus,
et benedictus fructis ventris tui Jesus.
Sancta Maria, Mater Dei,
ora pro nobis peccatoribus,
nunc et in hora mortis nostrae. Amen!

We worked our way around in simple harmonies, one of them sung by the small ones, backed up against my vocalization. We were all crying when we finished, even the little kids.

I hope you're not offended, I said to herself, just in case she was listening.

Then we turned to the *Salve Regina.* I noticed for the first time that Jane was not with us. But she had practiced with us, had she not when we returned from Europe?

Chuck intoned the hymn and the rest of us joined him.

Salve Regina, Mater misericordiae
Vita dulcedo et spes nostra, salve
Ad te clamamus, exsules filii Hevae.
Ad te suspiramus gementes and flentes
in hac lacrimarum valle.
Eia ergo advocata nostra,
ilos tuos misericordes oculos ad nos converte.
Et Jesum, benedictum fructum ventris tui
nobis post hoc exsilium ostende.
O clemens, o pia, o dulcis Virgo Maria

We really shook the arches of St. Ursula with that one.

Back in the pew I felt much better. Okay, we'd be senile fools in another forty years, but we'd live till then. Maybe we would even have the grace to laugh at ourselves.

I noticed that Jane had maneuvered herself into the front pew so that April was at the end of the pew, Jane next to her, and Peg cut off from her mother. I didn't like that at all.

Then my Chucky Ducky, looking trim and fit and adorable, came to the edge of the sanctuary, wearing a lavaliere mike, just as John Raven had.

> I suppose that I speak for all the family when I say that our father in great part made us what we are. He was a Cubs fan, I a Sox fan. He was born a Republican, though, through the grace of God, he subsequently converted. I was even before I was born, a yellow-dog Democrat. He was a baritone. I am a tenor. He was an artist and an architect, I am still in my heart of hearts an accountant. When I began to earn my living taking pictures, I claimed that I was a realist. He was, early and late, a pure romantic. He loved the military and took great pride in marching down Michigan Avenue in the armor of the Black Horse Troop. I for my part hated the military with an abiding passion. He never feared the return of the Great Depression. I have only just recently and still very tentatively rejected that prospect.
>
> So we argued before I reached the age of reason and continued to argue for the rest of his all too short life. Yet we never once quarreled. More than that I took it for granted that we should argue, that he expected us to argue, and that I would have been an incomplete firstborn son if I wouldn't argue with him. It was evident from the very beginning that my father delighted in arguing with me.

At this point Jane pushed her way clumsily over April and out into the aisle of the church. She sobbed her way toward the back, with her husband trailing behind. "You bitch," I muttered to myself. "You can push me around, but you can't publicly insult and humiliate my Chucky Ducky." Sensing my rage, Mary Margaret extended her arm around my shoulder. My husband continued his eulogy without a moment's break. Well, bitch, I accused her silently. You can make a huge scene but you can't fluster my Chuck.

One of my great surprises when I returned from military service in Germany was that he would ask my advice, and myself not quite twenty years old. Where did I think we should buy a house on the Lake? What did I know? Yet he was seriously interested in my opinion. This was a new dimension to our relationship. I had been promoted from the role of dialectical adversary to that of a senior advisor even though at that time my WQ—wisdom quotient—was lower than zero. I was now both adversary and advisor, roles which persisted until a couple of days ago.

Only later in life, much later, did I discover that he had polled the whole family about our beach-house-to-be and that we all had made the same choice. We each believed that we were the only one of the crowd he consulted. Each of us reveled in our role of the only coconspirator. I'm still wondering how he managed that consensus. Then I remember that his father had been a politician, albeit a Republican. Dad had inherited deft political instincts.

He knew how to preside over a family so that almost all the time we wanted to do what he wanted us to. He never laid down the law. A father-husband can be that relaxed only if he knows his precinct well from careful observation and analysis. I'm not suggesting that Dad deliberately played this family game. By nature and nurture he had absorbed his style almost automatically. How else can you be a good father?

Or a good president of a firm of brilliant architects?

Dad governed us all, even Mom I suspect, by compromise and consensus. As the father of a brood of my own and with a wife of my own. I have tried to use the same strategy, with what success it is not for me to say, though there is no way I can claim to be the paterfamilias as he was.

Only a secure and playful person can engage in Dad's family style. He had to know who he was and what he wanted out of life. He was quite incapable of manipulating his children so that they would reflect his own glory.

Dad also delighted in women. He knew how to respect and reverence them. One need only look at the paintings in his books to observe his candid mix of delight and reverence. I have tried to play that game his way too. Again others will have to judge with what success.

He also had great taste in women. I learned a lot from him there.

People have sometimes dubbed us the Crazy O'Malleys. Dad did not force any of us to fit that paradigm. But his family governance almost guaranteed our "crazy" style. We are men and women who experienced his faith and his love in childhood and were freed thereby to pursue our own destiny, always knowing that there would be a happy home to which we could return. He was beyond all doubt the craziest of all the O'Malleys.

Now we are separated from him, in Jesus' words, for only a little while. The Crazy O'Malleys have opened a branch office in the world to come. We all miss him terribly and we shall continue to miss him. For you, Mom, the loss of your permanent lover will be especially difficult. However, the family has a tradition to sustain. And in the months and years to come we will rally around the Good April and continue to be the kind of family you and Dad created. With your help and God's, we will prove that love is stronger than death.

Chuck walked back to his place with the pallbearers.

The congregation rose to give him a standing ovation. I hoped someone would report that to my ex–foster sister, the Wicked Witch of the North Shore.

Dear God, I will be glad when this terrible day is over.

Chapter Seven

Chuck

We waited quietly in the limo that would take us to Queen of Heaven Cemetery in Hillside. None of us smoked. Yet the atmosphere was dense with heavy emotion, grief, and anger combined. Peg and Rosemarie for one of the rare moments in life that they were together said not a word, behind their veils. The Good April was also silent. I took her hand.

"Almost over," I said.

Not really. There was still the ceremony at the cemetery and the lunch at Oak Park Country Club (which is not in Oak Park), the place where my parents and I had eaten supper after my honorable discharge from the Army of the United States.

"That was a very nice little talk," April said. "I'm glad everyone liked it. Dad always said our little Chucky has a way with words."

"Thanks," I said.

"I really think it's time that Ted do something about poor Jane. I'm sure she's stopped taking her pills."

"What pills?" we all asked.

"Oh, I don't know what they called them. Tranquilizers of some kind."

"What did she say when she left the pew?"

"I really didn't hear her very well."

"She said," Peg replied, her voice tight, " 'I don't have to sit through this shit.' "

Ah, I was now certainly another target. Perhaps Jane thought that as the oldest she should have given the eulogy. Her outrage was perfectly understandable. Yet the only one really hurt by it was Mom.

"What did she say to you, Rosemarie?" Peg asked.

" 'You don't belong here. You're an interloper in our family. You're not one of the family. I belong with Mom. I will walk with her.' "

"The bitch!" Peg shouted.

"I think she was probably jealous of you," Mom said calmly. "She certainly never had any reason for that."

Ah, but the thought that Rosemarie had replaced her must have haunted her life. Whether there was reason for such emotions was not to the point. Rather the point was that we had totally missed her jealousy.

"If we had paid closer attention to her throughout the years, we might have noticed it," I said.

"I can't remember her resenting Rosie when we were kids. She never did like me very much. She didn't mind Mom and Dad bringing a boy home from the hospital. But a second daughter. Before I was old enough to fight back, she'd slap me every chance she had."

"I don't recall that," I said. "But little boys don't see what's going on before their eyes."

"When Rosie kind of moved in," Peg went on, "she was already a popular young woman at Trinity High School. She hardly noticed you, did she, Rosie?"

"I didn't think so. Now I'm sure she felt such emotions. I can understand what happened. I was an extension of you and she was now outnumbered and, in her mind, outloved."

"She was always a little difficult," Mom said. "Very quick to take offense. We certainly tried to be nice. However, Peg darling, no matter how we tried, she never really accepted you. When I came home from St. Anne's with you, she told us to take you back. She said that many times in the next couple of years."

I had been clueless.

"Nonetheless, she's hurting," I said. "We should try to help her if we can."

"I'll have to ask Maggie Ward whether there's anything we can do," my wife said. "I think she'll say its much too late."

I shut up. This was not the time or the place to reopen the Jane question. If I had known about it, I might have suggested that she give the eulogy. That might have made matters worse. However, the few remarks in the car on the way to Hillside—three layers of suburbs west of Chicago—made my eulogy look pretty bad.

No, that was not true. Because Vangie had probably never been able to break through Jane's rage did not mean he was a failed father. It meant rather that in some situations there is nothing even the wisest parent can do. Rosemarie and I had tormented ourselves for years when April Rosemary had drifted away into the drug and commune underground. She managed to pull herself out. Jane never did.

That was too easy a comparison. I shouldn't be making any comparisons. What if this were my funeral and poor Rosemarie was trying to cope with a child who had resented us. Maybe Sean would be angry at us for the loss of his beloved Jewish sweetheart. It wasn't our fault. We had been kind and sympathetic to her. She seemed to have bonded with Mary Margaret. Then she went off to Israel and within a couple of months married a pilot in the Israeli Air Force. Sean Seamus had not recovered. Mary Margaret, with the wisdom of a younger sister, insisted that he would be all right, but what did she know?

So many things they can blame you for if they want to.

A faint drizzle descended upon us as we neared the cemetery. My gut was twisted up in knots. The ancients believed that the bowels were the place of emotion. Not a bad idea actually. Emotional stress stirred them up. I'd had a stomachache since the call in Moscow.

Funeral cortèges are intolerably slow. A ride to a cemetery was like a sentence in purgatory. Would we ever get there?

Finally, we made the slow turn off Wolf Road into the cemetery. Someone appeared from the cemetery office to propose that we have the burial services inside the chapel.

"I don't think so, dear. My husband couldn't stand those things."

We wound our way through the cemetery, which, like all such, was designed to create the impression of a maze. We were held up by another cortège that was slow in leaving. How dare they slow us down?

Charles Cronin O'Malley, you are becoming more of a cranky, crabby curmudgeon every day.

Finally, we pulled up to the spot—the burial plot my parents had bought forty years ago because they knew they should have one. Rather the Good April had insisted that they should buy one. How many memories must be flowing back from those days? We waited in the car until the mourners had been arranged around the tomb. I joined the other pallbearers in front of the hearse.

"Great talk," Vince whispered to me. "I could never have been that cool if someone walked out on me."

"Poor woman," I said.

Oddly enough, I was not angry at Jane or even surprised. Death seems to curtail surprises.

My sons, instrument cases in hand, were arranging themselves at the head of the open grave. The rest of the clan drifted in that direction. The small fry, under Mary Margaret's and Erin's direction, pushed their way to the front. Please, God, grant that this crazy move of the Crazy O'Malleys works.

We carried Dad's mortal remains to the grave site and lowered it to the stand on which they would rest until we had left and the coffin would be lowered into the ground. My brother Ed, perhaps another member of the clan whom the rest of us had forgotten, was going to preside over the services. In church he had not gone beyond the rhythms of the liturgy. I had never really understood him, though Rosemarie surely did. Mary Margaret had insisted repeatedly in the last couple of days that he was a totally cool priest, even if he was not as noisy as the rest of us.

The drizzle, which had become rain for a few moments, stopped. The iron cope of clouds began to move.

"We are at the end of the funeral services," he began, so softly that one could hardly hear him, "though for the family of John Evangelist the mourning will go on, as will life and love. My brother"—he nodded in my direction—"with characteristic grace described him perfectly in his eulogy. I always thought that Chuck should have been the priest . . . Sorry, Rosie . . . Now I'm glad we have laypeople like him in the Church who understand what our faith is all about better than we priests. Our dad was larger than life, though it took us a long time to realize it. So is our mom. So too are at least some of us. We will miss Dad . . . Dear God in heaven, we will miss him . . . But we will continue to laugh and to celebrate life the way he and Mom taught us to. Oh, yes, there'll be a bite of food to eat and maybe a touch of the creature to drink at Oak Park Country Club when we're finished."

Cool, Eddie, I thought. Like totally cool.

Then he began the beautiful graveside prayers of the Church. At Mary Margaret's instigation, the small fry answered with loud and enthusiastic "Amen" to each of them. I glanced around the huge crowd that had assembled. What would they think of this ultimate in Crazy O'Malley capers?

Finally, the closing prayers, definitive and conclusive. My sons produced their instruments. The sun began to break through the clouds. Nature and nature's God were cooperating.

"Eternal rest grant unto him, O Lord, and may perpetual light shine upon him."

"AMEN!"

"And may all the souls of the departed rest in peace."

"AMEN!"

Kevin Patrick raised his trumpet into the air.

"When the saint . . ." he began, then reprised it on the horn.

"Go marching in, go marching in, go marching in!" Rosemarie and I began our vocalization as the trumpet and sax joined us.

After the first stanza, Kevin Patrick spoke to the astonished crowd.

"We're going to march around the grave, like the ancient Irish did, then go back to the cars as we celebrate the victory of life over death."

I am just a lonesome traveller,
Through this big wide world of sin;
Want to join that grand procession,
When the saint go marchin' in.
|: Oh when the saint go marchin' in, :|
Lord I want to be in that number
When the saint go marchin' in.

All my folks have gone before me,
All my friends and all my kin;
But I'll meet with them up yonder,
When the saint go marchin' in.
|: Oh when the saint go marchin' in, :|
I will meet them all up in heaven,
When the saint go marchin' in.

Come and join me in my journey,
'cause it's time that we begin;
And we'll be there for that judgment,
When the saint go marchin' in.
|: Oh when the saint go marchin' in, :|
We will be in line for that judgment,
When the saint go marchin' in.

|: And when the stars begin to shine :|
Then Lord let me be in that number
And when the stars begin to shine

|: When Gabriel blows in his horn :|
Then Lord let me be in that number
When Gabriel blows in his horn

|: And when the sun refuse to shine :|
Then Lord let me be in that number
When the sun refuse to shine

|: And when the moon has turned the blood :|
Then Lord let me be in that number
When the moon has turned the blood

|: And when they crown him King of Kings :|
Then Lord let me be in that number
When they crown him King of Kings

|: And when they gather round the throne :|
Then Lord let me be in that number
When they gather round the throne

|: And on that halleluja day :|
Then Lord let me be in that number
On that halleluja day

|: And while the happy ages roll :|
Then Lord let me be in that number
While the happy ages roll

When the saint go marchin' in.
|: Oh when the saint go marchin' in, :|
Lord I want to be in that number
When the saint go marchin' in.

We sang all the way down to cars, joyously defying death and sending John Evangelist O'Malley on his marching way toward the world-to-come. With one final ruffle of drums from Gianni Antonelli the jazz group trailed off into silence. The mourners cheered enthusiastically.

"Great exit," Peg announced.

"Wasn't it thoroughly refreshing?" the Good April asked. "I'm sure Vangie is proud of that cute little group."

"Three of Sheridan's raiders," Rosemarie whispered to me, "and two of Garibaldi's drummer boys."

I had maneuvered matters so that Rosemarie and I were

sitting in the backseat and Peg and Mom were in the front seat. We sang "When the Saints Go Marching In!" all the way back to the country club. Exercising my right as a man falling in love, I permitted my unruly hand to creep under Rosemarie's skirt and up her nylon-coated thigh. She sighed in soft protest but did not banish my hand.

Wrong time for a man to fall in love again with his wife? Not the wrong time at all. Maybe just the right time. However, the mysterious cycle of falling in love in the life of the male of the species displays no respect for time or place. It just happens. Presumably the evolutionary process has selected for it.

I assume, though with no solid evidence, that a similar cycle affects the female of the species, though, as in all matters, she hides it better than does the male. Many women, I gather, reject the return of their mate's adolescent foolishness. The man then either gives up on romance or, in a few cases, finds someone else to fall in love with.

My Rosemarie is usually amused by my regression to the teenage years. She claims that I am most attractive when I am a "cute little boy." I reply that I was more than a cute little boy on that day in Lake Geneva in 1946 when I held her in my arms. She replies with characteristic smoothness, "You were simply adorable, Chucky Ducky, and irresistible."

At that point in our lives I didn't know how to be irresistible, fortunately for both of us.

If I didn't fall in love with her periodically, I would be a cad, an idiot, and a blind fool. My Rosemarie is breathtaking, radiant, glorious. She is more beautiful now than she was when she was my Bride. She denies this fact, though with what certainty I don't know. She tells me that her ancestor about whom she is writing a novel, another Rosemarie with similar genes, was drop-dead beautiful at sixty, but she rejects any argument that the same comment must be made about her.

I suspect that this is part of the conviction of Irishwomen that if you accept a compliment you might lose that which is the object of the compliment, a mean trick played by a jealous God. That is not the God we sang to at Queen of Heaven Cemetery.

Yet anyone who can live with a woman like her, absorb daily her beauty and brilliance and not fall in love with her is, to put the matter mildly, insensate.

Falling in love is distinct from both sex and love, though clearly involved with them. Good sex and deep love may persist in life, without the need—at least in the short run—of falling in love. But when you do fall in love both sex and love take on a new dimension.

Silliness, Rosemarie calls it. "You act silly, Chucky Ducky, but I like you when you're silly."

My fingers reveled in her thigh as we left the expressway at First Avenue and turned north. She had closed her eyes and pressed her lips together as we paused for breath between singing.

"Chucky," she whispered as my out-of-control fingers reached their goal, "Not now!"

Okay, not now. It was time to retreat anyway. However, my redeployment was slow and luxurious.

As I helped her out of the limo, she shook her head, as if in despair.

"You're terrible! And on this day of all days!"

"No better day."

She sighed loudly, but not, I think, in disagreement.

The dinner (or more recently lunch) after a burial is part of the Catholic tradition. Ours was different from most only that it was at a country club and the food was both better and less laden with calories. Despite my romancing of my wife in the back of the funeral limo, my stomach wanted only a few crackers and cheese and a sip or two of wine.

There was much hugging and congratulation inside the club. We all praised the exuberance of the quintet and urged them to turn away from their other careers and go national.

Many of the graveside mourners told us that it was the "most Catholic" burial they had ever attended.

"Burial," I said with apodictic theological confidence, "is only a prelude to resurrection."

My son, Deacon Jimmy, assured me that was a theologically correct assertion.

"It is also," I told him, "true."

"One other thing, Dad . . ."

"Yes?"

"You've done a good job of imitating Grandpa's family strategy . . ."

"So?"

"I hope I can do the same thing as a priest."

I thanked him briskly, lest I collapse in tears.

I cornered my wife and led her by the hand into the club's chess room, usually empty because there were no chess players among us.

"Chucky, darling, you are importunate!"

"Is that bad?"

"Can't you wait till this evening?"

"I'm in love with you," I protested. "I want to hug and kiss you."

So I did. And added a few special caresses.

"Importunate and impossible . . . You're not going to fuck me here at the club, are you?"

"No, but that's not a bad idea."

She ended our clinch and turned toward the door of the chess room.

"One more thing, Charles Cronin O'Malley."

"Yes?"

The full name usually meant I was in trouble.

"I have been proud of you in our marriage more times than I remember, but never as proud as I was this morning during your eulogy."

"Oh," I gulped. "Now I'm really in love with you!"

She shook her head in feigned dismay.

"And," I added quickly, "thank you."

"You're welcome!"

We rejoined the party, for it was a party, one last defiance of death. I hated Oak Park Country Club. It was once a center of anti-Catholicism, from which Catholics were banned. In the 1920s, led by one of the local monsignors, a group of Catholics founded Butterfield, as a Catholic rival which it was, only better. My late father had joined both at the same time, the first Catholic member of Oak Park. Now it was dominated by overweight Irish Catholic Republicans whom I couldn't stand. However, Peg argued that a) Dad had been the first Catholic member and b) there were three wedding receptions at Butterfield on this September Saturday afternoon.

The Good April was ensconced in a regal chair as befitted a reigning grand duchess and flanked by two lovely ladies-in-waiting, Peg and Rosemarie. They were both, I was convinced, slim and trim because they reinforced each other's willpower, an especially difficult task for my poor wife after her "elderly" pregnancy, which had produced the luminous Siobhan Marie. I was also convinced that they worried about their figures not because of their husbands but because of their own self-respect.

"Here's some healthy food for you, Chucky." The Good Mary Margaret handed me a plate. "Eat it slowly or you'll be sick again."

I didn't ask how she knew I was sick in the first place.

"You were sensational," she continued. "I was proud of you, especially when you kept your cool when dippy Auntie Jane walked out."

"Thank you," I said. "It's not an easy day . . . Poor Aunt Jane is deeply troubled."

"Nutty as a fruitcake," she laughed. "I don't think we've seen the last of her . . . Eat this stuff slowly, big fellow. We don't want you sick again . . . 'Scuse me. I gotta tend the kids again."

She would be as good a mother as her own mother.

"Wait a sec?"

"Yes?"

"Who is this Oriental woman I see with Sean Seamus?"

"Asian . . ."

"I stand corrected."

"Her name is Maria Anastasia and she's Luong. They're a tribe from Laos. She works on the trading floor."

"Ah . . . Serious?"

"Could be."

"Are they sleeping together?"

"No way, she's an old-fashioned Catholic."

"Like you?"

"Kind of."

"Sean has a taste for exotic women, doesn't he?"

"You've noticed?"

"Nothing wrong with that."

"Dad, she's a hell of a lot less exotic than I am. She was born in this country and went to Catholic schools for sixteen years."

"Yes, ma'am . . . What's her name again?"

"Maria Anastasia."

I nibbled on a bit of wheat bread with some kind of nondairy spread. My stomach lurched in protest. I put the dish of food on a table and rushed to the men's room. When I was finished I was utterly empty.

When I returned to the luncheon, I realized that my allergies had returned and myself without any tissues.

I whispered in my wife's ear, "Tissues!"

"Chucky, you look green!"

"Irish," I said. "Do we approve of this Chinese kid that's hanging around Seano?"

She produced a pack of tissues from her purse.

"She's very sweet . . . Chucky, are you going to pass out?"

"Probably."

Maria Anastasia, no last name given, approached me timidly.

"Mr. O'Malley, your eulogy was so beautiful that I want to cry every time I think of it."

True to her word, she began to cry.

And I sneezed.

"Thank you, Maria Anastasia, you're a woman of great good taste."

She blushed and, having delivered her compliment, turned away. Doubtless she would report to Sean Seamus. Well, I had done something right. It would take her a while to remember that I knew her name.

I searched for Jamie Nettleton, April Rosemary's husband and son of my commanding officers in Bamberg, John and Polly Nettleton.

"You look like you're going to die, Chuck," he said with less concern than would have been appropriate. "That was a wonderful talk today, I'll call Mom and Dad and tell them."

I sneezed again.

"Allergies," I managed to say between spasms. "If I take my allergy meds, will it make my stomach disorder any worse?"

"They won't make it any better." He laughed. "I seem to remember a story my mom tells about your stomach acting up one night in Bamberg."

"Defamation!"

"I was sorry about your sister acting out . . . My guess is that she's on medication and won't take it."

"Her husband is a shrink like you are!"

"I only work with kids . . . It's a good way to punish a psychiatrist if you refuse to take his prescriptions . . . Sorry if I'm intruding."

"Not at all, Jamie. That will help us to understand . . . I hope my daughter never does that to you."

Dumb thing to say, but he didn't seem to mind.

"April? No danger of that!"

I wondered as I searched out my wife for my allergy meds, if Ted McCormack had said that long ago about Jane.

"Maybe you shouldn't take them, Chuck, with your stomach as upset as it seems to be."

The words of a mother.

"I talked to Dr. Nettleton," I said proudly.

"What does he know? He's a shrink!"

But she fished the bottle of Bentyl out of her purse.

The "lunch" went on forever, largely because of the incorrigible inability of Irishwomen to say good-bye to one another.

Finally, the last of them left. My mother, my wife, my sister, and my daughter looked around the room to make sure they hadn't missed anyone and decided that it was time to "go home," which meant to the family house on New England Avenue. Mary Margaret collected her little sister from the room in which she had been napping. The little redhead hugged me fiercely.

"You were wonderful, Daddy. I was so proud of you!"

"Thank you dear. I'm always proud of you."

The "inner family"—Peg, Rosemarie, Ed, Vince, and I—went home with mother. Mary Margaret would turn Shovie over to Erin, our nanny, a young Irishwoman who had already bonded with Rosemarie in the common conspiracy against me, and return for the final phase of the obsequies.

Mom stretched out in her favorite chair.

"Well," she said, "I'm sure poor dear Vangie is very pleased with us. On the whole, we did very well."

"Except for Jane," Peg said sadly. "She certainly hates the rest of us."

"Especially me," Rosemarie added.

"Poor Janie." Mom sighed. "She's not herself. I really think Ted ought to do something to help her."

I told them Jamie Nettleton's diagnosis.

"That doesn't sound good," Ed said. "I wonder if there's anything we can do to help her? Maybe you could talk to Ted, Chuck?"

"For the moment," I said cautiously, "it's probably best to let him take the initiative. Life is probably difficult enough for him as it is."

"I don't think we've seen the last of her," my Rosemarie said thoughtfully. "She feels that we have done a terrible wrong to her that ruined her life. . . . Maybe she has a point."

"It's all in her imagination, isn't it?" Vince asked. "From not taking her pills?"

"She believes that I replaced her in the family. When I appeared, the family stopped paying attention to her."

Mom put her arm around Rosemarie, who was sitting on the ottoman next to her.

"But, Rosie, dear, that isn't true. It's not your fault. We never stopped loving poor dear Jane, did we, Chucky?"

"She thinks we did, which is the problem. I'm not sure that she can ever give that notion up, no matter how much of a mistake it is."

"She never liked me much," Peg said. "She always thought I was an obnoxious brat."

The conversation was circling aimlessly and was not healthy. Indeed it could not be healthy, not tonight or any night.

Then Mary Margaret arrived with a package from the drugstore.

"Bentyl," she said handing it to me. "Jamie said that you shouldn't take any liquor with it, but you don't drink much anyway, Chucky. Here's a glass of water. Take it now . . . It will make him sleepy, Rosie, so you drive home."

"I usually do, dear," my wife said, "but thanks for the warning. I may take some of them when we get home."

We turned away from our Jane problem and engaged in bittersweet reminiscences about Dad combined with reflections on how much he must have liked the various aspects of the obsequies, most notably the homily, the eulogy, and the concert at the graveside. Vince reported that the Catholic cemeteries people warned our funeral director that they would ban him if he tolerated anything like that ever again.

"I'll make a phone call on Monday," he said, "and change their minds."

"I think I'd better take you home, Chucky," my wife said from a great distance.

I must have agreed because I soon found myself in bed. I was supposed to be falling in love with someone, but I didn't quite remember who it was.

Chapter Eight

Mary Margaret

I didn't really want to go down to Rush Street with my Rosary College classmates. They insisted that I should get away from the family for a couple of hours. I decided that those hours would spare me more agonizing over poor Aunt Jane. The woman was a bitch, a sick bitch indeed, but still a bitch.

I don't much like the Rush Street scene. It's what we sociologists call anomic, that is normless. A large number of young adults mill around and try to impress one another, without much success. Men pretend they're tough. Women pretend they're silly. Everyone seems to be looking for sex of one sort or another and some are looking also for a spouse, a few with success despite the unpropitious ambience of the scene. They are, it seems to me, extremely fortunate. God presumably can work with any circumstances, especially when the hormones are sizzling.

I am too young to be looking for a spouse and my instincts tell me that Rush Street sex is hardly worth the effort. I figure that when I decide to look for a husband, I'll do it in other, and as yet unspecified, circumstances. So I sip my Bushmill's straight up (only one glass) and reflect on the horror of the scene.

Good dissertation material maybe. Someone has probably beat me to it.

I usually ignore come-ons. Sometimes I dismiss them with a withering stare. Occasionally I dismiss them with a wave of a hand. Rarely some thoughtful guy, somehow persuaded that a woman with red hair can be intelligent, initiates a sensible conversation.

Which can be a come-on too.

I would never come down to Rush Street with this boy Joey Moran, who stands around, as Chuck says, looking bemused and amused. He might fit in the scene and I might fit there, but not together. We'd be appropriate at a place like Petersen's ice cream store, where Rosie and Chuck used to hang out when they were kids and where they still hang out sometimes thirty years later. Rosie was already married and a mother when she was my age; but, like she says, times change. You'd better believe it.

They're both basket cases today, wiped out. I told them they were so tired that they didn't have to go to Mass. They were shocked, poor dears. They're so cute, they love each other so much. I hope that, if I marry, my husband and I will love the same way when we're that old.

Aunt Peg and Uncle Vince were the same age when they were married and he went off to Vietnam and was a prisoner of war. He doesn't talk about that much.

I'll be fifty someday and I may lose them. I don't want that to happen.

What if Joey Moran should ask me to marry him? Like now. What would I say?

I give the impression that I have all the answers. Ms. Take Charge. Good act.

So this guy comes up to me while I'm thinking about all these things, thirty or so, hair thinning, the hard eyes of an accomplished predator, bored smile.

Ted McCormack, Ted Junior as Aunt Jane always calls him.

"I didn't know I had such a pretty cousin," he begins.

"We missed you at the funeral," I snap.

"I heard you played jazz at the cemetery."

"Yeah?"

I am making it clear that this is not going to be a friendly conversation.

"Mother told us only at the last minute. We figured that she would make a fool out of herself again. We've seen that too often. Father has her on pills and sometimes she refuses to take them."

"Oh?"

"Did she misbehave?"

"Ask her."

His smooth manner disappeared.

"We never see much of you people . . . I don't quite know why . . . Michele and Jennifer are about your age, aren't they?"

"I'm in between them . . . I graduate in the spring."

"They both dropped out of college. Didn't like it. They have an apartment up in Wrigleyville. Close to where I live. Don't see them much. They have small temp jobs. Haven't settled down yet."

He seemed to be looking for sympathy. Wrong shoulder to cry on. Sean lived up there too, as do all the yuppies in the world. Halsted Street is a yuppie bar outdoors.

"Had to get away from Mother?"

His pale blue eyes flashed for a moment. This pretty little cousin had the occasional insight.

"I guess. Something went wrong, Mother has found it difficult to win acceptance in Kenilworth. It's mostly in her imagination. Maybe we should have stayed on the West Side. Oak Brook something like that."

"I would not be caught dead living in Oak Brook," I said.

"Chris is still at home, poor guy. He's finally getting married, a Polish woman who's in the same law firm. Nice girl, bright. Mother hates her."

This was family talk, not barroom chatter. I felt sorry for him.

"Do you have a boyfriend?" he went on.

"Not exactly. A guy hangs around. I went to grammar school with him."

"Your parents like him?"

I shrugged.

"If it's a choice between me or him, they might take him."

He thought that was very funny. Poor dolt.

"Whatever went wrong between our families must have happened when you moved to Germany. Mother is still terribly upset about that. She doesn't like your father's photographs."

"She didn't like Grandpa's painting book either."

"She said it was terribly embarrassing . . . You're pretty quick on the uptake aren't you?"

"I learned that in the diplomatic service."

He laughed again.

I sipped a little of my closely held Bushmill's Green. It's okay if you're going to sip whiskey all night. Sure clears the sinuses. When you walk up to a bar and say, "Bushmill's Green straight up," you create a certain impact.

"I should warn you," he said hesitantly. "Mother thinks her life will straighten out if she brings our grandmother up to live in Faith, Hope . . . That's our parish, you know."

"Faith, Hope, and Cadillac."

"Benz or BMW more likely these days," he admitted with a wry smile. "I hate it. When I go to Mass, I usually go down to Old St. Pat's."

So he was still a Catholic, if a predator.

"Nice place."

"Mother is trying to arrange to go over to Grandmother's house and bring her up to our house. She has two nurses, Big Bertha types, that will go with her."

"I don't think Grams wants to go."

"When Mother makes up her mind, she makes up her mind."

We chatted a few more moments and he drifted away, a confused and troubled young man. Dear God, why do You let parents do these things to their children?

I slipped outside and waited till the half-drunk jerk at the public phone finished his call.

"Hi, gorgeous!" he said to me.

"I hope she had enough sense to turn you down," I said, brushing by him. I half hoped that he would try something. He would be good black belt practice material.

"Chuck O'Malley," Chucky said on the phone.

"Your intermediate daughter. I'm in a public phone on Rush Street and don't worry I haven't knocked out any drunks yet. I had an interesting conversation with our cousin Ted Junior in the bar. He tells me that his mother is collecting a couple of tough nurses and some one of these days she's going to descend on Oak Park as the Wicked Witch of the North Shore. They will kidnap Grams and carry her off to a real neighborhood."

"What!"

"You'd better assemble some of the troops. Call Uncle Vince. Ask that nice Mr. Casey to put some off-duty Oak Park cops in front of the house. Alert everyone. She's obviously manic-depressive in a manic stage. She could be dangerous."

"Are you sure, Moire Meg?"

He's the only one who can use that outdated name—and only occasionally.

"If I wasn't sure, I wouldn't call you at this hour of the night. I'm going to sleep at Grams's tonight. I want to see a car with cops out in front when I get there."

Chapter Nine

Chuck

When Mary Margaret called, my wife and I were cuddled on the love seat in our parlor. I had removed her blouse and was playing the games a love-struck teen might play with his compliant sweetheart. I would take off all her clothes very slowly, behavior for a cautious and timid, but still determined, lover.

"Her name," Rosemarie muttered, "is Mary Margaret, not Moire Meg. It's a Catholic name. And she's a fanatical Catholic"—she giggled—"like you are, even if you've been fixated on my boobs since before I got them."

"God," I said, "in the interest of continuing the species made women's bodies attractive to men. We are genetically programmed to delight in your breasts and if you're honest about it you delight in our delight."

"Hmm . . . What did the intermediate daughter want? She wasn't in trouble was she?"

"Not hardly."

I told her Mary Margaret's message. She sat up and disengaged herself from me.

"Charles Cronin O'Malley! Do something about it!"

I eased her back into my arms.

"Woman, I will! Now be quiet for a few moments."

I called Mike Casey, the head of Reliable Security. He promised he would have a couple of off-duty Oak Park cops across the street from the house on New England Avenue within the hour; hopefully one of the cops would be a woman.

Then I called Vince. Peg came on the line at once. Were they playing hanky-panky at the same time by some kind of prearrangement? I would not put it past them.

"She's crazy," Vince snorted.

"Manic-depressive in a manic stage," I said, quoting Mary Margaret, "and she's not taking her lithium."

"Ted should lock her up someplace," Peg demanded.

"We can't get a restraining order against her until she actually does something," Vince said. "Then of course it will be easy."

"There will be two Oak Park cops outside and the rest of the department on call," I added. "Those two Irish furies will protect her. Mary Margaret will be there tonight and when she's not at Rosary tomorrow. We should take turns stopping in."

The Irish furies were Madge the cook and Theresa the housekeeper, women in their late sixties who together with the Good April were kind of a local branch of the Irish warrior goddess society.

While we were talking, my hand, as uncontrollable as ever, slipped back under Rosemarie's black skirt. The nylon was long gone so I encountered only delicious woman flesh, firm and disciplined by tennis and other forms of exercise, and sweetly responsive to my affection.

"Is Mary Margaret staying there tonight?" Peg asked. "I could ask Rita to go over and keep her company."

I thought about that.

"Let's hold off on that for tonight. We don't want to stir up worry for April."

"Right."

"Sorry to interrupt."

"Were they doing hanky-panky?" Rosemarie asked.

"Why should we be the only ones?"

It had been a difficult day at our house. We were both grouchy and groggy when we woke up. I was filled with drugs and Rosemarie's sleep was deep and troubling, filled with obscure dreams about her father. I vaguely remembered that it was Sunday morning and that we had to go to church. We had to hurry to make the twelve o'clock Mass. We showered and dressed quickly. It was only when we were hurrying into our clothes that I remembered that I was falling in love with my stately wife, now donning a svelte black suit.

There was no time to do anything about it. Moreover, I needed my morning cup of tea, maybe two cups before I did anything about anything.

We stumbled down the stairs and discovered our two daughters, in their Sunday best, reading the papers, Shovie concentrating on the comics and Mary Margaret frowning over the "Week in Review" in *The New York Times*.

"What are you two doing up so soon?" Mary Margaret asked, not bothering to look up from the paper. "You should have slept in. You're both totally whupped."

"We have to go to Mass." Rosemarie said sternly. "You should have awakened us.

"Chill out, Rosie, you went to Mass yesterday. You're both a shambles; Chucky looks like a man in drug rehab. God doesn't expect you to drag yourself over to church today."

"Since when have you become God's special messenger?"

Mary Margaret ignored her.

As we were about to leave the house and she was searching in her purse for the keys to our old Benz, Rosemarie stopped, shook her head in disgust, and returned to the parlor.

"Sorry, Mary Margaret." She kissed her daughter. "You're right as always. We old folks are just religious fanatics."

Our intermediate daughter brightened.

"Say a prayer for me."

"Me too." Shovie rushed over to hug her mother.

"That was gracious," I said as I lurched toward the car.

"Makes up for being graceless."

"Maybe I should apologize?"

"Don't be silly. You didn't say anything."

In front of St. Agedius, Packy Keenan renewed Mary Margaret's argument.

"You guys didn't have to come to Mass this morning!"

"We're religious fanatics," Rosemarie said.

"We'll compromise and not put any money in the basket," I said.

"My poor husband is finally awake."

She took my arm and guided me into church and down the aisle toward the front. The Crazy O'Malleys always sit in the front of the church, like they own it. Peg and Vince were already there.

"Family of religious fanatics," I murmured.

I thought about Rosemarie all through Mass, darting an occasional glance at her. I had lucked out. I knew nothing about what a wife should be when I married her—not that I had that much to say about it. She was elegant, graceful, gifted, a great mother, and exciting in bed. Poor Ted must have thought the same thing when he came home from the War to his beloved Jane. Why had I been so fortunate? I didn't deserve it. I sighed loudly. She glanced at me to warn me to behave in church.

How could I not fall in love with her again and again and again, even if she displayed the Irish womanly proclivity to be bossy.

The four of us stopped by Mom's house for a cup of tea. The starch had gone out of her. She had begun to understand that she would spend the rest of her life without her lover. She was stooped, lifeless, suddenly old. Yet she perked up when we came and insisted that she had made scones when she came home after the seven o'clock Mass because she knew we would want some with our tea.

So we drank the tea and ate the scones, I a vast number of scones.

"You're disgusting, Chucky," my sister said. "No one should eat as much as you do and not put on weight."

"He's just a pig," my wife agreed.

"Poor dear Chucky," my mother said with her usual sympathy, "he always burned off the weight because he was so intense and so active."

My sister and my foster sister, also my wife, ridiculed that theory.

"I'm pretty active," Vince, my longtime unindicted coconspirator, said. "I guess I'm just not as intense as Chuck."

"His real secret," my wife said in an irrelevant argument, "is that when some worry arises, he goes to sleep."

"Would someone please pass me the raspberry jam," I asked, dismissing their barbs.

When we entered our own house on Euclid, Shovie, Erin, and Mary Margaret were sitting on the porch in their swimsuits. Our pool—an extravagance that I had stoutly resisted—was scheduled to remain open by Rosemarie's fiat till October 1, then perhaps all year long.

"You guys should swim," Mary Margaret instructed us. "The water's great and you'll relax a little. Oh, by the way, a courier brought that big package in the parlor from the State Department."

We both dashed into the front room. We paused to look at the box on the floor. It looked battered.

"We should open it now," my wife insisted.

"What if all the films are wrecked?"

"We'd better find out now so we can stop worrying about the possibility."

She dashed into her regal office off the parlor and reappeared with a knife, a scissors, and a box cutter, all part of an expensive, inlaid, designed desk set. Nothing too good for Ms. Clancy.

She placed the box on a table, deftly opened it, and remove an X-ray-resistant bag.

"That's number five," I said. "Number one is at the other end. We should open them in the proper order."

"Why?" she asked, glancing up at me with some exasperation.

"Because, like you tell us all the time, Chucky is a neatness freak."

Our daughters had gathered behind us, both in robes so they wouldn't track water in the house.

I reached in the box and pulled out the bag on which I had placed the label #1.

"I am not a neatness freak," I argued. "I am an order freak."

They laughed.

I opened the bag with great care and removed the first roll. It was labeled 1-1, which seemed sensible enough. My women thought it was hilariously funny.

"I should go downstairs and see if it can be developed."

"I'll come with you."

I wanted to do it myself, but Rosemarie had signed on as my photographic assistant at the beginning of our marriage. "Our" darkroom was right next to "our" gym.

She flipped on the exhaust fan which drew any foul air out of both rooms.

I remember the day I told April Rosemary, after her marriage to Jamie, that she had been conceived in the darkroom. She laughed in great delight.

"Brilliant, Dad, brilliant!"

"I kind of thought so too."

She turned on the red light outside the darkroom and locked the door inside. I was cradling the precious role of film in nervous fingers of both hands. She turned out the lights in the darkroom and turned on the red safety lamp.

"You do it," I said, handing her the roll of tri x. "You're cooler than I am. Way cooler."

She didn't argue. In a few moments she removed the film from the developing tank and held it up to the red light.

I sat down on the easy chair she had provided for "our" darkroom and exhaled loudly.

"I'm too old for this aggravation," I admitted.

"You reacted the same way thirty years ago, Chucky Ducky." She planted a hasty kiss on my lips . . . "These shots look great. Let's go upstairs and have a swim."

Our red-haired daughters were waiting for us anxiously.

"Another Charles Cronin O'Malley miracle!" Rosemarie announced. "The lens cap was off the camera!"

Applause from my carrot-top daughters. I bowed modestly.

"April Rosemary and I will develop all the rolls for you, if you want," Mary Margaret said casually, too casually.

"When did she make the offer?" I said, playing for time. I knew that I didn't trust them to do this delicate work. I knew I couldn't turn down their offer. I knew finally that they would do a better job than I would . . .

"When I called her to tell her that the package had come from the State Department."

"A new alliance?"

"She finally decided that I am a totally cool little sister," Mary Margaret said with studied indifference. "Which of course I am, huh, Shovie, a totally cool big sister?"

"Totally," Shovie said with her usual woman leprechaun grin.

I saw a time, not too many years in the future, when these three wicked witches would take complete control of their parents' lives. This was but their first tentative grasp for power.

"Won't the chemical smell bother April Rosemary?" my wife intervened to help me form an answer.

"She says she's over being sick . . . We'll make three sets of proofs—one for each of you and one for ourselves to circle our favorite shots. We'll show you them only after you've made your own choices."

"Will one of you draft a text for your mother?"

"Well, I might try my hand at it." Her aquamarine eyes glinted with mischief. "We'll let you make the prints, Chucky. This time anyway."

"Well . . ." I pretended to weigh the decision.

"Tell him, Rosie, that he doesn't have any choice."

"He knows that, dear."

"Well, if you ruin any of them, I'll ground you till the day before the apocalypse!"

Many hugs and kisses for the new but already fast-aging paterfamilias. One provocative kiss from his wife. Whereupon he began to sneeze again.

"And I reserve the right to peek in," he gasped between sneezes, "while you're working to make sure you're doing it right."

Much laughter.

"You better take your allergy medicine, Chucky."

After I had swallowed my Bentyl I sought out my wife in her office. She was sitting behind her ornate mahogany desk poring over her notebooks from the Russian trip. I collapsed in the easy chair which was reserved for the dutiful consort.

"I think I can tease out three or four themes, kind of tentative till we make the print selections."

"Who's this 'we'?"

"I mean April Rosemary and Mary Margaret and myself."

"I don't get a vote?"

"You lost the franchise long ago."

"I have the feeling that there's generational change going on here. I have been eased into Grandpa-in-the-wheelchair role several years before I should be."

She looked up from her notebook and took off her glasses.

"You still get to take the pictures, don't you?"

"You're encouraging those brats in their coup d'etat."

"I'm part of it, Chucky dear. We have to take care of you in your golden years."

I was drowsy again. Jet lag still catching up. I must have yawned.

"Chucky, go take a nap. It will be good for you."

I was being dismissed from the empress's presence so she could do her work. As I fell asleep, I began to worry about all the responsibilities. There would be the thank-you notes to those who came to the wake, to everyone who had helped with the services, legal matters regarding probate, the trip to DC to take pictures of the Gipper, Joe Raftery, and, what else, oh, yes, Jane.

When I woke up I realized that I had forgotten about Maria Anastasia. Perhaps, however, she would not be a problem. We had red-haired Latino grandchildren, we could cope with red-haired Luong grandchildren. Still I needed a long rest, maybe a year or so devoted entirely to malted milks and falling in love with my wife. For supper I would take her over to Petersen's to begin the fun.

Later, after we'd returned from the ice-cream parlor, given the appropriate cautions to Mary Margaret for her venture to Rush Street, and put an exhausted Shovie to bed, I took my wife's hand and led her to the love seat in our parlor.

"In here?" she said dubiously.

"More room."

She sighed in mock resignation.

"Well, it took you long enough to get to this falling in love business."

"I needed the two malts to revert to my teen perspective."

We joked that falling in love again was a regression to teenage fantasy. In a way it was. The person falling in love is certainly caught up in an infatuation. However, he is also a more or less experienced adult. He has a clear idea of what's happening and some confidence that he can carry it off. He also has useful insights about how to respect his beloved so that she doesn't become a fetish—nor a surrogate Playboy Bunny. Hopefully he no longer feels it is necessary to prove his masculinity. Above all, he knows that his wife likes to play the game, in her own fashion.

We were making good progress in the game when Mary Margaret phoned us. I made the right calls before I returned to the game, though in a dark attic somewhere in my brain I realized that Jane was going to be a big problem. Now, however, my focus was on my wife.

She giggled as I unzipped her skirt and, oh, so slowly slid it down off her hips.

"Got the woman down to her skivvies?" she said with a long slow sigh. "I don't remember you ever did that as a teenager . . ."

"Thought about it often."

"Why, Chucky?" She snuggled closer to me.

She shifted her position on the love seat so that she lay supine against my chest. What more could a man ask for from his wife?

"Why what?"

"Not why do you love me. I know that you do and I take you at your word about the reasons. Not why you enjoy sex with me. I'm a good lay. Not even why you fall in love with me over and over again. The logistics are easier if you fall in love with your wife. But why now? Is it because we lost Vangie?"

I drew my fingers across her belly. She gasped with pleasure. I did it again even more slowly.

"Let's say a man works in an office. They, whoever the evil 'they' are assign a new woman to his staff. She's pretty and bright and fun. Suddenly he's head over heels with her. He doesn't understand why. She's attractive, appealing, seems to like him. He doesn't want to fall in love with her. He's happily married. He knows the dangers and takes no chances. Why does this particular woman knock him over at that particular time? He doesn't know and he doesn't want to find out. If he's like me, he's not sure he's up to it with any other women but his wife. That's that, right?"

"I should hope so."

"So I'm sitting next to my wife in a car. She's driving, of course, since she is convinced she is a better driver than I am. I notice how beautiful she is, how poised, how intelligent, how funny. I think to myself that she's an irresistible woman. I bet she would be good in bed. I bet she'd be fun to neck and pet as we used to say. It would be really great to feel her up and to take off her clothes. She'd be wondrous, mysterious, challenging. I want her the worst way. I'm infatuated."

My fingers crept up toward her black bra, lavishly decorated with lace. That would have to go soon.

"But, Chucky Ducky, you've already had her hundreds, thousands of times for almost thirty years."

"It's different. She's suddenly mysterious again . . . I think that's a perfectly reasonable reaction. Only an idiot thinks he knows all there is to know about a spouse, no matter how many years he's known her. I rediscover you again to discover you for the first time. Okay?"

"Sure it's okay. Have I ever said it isn't? But does it have something to do with Vangie's death?"

I slipped a finger under one of the straps.

"Probably because I was knocked over by the grace with which you cope with loss."

She rolled over and lifted herself to my lips. She then pressed her breasts against my chest and devoured me with passionate kisses. I may not survive this, I thought to myself.

Chapter Ten

Rosemarie

The trouble with revolutions, they used to say back in the 1960s, is that even revolutionaries have to sleep. So it is with young love, even superannuated young love, lovers have to sleep.

Chuck and I ended up in our pool, quite naked, at a not-so-small hour in the morning. We collapsed into our marriage bed, destroyed altogether as the Irish would say. Ecstasy lasts just so long, then you must sleep. And you wake up the next day feeling like you'd played a tennis match for twenty hours. Poor Chuck is still deep in sleep. What started out as his infatuation became my infatuation. The pleasure was so strong that I cannot concentrate on my Russian notebooks or even think about the rest of the day. I should be making plans for our shoot at the White House at the end of the week.

Our combined misbehavior is likely go on for a long time, all winter I hope.

In public my husband seems—and actually is—a talented, befuddled little boy, appealing, adorable, and clueless. As a lover, he is a powerful, challenging, and electrifying adult man whose passion calls forth from me all my resources as an adult women. When that happens it's Katie bar the door!

After years of marriage, many women are furious at their husbands if they get into playful moods. That's over with, they say. We're too old for it. I suspect they never learned to like sex all that much. I learned early with Chuck's patient help to delight in my husband as a lover. I was always a risk taker. I listen to other women when they complain and feel sorry for them. I discuss such matters only with Peg who, as in all things, agrees with me completely.

"What other point is there in having a man around the house?" she says with only some exaggeration.

Mary Margaret called from April's house when she arrived to assure us that the car with two cops in it was already outside. Chuck and I were in an advanced stage of the game and my answers to her must have been strained. She didn't seem to notice. Or if she did she didn't say anything.

There are many advantages of mutual infatuation at our stage in life: no fear of pregnancy, no guilt, and no danger of failure to satisfy.

Thank God for it.

Yes indeed. If I can still be infatuated with my husband and he with me then that is a great grace from God which I don't deserve but I will cheerfully accept.

But I have to get on with my work. April Rosemary will be here in early afternoon to begin work on the proof sheets. I have to call the White House. Now I'd better wake up Chucky. I think I wore him out, poor dear man.

Chuck went back to work in the darkroom and I began to prepare the Irish stew we would have for dinner. Except for the day when she had a late-afternoon class, Erin would kind of drift into the kitchen to help me with dinner.

Erin was a thin waif of an Irish child, with lustrous blue eyes and jet-black hair—quiet, gentle, and inoffensive. She was studying for an ME in education at Rosary College. Our daughter had found her there, took her under her wing, and brought her home to be our "Shovie Sitter." The situation was very different, but I remember how Peg had brought the obnoxious little Clancy brat home.

"It's not part of your job description, Erin," I said gently when this process began.

"Sure, am I not being selfish now? Don't I want to learn to be a good cook like yourself?"

I didn't doubt that explanation. I also suspected that she felt obligated to demonstrate something more in gratitude for what she felt we had done for her.

"Well, I'm sure you don't need any instructions on how to make Irish stew . . . What did you think of the wake and funeral?"

"Your family is ded friggin' bril. You were all wonderful. I has happy to be here with you. I learned a lot about how to react to death."

She kept her eyes on the carrots she was cutting.

"You were a big help to us," I said, somewhat embarrassed by the strength of her reaction. "You're a grand addition to our family altogether."

"I was the youngest of twelve," she said, revealing just a little about herself. "They all loved me, but I kind of got lost in the shuffled deck, if you take me meaning. I don't know why you're so good to me . . ."

Tears slipped down her flawless complexion.

"In my case," I said, "as I'm sure you know, I was taken in too."

"Doesn't herself tell me that? I think they were lucky you came along. Herself says so too."

"After you get your degree in spring, will you go home?"

"I think I'll stay here in America for a while, find meself a decent teaching job, and save meself a bit of money."

"Well, I hope you won't move out on us!"

"I couldn't impose on you anymore . . ."

"Would you ever listen to me, young woman? Won't our feelings be hurt if you move out?"

She threw her arms around me and hugged me as the tears poured out of her luminous blue eyes.

Well that settled that.

CHAPTER ELEVEN

Chuck

I didn't think Rosemarie's swimming pool was the answer to our wintertime in Chicago. She has tons of money she inherited from her mother and which grew huge with investments (about which I did not want to know) since 1946. If she wanted a year-round swimming pool in our backyard, that was all right with me, especially since it was her house too. She had asked me what I thought, as she always does, and I said it was a crazy idea and that our house would smell like a high school locker room. So she had it built anyway—sliding glass panels and all.

Nonetheless, it might serve some useful purposes as I had discovered the previous night.

She was not home when I entered the house. A note on the table said she had gone shopping. April Rosemary was downstairs, working on the proof sheets and I must not disturb her.

Rosemarie shouldn't have gone off to the store. She should have been home waiting for her lover. I sighed and slipped into my chair in her office and drifted off to sleep. She may have been in my dreams, but she was not a scary presence.

The phone rang from a great distance.

I fumbled for it.

"Chuck O'Malley."

"Dad, come quick, the crows have landed."

"I'll be right over."

I staggered to my feet, scribbled a note for Rosemarie, ran down the steps, jumped into my car, and raced over to New England Avenue.

I arrived at the same time as four Oak Park squad cars, lights twirling. A bunch of cops piled out, including the chief of police himself, and followed me into the house through the open door and into bedlam. The two young off-duty cops had cornered Jane's nurse/thugs—one of whom was a nun—in a corner of the room and was keeping them at bay. Jane, screaming curses like a she-demon from hell, was struggling to tear April out of the protective arms of Madge and Theresa. Mary Margaret, in jeans and her red University of Moscow sweatshirt was on the floor groaning.

"Get that crazy bitch off my mother!" I yelled at the cops and knelt over my daughter.

"I'm all right, Dad," she said in a woozy voice. "Help Grams!"

Four cops pulled Jane off April with considerable effort. I embraced the Good April, who was shaking like a palm tree in a hurricane.

"It's all right, April, it's all right."

"Poor dear Jane," she confided to me as though it were a secret, "is nuttier than a fruitcake. I will never leave this house. Never."

"She won't try again, I promise you that."

"Take these witches downtown and book them!" I screamed, holding April as tight as I could. "Charge them with illegal entry, disorderly conduct, assault and battery, attempted kidnapping, and whatever else you can think of. Get them out of here. My father was buried on Friday. My mom should not have to put up with this."

Cops were milling around, shouting orders, barking into their walkie-talkies, and generally increasing the chaos. A young woman cop knelt next to Mary Margaret and murmured something.

"That's my daughter! Be careful of her!"

The woman looked up at me and grinned. "Why am I not surprised?"

"Ambassador," the chief asked me, "who is this perpetrator?"

I almost looked around to see who the ambassador in question was.

"Jane O'Malley McCormack, my sister. I'm afraid that she has not been taking her medication recently. You may need a sedative to calm her down. I'll phone her husband in a minute."

"I think your daughter might have a concussion, Ambassador," the young cop said to me. "I'll call for an ambulance. She should be under observation for twenty-four hours."

"Gotta go to DC and see the president," Mary Margaret protested.

The cop looked up at me.

"That's true, ma'am, but not tomorrow."

You never lose any points by treating a woman cop, no matter how young, with respect.

"I'm all right, Chucky, really."

"For the first time in your twenty-one years you'll do what you're told."

"Yes, Daddy."

I grabbed a phone and called Peg.

"Get over here to Mom's. Jane has been on a rampage."

"Right there."

Then I called home. No answer.

Madge and Theresa were calming April down. She had stopped sobbing.

"I'm not leaving this house," she insisted again and again. "No one is going to make me leave."

"No way, April, no way."

The reserves arrived just as the cops were dragging Jane out of the door—April Rosemary, Peg, and my good wife. Peg ran to Mom; my wife and daughter knelt next to Mary Margaret.

"I have a concussion, Rosie. Your husband is making me go to the hospital."

"Who hit you on the head, M. M.?" her big sister asked.

"Aunt Jane, with that table lamp by the door."

"That sick, crazy bitch."

"I'll be okay," Mary Margaret insisted.

"She might have killed you!" my wife was crying now. "Chucky that crazy woman might have killed her!"

"Chief," I shouted, "add attempted murder to the charges against my sister. Bring that lamp on the floor along as evidence."

The cops were struggling with Jane's co-witches.

One protested, "We're both nurses, you can't arrest us!"

The other shouted, "I'm a nun! Leave me alone."

"Poor little Moire," my mom crooned sadly. "She's such a sweet little thing. Jane should really be put away."

"I'll be okay. I have to go to DC to see the president."

"Ambassador, the ambulance is here. Will you want to ride down to Oak Park Hospital with her?"

"Her mother and sister will ride with her. You'd better go too."

"No way I wouldn't, sir."

"Thank you, ma'am."

"Peg," I shouted, "call Vince!"

"I already did. He's coming home. Rita will pick him up at the L."

Outside Jane was still screaming curses. Doubtless the whole neighborhood was watching. Even for the Crazy O'Malleys, this was quite a show.

Two medics appeared with a stretcher.

"Looks like a concussion to me," said the woman cop, moving her hand in front of Mary Margaret's eyes.

"I'm fine," she protested. "Gotta go to DC and check out the president."

"If you can't come, we'll cancel."

"Don't do that."

They lifted her carefully onto the stretcher.

"I have a test tomorrow," she protested.

"It will be all right, hon," April Rosemary assured her. "Uncle Vince will sue them if they don't let you take the test."

"Chucky," she instructed me, "you stay here with Grams. I should have pushed Aunt Jane down the steps. I'll see you at the hospital."

Rosemarie winked at me. Our daughter was coming out of it.

I picked up the phone next to the Good April and called Dr. Kennedy at the hospital. Fortunately he was there.

"Hit her over the head with a lamp? I'll be at the emergency room when they get there."

The house was suddenly quiet. The crazy women were gone. The cop cars were leaving. The ambulance whirled away with its sirens blazing. A full-fledged Oak Park scandal. Only Peg and I and Madge and Theresa were still there, all hovering around Mom.

"Well, Chucky dear," she said, her Panglossa mode returning, "you certainly are good at working in a crisis. You must have learned that when you were working for poor dear Mr. Kennedy, God rest him."

"Have I forgotten anything, Peg?"

"Call that moron Ted and tell him what happened."

I looked up Ted's number and dialed it. The woman who answered the phone was not patient with my plea that it was an emergency and I had to talk to him immediately.

"I'll take your number and Doctor will call you back."

"Tell him that his wife is in jail at the Oak Park Police Station. That should get him to the phone."

Then Ted's voice, anxious and guilty.

"What happened, Chuck?"

"Your wife and two aggressive women came to Mom's house to kidnap her. She's in jail under charges of disorderly conduct, assault and battery, and attempted murder."

"Murder?" his voice wavered. "Whom did she try to murder?"

"My daughter Mary Margaret, whom she hit over the head with a lamp. She's in the hospital now under observation."

"I will have to put Jane in a mental institution for treatment . . . I'm sorry, Chuck, more sorry than I can tell. Also for the show at the wake and funeral. I have no control over her. She swears she takes the lithium. I never know whether she's done so. She seemed quite composed this morning."

"She was dragged out of here under restraints, shouting at the top of her voice. The street is filled with interested observers."

Peg went over to the window to investigate.

"I've done everything I can, Chuck, though it seems that's not enough. She has been fine for the last few months. She took her lithium every day. Your father's death brought on mania, and typically manics will not take their drug at that phase. She came home from your house, no, your mom's house, in a highly manic stage. I made her take the medicine, but she wouldn't swallow. People like being manic."

He sounded so sad that I felt sorry for him. When he came home from the War to marry his sweetheart, he could not have anticipated that this lovely young woman whom he loved so much could become a raving loony.

"Regardless, I have a traumatized mother and an injured daughter."

"I'll pay whatever bills you have, Chuck."

"Damn it to hell, Ted, I don't want your money. I just want your wife to leave us alone."

"I understand . . . I'll promise that what happened today won't ever happen again."

How could he keep such a promise?

"I assume Vince will ask for a peace bond."

"Of course. I understand. I would even understand if you press charges . . ."

"She's at the Oak Park Police Station. Vince will be there shortly. You'd better bring a lawyer. I think the cops have sedated her for her own good."

"I understand . . . I never expected this to happen, Chuck. I have always admired your family. Whatever happened long ago is in her mind, not in the real world. I'm very sorry."

"So am I."

"You didn't cut him much slack." Peg had picked up the violin she keeps at Mom's house and was tuning it.

"I feel sorry for poor Ted. His heart is breaking, but we don't give him slack till he tells us how he's going to control her."

"What if he can't?"

"Then they have real trouble."

"Are you going to play some Mozart for me, Peg dear?"

"A lot of Mozart, darling."

"I think I'd better see how my daughter is doing," I said.

"She'll be fine, Chuck," Peg said as she tightened the strings on her violin. "We all have pretty hard heads . . . Vince will take care of things one way or another and be in touch."

I stopped at Petersen's on the way to the hospital and purchased four chocolate malts with whipped cream. They put them in a bag which did not identify the source. I ambled into the hospital, strolled up to the reception desk, and smiled broadly.

"Ambassador O'Malley, you sure look better than the last time you were in here."

"My daughter is in for a bump on her head."

"Room 414. Mrs. O'Malley is up there with her."

I almost said, "Ms. Clancy." But I decided not to try my luck.

Various white-clad and blue-clad hospital staff smiled at me on the elevator in the corridor on the fourth floor. The secret of being a good smuggler is to act like you already have permission for whatever you're carrying. Then I remembered that Room 414 was the place where I almost died of pneumonia and had a visitor from another dimension.

I paused at the door of the room. Mary Margaret was lying on the bed, a large ice pack on her head, clad in an unappealing hospital gown. My wife and April Rosemary were sitting next to her, the former holding her hand.

"Stop talking dirty," Mary Margaret said wearily, "Ambassador Daddy's here and he looks like he's going to issue orders."

I said nothing for a moment because I'd been poleaxed by my wife's beauty as she leaned over her injured child. The brew of chaos and hatred of the afternoon was swept away by my love for her.

"I just brought good junks," I said, removing the malts from their secret container.

"Chucky, you're so sweet!" Mary Margaret smiled. "Rosie, isn't he sweet?"

"He's a wicked little boy who used to like to sneak candy into church and ice cream into the movies."

April Rosemary was the one to be responsible while I distributed the malts.

"Dr. Kennedy did a brain scan. He says he thinks my kid sister is fine. He'll be here in a few minutes, so we'd better dispose of our malts in a hurry."

"He's had to cope with Chucky before," my wife said, "and in this very room nothing will surprise him."

"How you doing, M. M?" I asked. "You look great."

"I do NOT look great," she protested. "I look awful. I feel awful. I should have ducked when crazy Aunt Jane swung that lamp at me. I'll never be the same again when I see a lamp. BUT I'm going to DC on Thursday, got it Chucky, Rosie? AND I'm getting out of this place in the morning . . . Are you going to give me one of those calorie machines, Chucky?"

She was sufficiently feisty to convince me that she was all right. We proceeded to dispose of our contraband.

"Rosie," Mary Margaret asked, "I remember how you looked at Shovie when you brought the poor little squalling brat home from the hospital, kind of like adoring her the way the Madonna does in those pictures. Did you look at me that way?"

"She sure did," April Rosemary said, "only you weren't wailing. You were a smug and contented little dickens."

"Hon, that's the way all mothers are with their children. They do adore them and love them and hope they are happy and have wonderful lives. We can't help ourselves."

"So Grams must have adored Aunt Jane when she was a baby?"

Uh-oh, I thought to myself as I leaned against the hospital window that looked out on Harlem Avenue.

"I'm sure she did."

"So what does it do to her when Aunt Jane breaks into her house and tries to kidnap her."

Silence.

"Chucky?" she looked at me.

Why me?

"God gives us kids for only a little while. We feed them and love them and then take care of them. Then we have to let go of them and turn them over to God. We do all we can, maybe we make some mistakes, then they're out of our hands and on their own. We laugh when they laugh and cry when they cry, but we can't live their lives for them."

"We break their hearts like I did," April Rosemary said sadly, "but they take us back when we come home. I say to myself that I would never do that if one of my kids freaked out. But I know I would."

"So," my wife finished, "Aunt Jane has been breaking her mother's heart these last few days and probably a lot longer. She's mad at her. But she still loves her."

Mary Margaret sighed. "It's hard being a mother."

"Parent," I said.

They all thought that emendation was very funny.

Rosemarie took over.

"Aunt Jane has an emotional disorder . . ."

"She's a manic-depressive. I know all about that. A couple of kids in my class take lithium every day and they're fine."

"They're very fortunate, hon, that they discovered the problem early. Parents and doctors weren't so sophisticated when we were growing up. Aunt Jane seemed cheerful all the time. Maybe a little too cheerful. Anyway, she's fine when she takes her medicine. Sometimes she doesn't, especially when something terrible happens like her father's death. That's why she went kind of crazy. Uncle Ted will get her back on the medicine and she'll be fine."

"She'll still hate Oak Park."

"No one has to like Oak Park."

Fortunately for all of us, Mary Margaret didn't ask *why* Jane hated Oak Park.

"Well, her kids are creeps."

"Just a little different from us."

"A *lot* different . . . Speaking of different. There's a person at the doorway, looking amused and bemused."

She pulled the sheet and light blanket up to her neck.

It was the ineffable Joey Moran. Carrying a bouquet of flowers. No roses.

"Street fight?" he said, slipping across the room to the edge of the bed, and handed her the flowers. "Mr. O'Malley, would you mind if I kissed your daughter very chastely?"

"What do I know?"

He did kiss her. It was not an excessively chaste kiss.

"You gonna be all right?"

"I just had a slight setback."

He kissed her again.

"A mite better . . . And he's Ambassador O'Malley."

"Here, dear," Rosemarie handed her half-full malt to Joe. "Ambassador O'Malley likes to smuggle contraband into the hospital."

"Should I call you Ms. Ambassador, ma'am?"

"Try Mom for size!"

Before everyone could express proper outrage over my outrageous comment, Dr. Kennedy in his white jacket entered Room 414. I thought I smelled the roses that my mysterious friend had brought to me. No, she had brought the smell of roses.

The women tried to hide their contraband. Poor Joe Moran continued to sip his.

There was definitely a smell of roses. My visitor had always been a showoff.

"Still breaking the rules, Chuck?"

"I found them at the nurses' station," I pleaded.

"And you, young woman, how do you feel?"

"I want to go home and I want to go to DC on Thursday to scope out the new president."

"I don't think there'll be any problem about DC. There's no hint of a crack on that fine skull of yours. But we want to keep you overnight, just to make sure there are no complications."

"I'm FINE!"

"You do what Dr. Kennedy tells you, Mary Margaret O'Malley."

"Yes, *Daddy*."

The doctor felt her pulse, then took her blood pressure.

"Vital signs all normal."

"Hmf . . ." She glared at poor Joey Moran.

"We'll see about things tomorrow morning. In the meantime, Ms. O'Malley, I would urge you while you are in the hospital to do what your father says and not what he does."

"Yes, Doctor."

Rosemarie gave the keys to her Bentley to our firstborn. "April Rosemary, you'd better pick up your car and get home to your kids and husband."

"Good idea, Mom. He'll be interested in the details."

"I'm sure he will."

"I'll leave too, Mrs. O'Malley," Joe Moran said. "I don't want to raise your daughter's blood pressure."

"As if you could," she said affectionately as he kissed her good-bye.

I caught Rosemarie's eye. She smiled faintly. Sure marriage.

"Okay, you two can go home too," our daughter informed us, after her young man had left. "I need to get my sleep."

"No way," I said.

"Absolutely not."

"You should get some supper and some sleep. There's a lot of work to do."

"You're babbling, Mary Margaret," I said. "We have nothing to do tomorrow."

"You're babbling, Chucky. You have your Russian book to do."

I had forgotten about that.

"Come on, Chuck," Rosemarie told me with a wink. "Let's go down and get a bite to eat."

"I'll call . . . and get some pasta."

While we were waiting in the lobby for the pasta to show up, we discussed the events of the day.

"You know the shrink stuff," I said. "What are Jane's chances?"

"Not too bad if she takes her meds," Rosemarie replied. "She can lead an even if uneventful life. Maybe one of those creepy kids will marry and have a child she can adore. I'll ask Maggie, but I think the combination of bipolar and resentment can be pretty potent, unless she sticks to her meds. I'm not sure what will happen to Ted. Poor guy has probably done his best. I don't know what joy is left in his life."

"His father's spirit continues to haunt him after all these years."

"I suspect he has grounds for an annulment," she went on. "He's probably too much a straight arrow to ask for one."

"Very grim . . . Can we do anything?"

"Probably not, but, being who we are, we will probably try . . . What happened with Joe at lunch the other day?"

"I forgot all about it . . . It seems like a long time ago."

"A crazy aunt does not bang your daughter on the head every Monday afternoon."

So I told her the story. Among my wife's many virtues is that she listens silently to a story. Unlike other women, she saves her questions for the end. I fall more in love with her as the hours pass. Won't do anything about it tonight.

"I have to call Erin and tell her we won't be home tonight and hold a conversation with Shovie. She's entitled to an explanation."

The pasta came. I slipped into a small conference room that had sort of become a room reserved for the Crazy O'Malleys on their various visits to the hospital. I figured that if I were a gentleman, I'd wait for my wife. But I was hungry.

She was so used to my gluttony that she did not even notice that I had started to eat without her.

"Shovie is not happy with us. She should be at the hospital too to make sure that they take good care of her sister. I told her that Mary Margaret had thrown us out of her room so she could sleep. Shovie said that she must be all right. Erin said that they'd both pray for Mary Margaret. Poor Erin could not have been more concerned about her own sister."

She sat down at the table and opened her Diet Pepsi.

"How did you explain the accident?"

"For the moment Mary Margaret fell and hit her head on a lamp—minor change in the order of things . . . Erin is putting her to bed."

She removed the cover from her plate of linguini à la Genovese.

"Yum . . . Where were we? Oh, yes. Why you, Chucky Ducky? Why does this Bride Raftery person, living or dead, real or only in poor Joe's mind want to bring you into the act? You're not an internationally known detective. Nor are you reputed to be a psychic. You are a picture taker with the heart of an accountant—which is nonsense of course—and an unemployed ambassador whom the State Department keeps on their list because they might want you to do something sometime . . . Why are you selected to play the role of a medium in this business?"

"Good point," I said.

Heavens, she was beautiful when she put on her thinking cap.

"It must have something to do with your picture taking. She links you with your books of pictures, which she knocks off the shelves to remind Joe that's what it's about."

"Fair play to you, Rosemarie . . . What do you think?"

"I think she and her daughter are probably dead, the victims of a cruel and vicious murder. I think that Joe's troubled soul has conjured this whole story. I think Maggie Ward would suggest that it's a wild-goose chase."

"I can't disagree."

"But what if I'm wrong?"

"I ask myself the same question."

We both remained silent.

My wife lifted her lovely shoulders.

"You will read the file and then give it to me."

"I don't think there is a rush."

"Probably not, Chuck, but . . ."

"But if Bride Mary O'Brien is still alive, there might be a rush."

She nodded solemnly.

"I don't like this sort of thing, Rosemarie. The uncanny makes me feel uncanny."

"We don't have much choice. Joe Raftery is from the neighborhood."

At that moment, speaking of the neighborhood, Peg and Vince arrived. We wouldn't tell them unless we needed their help, especially Vince's, as our probing went on. Deep down in my brother-in-law's Italianate soul there was not merely dislike of the uncanny, but fear of it.

"We heard you ordered from Farnese when we went in there, so we brought along our own supper."

Vince had his usual spaghetti and meatballs and Peg, always the soul sister of my wife, brought linguini à la Genovese. They also provided a bottle of Chianti, substantially better than the Dago red of our youth.

"How's she doing?" Peg asked anxiously.

"She ordered us out of her room, so she could sleep."

"Her mother's daughter . . . No hairline fractures?"

"None. They're keeping her overnight for observation."

"Routine. But if it were Rita, I'd be a wreck."

Rita was their youngest—Marguerita, named after her mother, just as our daughter was named after her aunt.

"And Mom?" Rosemarie asked.

"Pretty shook up, as are Madge and Theresa. They cringe every time a car goes by. The Good April seems so vulnerable and fragile. She praises all of us for being so quick to respond and worries greatly about 'poor little Moire Meg.' Maybe when she gets out of the hospital tomorrow she should stop and say hello. Are you still going to visit Mr. Reagan?"

"Only if Mary Margaret is well enough to come with us. Dr. Kennedy says she seems okay. But I'm not going there to 'scope out' the new president, unless she comes with us. And that's final."

That settled that.

"After all," Vince chimed in, "he's a Republican!"

"I'm worried about April," Peg went on, toying with her linguine. "She recites the same lines, still Dr. Panglossa with bit of the old flapper thrown in. But she's tired and fragile and lonely and sad. I'm not sure exactly what's wrong with her heart, but it's not as good as it used to be. This crazy business with Jane might be just too much for her."

"Are the cops still out there, Chuck?" Rosemarie asked.

"They sure are, including that young woman who was so nice to Mary Margaret. Since Jane is not likely to reappear for a long time, they're there for morale purposes. I suppose by tomorrow April will be inviting them in for cookies and tea. I told the chief to tell them that it was okay. And, Vince, what about Jane?"

He spread his hands out in that marvelous Sicilian gesture which, I think, means what can I tell you, especially in this perverse and fatalistic world. I have tried to imitate it often with little success.

"Poor Ted. He's such a good guy. He still loves her or maybe loves what she used to be. We're not going to file charges against her for the present, though we hold open the possibility of filing before the statute expires. I'll need some evidence from Doc Kennedy about the injury done to Mary Margaret. We have the testimony of the cops, of Madge and Theresa, as well as yours, Chucky. We could nail her on felony charges, but I don't think anyone wants to do that unless we have to."

"We might have to," I insisted.

"Certainly . . . I told Ted that and he understood. He wants time to get her back on her medications. Right now she's on her way to a private sanitarium up near Deerfield. He won't let her out of there until the doctors in charge are convinced that she will stay on her pills."

"How can they know that?" Rosemarie asked.

"They can't. Ted says he will have full-time nurses on her after she comes home. Moreover, he'll bar any contact with Father Delahaye, some sort of weird religious order priest who told her that she was bound in conscience to free her mother from those who were keeping her prisoner."

"Can we do something about him?" I asked.

"I can and will talk to his superior and tell him that we will depose Father Delahaye and the superior if it comes to a civil case. In the present climate of the Church, priests are scared stiff of suits."

"It will get worse," I said, "when all the sexual abuse stuff comes into the open . . . Can we do anything with the rest of Jane's children?"

"Ted brought Chris along, an estate planner at a Loop law factory. Obnoxious punk, combination of patronizing smile and a bored yawn. He told Ted not to pay any attention to me, I was merely a Daley hack. His firm would teach me how hardball is played in the big leagues."

"Tell them what you said," Peg urged.

"I told him that if they really wanted to play hardball, we'd go for attempted murder. Your cousin, I said, is over at Oak Park Hospital with a possible skull fracture. Your mother hit her over the head with a lamp. It's a miracle she didn't kill her. They could plead insanity if they wanted. Otherwise, she'd do serious jail time. He tried to answer that, and Ted told him to shut up. So he yawned again."

"Mary Margaret says the kids are creeps," I said.

"Could we really do that?" Rosemarie asked with a contemplative frown.

"We can and we will if they don't keep her away from us."

"In other words," Rosemary summed up, "we don't want to play hardball just yet, but Ted knows we're prepared to do so."

"Yes, the poor guy. He knows you have no choice."

"He never should have moved away from the neighborhood," I said.

"She probably wanted to move," Peg added. "Get away from me and Rosie."

"I figured you'd want me to do it this way." Vince looked uneasily around the table. He had never quite understood the dynamics of Irish family decision making.

"Certainly," Rosemarie said, feeling no need to ask my opinion.

"They sedated her at the police station as you know, so she wouldn't do any harm to herself. It would have broken your heart to see what a pathetic lump she was . . . I remember." He trailed off.

"So do we all," I said.

My wife and I returned to our daughter's room.

"Mary Margaret is restless," the floor nurse told us. "She has a tiny fever, nothing serious. But she's lonely and confused."

"Where have you two been?" Mary Margaret demanded when we entered the room, dark save for the monitor on the wall.

"We were having supper downstairs with Aunt Peg and Uncle Vince," Rosemarie replied.

"You told us to get out and leave you alone," I pointed out.

"You should have known I didn't mean it . . . I'm scared. Aunt Jane is chasing me with that lamp."

"Aunt Jane is locked up, hon. You're dreaming."

"Regardless . . ."

Our mature, self-possessed daughter was weeping. Damn Jane and her sick envy.

"We'll stay here all night, hon," Rosemarie said soothingly.

"You'd better . . . I want to go home."

"First thing tomorrow morning."

Rosemarie sat on the chair next to the bed and took our daughter's hand in her own.

"Chucky, will you close the door, please. Aunt Jane might not know it's my room."

"Sure."

I closed the door.

"Rosie . . ."

"Yes, hon?"

"Remember when I was a real little kid and I'd have a cold and you and Chuck would sing me to sleep?"

"You want us to do it now?"

"Kind of soft, so you won't disturb others, huh?"

So we sang our "intermediate" daughter to sleep and exorcised all visions of the Wicked Witch of the North Shore coming after her with a lamp.

Chapter Twelve

Bride Mary O'Brien was born in 1941 in a small hamlet in West Galway on the River Suck [sic!] above Ballinasloe on the Roscommon border. The circumstances of her birth were not promising. Ireland was in the Emergency, a period of economic stagnation as Mr. De Valera, the leader of the country, argued that every possible sacrifice was essential to keep Ireland neutral in England's war with Hitler. So neutral was Ireland that, although many of its sons were fighting in the English armed forces, Mr. De Valera went to the German embassy to sign the sympathy book at the time of Hitler's death.

However, Emergency meant poverty, especially in the West of Ireland, and more especially for those who lived on poor land like her father's. Bride Mary was the only child of James O'Brien and Brigid Mary Slaney, who married late in life as was still the custom in the West in those days. Her mother was 42 and her father 58 when she was born. The neighbors said she was a stubborn, headstrong little girl who fought with the other children in the hamlet, defied the older people, and charmed everyone with a mischievous, crooked smile. She was a troublemaker at the National School in Newtown, to which she walked every day because her parents were too poor to afford even a bicycle. She was by far the brightest child in the school but also the most troublesome. She made fun of the teachers, the principal, and even the parish priest. The last named, a stern, dour old canon, unaccountably was fond of her. He had a reputation for never laughing; but he did laugh at her jokes, her insults, her dirty face, and her threats.

Astonished to discover she had an audience, she would often visit him in the parish house and request that he tell her stories. The canon, who seemed to have a collection of fairie stories from the old days, was delighted to do so. People said that she reminded him of his mother or of a sweetheart from long ago.

Bride Mary's parents, conscious of their position at the bottom of the social ladder, were not happy with this sign of favor. What will people say? Who do we think we are? None of this opposition had the slightest effect on Bride Mary or on the canon either. She continued to do well in her studies, but acquired no other marks of a civilized respectability. Moreover, while her parents were English-speaking, she caught on to the Irish language in class and loved it. She spent what little time she had between school and work on the farm with a gang of Irish-speaking kids who roamed the fields around Newtown and even invaded Ballinasloe on Saturdays to pick fights with the townies and yell insults at them in Irish.

The Irish language lacks obscenities and scatology, so in the Ireland of that day, the Irish-speaking ruffians had to spice up their insults with English four-letter words. They were mostly children of men and women who, like Bride Mary's parents, had to marry late in life because of the poverty of the Great Depression and lacked the vigor to tame their bright and charming young hellions. When they were not in school and not working their family farms and not tormenting the respectable citizens of Ballinasloe, they played in the reeds and marshes along the Suck, chasing birds, scaring fishermen, begging money from the occasional tourist, and, if one were to believe the gossip, being free with their sexual favors to one another.

The gossip was probably defamation. The prudery of Ireland at that time made sexual play among the young almost impossible—and it was a good thing too they themselves would later say when they began to worry about their own offspring. Yet perhaps Bride Mary's group was an exception to the national norms. Perhaps their crimes did not go further than naked play and swimming in the Suck under the full moon. Perhaps.

At twelve, Bride Mary and her class would leave the National School in Newtown either for the Secondary School in Ballinasloe or to return to their farms as full-time workers. Her teacher insisted that she was a young woman of enormous talent and should go on to Secondary School. Brigid Mary and James O'Brien worried that people would say that they were putting on airs if they sent their daughter into Ballinasloe for school. The next thing the priest and the teachers would be telling them that she should go to Galway for university.

Galway might just as well be in Nigeria as far as the O'Briens were concerned. They had never visited the city and did not intend to do so. They had traveled a couple of times "down the line" to Athenry and returned disappointed with the venture. Travel cost money and it afforded little pleasure. Athenry, they told their neighbors was no different from Ballinasloe, though the people in the former town put on a lot more airs.

Brash and irresponsible hellion that she was, Bride Mary had come to enjoy school. She loved to show off her intelligence, which, she realized dimly, was considerable. She also loved the praise of the teachers and the canon. She didn't give a fig (she would have used a stronger word) for the envy of her classmates. Yet she was of two minds about more school. She loved her elderly (as she saw them) parents dearly. She knew they needed her help on the farm. Her Irish-speaking gang, especially Colm, with whom she thought she was in love, would not be going on to school. There was not that much point in more education. She would eventually marry someone from her part of Ireland and settle down to a life like that of her parents, though perhaps a little less difficult. She wanted a different life, the kind of life portrayed in the books she was reading; but there was nothing in the world around her to suggest that such a life might be possible.

Then the canon changed everything. He came by their farm one Sunday afternoon in April and informed her parents that the nuns in Galway were offering Bride Mary a complete scholarship—board, room, tuition, everything for a secondary education. She would have to maintain a high average and her behavior would have to be exemplary (a stern look at Bride Mary). However, he had no doubt that she would live up to both requirements. The nuns were women who demanded prompt reaction to their generosity. He would phone the nuns tomorrow with their acceptance.

The O'Briens were devastated. What will people say? Brigid Mary asked immediately. Why should a daughter of ours go off to the nuns in Galway? She'll never come home again, her father protested. She'll think she's too good for the likes of us. Bride Mary was too frightened to speak. Galway was a chance for a different life, one of limitless possibilities or so it seemed. But it was also an unknown, so terrifying that it overwhelmed her. She wanted to stay where she belonged.

What do you want to do, young woman? the canon asked imperiously. I don't know, she stumbled. Do you realize what a great grace this is? She didn't know what he meant, but she said yes, because that was what you said to the canon when he asked a question that way.

Well then, that settles it. It's off to Galway with you in September.

After the canon left, all three O'Briens clung to each other and wept. Great was their grief all summer long and it was a wet and grim summer. The Emergency had ended almost a decade earlier, but Ireland was still a poor and stagnant country. Could her parents survive without her there to help them on the farm? But she had given her word to the canon, her father said, and she must keep it.

Her friends ridiculed her good fortune. Who did she think she was? She wouldn't last a week with the "swells" in Galway. She'd come home in disgrace. Or, alternatively, she would become a grand lady.

It is possible that she lost her virginity to Colm that summer or maybe the next one. She never mentioned him in her later letters and apparently never wrote to him. Inquiries about him reveal only that he migrated to England and never returned to Ballinasloe.

We do know that she wept all the way to Galway on the train trip from Ballinasloe. She was awed by the city when she arrived. Though in 1954, still the time of a stalled Irish economy, Galway was a drab, dour city even in the bright afternoon sunlight, her busy eyes drank in the people, the buildings, the cars, the Green in front of the station, the young people her age who were coming to town to begin their university education. This she thought to herself was even more terrifying than she had expected: it might also be something like paradise.

Two nuns waited for her at the train station, tall, slender, stern-looking women. She had heard many stories about how ferocious nuns were. She realized with a sudden insight that she was a dirty farm child in old clothes and with manners these elegant women would detest. She felt naked and wanted to turn and run.

You're Bride Mary, are you not? they asked. Yes, s'ter, she said, as if she were pleading guilty to a criminal charge. They both embraced her and said that she was most welcome to Galway. They were proud to have one with such sterling academic credentials join them. They were sure she would be happy.

Bride Mary was astonished: she began to cry again. They took her to a tiny ice-cream store just off the Square and bought her a cup of tea and a dish of ice cream, the latter a delicacy she had never experienced. Bride Mary realized in that ice-cream store that her life had changed forever.

Unlike her contemporary the Irish writer Edna O'Brien, convent school was a pleasant experience for her. Most of the nuns were kind, sensitive women, despite their stern moral code which Bride Mary discounted as the result of the fact that they had always been nuns. Her school uniform hid the poverty of her past. Shrewd peasant that she was, she studied the manners of the girls who seemed to know how to behave and acquired the polish of a "nun's girl." She couldn't hide Ballinasloe and didn't want to, but celebrated its glories in terms she began to believe herself.

Some of the more snobbish girls treated her with contempt, but many of her fellow students delighted in her quick wit and impish eyes. She decided that she had better conceal the hellion and the hoyden that she really was. The nuns, whom she loved, wouldn't appreciate it. It would be the death of the poor old canon if she were sent home in disgrace. Slowly and without any conscious intent she became the leader of her form. The implicit rules of friendship she had learned on the banks of the Suck applied in Galway too. You had to be eager to help people and to console them when they were discouraged. She seemed to have a natural aptitude at caring for others, so much so the girls said that she would be a nun someday.

As much as she loved them, she did not find that vocation attractive. I guess I like boys too much, she said. Bride Mary seemed to her friends to understand what sex was about. Boys will take whatever they can get and then drop you, she pontificated. It isn't worth much if there's not some commitment involved. The nuns said the same thing, but here was someone who seemed to know from experience that made her confident, though she never described that experience. She charmed the boys from the Brothers' school during the brief contacts which were permitted, but kept them at bay.

We have a picture of her at that time of her life. She is wearing the uniform skirt and black sweater of the school and knee-high socks. She is about fourteen at the time with the full body of a woman, long black hair, and a crinkling, happy smile. Though the other young women in the picture are certainly not unattractive Bride Mary O'Brien even then stood out, a beautiful, mischievous young woman whose eyes knew perhaps too much.

She luxuriated in the comforts of the school, indoor plumbing, bathtubs, a comfortable bed in the dorm which, while chill by the standards of most of the students, was blessedly warm to her, especially under a big blanket.

She did well in class, knowing the answers but remembering to be deferential to the nuns and restrained so as not to offend her classmates. She was often told that she was the smartest student in the school. She dismissed the compliment by arguing that she was only a peasant from the bogs.

The nuns knew she had no money of her own, so they provided her with small tasks the pay for which enabled her to buy such things as underwear and the occasional chocolate or biscuit. If she envied the more affluent young women, it never appears in the letters she dutifully wrote to the canon and her parents, letters which were mostly straight factual descriptions of the school and its people. We have no idea what the impact of her letters was on James and Brigid Mary O'Brien.

She found an outlet for her energy and, as she admitted herself to the canon, her destructiveness on the canogi field, a woman's version of the male combat of hurling. Her long hair trailing behind her, one of her friends wrote, she rushed up and down the pitch like a womanly Finn MacCool.

Under the guidance of a young nun, she drifted into the world of books and began to read with the same ferocious passion that she demonstrated on the playing pitch. She wrote long letters to the canon about what she had read in both English and Irish. We know that she delighted in Brian Merryman's poem "The Midnight Court." We would like to know where she found it in Galway because it certainly wouldn't have been in the nuns' library. We would also like to know how the canon reacted to her reading such sexually explicit and anticlerical material. Maybe he understood that those were themes you couldn't avoid if you delved into Irish-language literature.

We know that Bride Mary returned to her home above Newtown at Christmas and in the summer and that she worked diligently on the farm with her parents. The canon notes in his erratic journal that she returned in the same clothes she had worn when she went to school and worked just as hard as she ever did. However, she spent more of her free time, such as it was, reading than with her Irish-speaking ruffian friends, much to the canon's delight.

When she was fifteen, in the middle of a dark cold winter with the winds blowing all the way over from Newfoundland and the waves beating against the shores of Galway Bay, her father and mother both died. Brigid Mary Slaney O'Brien was only in her late fifties when she died of an untreated cancer that had rapidly consumed her whole body. Two months later her father collapsed with a massive stroke. At Easter the old canon passed on, leaving her a legacy. The farm we know was sold though: after all the encumbrances were paid, Bride Mary inherited only a little more than a hundred pounds.

We have no record of her reaction to these three tragedies, because there was no one left to write the letters to, though the canon had saved the ones to him and the ones to her parents.

We have no letters for her remaining years, but she did keep a journal which she must have left behind when she graduated from the Secondary School. It doesn't tell us very much about her life. The nuns, aware that she had no home, invited her to spend Christmas and summer as their guest, perhaps because some of them still had some hope that she would join them in the religious life. They must have decided that it would only be fair if she were permitted the same freedom that young women her age were granted by their parents. Her journal makes it clear that she wandered around Galway—city and county—with some degree of freedom, usually in company with her classmates. She describes, perhaps with too much poetry, some of the beautiful places she visited and even the Galway races.

She also met many young men her age and older at parties and dances. She did not tolerate fools or predators easily. Such young men are dismissed abruptly. There are also some "nice boys" of whom she is fond, but she warns herself that she does not want to become "involved." We do not know whether any of these summer romances became serious.

We do know, however, that she did attend dances with her friends. We have a picture of her in a quite chaste strapless gown with a dancing card on her wrist. Her long hair is piled up on top of her head and she looks like a self-confident young noblewoman. The glint of mischief is still in her eyes. There is no hint of Ballinasloe in her demeanor.

Occasionally, she philosophizes about herself, not with much depth but with considerable pathos.

Back from the dance. It was fun. I had no trouble filling my card. The parents who chaperoned tell me that I'm darling. My friends say that they're proud of me. I feel like a fraud. I'm still a kid from the Suck River who grew up without inside plumbing. I'm an Irish-speaking hellion with a veneer of civilization pasted on me by the good nuns and my friends. I suppose that as my life goes on I will become more of a fraud and forget my dear parents whom I loved so much and I will miss so much and the wonderful canon who told me toward the end of his life that I reminded him of a sweetheart who died of the flu.

I am sad when I think about them. The canon said that when I left the Suck behind and came to Galway, I leaped from the feudal world into the early-modern world—early twentieth century, he said with a twinkle in his eye. I shall of course go to university next year. The nuns are sure I'll win a scholarship. Then perhaps to America. I don't know about that however. I'll have time to think about that.

I'll have to find a job somewhere in town and a place to live, probably with other students. I'll miss the convent. The nuns have permitted me to become a woman, though still a very young one and in most ways very inexperienced. No that's not fair to them. They have helped me to become a woman. Yet I can't remain here. It would not be fair to them because I do not plan to join them, as much as I admire them. And I must spread my wings and learn to live on my own. That thought excites me and frightens me.

I believe in God, though perhaps not the same God the nuns believe in. I know that You are a God of love and that You will take care of me. I trust my life to You.

I wonder why I'm crying as I read these words. Perhaps because if you're Irish you know that dreams never come true.

We find a yearbook from the school which tells us that she graduated with high honors and then matriculated at University College, Galway.

I put the file back into the folder. Bride Mary O'Brien was a fascinating young women. She had deserved a longer life. But who is to say what anyone deserves. She was correct that if you're Irish, dreams never quite come true. But if you're Catholic, you know that in the long run, the very long run, they do come true.

Chapter Thirteen

Mary Margaret

Well, they finally let me out of the hospital this morning. After taking my blood pressure and temperature several times, asking me to tell them how many fingers they were holding up, and the names of my nieces and nephews, and if I had seen *Raging Bull* and liked Billy Joel, they said I could go home if I promised to be careful. There was some difficulty because I named an extra niece, April Rosemary's unborn daughter Polly. I knew about her because the pictures say that it is a daughter and she's going to be named Polly after her Grandma Nettleton who was one of Chuck's commanding officers when he was in Bamberg (stories about which we hear often, always in slightly different versions). I did this deliberately to bait them because I was tired of being treated like some kind of freak.

Chuck and Rosie showed up about then to take me home and confirmed the expectation of Polly II.

They warned me to be careful and not to take any chances in the next couple of days, like playing tennis. I agreed so long as it is all right for me to fly down to DC with Rosie and Chuck on Thursday.

I have class this afternoon and already missed too many.

Then Rosie had to hold my arm as I walked out to the car.

"I am totally all right," I insisted. "I'm young and resilient."

"You missed the last stair," she said.

"It shouldn't have been there."

I insisted that we stop at Grams's on the way home. She was presiding over a nice little tea party for herself, Madge and

Theresa, and the two off-duty women cops who were supposed to be outside in the car protecting her from any return attack by crazy Aunt Jane.

"It's all right, dears," Grams says. "Poor dear Jane is locked away in the loony bin and she can't get out."

Trust Chuck to say something gross. He picks up the lamp, examines it carefully, and says, "Lucky it didn't break!"

Grams and Rosie immediately shout, "Chucky!"

This is what he wants to hear and he grins like a silly little boy. I just laugh.

Grams hugs me and proclaims me a heroine for saving her life. I thank her, but I'm no heroine. Crazy Aunt Jane rolled over me like she was a tank. I hope she stays out of my dreams tonight.

Then we go home, I change into a suit, and lump on my head and all I drive over to Rosary. Rosie and Chuck insist that they will drive me and I insist that I can drive myself. They follow me over just the same. My classmates applaud as I walk in just as the session begins. Even the teacher applauds. My face, always prone to blushing, turns very warm. I nod and smile but ignore them. I am totally no heroine.

I drive home at three-thirty. Shovie is waiting for me at the door, jumping up and down with joy. She hugs me, then bursts into tears. "I thought you were dead," she sobs. Our family, excepting me, are prone to tears. Chucky is the worst weeper of all. Poor little Shovie has death on her mind. Like we all do these days.

Chucky and Rosie are in her office working on their book.

"I'm going down to the darkroom to work on the film," I say.

"Young woman, you certainly are not!" Rosie jumps up from her desk.

"I certainly am!" I say firmly.

Mothers and daughters bond by fighting.

"Don't ruin any of the film," Chucky mutters, just stirring up the pot, which he loves to do. Like I say, he really is a silly little boy. Compared to him Joey Moran is a grown-up.

"You need a nap," Rosie says.

This is true. I do need a nap. BUT I have to start to catch up with April Rosemary's work in the darkroom. We're buds now, which is neat, but we still compete on some things, like all sisters do. Except maybe Rosie and Aunt Peg who are codependents.

"I do not need a nap!"

She ponders this and then comes up with a compromise.

"I'll come down and work with you."

I probably need someone to keep an eye on me, though I won't admit that.

"Suit yourself," I grumble.

"It's all right if you two argue down there, but don't destroy any of my precious film. I'll fire you both."

We both dismiss him with loud sighs of protest and loud cries of "Chuck-KEY!"

We work smoothly and effectively, just to show Chucky. The chemicals get to me just a little so I'm glad Rosie is with me.

The phone rings. She answers it promptly even though we're in the darkroom.

"O'Malley residence."

She hands the phone to me in the dark.

"Some boy . . ."

"Where have you been all day, Joey Moran? I could have been dead and buried!"

Rosie whispers that he's been calling all day. I know THAT.

"Sure I went to school . . . I'm totally recovered . . . I'm in the darkroom with Rosie working on the films from the Russian shoot . . . I certainly am going to DC. I can't play tennis till next week . . . Only a little headache . . . Bad dreams last night . . . Crazy Aunt Jane coming at me with the lamp again . . . Well . . . Only for an hour or two. We can watch *Star Trek* . . . I have to get a good night's sleep . . . thanks for calling . . . Bye."

"You're as bad as your father," Rosie tells me. "I'm astonished that such a nice boy puts up with your guff."

"He says he loves me."

"And that act at the hospital about the unborn niece. You were just making trouble."

"Apples don't fall that far from their trees!"

We both laugh because we know that I inherit the contentiousness from her and the childishness from Chucky.

We hang up the films we've just finished.

"Let's do some proof sheets," I say.

"We should do all the developing first."

"You always want to defer gratification," I reply.

We both laugh because I know that she wants to see some proof sheets too. Also I know—though she doesn't know that I know—that she and Chucky aren't deferring gratification much these days. They're gaga about one another. Again. Maybe death does that to people. I think that's very healthy. It is also very healthy that I think it's very healthy. I hope that when I'm almost fifty my husband and I have the same sort of romance going.

Might it be that way with my current nuisance? Would Joey Moran be gaga about me in 2010? Well, that would be up to me, wouldn't it?

Then the phone rings. She grabs it again. Like Chucky says, its her house.

"Another boy."

"Mary Margaret O'Malley," I tell the caller.

"It's Ted."

"Ted who?"

"Ted McCormack . . . I called the hospital. They said you had been released. I just thought I would check."

"I'm okay, Ted. Working in the darkroom."

"I wanted to apologize . . ."

"You didn't hit me over the head with a lamp."

"She might have killed you."

"Well, she didn't kill me. Even if she had, it wasn't your fault."

I'm using my responses to tell Rosie what's going on.

"Well, can I at least say that I'm sorry it happened . . . Mom really flipped out this time. No one expected she'd be so violent."

"How is she doing now?"

"She's in Valley View, sedated like a vegetable. Dad says she looks terrible. So does he . . . Jenny and Micky said they're sorry too. The three of us wonder how much we missed by drifting away from you guys."

I feel tears sting at the back of my eyes. If I'm not careful, I'll become a constant weeper like the rest of the family.

"Well, we're all young enough to correct that," I said.

"I hope so . . . We had a family meeting this morning. Father was very candid about everything . . . My brother Chris was a bastard as usual . . . His firm should play hardball with you guys and teach you a lesson."

"I don't think Chris knows what hardball is here on the West Side."

"Chris is pretty good, I think, at estate planning. After that his view of what happens in court is based on television and films."

"I hope your mother recovers quickly."

"So do I. Father says it's likely to be a long haul . . . Well, I just wanted to say I was glad you're feeling better. Micky and Jenny will be too when I tell them."

"Give Micky and Jenny my love," I say almost choking on my words.

"Well!" Rosie says when I hang up. "Does that young man have a crush on you?"

"He has a crush on the O'Malley clan," I say. "He thinks he and his sisters might have missed something. He heard about the saints marching in."

"Poor kid."

"Yeah . . . Do you think our clan and their clan have a chance of ever being friends?"

"Father Raven says that forgiveness is what Christianity is all about."

Chapter Fourteen

Rosemarie

"She doesn't know what we are doing, does she?" Chuck said to me as we fell into each other's arms as soon as he had closed the door in our room in the Hay-Adams Hotel.

"Certainly she knows what we're doing. She's a very perceptive young woman. She doesn't quite understand what happens that makes two people our age fall in love again simultaneously. But she approves."

We pawed one another, crazy with desire. Since we had boarded the plane at O'Hare I wanted nothing more than to be naked with him. I told myself that I was too old for such feelings and that even when I was younger they would have been inappropriate. I was a grandmother almost fifty years old. I was past the time in life when sexual abandon was suitable. My obsession with my husband was undignified. We were in DC on serious business—a portrait of a president. I knew we could defer romance just like we could defer a forest fire. I was a she-animal in heat. I should be ashamed of myself. That thought enflamed me even more.

As we kissed and caressed, I unbuttoned the top of my beige knit autumn dress and pushed my bra straps off my shoulders. Chuck finished the process of stripping me to the waist. I cried out with joy, not loudly enough, I hoped, to be heard in the next room, much less down the corridor where our curious daughter was doubtless reading a book. And wondering . . .

The week had not been easy. The Good April seemed more ethereal every day. Mary Margaret's nights were troubled by angry dreams. I had to tell her that she should be furious at Crazy Aunt Jane. Her anger did not mean that she did not forgive her. I also brought her over to see Dr. Kennedy about the trip to DC, despite her angry protests that she felt "fine." He approved the trip and asked her about sleeping at night.

"Fine."

"No bad dreams?"

"Only a couple . . ."

"Mary Margaret Anne O'Malley!" I warned her.

"All RIGHT, Ro-SIE . . . Terrible dreams, Dr. Mike, all confused and angry and violent . . . I don't sleep much . . ."

"You might perhaps want a couple of counseling sessions with someone," he said tentatively.

"I'm FINE!"

Mike Kennedy, who had teens of his own, did not make an issue out of it. Mary Margaret was not a teen anymore but sometimes she regressed.

She sulked as we drove home.

As we pulled up in front of the house, she said sadly, "Trees are beginning to change colors."

"It happens, hon."

We made no move to leave the car.

"I don't suppose that your friend Dr. Ward would see me once or twice."

"It's probably against the rules, but Maggie doesn't always keep the rules."

"Could you call her and ask?"

"It would be better if you did."

"Will you sit in your office with me while I call her?"

"Sure . . . That's what mothers are for."

"Okay. Let's do it now before I change my mind."

We went into my office—The CEO's office as Chuck called it. I gave her the number and she dialed it.

"Lo, Dr. Ward. I'm Mary Margaret O'Malley. Rosie's daughter. I wonder if I might come over and see you a couple of times . . . My crazy Aunt Jane tried to kill me with a lamp . . . Chucky and Rosie and I have to go to DC to take the president's picture this week . . . Next Monday afternoon? Good, I don't have class then. Thank you."

"That wasn't hard, was it?"

"She's a nice lady . . . I am SO mad at Crazy Aunt Jane!"

"She could have killed you, hon."

"She could have made me a vegetable for the next fifty years."

I shivered. I'd never thought of that. I hope that Vince could keep that crazy woman locked up forever. I didn't think she was so crazy that she didn't know what she was doing.

"Well," my daughter perked up, "back to the dungeon. April Rosemary is coming over, probably with her kids. You can play grandma."

My children think they can waltz into my house with their kids anytime they want to and I won't object. They're right of course. April Rosemary has trained Johnny and April Nettleton to adore their grandmother. I have no resistance to them at all, at all.

That evening Chuck and I went through the proof sheets, this time just glancing through them hastily and marking some of the more promising shots. We viewed them on a huge magnifying screen. We did it together in the darkroom because we had learned that our tastes in such matters were similar. We distracted ourselves in the process with remote but delectable foreplay.

"Charles Cronin O'Malley! We are here to work! You're distracting me! . . . Ouch! Stop it! Mary Margaret is upstairs. What if she walks down to see what we're doing?"

"The door is locked and she knows better than to do that!"

"We have to finish these proof sheets!"

"We'll finish them," he said innocently. "A little petting does not interfere with my artistic judgment."

"It does interfere with mine."

"That's because you women are more easily distracted by pleasure than us men."

"Stop it!"

"Do you really mean that?"

I considered for a moment.

"Certainly not!"

"I figure," he went on, "that this is an important turning point in our life and we must make the most of it."

"Entering our golden years and losing Dad?"

"Falling in love all over again seems a wise response, though I don't think either of us planned it."

I didn't disagree. There was too much sweetness between us not to seize it, cling to it, revel in it whenever we could.

We did manage to go through the proof sheets and choose more shots than we could ever use. My thoughts about the text were shaping up.

"I think we should make your remarks at the embassy one of our major themes, implicitly, indirectly, so the reader will decide for herself that this is a society which is falling apart."

"Despite the obvious fact that the ordinary people are wonderful?"

"Right!"

"Maybe I'll say something like that to the president when we see him."

"He might not like to hear it."

"We'll see . . . Do you want to go upstairs or shall we continue the game down here?"

"Why should we have to choose?"

By then I had become pretty wanton. In fact, I seemed to be pretty wanton all day, every day. Chucky had started it. The abandon in my response astonished me. We were both fighting age and death. The pain of death and the threat of more death didn't go away but somehow we trumped it.

"Woman, you'll be the death of me!"

"Charles Cronin O'Malley, I'll be the life of you!"

Our concerns about Crazy Aunt Jane, as everyone called her, and about poor April continued. Ted had told Vince that Jane was not responding well to treatment. She fought off all medication, refused to talk to the psychiatrist, and cursed Ted when he came to see her.

The Good April, we all agreed, was "failing." We set up a system by which various members of the family with their children would keep her occupied over the weekend. No one was quite sure what we could do for her. The truth I feared was that we could do nothing for the present except be around.

Our baby was displeased that we were going away again without her and this time we were taking her "big sister" with us. We promised her we'd be back by Saturday morning and immediately drive down to the Lake for the rest of the weekend. She would stay with Peg, who would spoil her rotten.

On Thursday morning, Chucky appeared in the parlor with his luggage, the photographic equipment, and the tickets—all ready to drive up to O'Hare three hours before plane time.

"Give me the tickets," I demanded. "You'll lose them."

He didn't say, because he had learned better, that if my daughter and I didn't hurry with our preparations, the tickets would be worthless. He simply smiled smugly and continued to read a biography of the film star turned president. Judging from the expression on his face, he didn't like what he was reading.

He should not have worried about our catching the plane. We were on board with ten minutes to spare.

On the trip to DC Chuck continued to read the book about Reagan, making all sorts of guttural sounds. Mary Margaret struggled with a calculus problem. I read the first two files about Bride Mary O'Brien, which I found somehow disturbing. We were getting into dark and deep waters with this one.

At supper that night, in the ornate and old-fashioned restaurant of the Hay-Adams, Chuck became expansive for Mary Margaret's benefit.

"Ike was the first president whose picture I took. It was a kind of candid-camera thing of him at the top of Mount Suribachi on Iwo Jima. He was on his way to Korea in fulfillment of a campaign promise that he would go to Korea. The implication was that he would go there and end the war, but it was much more difficult than that to end the war. It's interesting how many times the Republicans have won an election because the Democrats got themselves into an overseas mess. In 1952 it was Korea, in 1968 it was Vietnam, and this time around it was the Iranians taking our embassy staff hostage. We're not very good at getting out of messes we should never have gotten into in the first place.

"Anyway, I was over there for *Look* and was exhausted and airsick and worried about my pregnant young wife. I didn't like Ike, mostly because I don't like generals—with the exception of Radford Mead who was top CO in Bamberg—but also because he seemed a mean, authoritarian human being. My picture was on the cover of the magazine and my first child was born without me . . ."

"And his young wife," I interjected, "did very well without him."

"Ro-SIE," Mary Margaret said, "let him finish the story."

"Anyway, the picture was controversial. I thought it caught him as a nasty CO. A lot of people liked it, including Ike himself, for some strange reason. Some Republicans said I was probably a Communist. I was a smart-ass and said that at the present time I was not a member of the party. Then my colleagues in the media wanted to know whether I ever was. I said that I had been a Cook County Democrat since I was conceived."

"He has always had this ability," I informed our daughter, "for getting in trouble with his clever little mouth."

"So then Jack Kennedy wanted us to go to Bonn as an ambassador because he liked my work on Germany and my dissertation on the Marshall Plan, so I asked him if I could do a formal portrait before I left. I managed to get one of Lyndon Johnson in the little room in the Senate Office Building, where he preyed on every young woman he could lure into the room. It's a good thing I did because he was so angry at me when I resigned from Bonn and refused to go to New York for the UN that he didn't talk to me for years . . . I still can't figure out why anyone thought I would be a good diplomat."

"Very effective wife," I commented. "That's what all the news magazines said, usually with a picture of me in a swimsuit."

"I caught Jack Kennedy perfectly, a tall, handsome man, with probing eyes and a sense of vision. I didn't get what we didn't know about then. His terrible health and his obsessive pursuit of women, a habit that he had inherited from his father and grandfather. For all of that, however, he saved us from nuclear war at the time of the Cuban Missile Crisis, which I don't think any other president in our time could have done."

"I was three years old then, wasn't I?" Mary Margaret asked. "Little brat babbling in German. I think maybe I vaguely remember all the excitement."

"I'm glad you kept up your German," the proud mother said, "but you never were a little brat."

"My shot of Lyndon Johnson showed a shrewd man from whom you wouldn't want to buy a used car or a used war. Tricky Dicky Nixon was tough, because I didn't want to present him as the truly odd man he was. I don't think I was successful. He came through looking like a crook. Gerry Ford was a great subject—a handsome ex–football player who was never elected president—but a nice man if not very bright who inherited the Nixon mess. Jimmy Carter was in a way the opposite. A nice and very bright man who should never have been elected president. He thought he could cope with Washington the way he coped with Atlanta and handle Congress the way he handled the Georgia state legislature. Then he got caught up in problems that he had inherited—inflation, unemployment, Iran. When we visited him to take the picture, he already seemed to know that he was sinking beneath the waves. Bonzo buried him. So there we are—the United States since 1952. I have a hunch it's going to get worse before it gets better."

"What's he like, Chucky?" Mary Margaret asked, a leading question because she loved to hear him talk, an inherited trait, I fear.

"He was a sports reporter and a second-rate movie actor. He played George Gipp in *Knute Rockne: All American* and *Bedtime for Bonzo.* He was born in Tampico, Illinois, and went to Eureka College. He was baptized a Catholic and married the movie actress Jane Wyman in a Catholic church. He dumped her after eight years and married the present Mrs. Reagan when she was six months pregnant. He became active in the Screen Actors Guild and cleaned out the Communists. About then he converted to the Republicans. Then he ran for governor and was elected. He had a couple of tries at the presidential nomination and finally won it. He wasn't a very good governor but Jimmy Carter wasn't a very good president. Reagan is the 'Great Communicator'—the first movie actor to become president of the United States. He's mostly style, but it's very good style. In presidential politics from here on in, style will be important. No more Harry Truman or Lyndon Johnson or Dwight Eisenhower."

"You're a little too hard on him, Chucky. He wasn't raised Catholic, so he's really not fallen away."

"He's a fallen away Democrat," he complained.

"Our generation," I explained to Mary Margaret, "will never get over the death of Jack Kennedy. There seemed to be so much hope, so much promise."

"Maybe you expect too much from presidents," Mary Margaret said. "They have not been all that great historically, have they?"

Chucky stopped eating his chocolate ice cream dessert.

"You are entirely too young, Mary Margaret, to have acquired that kind of wisdom."

We all laughed. After supper we walked around Lafayette Park and down Pennsylvania Avenue. Then we put in a call to Shovie at Peg's house.

"They're spoiling me rotten, Mom," the child assured me, "like they always do."

I felt a twinge of sadness for my sister. I had four grandchildren and two more coming. She didn't have any yet, though it was possible that Charley, her daughter, was expecting. It didn't seem fair.

Then we went to our rooms and Chucky and I began our dance again.

When we had finished we lay side by side on the couch in the parlor of our suite, exhausted from our efforts and complacent and holding hands.

"I hope I didn't hurt you?" Chucky said.

"Not at all, my darling. You'd never hurt me . . . It was strenuous exercise."

Such interludes in a marriage could not go on forever, no

matter how much a couple might enjoy them. Eventually marriage relations would settle back to an ordinary routine, which in our case was certainly satisfying. A man and a woman cannot spend all their time in making love and preparing for it. They cannot live indefinitely in a condition of semitumescence. However, they must, I assured myself, make the most of the situation while they could in the hope that it would enhance the routines to which they must return.

Right?

"What do you think God would say about us?" I asked.

"Who?"

"GOD!"

"Oh, Him . . . or Her as the case may be . . . I think God would be pleased because we are trying to love each other without restraint for a little while just as He loves us all the time. One of the advantages of being God is that passionate love never tires God out."

I sighed.

"It must be fun to be God."

"My problem, Rosemarie, is that you are so beautiful. You're irresistible with your clothes on, awesome when you're naked, and overwhelming when you're at the height of pleasure."

"That was a very nice compliment," I admitted. "Chucky we're both all sweaty and sticky. I think we need a shower."

So I led him off to the shower.

There is little autobiographical information about Bride Mary O'Brien from her years at the University College Galway. She no longer wrote letters back to Ballinasloe because there was no one there to whom she owed letters. Nor is there any trace of her ever returning to that town. She did write a paper for one of her classes on the annual horse fair in Ballinasloe but she may have been describing it from memory. It was later published in a small Galway paper under the pen name of Kathleen Ni Houlihan, a figure from Celtic mythology who represents the Irish people. Galway had become her home. When she pedaled her bicycle out of town she apparently chose to ride north along Loch Corrib or west into the Gaeltach around Spidal and Carraroe. Such are the reports from her college friends and classmates.

Jean Lawton, who shared a room with her through the college years, tells us that Bride Mary was fun-loving, a natural leader, and a sensitive friend. Jean is a Protestant from Ballina in County Mayo, one of the few such by her own admission. Bride Mary was fascinated because she had never met a Protestant before but also very kind to a young woman who was not sure that she'd be accepted by her fellow students. Bride Mary studied very hard and played at least as hard. Her crowd had the reputation of being wild and may have on occasion too much of the creature taken. However, they harmed no one and whatever sex they indulged in was very discreet. It was still Ireland in the late 1950s and early 1960s. Bride Mary had many boyfriends, but as far as Jean could tell us she was intimate with none of them.

She planned to leave Ireland as soon as she could. There was no future for young people in Ireland. If she could arrange it, she would migrate to America and stay there. She thought that perhaps she could enroll in an American university and earn a degree that would enable her to teach in a higher educational institution. She didn't care whether the school at which she would teach would be Catholic or not, distinguished or not. She simply had to teach people who were at the same age she was now. That way, she told Jean with one of her huge laughs, she'd never become old.

Her friends did not take these plans seriously. They could not imagine Bride Mary anywhere else but in Galway. The city and its life absorbed her. She particularly enjoyed the Galway races and the dances out in Salt Hill on the nights of the races. America was all talk, they thought. Many of their classmates would strive to emigrate to America and succeed. Somehow it didn't seem to be the kind of thing Bride Mary would do.

She was very frugal. She spent little on clothes, though she always managed to look chic. With a figure like hers that was easy, Jean told us. She saved most of the money she earned as a waitress in a restaurant on High Street, where her good spirits charmed especially American visitors. The money from the restaurant and her tiny legacy from the sale of her farm and from the canon's estate were destined to pay for her trip to America.

Though she was exuberant, there was always a part of her, Jean would tell us, that she kept hidden. Probably the penury of her early life. Certainly she did not want to talk about the "gang" to which she claimed to have belonged.

In the last year and a half of school, she grew increasingly rebellious, though more in words than in deeds. UCG was not yet a center for the student unrest that came to Galway in the late 1960s. In the pubs late in the day, Bride Mary would argue that there were two things wrong with Ireland—the Catholic Church and the ruling class. The Church not only wanted to keep the Irish people poor so it could control its parishioners, it also wanted to prevent them from having any fun. The Church and the ruling class conspired to exploit the ordinary Irish people. It might take a revolution to change that. The young people of Ireland should lead the revolution.

Then they would order another round of Guinness.

She was serious, Sean Cailaigh, part of Bride Mary's crowd, told us. She was a deep one. If she had stayed in Ireland, she might have become involved in radical action. And not the kind of action that the lads up in the North were doing. She might throw a bomb someday, but it would be at a church or a millionaire's house, if she could find one. She was still a Catholic of course and went to Mass every Sunday, every day in Lent. But she hated priests and especially Michael Brown, the bishop of Galway, who was building his big cathedral then on the site of the old jail.

Was she free with men? Well, only up to a point if you take me meaning. I don't know whether she was a virgin or not. I never had the opportunity to find out, as much as I would have liked to. But she lived a virginal life, for whatever that's worth. Now that I'm a little older and with daughters of my own, I'm inclined to respect her for that. I never did think she'd leave Ireland. She talked about America, but she wouldn't even get on a train for Dublin. Galway was big enough for her. I saw her teaching in a secondary school, maybe one run by nuns. She'd marry only in her late twenties and still produce a large brood of kids for whom she would be a wonderful mother. I was destroyed altogether when I heard she had flown off to San Francisco from Shannon with hardly a word of good-bye to anyone.

An t'ather Tomas O'Callaigh, a priest with whom Bride Mary debated often at the Irish-speaking town of Spidal, told us that she was a grand one for the arguments, especially in the Irish language, which is especially shaped for arguing. She blamed the frigging Brits, as she called them, though herself using a word that's a might stronger, for crushing the Irish language and the Irish culture out here in the West. She blamed the Church for accommodating itself to the Brits. I can't say I disagreed with her at all, at all, and herself knowing that, but we still had great arguments. I wish she had stayed here. She could have done great work in Galway, particularly here in the Gaeltach.

Professor Liam O'Haydin, who taught her philosophy, had a much less benign picture of Bride Mary. She was an uncivilized and contemptuous young woman, typical of the kind of crude child we enroll here at the present time. She was bog Irish from the River Suck, a group which has created nothing but trouble for four hundred years. They are too lazy and indifferent to improve themselves, which is fortunate, because if one of them does obtain a bit of education, their undisciplined minds and rude manners greatly disrupt the peace of a classroom. It is a good thing for Galway that she apparently emigrated to America.

Eoin O'Leary claimed that Bride Mary and he were in love and had discussed marriage. We were not lovers, he said, though it would have been very nice. I still miss her though I am happily married. I was sorry to hear of her death.

All our Galway contacts found it very hard to believe that such a vivacious and ebullient young woman could simply disappear from the face of the earth. Save for a letter or two after she flew to San Francisco, no one ever heard from her again.

Chapter Fifteen

Dressed in raincoats and carrying umbrellas we lugged our equipment through Lafayette Park, across Pennsylvania Avenue, and around the corner to the entrance of the West Wing, a driveway protected by National Park Service Police in a guardhouse. These folks were very considerate of those who were on their list and quickly dismissive of those who were not. We waited patiently in line for some time, then were quickly dismissed. Our names were not on the list. No one had ever heard of an Ambassador O'Malley who was to take a picture of the president.

"Ambassadors," the guard sneered at me, "don't take pictures. I don't suppose you have any evidence that you are an ambassador?"

I just happened to have the diplomatic passport that the State Department issues me for auld lang syne or some similar reason. I just happened to have it because, as I tell my priestly brother and my soon-to-be priestly son, it confers almost as much clout as does a driver's license displaying a Roman collar in Chicago.

The redneck cop was not impressed.

"I don't care who you are. You're still not getting into the West Wing unless your name is on my list. And it's not on my list."

I felt like someone who had made reservations at a restaurant and then is told by the maître d' that his name is not on the list. I suspected that if I could see the list I would find my name.

"We spoke to Mr. Deming earlier this morning. He said we should come right over. I'm sure if you would call him . . ."

"We do not call West Wing personnel unless they call us, sir. Would you please give way for those who are next in line."

"Come on, Chucky," my wife said, "let's not argue with this Republican."

So, we lugged our stuff back across the park as the rain beat down. I wanted to go to the airport and release our story to the Chicago media. Rosemarie insisted I call Mr. Deming. The expression on our daughter's face suggested our ancestor Grace O'Malley about to launch a raid against the hated O'Flahertys.

"Chuck, where are you?" Tom Deming demanded.

He had been one of my junior staff in Bonn a long time ago.

"In the Hay-Adams."

"Too much rain to carry your equipment across the park? You should have called me before."

I had adjusted the tone of my voice to suggest scarcely controlled rage.

"We have carried the equipment over and back. One of your cops would not let us in because our names are not on the list."

"You are certainly on the list. I'll get a Secret Service car and pick you up."

"We're going back to Chicago," I said, a sullen little boy.

"Don't do that. The president will be terribly disappointed. He wants to meet you."

I was not impressed. I had been in the White House and indeed the Oval Office often enough. It was no big deal.

"I'll be right over," Tom Deming said, and hung up.

"Chucky," my daughter informed me, "you can be a real hard-ass."

"Only when dealing with one of the same persuasion."

I had begun the morning in an excellent mood, the reaction of every man to high quality sex, especially since, after thirty years, I had made a little progress in understanding a woman's perspective on the matter. I was, not to put too fine an edge on it, proud of myself. The glow in Rosemarie's eyes was enough to confirm my suspicion that I might be now a somewhat more than adequate lover. I tried to temper my elation with the caution that I had a long way to go.

My wife was so unbearably lovely.

Then the rain and the wind and the mud of Lafayette Park and the falling leaves and the redneck cop had ruined my day. Why, with all the troubles back home, had I come to Washington? To take a picture of a Republican? Charles Cronin O'Malley, you gotta be out of your mind! After every high, there comes a low. Better to avoid the high? Not when the high was my Rosemarie.

We waited in the lobby of the Hay-Adams until a nondescript black Ford with a radio antenna appeared. The doorman saluted, waved the car up to the doorway, and held up his hand to block the cars that might pull in behind us. These nondescript Fords apparently had a certain cachet of their own.

Tom Deming, with more weight and less hair than when we had known him in Bonn fifteen years before, popped out.

"Mr. Ambassador!" He pumped my hand. "You never change! And Mrs. O'Malley, you're more beautiful than ever! And this young woman must be Moire, the redhead, German-speaking tot who won all our hearts at the embassy. We all said that you would grow up to be a stunning woman. We underestimated the truth."

Mary Margaret was so pleased with his grace that she did not correct him by insisting on her "real" name.

"I assume that our name was on the list and the redneck cop just didn't like our looks?"

Tom was loading our equipment into the trunk of the Ford. He looked up and smiled again.

"That man has been transferred to other duty."

"I hope in one of the Park Service's glaciers."

"How is the rest of your family, Ms. O'Malley . . . Or should I say Ms. Clancy."

"Rosemarie, Tom . . . Kevin Patrick and April Rosemary both have two children and soon both will have three. Jimmy will be ordained in the spring. Sean is considering his options, though Mary Margaret here says they have narrowed to one lovely young woman. We also have a five-year-old redhead who is pure delight."

Tom and the Secret Service driver loaded our stuff into the trunk. I ensconced myself in the middle of the backseat between my wife and daughter.

"And you write stories and the ambassador takes pictures," he continued. ". . . The delay is fortunate because the first lady has an appointment this afternoon and she won't be able to be present."

"Oh?" I said. "She involves herself in such matters?"

"She does indeed."

"She would attempt to tell me which poses to take?"

"She would indeed."

"So."

Should that happen, we would pack our things and decamp. No one tells Chuck O'Malley which shots he can take, not twice. My Rosemarie was smiling her "such-a-cute-little-boy" smile. Witch.

Beautiful though.

The Secret Service car went around the East Wing and pulled up to the back gate.

"Car seven with Ambassador O'Malley and family," the driver said into his mike.

The gate opened. We drove through it and stopped. An officer peered in the backseat and smiled at the two lovely ladies, more than the idiot at the gate to the West Wing had done.

"They're the family," I said, pointing cross-armed at my wife and daughter.

"Welcome, Mr. Ambassador, it's good to have you back."

That's better. We pulled up under the steps to the low-slung diplomat's door which would bring us to the ground floor. A flock of White House ushers swarmed out of the door, some with umbrellas, some to carry our bags. We were whisked through the rooms to an elevator.

"We'll take a closer look when we leave, hon," Rosemarie assured our daughter.

They led us along the portico to the West Wing, into a waiting room outside the Oval Office.

"You can go right in, Mr. Ambassador," said the woman at the desk next to the door of the Oval Office. "The president is waiting for you."

We walked right into Ronald Reagan's tidal wave of geniality.

"Chuck O'Malley, I'm glad to meet you! What wonderful photos." He held up a copy of my portrait book. "You have to make an old actor look as good as these people do . . . I don't think the Oval Office has ever had two such beautiful Irishwomen in it at the same time. I recognize you both from your pictures. Wonderful! Come in! Let's relax and have a cup of tea before we go to work!"

My first reaction was that "the Gipper" and "Bonzo" had aged, as we all do. He didn't look his seventy years but he was not nearly as young as he seemed on television. His hair could not possibly be as black as it was unless it had been touched up. Everywhere.

He was wearing a dark blue business suit, white shirt, and red-and-blue tie—actor and athlete as CEO.

"They tell me you're just back from Russia. What was it like? Did you bring any of your photos along?" he asked as an usher poured our tea. There were exactly three cookies on the White House china plate, something like the ration you'd receive at St. Ursula's convent in the old days when the Good April and I went over to do battle with Sister Mary Admirabilis, AKA Sister War Admiral.

"As a matter of fact, I did. Would you like to see them?"

I reached in my film bag and pulled out half a dozen pictures that I had secretly printed up the night before. My wife and my daughter gasped. Good! I'd fooled them.

"I'd love to see them."

His geniality and charm were authentic, not just an act for television. He was not a mean man hiding behind a smile as Ike had been.

I spread the pictures on his desk, images of peasants in front of log houses, workers coming out of factories, kids playing in the mud, an orthodox priest.

The president became serious.

"Good people," he said. "You can tell by looking at them, but so poor."

"Only a step above a third world country. In Moscow you see better clothes but still they're poor . . . I hardly need tell you, Mr. President. Socialism doesn't work. The man who said he'd seen the future and it worked was dead wrong. Nothing works—airplanes, rockets, steel mills, health care, collective farms. They're spending their gold reserves to buy grain to feed their people."

"As I have said, it's an evil empire. Very dangerous."

I gathered up the pictures.

"It will implode within the decade," I said. "The middle-level apparatchiks who are going to replace the present gerontocracy will cancel out the Bolshevik revolution, the non-Russian republics will break away, and the occupied countries in Eastern Europe will free themselves."

I gathered up the pictures, surreptitiously confiscated one of the three cookies, and began to unpack my equipment.

The president sat at his desk, his face furrowed.

"That's an original perspective, Chuck. No one has suggested it to me."

"Not so original, Mr. President. Willard Mathias of the Office of National Estimates wrote in 1954 that Communism's inability to produce sufficient consumer goods and resistance to sharing power with a growing class of professionals and technocrats will ultimately destroy the party's power."

"1954! That was twenty years ago!"

"Almost thirty."

My wife and daughter, dutiful and uncomplaining members of the team (for the moment) began to unpack the lights and the screens for the picture taking. I didn't normally use such paraphernalia, but for a president of the United States you had to create the impression of a real professional photographer.

"I've never heard that from any of our people. They think the empire will endure for decades, perhaps even centuries."

"Only if they can make it work. The new leadership, which will certainly emerge during your term of office, will try to make it work, but they won't succeed."

He shook his head dubiously.

"I hope you're right. I'd like to believe you're right. But it all seems too easy . . . The Cold War has gone on for a long time . . ."

"By 1990 it will be over. You can claim victory."

"Have you told this theory to any of our people?"

"As you said, Mr. President, the Cold War has gone on for a long time. A lot of folks wouldn't know what to do if it ends."

We proceeded with the picture taking. He was an easy shot. There was not much difference between his public persona and his private self. He *was* the Gipper. His philosophy of administration was that he figured out what needed to be done, selected the men to do it, then did not interfere with them. It made for a relaxed presidency and a relaxed president, one who could watch movies every night.

My wife and daughter shuttled back and forth with the color and black-and-white cameras, reloading the one as I shot with the other. They were charming assistants and quiet and self-effacing—rare behavior for both of them.

In the lens of my Hasselblads he emerged as a handsome, genial, elderly Irishman who did not like to worry about the small print. I wondered as I snapped away how much there was there. He was mildly interested in my scenario about the Soviet Union but would never question the CIA or the State Department to determine if there were men in either agency who agreed with me. Maybe our most genial president, perhaps even the most likeable, but far from the brightest. I wondered whether John Hinckley Jr.'s assassination attempt the previous March had slowed him down or whether he was at that age in life where we all want to slow down, if only just a little.

After the shoot was over, his secretary brought in a large box of White House souvenirs for our family. We thanked him for his thoughtfulness. None of us hinted that some of the family—especially Father Ed—would not want a remembrance from this particular White House.

"We'll send them off to you in Chicago," he said. "No point in burdening you with more luggage . . . You must come back sometime for dinner . . . Mrs. Reagan would love to meet you . . . Have you ever been here for dinner, Mrs. O'Malley?"

"Only once, Mr. President. On the night John Kennedy said to a bunch of artists and writers that the only night there was more talent in the room was when Thomas Jefferson dined alone."

"Then you must certainly come again."

None of us were about to hold our breath waiting for an invitation, yet no doubt his offer was sincere. At the moment.

On our way back to the hotel, Tom Deming said, "You won't find many people in the government who believe that the Soviet Union is about to implode."

"None at the embassy in Moscow," I replied.

"You said in effect that thirty years of Cold War has blinded us to the weakness of our enemy?"

"I don't doubt that the facts are reported accurately," I replied. "I doubt that the dots are connected."

"This administration will never believe it, even if all your predictions turn out to be right."

"That's what I'm afraid of."

At the Hay-Adams, my wife informed me that I needed a nap, a "nap nap. You're always exhausted after a shoot . . . Mary Margaret and I will do a little shopping. We'll call Peg and talk to Shovie."

A limo would pick us up at seven. We'd fly out of National at eight-thirty and arrive in Chicago a little before ten.

I did need a real nap. My hormones were quiescent.

The United States, I realized, was slipping into another era of peace and prosperity, both deceptive. However, the public wanted to be tranquilized. Our new president was the perfect leader of the time.

The JFK dinner that Rosemarie had mentioned to the president belonged to a different world. We were fortunate to be part of it. Then I glided away to the land of Nod, wondering how come a punk kid from a two flat on the West Side could become as familiar with the White House as I was.

I solved a lot of international problems before I was wakened by a demanding telephone. I couldn't quite figure out where I was or what time it was as I reached for the phone.

"Chuck O'Malley."

"Peg, brother. Mom's in the hospital. They think she's had a heart attack."

Was this message nightmare or reality?

"What happened . . . ?"

"She had pains in her chest and trouble breathing. I called for the ambulance. Friday afternoon, not too many doctors around. She's resting comfortably. They're controlling the pain with medication and watching her closely. Mike Kennedy was playing golf at Butterfield, but he's on his way in."

"Are you at the hospital?"

"Sure. Father Ed is here too. Rita is taking care of Shovie. When do you get home?"

"Peg, where am I?"

"You're at the Hay-Adams hotel in DC. You photographed the president this afternoon."

"Indeed we did," I admitted, not at all sure the charge was true.

"Is Rosie there?"

I looked around the bed.

"No, I think she and Mary Margaret went shopping."

"Have her call when she returns. We're in Room 414."

Naturally. I hoped the smell of roses was still there.

"Our flight is at eight-thirty," I said. "Maybe we can get an earlier flight."

"They say there's no immediate danger."

I struggled out of bed and took a shower to wake up. It didn't do much good.

I sat in an easy chair in the parlor of our suite. We had a suite because Rosemarie had arranged the travel plans. I had long since given up arguing about the cost of such luxury. I began to leaf through another file in Joe Raftery's story about Bride Mary O'Brien.

I couldn't concentrate on the story. The image of the vibrant young flapper who had snatched Dad out of his Irish bachelor's life would not leave me. Why did any of us have to die?

Rosemary charged into our suite, filled with vitality and descriptions of the brilliant shopping coups she and Mary Margaret had accomplished. She was, I knew, ready for more love.

"Call Peg at Room 414 at Oak Park Hospital," I said. "Mom's apparently had a heart attack."

Rosemarie slumped into the chair next to the telephone.

"You're sure?"

"Yes, ma'am. Rita's taking care of Shovie."

She punched in the number with which we were all too familiar. Her conversation was brief and whispered.

"She's had another attack," Rosemarie murmured. "Serious. Dr. Kennedy is with her."

"Can we get on an earlier plane?" I asked.

"Too late for that, Chuck. We'd better start to pack. I'll tell Mary Margaret."

She picked up the phone.

"Better tell her face-to-face."

She put down the phone and smiled.

"Right as always, Chucky Ducky."

It seems likely that Bride Mary O'Brien entered the United States illegally. She had somehow obtained a student visa on the grounds that she had a scholarship to the University of California at Berkeley. In fact, she had earned no such scholarship. All she had was an admission to the comparative literature department at the university with no promise of aid. In those days there was a steady stream of young Irish university graduates who outsmarted the consular bureaucrats of the State Department, who were probably not too interested in barring such bright and charming young people from the United States.

She seems to have predecessors already in Berkeley because she easily found a job in a bookstore and a bed in an Irish commune. Apparently the "commune" was not ideological and did not encourage sexual relationships. She matriculated at the University of California at Berkeley in a literature department which, even at that time, was more interested in radical political action than in academic matters. The Free Speech Movement, it will be remembered, began in Berkeley in 1963, long before campus demonstrations spread to most other campuses in the country. Already an Irish radical, Bride Mary fit in with the spirit of the time at the university and in her department. She seems to have marched in demonstrations, blocked cars, shouted obscene epithets at police. We know this from testimony of a young woman, also an illegal Irish immigrant who shared a room with Bride Mary after they both had earned enough money to move out of the commune. Our investigations were unable to uncover other members of the commune. Like so many radicals of the day, they quickly melted into the mainstream of American life.

Bride Mary was arrested for disorderly conduct on at least one occasion. She almost certainly would have been deported if she had not persuaded the Irish-American cop who had arrested her to give her a second chance. After that, her friend tells us, she avoided all demonstrations where there might be arrests. Yet in those turbulent days on the east side of the Bay she had some close calls.

She dropped out of school and out of the radical movement at the same time. She began working full-time at the bookstore, then sometime in 1965 went to work part-time for a real estate company that catered to people who wanted to move into the East Bay area. She must have been very good even at the beginning because she was able to buy a condo in the Berkeley Hills, some distance away from the university.

Her roommate had no explanation for this sudden change in lifestyle and profession. She said she wanted to make some money so she wouldn't be just an impoverished Irish immigrant. The roommate thought there was a possibility that one of her faculty mentors promised her a job in the department if she would sleep with him. Shortly after she left the university she told the roommate that the radical faculty members were not interested in principles or ideals, only in exploiting as many women as they could collect. All this radical shite, she said, is about using women who think they're rebels. They're a bunch of frigging hypocrites.

After this it becomes more difficult to trace Bride Mary O'Brien. She worked for several different firms. Her colleagues said that she was friendly enough, but reserved. Her brogue indicated she was from Ireland, but she refused to say where she came from or when. She was scrupulously fair to her customers, warning them away from properties that were overpriced or had hidden problems. In fact, an employer said that she went beyond the ethical requirements of the profession in protection of her customers. Yet no one wanted to fire her because she was so successful. Her charm and integrity were transparent. All her clients liked her. About her private life, she said almost nothing. They thought she lived with a man for a while but ended the relationship quickly. She did not socialize with her professional colleagues. She did take classes at a local community college in accounting and finance and also in wine making. When she moved on to another company, they were all sorry to see her go. Characteristically she took none of her clients with her.

Then they heard that she had married Joseph T. Raftery, an extremely successful developer in Marin County, in a small church wedding, though she had never seemed all that much interested in religion. He was ten years older than she was. Later they set themselves up in the wine-making business and had a child.

To a person they were sad when they heard of the probable death of her and her child. They couldn't imagine who would want to kill Bride Mary O'Brien unless it were some drug-crazy hippies.

Chapter Sixteen

Mary Margaret

Rosie and I had a great time shopping in DC. Chucky was back in the hotel sleeping and we didn't have to worry about him getting lost. So we relaxed and enjoyed ourselves, even if we didn't buy much—and only some things that were on sale. We decided that we didn't much like the new president. He was a nice man with a lot of charm, but he wasn't very bright and didn't seem like he'd work very hard at being a president. Jack Kennedy, Rosie said, would have listened very carefully to what Chuck had to say about the Soviet Union, because he knew Chuck was very smart and almost always right about political things. Lyndon Johnson, when he was looking for solid advice before he withdrew from the presidential race, called Chucky in with a bunch of much older men. He also wanted Chuck to go to the UN, as did Jimmy Carter. Bonzo over there wasn't curious enough to pursue Chuck's notion that the Soviet Union would implode in between five and ten years.

"What's more, when it happens he won't even remember that Chuck predicted it."

"You think he's getting senile, Rosie?"

"Not yet, but I don't think he bothers to listen to things that don't fit his impressions about the world."

"Scary!"

"Maybe not. The United States has been lucky so far in our history. Maybe our luck will hold out."

"It's a shame that no one will pay attention to Chuck."

"Don't count your father out, Mary Margaret. We're going to

make the argument pretty loudly in our book and in the article I'm doing for *The New Yorker*."

Then we arrived at the hotel, a totally neat place, and Rosie went upstairs to wake up Chuck. Then she came back to my room to tell me about Grams.

"Damn crazy Aunt Jane!"

"My very thoughts, hon."

Dad called again from National Airport. Aunt Peg said that Grams had had a second attack and was in intensive care. We tried to work on the flight back to Chicago, which seemed to go on forever. He called again as soon as we landed at O'Hare. Aunt Peg said things did not look good. We should come right to the hospital. Shovie was sleeping soundly at their house and Rita was keeping a close eye on her.

Rosie drove us to the hospital, of course. Aunt Peg and Uncle Vince and Father Ed were waiting for us in the intensive care room. Grams was breathing on a ventilator. A monitor was beeping above her. Aunt Peg had been crying. Her eyes were red and her pretty face was lined with sadness.

"They say touch-and-go," Father Ed murmured. "At least another day or two before she'll be out of the woods."

"Peg," Rosie said, "why don't you and Vince go home and get some sleep. If there's any turn for the worse, we'll call you right away."

"Damn Crazy Jane," Peg whispered.

"I know how you feel, Peg," Father Ed said. "I feel the same way, but it won't do us any good to blame anyone, especially since poor Janey is out of her mind."

"It's not easy being a Catholic, Aunt Peg," I said, not having enough sense to mind my own business, especially since I wanted to kill crazy Aunt Jane too.

Aunt Peg hugged me and said, "You and Rita are the only ones in the family with any Catholic sense left."

"Maybe," Chucky said, "we can say the Rosary, then Peg and Vince can go home . . . Maybe, Mary Margaret, you can lead us since your aunt thinks you have some Catholic sense left."

This was Chucky at his deft best. He gave us something to do and he put a time limit after which Aunt Peg had to go home. I am as capable of leading the Rosary as anyone else. Halfway through, Grams lips seemed to move. Maybe it was a turning point. I thought I smelled roses, which wasn't possible because there weren't any flowers in the room.

Chuck and Rosie were a mess all weekend. They didn't sleep much and were back and forth to the hospital every couple of hours. I told them not to worry about Shovie. I'd take care of her and make sure her homework was done and take her to Mass on Sunday. Poor little kid needed to have someone around from her family, though Erin, our probably illegal babysitter, was now almost a member of the family.

Seano was hanging around the house when I arrived to pick up Shovie for Mass on Saturday afternoon.

"You look terrible, Seano," I said. "What's the matter? Maria Anastasia drop you?"

"Yeah," he said sadly. "She decided to marry a boy who is Luong like she is. Her parents talked her into it. He seems to be a good guy. I haven't had much luck with my romances, have I, sis?"

"Bitch!" I shouted.

"Sis!"

"Too much pent-up anger," I said. "And too many geeky people picking on my family!"

"It's for the best," he said. "Esther is happier with her Israeli pilot, and Maria Anastasia is better off with her Luong prince. Neither one of them ever made any promises to me."

"Everything but . . ."

"That doesn't count, sis . . . I'm pretty low now, but I'll pull out of it . . . Maybe start looking for someone Irish . . . Just like you."

"I'm NOT, totally NOT, looking for anyone from any ethnic group!"

We both laughed.

Sean Seamus would be all right. I just hoped that whoever his next love would be, and of whatever ethnic group, would appreciate what a wonderful young man he is.

By Sunday night Grams was off the ventilator and talking.

"Well, I'm just so sorry to have caused so much worry. I'm

fine now. . . . I started to feel better when I heard poor dear Mary Margaret leading the Rosary. Wouldn't she make a wonderful priest!"

"They'd have to ordain her a monsignora!" Chuck, always the wise guy, had to say.

So that was the end of that. Now all we had to do was finish the proof sheets for the Russian book, work on the portrait of President Bonzo, and write thank-you notes to all the mourners. The family was not ready for another death, though we wouldn't have much choice about it. Grams was back in her flapper mode, but she didn't look like she'd last too long. Everyone dies someday.

On Monday afternoon I walked from school to my appointment with Dr. Ward, so I could think over what I would say. Her office was at Lake and Harlem in an old building in which every doctor in Oak Park seemed to have an office. I wore the fawn suit I had worn to the White House. You go see a shrink for the first time, Rosie had told me, you look your best. I figured she knew what she was talking about.

Maggie Ward was a gray woman—gray hair, gray eyes, and a gray dress. But it was a happy kind of gray, a gray that made you want to relax and maybe smile a little. She had to be really good to deal with Rosie.

"I must ask you one question at the beginning, Mary Margaret," she began. "Is it your mother's idea that you should come to see me?"

"You must know Rosie better than that, Dr. Ward. Dr. Kennedy said I might need some counseling. It seemed to me that he might be right. Rosie is sky-high on you, so I knew you'd be good. I asked her whether she thought you would see me and she said I should call and ask. Which I did."

She smiled and I knew we'd be friends.

"You have not been entirely absent from our conversations. I'm happy to meet you in person."

"I know Rosie would say only good things about me," I said, "so I'm not worried . . . The thing is I totally want to kill my Crazy Aunt Jane. She hit me over the head with a lamp and might have killed me. They thought I might have a fractured skull, but it was only a brain concussion, which is bad enough, and she beat up on my poor grandma and probably caused her heart attack. I hate her so much that if I were a vampire, I could already taste her blood."

"You would not actually kill her, would you Mary Margaret—even if you could get away with it and not be caught?"

"No, of course not. I'm a Catholic. We don't kill people. I even believe that the Pope is right: we don't kill people in wars either."

"But, if the Pope gave you permission, would you kill Crazy Aunt Jane?"

"She's a sick lady. Bipolar. She won't take her medications when she's on her high, which she was when she hit me . . . I hope I will take my meds when I go bipolar."

"May I make a small prediction about you, Mary Margaret O'Malley?"

"Be my guest!"

"Whatever else you may do in your life, you will never, I repeat, never go bipolar."

We both laughed at that.

"The problem is that I'd like to be able to kill her. I bash her brains out in my dreams."

"Your grandmother is recovering this morning."

"Out of danger, they say. Still I don't think she'll be with us very long."

"You're probably right . . . We all die sometime."

"I won't. I'm young and convinced that I am immortal!"

"No, you're not! . . . Let me see if I understand you. You won't kill Crazy Aunt Jane although she richly deserves it. Yet you worry because you have homicidal dreams."

"And daydreams too . . . If somehow she turned up at Oak Park Hospital last night, I would have wanted to push her down the stairs, then kick her in her fat stomach at the bottom of the stairs."

"Your daydreams are vivid."

"Day and night dreams both."

"You think they're sinful?"

"No, but I shouldn't have such thoughts, should I? I mean when I'm awake isn't that anger wrong?"

"Do you have a boyfriend, Mary Margaret?"

"Not exactly a boyfriend. There's this boy who you could call a friend who kind of hangs around. Chucky says that he looks amused and bemused."

"Nice boy?"

"So nice that if my parents had to choose between him and me, they'd choose him."

"Do you think you might marry him someday?"

"I don't know . . . Maybe . . . If someone better doesn't come along."

"Which I interpret to mean 'yes.' "

"For the sake of the argument."

"You have daydreams and night dreams about going to bed with him?"

I could see why Rosie says she's a witch. She was backing me into a corner.

"Sure . . . Like Chuck says, if we didn't think that way, the species would have stopped existing long ago."

"I see . . . Now do you consider those thoughts to be wrong?"

"Maybe if I waste my time on them all day long."

"You're not about to hop into bed with him?"

"Not for a long time."

"How long?"

"Deponeth sayeth not."

"You see where I'm going?"

"Sure, I see where you're going."

"Tell me."

"You're saying that the species wouldn't survive unless we became angry when someone beats up on us or some of our family. It's only wrong when it turns into the desire for revenge."

"Can you give me an example of that?"

"What about the people who want to go to the execution room to watch someone die because of what the person has done to their family?"

"Why do they want to do that?"

"They say because they want closure . . . But they'll never get it, will they Dr. Ward?"

"No, Mary Margaret, they never will. They should learn to transcend their anger, which is not only good Christianity, it's good mental health. Now tell me about what happened when your crazy Aunt Jane bopped you over the head."

So I did. And felt a lot better. We agreed that I would come back once more in two weeks to talk about it all again.

I felt fine when I left to walk back home.

Except that I had admitted that I actually might just marry Joey Moran.

Chapter Seventeen

Chuck

As I slurped up my breakfast on Monday morning, I felt very sorry for myself. The house was deserted. Mary Margaret, Shovie, and Erin were in school. My wife, smelling of shower soap and her favorite scent and fully clad in her black business suit, was off on a visit to Dr. Ward. Her mood upon returning from such a session would be unpredictable. She had confided in me that Mary Margaret had a session with Dr. Ward to "work through" Aunt Jane's head-bashing exercise.

"Sleep in, Chucky Ducky, you need to recuperate from your sleep deprivation."

Her implication was that if I were of the superior gender, I would not suffer from sleep deprivation. How could I sleep in when there was so much work to do? And she had deprived me of my English muffin with raspberry jam, the preparation of which was an element in the spousal vows that my wife had made to me. More time for Maggie Ward than for my English muffin!

My obligations included developing the rolls I had taken at the White House and preparing versions of the portrait for *Newsweek*, for the White House Press Office (which would never use them), for *The New York Times*, which wanted a complete collection (for reasons that escape me), and for the next volume of my collection of portraits. Then I had to return to our neglected Russian films and confer with my wife about our book. It was necessary to produce that book soon, so that my warning about the implosion of the Soviet Union would be on the record before it happened.

We must divvy up the list of people who had mourned with us and send them notes of gratitude for their sympathy; I would certainly visit my mother at Oak Park Hospital before the day was over. She would probably come out of intensive care sometime today.

And I was too tired to do anything except pour my second cup of tea and consider the wisdom of making my own English muffin. I was home from Moscow less than ten days. I had not kicked the jet lag. I had been through several wrenching emotional experiences and I was now the titular head of the family (which together with the required fare would earn me a ride on the Chicago subway). That meant that the women in the family would go through the motions of consultation before they did whatever they had already decided.

The weekend had been a nightmare of rushing back and forth to the hospital and trying to snatch a few moments of sleep as the Good April improved. Poor dear woman, her burdens were simply too heavy. Yet she had bounced back when she heard the luminous Mary Margaret leading the Rosary, accompanied by the smell of roses which might have been a message from someone. Flappers are pretty hard to kill, even when crazy Aunt Jane invades your house with two storm troopers.

Mary Margaret the favorite grandchild? She and April were as unlike as two women could be—Dr. Panglossa over against my daughter's clear-eyed, tough-minded realism. What did I know about such things, save that I was now toasting my own English muffin.

To add to the list of responsibilities about which I could do nothing, was the sad tale of the abrupt end of Sean Seamus's romance. He was twenty-five, going on twenty-six. His brother Kevin was about to become the father of a third child, his brother Jimmy was about to be ordained. All Seano had was the thrill of the trading floor without the booze and women with which many of the young traders whiled away their afternoon free time.

Why did he choose to fall in love with women from other

cultures whose loyalty to their heritages would prove stronger than their affection for him? Why couldn't he be sensible like Mary Margaret and pursue a spouse from across the street or down the road?

Like I did.

By the time I was his age I was already the confused father of a daughter and three sons.

I had never been twenty-six, had I? No, not really.

Then there was my wife. Sadness, sleep deprivation, responsibility had terminated prematurely our silly romance. Wrong time, wrong place. Only she had been swept up in the falling-in-love-again dynamic and enjoyed it too much to quit prematurely. One more impossible job.

At that point the wife in question swept into the kitchen.

"Still eating breakfast, Chucky? Ick, your hands are sticky! Come on there's work to be done!"

"I had to make my own English muffin. This could constitute grounds for seeking an annulment of our marriage contract."

She laughed.

"Well you can punish me in bed tonight for that omission . . . Ugh, your lips are sticky too. You haven't taken a shower yet. Come on, lover, it's a gorgeous day."

"It's raining."

"Just a light rain and that's beautiful too . . . I know what you need before you go to work in the darkroom. You need a brisk swim to wake you up . . . That's why we bought the pool, so you could get some wake-up exercise. Come on, I'll swim with you."

"Without any clothes?"

"Chucky Ducky, this is Oak Park on an autumn morning . . . Come on let's go."

She bounded up the stairs as I trailed behind her. She had removed her dress before she reached the head of the stairs. However, this was to be exercise in the name of health and vitality, not lovemaking, though she did insist on continuing the kisses as we swam. Then allegedly invigorated but only more weary, I accepted my banishment to the darkroom. In shorts and a University of

Chicago tee shirt, she retreated to her office to work on her Russian notes.

It was not hard to find a half dozen shots of Bonzo the President that would serve various purposes—handsome, genial, dedicated, and just a trifle empty. I had merely to hint at the hollowness of this hollow man. Indeed the hint had to be so subtle that most Republicans would not notice it and yet sense somehow on the edge of their teeth that the picture was a little wrong. Mrs. Reagan might think the portrait to be perfectly wonderful.

I did not create the emptiness. It was there. I didn't even accentuate it. I would not use the shots that made him look like a perfect idiot. He was not that either. He was just a hollow man with no interest in new ideas, like my prediction of the collapse of the Soviet Union and the evil empire.

When I'm at work in the darkroom I forget about all the things I'm not doing that I should be doing and do not notice the passage of time. So it was late afternoon when I ambled up to Rosemarie's office to show mommy my handiwork.

"Rough prints," I said, spreading them out on her desk over her Russian notes.

"Chucky! I was beginning to worry about you! . . . Let me see . . . Oh, my, they're very good, aren't they . . . We certainly don't like the man very much, do we? . . . But no one at the White House will get it . . ." She shuffled the shots around and reordered them . . . "This one for your book . . . This color one for *Newsweek* and this one here for the *Times* and the White House . . ."

Thirty years of marriage will not produce such agreement unless there is some sharing of fundamental tastes. I had lucked out.

"You are a genius, Charles Cronin O'Malley," she said as she gently caressed my arm. "A dangerous genius. These shots are just like your portrait of LBJ . . . I wouldn't buy a used car from this man . . ."

"Or a used antimissile system."

And I suddenly fell in love with her again. She did have excellent taste, did she not?

Then the magic of the moment was broken by the sound of

the thundering herds coming home from school. They (Mary Margaret, Erin, and Shovie) bounded into the office of the materfamilias and made the appropriate approving sounds about Daddy's work.

"Got 'em!" Mary Margaret shouted triumphantly.

"I don't like him," Shovie said. "He's scary."

"A bit of a gombeen man, isn't he?" Erin whispered.

"Women of excellent taste . . . I'd better get back to work."

I had finished the portraits for *Newsweek* by suppertime. They'd love them. We had a full house at supper, all the residents and Seano, who had come to play with his beloved Shovie. We were all in good spirits and the meal was festive. My wife, who insists that in our house she is the cook, had made delicious spaghetti and meatballs which we consumed frantically as we argued about the fates of the ill-starred Chicago sports franchises.

I noted that Seano was guardedly considering Erin's aboriginal Irish beauty. Whenever she spoke he listened intently. For her part she avoided looking at him.

There were dangerous possibilities in the chemistry of that nonexchange. I cornered Mary Margaret before we left to visit the Good April at the hospital.

"Warn your brother that she's a very vulnerable young woman, not to be used as a second fiddle."

"You noticed too, did you, Chuck! Of course Rosie caught it. Erin is superficially vulnerable all right, but beneath she's as tough as any of us Crazy O'Malleys. She can take care of herself. Seano is such an idiot. I've been talking to him about her and he's never bothered to look till now."

Machinations within machinations.

"I take it that you and my wife approve even at this early stage."

"Sure! Why not! He won't hurt her, Chucky. He wouldn't dare. But I'll warn him just the same."

The Good April had regained some of her color and seemed bright and upbeat.

"It was all so silly, dears. I'm fine. The doctors say I must take it easy for a few weeks and watch what I eat and I'll be just fine. I'm sorry I caused all that trouble."

"Loving you is never any trouble for us," my wife assured her.

"Aren't you sweet, Rosie? I'm so glad that Chuck finally married you. It was a long struggle, wasn't it?"

"It was, Mom, but he's worth it—some of the time anyway."

Much laughter.

"Did you bring along any of your pictures of that awful president of ours, Chucky dear?"

"Sure did!"

I pulled several of them out of my leather folder and passed them over to her.

"Bonzo the President." She sighed. "What a terrible empty man! I'd make a better president!"

April Mae Cronin O'Malley was a lifelong Democrat and fiercely partisan, the only dimension of her personality where Panglossa was firmly banished.

"You certainly would, April," Rosemarie agreed. "So would Shovie."

"Poor dear little child. She's so nice when she comes to visit . . . What about our sweet little Mary Margaret? Is she engaged to that darling Joey Moran boy yet?"

Rosemarie looked at me. I'm the head of the family. I must answer that conundrum.

"I think that they have an implicit and unspoken agreement to let their friendship continue in an open-ended way. Are they formally engaged? Not yet and not for a long time perhaps. Will they eventually marry? Don't anyone bet against it."

"Well, there's no hurry . . . I always thought your generation married too young . . . It was all those wars . . . Anyway, I'm glad you did, dears. Chucky was about to become a typical Irish bachelor like his father, God be good to him."

"In some ways," my wife said, "he is and always will be a typical Irish bachelor. He can't even make an English muffin with raspberry jam without my help."

They both laughed at my discomfiture. Once more what

John Knox had called the monster regiment of women had conspired to put me down.

Nonetheless, I did not reject Rosemarie's suggestion we stop at Petersen's for "dessert." Indeed, as we sat next to each other in the booth, my wife cuddling close to me more than was necessary given the dimensions of the booth, I realized that my infatuation with her was not waning.

"What do you think, Chucky?"

"About what?"

"Mom, Aunt Jane, Seano—for starters."

"I'll answer in reverse order: It would not be a terrible mistake for that twosome of black Irish aborigines to fall in love. We can have no impact on Aunt Jane. I wouldn't be surprised if she stays forever in that hospital. I don't think she wants to live a normal life anymore. Mom . . . I hate to say this, Rosemarie, my darling, she's a game fighter but I don't think she'll be with us for long. She's so frail . . ."

"She wants to see the next crop of great-grandchildren and Jimmy's ordination. Maybe Gianni's wedding. Not necessarily Mary Margaret's. Then she'll be happy to join Vangie and tell him how wonderful they all are."

"And we become the elderly grandparents . . ."

"Not a bad role . . ."

Usually my hand finds its way to her thigh in this booth in the ice-cream store. This time she beat me to it.

"Woman, you are really infatuated."

She shivered with delight.

"And I love it . . . And you."

"We're fighting off old age and death," I said solemnly.

"If you say so, Chucky Ducky."

Back at home, she went to her office to finish a draft of her manuscript on Russia and I went up to our bedroom. I wanted to deal with sleep deprivation, but I knew that would not be permitted. In truth, I did not want to sleep at all. I wanted to ravish my wife again. I delved into the Bride Mary O'Brien files as a distraction from my imperious hunger for her.

Finally, she appeared in a gossamer white gown that made my eyes pop open.

"Rosemarie," I protested, "that is a scandalous gown! I'm surprised at you!"

"I may let you take one of your obscene pictures of me in it." She spun around and the thin fabric spun with her. It was husband bait.

Then she lay on the bed next to me, her belly down, her face on top of mine.

"You don't know what a wonderful man you are, my sexy darling. You were perfect with that impossible president, you were a tower of strength for all of us through the weekend. You were good to poor Seano. You calmed me down—and our daughters too. You were so sensitive to April—and all the while you're practically dead on your feet. I've never loved you more . . ."

She covered me with kisses.

I doubted all of these charges.

"I'm pretty good at submitting to attacks by sex-crazed women," I said.

"Don't tear my gown."

"I have to save it for the shoot."

We know about the courtship and marriage of Bride Mary O'Brien and Joseph Thomas Raftery almost entirely from his testimony. They both had learned to be cautious about sex and love. As with many people at their ages in life, they were wary of the dating game and skeptical of the advantages in an intense love affair. Both had been burned before and knew all the dangers of intimacy. Yet they both desired intimacy and family before they grew older.

Joseph Raftery, reflecting on the neighborhood in Chicago where he grew up, remarked to us that the support of family and friends, of the Church and the local community helped the young couple before they made their choice of a spouse and after marriage in working through the adjustments of the common life. It wasn't perfect, he said, but better than two people passing in the night who suddenly decided to go for broke in the marriage market.

Neither of them were exactly looking for a mate. Indeed they approached most possibilities of intimacy with a guarded suspicion. Yet when they met at a seminar in which Joseph was lecturing about the difficulties the real estate industry might face in the future, they were instantly and powerfully attracted to each other. It was, Joseph said, like a flame leaped out of me at the podium and her in the audience and set the whole world ablaze. I would have taken her to bed that night if she had not been much wiser than I was. We've got to take it slowly, Joe. Too much too fast won't be good for either of us and we might ruin the possibilities in our relationship. He realized that was what a girl from his neighborhood in Chicago might say.

Raftery agreed with her, though by his own admission reluctantly. Did I want an explosion of passion with her as object or did I want a wife with whom I could share my life? I wanted both, but I was aware that this might be my last opportunity.

So they dated cautiously and carefully and discovered that they both wanted the same things in life, that they shared the same religion in which she was more devout or at any rate more punctilious than he.

The ardor between them became unbearably intense. One night she said to him, Joe would you be after planning to marry me. Next week he said. Then come to bed with me before we both perish with the heat. Their union, Joe reported, was relaxed, considerate, graceful. He knew that he could not let her get away. They were married a month later.

Their common life developed as naturally as had their physical love. They both respected each other, were careful of each other's feelings, and dealt with problems forthrightly. I would try to hide my complaints, Joseph told us; she wouldn't let me get away with it. I was in a permanent state of sexual arousal until the day she disappeared. As far as I can tell she responded to me with similar emotions. We both wanted children but it took us a while to conceive. I became uneasy about this little invader who made my wife sick in the morning and who was distorting her lovely body. But once Samantha was born, she made the bond between us stronger than ever. Then the dream stopped.

When members of a family are murdered, an investigator immediately suspects the survivors. In this case one must ask what Joseph Raftery had to gain by the (presumed) death of his wife and child. He was a rich man. While the money that he might inherit from Bride Mary was not insignificant, it would add comparatively little to his net worth. Their vineyard was moderately successful, but their lifestyle did not depend on it. He had financed it with his own money, so they had no apparent debts. We carefully investigated all possibilities but could find no motive for him disposing of his wife and daughter.

The circumstances of the crime are equally baffling. Joseph left their home at the edge of the vineyard to drive to San Francisco at ten o'clock in the morning. A fruit salesman stopped at the house at eleven. It was a routine stop by a man who had sold fresh fruit to them for a couple of years. At that time of the year there were no workers in the vineyard. At twelve-thirty one Raul Gonzalez, the foreman of the vineyard workers who worked at St. Brigid's Winery as it was called, stopped by to discuss plans for the coming season with Mr. Raftery. He found no one at home. Mr. Raftery's car was not there, but Mrs. Raftery's was present. She was not in the house nor in the vineyard offices. Mr. Gonzalez assumed that all three had gone somewhere, probably to San Francisco together.

The Raftery home was at the end of an unpaved road some two miles into the vineyards from State Highway 121. The Gonzalez family lived at the intersection of the two roads. Mrs. Gonzalez was in the house all that day and swore that the only car to come out of the vineyards and come back in were her husband's car and Joseph Raftery's car. She also swore that he had stopped at her house a little after ten and said if he missed Raul, he wanted to talk to him that evening.

Raftery had in fact driven to San Francisco to discuss with his business advisor the sale of land he owned beyond the Berkeley Hills to a developer who wanted to construct a new subdivision. The advisor, a John Chamberlain, told him that the developer did not have a good reputation and would probably make a mess out of this precious land. Raftery agreed and drove back to the St. Brigid's

Winery, arriving about three-thirty in the afternoon to discover that his wife and child were missing. The time frame of his return fit what would be required for a drive into the city and back with a lunch in between the two trips.

Immediately the State and Santa Rosa County Police began urgent investigations. They suspected that a group of hippies had come in from the hills behind the vineyard, robbed the house, and taken the mother and child away with them for their own amusement. However, there were no signs of a struggle in the house and nothing had been stolen, not even Mrs. Raftery's jewelry. Moreover, a careful search of the area revealed no bands of wandering hippies. The press speculated about another Patty Hearst kidnapping but at that time there were no revolutionary communes in that part of California.

The local authorities and State Police carried on widespread investigations with professional diligence, especially because the media coverage was extensive and persistent. At first they had made Joseph Raftery an instant suspect but his "alibi" was airtight. Even now some of the detectives who worked on the case and keep the file on it open suspect Mr. Raftery, but they do so only because of their conviction that it is ALWAYS the spouse. At one point they dug up some twenty mounds in the vineyard searching for bodies but found nothing.

Having followed Bride Mary O'Brien from Ballinasloe to the valleys north of San Francisco, we have found nothing to explain her disappearance. We append the documentation we have collected and the photographs of her at various stages in her life.

We conclude that she and her daughter Samantha Brigid Raftery are probably dead. Otherwise, we would have heard something about them from someone. However, probably does not mean certainly.

Chapter Eighteen

Rosemarie

"Something wrong, Rosie?" Mary Margaret asked when she returned from classes at Rosary. "You look spaced-out."

I was in fact daydreaming about passion with her father. I could hardly tell her that, though heaven knows she might suspect.

"I was thinking about a lot of things," I said, "instead of working on this Russian manuscript."

It was a perfect early October Indian summer day.

She flopped down on the couch in my office.

"All right if I use the pool?"

"Whenever has it not been all right?"

"Ask Erin to join me?"

"I didn't know she swims."

"She doesn't but I'll teach her."

"What strange social-class sensitivity made you think I'd say no?"

"I knew you wouldn't but I thought I'd ask."

"Well we can't have Seano falling in love with a nonswimmer, can we?"

Mary Margaret laughed.

"Poor Erin doesn't know how closely we're watching them."

"Tell me, daughter of mine, did you adopt that poor waif as a possible sister-in-law?"

"It wouldn't be the first time, someone in the family did that, would it?"

"And with happy results!" I said as I blushed.

"I can't dispute that." She grinned. "Hey, why don't you join us?"

"If not today, then tomorrow."

I worry about Mary Margaret. She's tough and sophisticated but also kind and generous. She thinks she has everything under control. I never thought that at her age. I knew my life was out of control. I suspected even then, I think, that I was an alcoholic. She has many advantages I didn't have. She has spent her whole life in a cocoon of family love and support. I don't begrudge it. I am part of it. She says she can take care of herself and I don't doubt that she can. At her age if you can't take care of yourself, no one can. Her mother can't protect her any longer. But mothers worry just the same. It goes with the job description . . . I couldn't protect her from crazy Aunt Jane. We could have lost her, oh, so easily. We didn't thanks be to You. But I still worry.

She is also a conniver, worse even than Aunt Peg, who connived with April to unite Chuck and me. But what if they were wrong. We came awfully close over my drinking. Or maybe it wasn't close at all. What if Seano and Erin are not suited for each other? You take a terrible chance if you try to set up romances. Yet how else can many young people, however attractive, find spouses unless their friends connive? I would certainly not be able to talk Mary Margaret out of her conniving. Erin is a sweet, pretty young woman who loves kids. Like I say, mothers worry. That's what they're for.

I had a terrible crush on Chuck in those years so long ago when they lived in that terrible two flat on Menard Avenue. I still have a crush on him. Did I have any hint of what that crush would lead to, especially my drinking? If I had known, I would have run. What if I had a hint of the games we play with each other now? I would have been terrified, but also perhaps a little curious. I still might have run. Foolish speculations . . . As I think of the games, of the laughter, the surprises, the cries, and the enormous pleasure, I dream of Chucky inside me and my body begins to prepare. I feel heavy, sinking into a delicious lassitude . . .

The phone rang and stirred me out of my reverie. It was Ted McCormack, poor dear man.

"I heard that Mom was in the hospital over the weekend . . ."

"She apparently had two heart attacks, one quite serious. However, she's off the ventilator and out of intensive care. Her color is improving and she seems peaceful. She'll probably be in Oak Park for several more days."

"Long-term prognosis?"

"Guarded."

"I'm sorry, Rosie."

"We all are."

"I'm sure that Jane's episode might have caused the attack . . ."

"It didn't help, Ted. But we don't blame you or her. Things happen."

"Please keep me informed . . . She's a magic lady."

"All of that . . . How's Jane doing?"

"Still pretty much of a vegetable. When they try to take her off sedation, she becomes manic, refuses her meds, demands that they let her leave, threatens them that her son Chris will file suit."

"Will he?"

"He doesn't like me very much, Rosie. He might. He'd lose but it's the kind of trouble our family doesn't need right now."

I remembered the old days when Chucky and I were allies in fighting off Ted's father when he wanted to prevent the marriage. Who could have known?

I promised Ted I would stay in touch. I felt a little guilty about not calling him over the weekend.

The intercom buzzed from the darkroom. My husband in a manic mood, not the sort of mania that suggested sexual hunger.

"Rosemarie, are you busy?"

"I'm always busy, Chucky Ducky."

"Doing what?"

"Daydreaming about you."

That was true, but I suspected at the moment irrelevant.

"Could you come down here for a moment?"

Boy child wanting to show something to Mom. Or maybe now to Grams.

"I'll be right down."

I knocked on the door to the office, which was an antechamber.

"Come in!" he bellowed.

Chucky glanced up at me as I entered the office. In one swift glance he tore off my clothes and reveled in my nakedness, ravaging me in his imagination. Husbands are not supposed to look at their wives that way—not after thirty years of marriage. However, he had other things on his mind.

"Did anything strike you as peculiar in the file on Bride Mary O'Brien?"

"The whole file is peculiar," I said, sitting down at the metal table that served as his desk.

"Any dramatic changes as the story went on?"

I pondered.

"Well, it seems to me to take on a different tone after Bride Mary quit Berkeley and became a real estate agent. She calmed down and became an adult very quickly."

"Precisely," he said, pleased that I had spotted the same anomaly he had. "Almost as if she was another women?"

"Is she another woman?" I asked, spooked a little. The waters were getting deeper.

"I was looking at the pictures," he said, his hands on two prints on the table, facedown. "Suddenly I realized that this woman"—he turned up the photograph—"is the Bride Mary O'Brien of Ballinasloe, County Galway, and this woman"—he turned over the second photo—"is the Bride Mary O'Brien of Santa Rosa County, California!"

The photos were blowups of the faces.

"The second one is blond . . ."

"Sure, sure," he said eagerly, "but different noses, different chins, different foreheads. Both pretty, but not the same woman."

There was no arguing the point.

"Curiouser and curiouser . . . What does it mean?"

"I don't know . . . There was some kind of identity change after this one"—he lifted up the woman with the long black hair—"quit Berkeley and this woman began to sell real estate in Marin County."

"Why?"

"I don't know yet. I'll have to figure it out. They both may be dead, for all I know . . . Yet if I'm Joe Raftery's wife and I want Joe to understand what happened to her, I'd bug him to talk to his high school buddy who is a photographer and likely to spot the differences in the pictures."

"Living or dead?"

"Probably dead . . . It's the kind of trick the Feds would play, as we learned from the cowboys who infested the embassy in Bonn when we first arrived there. Give a woman a new identity because she knew too much. Then become worried that she might spill the beans. Lift her from her home, probably in a chopper, take her a hundred or so miles over the Pacific, and push her out the door. You remember from our days at Bonn that they were doing that sort of thing back then. Why change?"

"You put a stop to it."

"All that meant was that they covered their tracks better so I didn't find out . . . I don't know what's happened. I have to presume that all three of them are dead. This is all instinct, Rosemarie, I smell a trick . . . Besides the Bride Mary of Ballinasloe and the one Joe married seemed like different people even in the story."

"What happened to the first one?"

"If they follow their usual tricks, she's dead too. Both Bride Marys are dead."

"Why kill the little girl?"

"Why not? These people are thorough. She could have told them that some men in dark suits came and took their mother away."

"Maybe they're holding the child as a hostage so that her mother won't try to escape."

"That assumes they didn't kill her. I can't imagine why they didn't if they viewed her as some kind of threat. They don't take chances out of pity."

"Maybe they owed her. Maybe their bosses said that they couldn't kill a woman who had done good work for them . . ."

"Maybe." He thought about it for a moment. "You can never tell what the bosses will do and when they mean what they say."

"What can we do about it?"

I felt very sick. We'd learned in Bonn how brutal some of our "cowboys" could be, killing some of their own people on thin evidence that the victims had been "turned" by the other side.

He sighed.

"Right now, it doesn't seem like we can do much. We don't have enough evidence to create a public scandal. I don't know how we can get it. Moreover, if Bride Mary O'Brien and her Samantha are still alive, we might endanger their lives. I'll have to work on it."

"We've always been a team on these things, Chucky."

"I know that."

"No moves without me."

"I understand," he said reluctantly.

It sounded dreadful and dangerous. We had pulled capers off before, but we were too long in the tooth for it these days.

I stood up to leave.

"Where you going?"

"To swim with the girls."

"Which girls?"

"Mary Margaret, Erin, and Shovie."

"We let the babysitter into our pool now!" He feigned shock. He knew as well as I did that she was afraid of the water.

"Mary Margaret is teaching her how to swim. And it's my pool!"

He stood up quickly and took me in his arms. Holding me close with one arm, he slipped his hand under my tee shirt and captured my breast.

"Chucky, you're groping me!"

He probed underneath my bra and found some warm flesh, then a firm nipple. His fingers were demanding, but so tender, so delicate. Unbearable sweetness surged through me.

"Stop it!" I protested weakly.

Then he kissed me, oh, so gently. I became putty to which he could do anything. Chuck's great skill as a lover is that he treats my body like a chalice.

"Just a taste for tonight," he said, aware of his power and confident of it. This was all too much.

"I can hardly wait," I said sarcastically as I slipped away from him.

"It's all your fault. If you weren't so beautiful, I wouldn't want to play with you every time I see you."

"You're gross!" I said, leaving the room and closing the door firmly.

He laughed. He knew how he had turned me on and delighted in it. Now it wasn't merely screwing the poor defenseless matron, but keeping her on an edge for much of the day.

This has to stop. He strips me mentally every time he looks at me and gropes whenever he sees the slightest chance. I must tell him that it has to stop.

I won't because I love it.

I leaned against the outside wall of the darkroom and tried to control my breathing. I would have to wait till night. That was all right. There is joy in waiting.

So I put on a swimsuit and a robe and rushed downstairs to the pool. Shovie was sitting on the side screaming instructions at Mary Margaret, who was trying to teach Erin to float. Both young women were wearing bikinis. Erin had a gorgeous little body which her drab clothes usually hid. More sweaters were in order if Mary Margaret's plot were to succeed. She and the children she would bear would be interesting additions to my growing family of grandchildren.

I slipped into the pool. The cool water quieted my passions but did not extinguish them completely.

Chapter Nineteen

Mary Margaret

"Hey, Rosie," I shouted as she towed Shovie up and down the pool, "Erin and I are going up to North and Harlem to have a drink tonight with Sean and that Joey Moran boy. After we put Shovie to bed."

"You're too young to drink in a bar," she shouted back before she and Shovie dove beneath the surface of the pool.

"I have my driver's license, my passport, and my Baptismal certificate," I yelled. "They all say I'm twenty-one, which I am."

"You're not twenty-one," she insisted. "How can a young woman like me have a twenty-one-year-old daughter?"

She was wearing her two-piece swimsuit and looked totally bitchin'. I wondered if Chucky knew how lucky he was. Probably he did.

"And Erin is already twenty-two."

"What would her mum say about her going to a local pub?"

"Me mum and da go to their local, Mrs. O'Malley," she said meekly, not at all sure that she wanted to risk her employer's displeasure.

"Well"—she splashed us—"I suppose you'll be safe, though I don't think that Joey Moran could fight his way out of a wet paper bag. I'm glad you're black belt."

"Ro-SIE! Don't be mean about poor Joey Moran."

"Did she say yes?" Erin whispered.

"I didn't ask her. I TOLD her."

"I hope she won't be upset with me."

"No problem. Like I tell you my mom is totally cool."

"And very beautiful."

"Yeah, well she works at it and she says she has good genes. I hope I inherit some of them."

Rosie produced a Kurdish dish called kavruma for supper. For Turkish wedding feasts, she assured us. Chucky devoured it like he had been fasting for a week.

"I really like this foreign food," he said between gulps.

"Charles Cronin O'Malley," she said, "the girls are going over to North Avenue for drinks after they put Shovie to bed."

"Not Shovie?" he said, looking up in surprise.

"I said after they put her to bed. She can't go to the bar if she's in bed."

"Hmm . . . By themselves?"

"I think they said they might meet that kid that hangs around here and Sean at the bar."

"What Sean?"

"OUR Sean."

This was all part of Chucky's act.

"Well why don't we go along with them and share in the fun?"

"Chuc-KY! You're too OLD!"

He pretended his feelings were hurt.

"WELL, you and Rosie can walk over to Petersen's. That's your style anyway."

"They can-NOT!" Shovie protested. "They gotta stay home with me after you put me to bed!"

"Are they ever serious?" Erin asked as we left the house.

"I told you when you came on board that we are the Crazy O'Malleys."

We walked slowly up to North Avenue. The boys would drive us home. It was a soft, quiet Indian summer night with a bit of a haze in the air, which covered a modest full moon. Perfect for romance. I hoped not too perfect. We were both wearing skirts and sweaters, mine light blue and hers light green. At first she seemed self-conscious, but she'd relaxed by the time we met the boys, who were waiting for us in front of the bar.

"Two gorgeous-looking woman," Sean said enthusiastically when we met. He did not, thank heavens, try to kiss either of us.

"If you like Irish," Joey Moran said with that damn mischievous twinkle in his eye. He might be a major problem for me tonight.

We sauntered in. The bar was not like those down on Rush Street. There were some young people around but also some older folk, a few looking for pickups and more seemingly contented middle-aged folk. Everyone's eyes turned to us when we walked in. It was time for my act.

"A double Bushmill's Green," I said to the bartender. "Straight up!"

"A young girl shouldn't be drinking that stuff," he said with a leer. "Let me see your driver's license."

He was Irish-American, red-faced, and overweight.

I pulled out my wallet and flipped the driver's license open, my passport, and my copy of my Baptismal certificate from St. Ursula Church and laid them next to each other on the bar.

"Now," I said with a touch of anger, "will you please give me my Bushmill's Green, straight up?"

Erin showed him her passport without his asking for it and wondered if he'd ever have a small pint of Guinness? I have never figured out the difference between a small pint and a pint, but who am I to criticize the funny way the Irish talk.

Sean ordered an Amstel light and goofy Joey Moran said he wanted a Diet Coke on the rocks.

The bartender brought the others the drinks they ordered. My whiskey had ice in it.

I stared at him dyspeptically.

"Are you a focking eejit or you just plain deaf. Only a focking eejid pollutes good whiskey with ice, especially when these three people will confirm that I ordered it straight up."

I stared him down and he went back to his whiskey bottles and poured me a drink straight up. I watched him to make sure that he didn't take the ice cubes out with his fingers. We adjourned to a table.

"Well, I said, no one will think of harassing us in here."

"I didn't know you drink whiskey," poor Seano said, kind of goggle-eyed. "You never drink it at home."

"Seano, love, I'm not home . . . besides this is sipping whiskey, isn't it Erin?"

" 'Tis. Don't they say it's very powerful stuff?"

"It clears the sinuses," I said, taking a very small sip, lest I humiliate myself with a coughing fit.

"I don't suppose you'd ever let me have a tiny sip, would you?"

"Very tiny," I offered her the drink.

She did have a coughing fit.

"Guys?"

"Well," said my big brother, "I've never tasted it before."

His eyes blinked as he took a big sip.

"It does clear the sinuses, sis, it does that."

"Joey?" I offered the tumbler to my amused and bemused swain.

"I'll stick with my Diet Coke"—he lifted his glass—"on the rocks."

Brat.

We had a very nice time. No one in the bar dared to bother us, that's for sure. We talked about anything and everything, school, Ireland, America, Reagan, television, films.

"You do that act," Sean asked carefully, "to keep the hasslers off, don't you, Mary Margaret?"

"A redhead with an Irish temper who drinks Bushmill's Green straight up is patently not a woman to trifle with."

"I could have told them that," dumb Joey Moran said.

"Have you ever done it with your da an' mum present?"

That was a marvelous idea. Why hadn't I thought of it?

"I wouldn't be caught dead in a bar with Rosie and Chuck. They're old. Petersen's ice cream shop is their speed."

"Let's go there later," Joey Moran said. "It's about my speed too."

He was telling the truth, though sometimes he said stupid things like that just to egg me on.

The chemistry between my brother and Erin Ryan was sweet. It wasn't like that between Rosie and Chuck—which will blow you right out of the room—though it's sweet in its own way. Poor Seano was happy and relaxed with a nice, pretty Irish girl who would never be mean to him. For her part, she glanced at him occasionally and with a quick smile. Okay, I had done my part. The rest was up to them.

I could not leave without finishing my drink. I should never have ordered a double. My sinuses would be clear for the next five years. Yet I walked straight and confidently to the curb to wait for Sean's car to pick us up. Well, I had found my limit with whiskey and that was useful knowledge.

I also walked a straight line into Petersen's though I was feeling a little woozy. I thought I had gone over the deep end when I saw Chuck and Rosie sitting in their favorite corner booth, looking dreamy eyed at each other.

"Who's watching Shovie?" I demanded, perhaps too shrilly.

Everyone laughed, everyone in the whole ice-cream shop. We pulled up chairs by their booth and Chucky, the big deal impresario, ordered a round of double malts with whipped cream.

The impossible Joey Moran giggled at that.

Rosie was still laughing at me. Did she know that I had too much of the drink taken? If she did, she'd never say anything.

"Jimmy came in from the seminary for some meeting and decided he'd stay at the house. So he's watching Shovie."

I drank my malt slowly and carefully. I said nothing because I was afraid I might say something stupid. Everyone had a lot of fun and we sang a couple of songs, which is what the Crazy O'Malleys do when they go to Petersen's. Then stupid Seano had to tell his story of how I had established "credibility" at the North Avenue. I was acutely embarrassed.

"You don't hassle a red-haired woman who drinks Bushmill's Green straight up!" I insisted piously.

Rosie smiled. Chucky, the boor, howled. I suppose Rosie was worried just a little bit about whether I had inherited the alcoholic gene. It was time to reassure her.

"WELL, at least I learned what my limit is tonight. Downtown I always drink one straight up. Here I was showing off for the locals and it was a bit much. Never again, and you stop laughing at me, Joey Moran, with your diet cola on the rocks."

"You weren't a bit fluthered at all, at all," Erin said, defending me.

"Only a tiny bit," I said. "That's why I shouted when I saw my parents sitting here waiting for me."

Soon the parents withdrew. They both had busy days ahead of them. They also wanted to give the boys a chance to kiss us good night.

Good old Seano was so gentle and so sweet with Erin that it almost broke my heart. My own swain is not a great one for passionate kisses either. So he was even more gentle than Sean. The whiskey still inside me took over and I responded more passionately than I had ever done to any boy.

"You're fun, Mary Margaret Anne O'Malley," he said with a laugh. "And you're also wonderful."

I tried to think of something funny to say, but the words wouldn't come.

All I could manage was, "Thank you, Joey Moran."

Erin and I went to our rooms silently, both of us with our own dreams.

Chapter Twenty

Chuck

After supper my wife pleaded work to finish on her desk and I said that I would go downstairs and think about the mystery of the two women named Bride Mary.

I did not want to think and I don't think she wanted to finish any work. My impulsive assault on her breast earlier in the day had kind of knocked us both out. How does one live in the same house with a woman who infatuates you and whose body is available for play all day—especially if you have work to do. Doubtless she had similar questions.

My first move was to make a call to DC to a man I knew in my completely crazy adventure in Vietnam. He had left government service a few years later and was the CEO of an important consulting firm, which in his case didn't mean working with spooks. He knew just about everything on the subject, however.

After an exchange of pleasantries and my telling him about taking pictures of the president, I said to him, "Whitney, I have a couple of questions to ask in this conversation which has never occurred, okay?"

"I was here watching TV all night and waiting for my wife to come home from a gala at the Kennedy Center."

"When I was in Bonn, some of the spooks executed their own people because they suspected the Stasi had turned them. Does that still happen?"

"Were the victims American? That doesn't change the morality of the action, but from the point of view of their employers it would make a big difference."

"Germans."

"I imagine that those cowboys were not employed with the Company for long."

"Company" was what the insiders called the CIA for whatever twisted reason.

"If the people whom they terminated with extreme prejudice were Americans and indeed fellow agents?"

"They themselves would be dead in a week. You can't do that without explicit permission from the top and that is almost never given. That doesn't mean that some rogues don't try it, but they themselves will end up sanctioned."

"Sanction" meant the same thing as "terminate with extreme prejudice." Murder in other words.

"You sure?"

"Absolutely. Through the years the rule has always been that if you sanction one of ours, we'll sanction you. Everyone knows that."

So maybe there was still some hope for the second Bride Mary O'Brien.

"What about the occasional agent that seems to disappear from the face of the earth?"

Silence for a moment on the other end of the line.

"Chuck, I will answer your questions because I know you are always on the side of the good guys. But I won't ask you any, as much as I would like to. Fair enough?"

"Absolutely."

"I know of an aviator who vanished during the Vietnam War, under very mysterious circumstances. His friends claimed that he was never shot down, till someone told them to shut up. He went underground, ended up at GPU headquarters in Moscow. Fooled them for years. Then our people ordered him to come in out of the cold. They were afraid he'd be caught and the Commies would eliminate all the, uh, resources he had. I don't know the details. The Russians thought he was dead. When he came back here, they told him that they would take care of him for the rest of his life, but they had to give him a new identity, even some plastic surgery. He could never see his family again. He knew that this would happen when he took the assignment. The family somehow is convinced that he is still alive. The Feds brush them off. They also quiet down any congressman who takes an interest. He lives near his family, so he can see them from a distance occasionally. Our people encourage that because they believe it keeps the agent in the reservation. He never remarried. I heard recently that now, twenty years later, his resources from Russia are all dried up. They may release him. Too soon to know . . . Brave, patriotic man."

"Resources" meant agents, human agents. It's easier to pretend that you're losing something abstract than a human person.

"You ever talk to him?"

"Yes."

"What does he say about Russia?"

"Same thing you told Ronnie the other day."

"You heard about that?"

"Everyone in the business heard about it. Some of us think you're absolutely right."

"Is the present crowd strong enough to prevent any sanctions against an agent who is as brave as your friend?"

"No termination, maybe hide him for a while. Some of those guys broke the rules for Dick Nixon and lived to regret it. Never again."

"You're sure?"

"Look, Chuck, you know that I don't like the business. That's why I got out of it. There are, however, a number of good reasons why we don't sanction our own. First of all, we are Americans, we are the good guys, we wear the white hats. We stand by our own. We bring out our wounded and dead, right? If we were Russians, we'd simply liquidate them and be done with it. That's not the American way. Secondly, if we did terminate the pilot I was talking about, the word would get around pretty quickly and no one would ever take risks like that again."

"What if he simply told your friends someday that he was going back to his wife and family?"

Silence.

"Well, there'd be some cowboys who would want to terminate

him. Too much of a risk, they'd say. He's gone rogue. Can't tell what he might do."

"Then?"

"Then they would be told firmly that they wouldn't themselves last another week."

"Ugh," I murmured.

"That's why I got out of it Chuck. I hate the cowboys. But even they don't want to die. Maybe we'd lock the pilot up for a time, then we'd let him go. He's not about to do that, however. He's a real American patriot."

"I guess so," I said.

Or a flaming nut. But what did I know?

I thought a long time about our conversation. Bride Mary and Samantha were most likely still alive. I could threaten the Feds, who knew me well enough from Bonn and Saigon not to mess around with me, that I'd go public with the whole story. I didn't think they'd try to sanction me, but I would build in all the safeguards that would make it pretty certain that they wouldn't try.

"We don't fuck around with Charlie O'Malley," a spook had told me in Saigon. "He's a crazy little bastard and very dangerous."

I was and still am very proud of that evaluation, but it gives me credit for a lot more courage than I really possess.

I needed one more piece of evidence to lock it up. I didn't have to know what Bride Mary O'Brien II had done for the Feds. I needed some evidence however, that they had pulled the switch. Then I could go ahead with the almost diabolically clever scheme that was turning around in my head.

I had to turn off the scheming machine or I wouldn't sleep at all. There was one cure for it and she was upstairs. I glanced at my watch—11:30. What an idiot I was! I claimed that I was infatuated with her and had forgotten about her.

I hurried up to our room, which was dark, undressed quickly, and slipped into bed. I was in deep trouble. She wasn't wearing a nightgown. "Sorry to be late," I whispered.

"Chucky Ducky, I love you so much I'd wait for you forever!"

Then, sentimental fool that I am, I began to cry. She did too.

Chapter Twenty-One

Chuck

The next morning after an inexcusably late breakfast, I returned to my darkroom office and called my friend Whitney again.

"Whit, when I was in Saigon and the Feds were closing in on me one of them said that they would hold me and my pictures in a comfortable safe house—Rosetta House, I think they called it—on the coast above San Francisco. They even said a Mr. Jackson ran it, a perfect host they told me."

"Yes?" Whit said evenly.

"Ah, I suppose they've closed it down, haven't they?"

"They have not."

"Interesting."

"Chucky, don't . . ."

He hesitated.

"Don't worry. I won't try to knock it over. I just need to know that it's still there."

"Be careful . . ."

"My middle name."

Then I had another brilliant idea. It was eleven o'clock. Too early to make the call. I flipped through the notes in Joe Raftery's files and found what I was looking for. Splendid! If my guess was right, it would confirm my hunches. I didn't see yet how I might use the information, but I'd know most of my speculations were right. What would I do for the next hour?

I rushed upstairs, found my swimming trunks with some difficulty, threw a robe around my shoulders. Only then did I look out the window. It was still gorgeous Indian summer weather.

"Rosemarie"—I burst into her office—"I think I'll swim in your pool."

She glanced up from her work, frowned to let me know that I had broken her train of thought, took off her glasses, and said, "I suppose I'd better join you, so you don't drown yourself . . . Couldn't you find a better terry-cloth robe than that one?"

I raced off to the pool and dove in. Clumsily of course. The water was inappropriately cold. I sputtered, thought about climbing out, and concluded that my wife would ridicule me if I did. After I swam a few lengths I adjusted to the temperature. Yet the good Rosemarie's plan that I do it every morning to wake me up would not work, not unless she notably raised the temperature of the water.

She arrived at poolside in one of her many two-piece swimsuits and a terry-cloth robe hanging open, of course. She tossed a second one on a chaise.

"For you," she said.

"The water is too cold," I shouted.

"You'll get used to it." She cast aside the robe and did her usual perfect dive into the water and emerged swimming an equally perfect Australian crawl.

After showing off for perhaps fifteen minutes while I struggled along in my ungainly backstroke, she tried to dunk me. No, that's not accurate, she dunked me and held me down. I struggled free and went after her to no avail. We wrestled, shouting and laughing, sputtering and pushing. It was a reprise of an old game we'd played for the last forty years. I always lost, though there was a special sweetness in losing these days.

She then decided that we had played enough and it was time for lunch.

"I'll make a nice fromage and jambon for both of us," she informed me, as she climbed out of the pool, "and brew some mint iced tea."

"I'd like a ham and cheese instead."

"Charles Cronin O'Malley, get out of the pool and dry off."

"No!"

"I said yes."

So I cautiously ascended the ladder and grabbed for the robe she'd left next to it. I thought that I would shiver till the day before the last judgment. I sat at one of the expensive tables that provided "accent color" (her words) for the pool. "I'm hungry," I yelled as she ambled into the house to reappear a little while later with a tray of three sandwiches, one for herself and two for me.

"I made hot chocolate as well as iced tea," she said, "because I knew you'd be sitting here shivering."

"BELGIAN hot chocolate, I hope."

"Naturally."

In the early days of our marriage, my good wife had determined that she would become a gourmet cook, one cuisine at a time. We had French food every night of the year, then pasta, then Middle Eastern food. I didn't mind because there was always plenty of it and it always tasted good.

I gobbled half a sandwich, washed it down with hot chocolate, and sighed contentedly.

"Country club life in my own backyard." I sighed.

"My backyard," she reminded me.

"Your backyard."

"Now, Chucky Ducky, tell me what mischief you have been cooking up down there in your fantasy cave."

So I told her what I had learned.

She listened attentively and respectfully.

"Remarkable," she said. "As always, I'm impressed when you put on your gnome disguise. What do you propose to do?"

"I'm not sure yet."

"You'll probably go after that secret office on Mass. Avenue. This is the sort of thing they'd do. Your friend Colonel Chandler still works there, doesn't he?"

"I think so."

"It could be dangerous."

"Not really, not when I have all the dominos in place. I'll check it all out with Vince."

"I'm in it," she said.

"No way."

"We're not having this argument again, Charles Cronin O'Malley. I let you go off to Vietnam alone and you almost got yourself killed in the South China Sea."

This was the literal truth.

"This is different."

"No, it isn't. We've done these things before, too often if you ask me, but it's part of the package that comes with being your wife. I'm in."

"One of us should be around, just in case something goes wrong."

"I thought nothing could go wrong."

"Accidents always happen, Rosemarie, even on the Congress Expressway."

Chicago Democrats never call it the Eisenhower Expressway.

"Which doesn't prevent us from driving it together."

"We'll see what Vince says."

"No, we won't. I'm prepared to lose you someday, Chucky Ducky. Maybe when you're as old as Vangie, but not now."

"You're claiming that you're my good luck charm?"

"The kids are old enough to take care of themselves. Peg would love to have Shovie as her own. If you're not afraid, then why should I be afraid?"

I gave up because I knew I was going to lose the argument. In truth, she was my good luck charm. After all I hadn't died in the South China Sea. God had sent the Marines to rescue me from it at the very last minute because of her prayers. Or so she claimed.

"I have to make a phone call," I said.

"I'll come with you."

We went to her office.

First I called Vince. He wasn't in the office but Charley, my namesake, was.

"Student Affairs Offices usually handle that sort of thing, Uncle Chuck. If they don't have one, they'll direct you."

"How're you feeling, Charlotte?" as my namesake she deserved her real name.

"Wonderful! Very happy! Can hardly wait. Neither can Mom. She wants to be a grandmother the worst way."

"God bless all of you," I said.

At ten-thirty West Coast time, I called the University of California at Berkeley and asked for Student Affairs. I told them that I was Thomas Jackson of the Immigration and Naturalization Services and I wanted to ask about one of their students. A very polite woman of Asian persuasion answered a phone.

"We are very private about our students, Mr. Jackson."

"I understand that and applaud it. A question has arisen about one of your students. Some of our records show that she has a student visa, but others claim that she has a green card. I'm convinced it's a green card, which is much better for her."

"I cannot tell you that, sir. But I can tell you whether she is enrolled here at the university under approved rules."

"Very well. Her name is Kathleen N. Houlihan."

I had to spell the name for her. I didn't bother to tell her that she was the symbol of Ireland.

"We have no name like that in our files," she said. "Has she married, do you know?"

"Possibly . . . We believe that she is in the Comparative Literature Department."

Another pause while the computer in the bowels of Berkeley whirled through its subbasements.

"We do have a woman student named Kathleen N. H. O'Shea. Her husband is a certain Sean O'Shea. She is in the university legally. She has been a student here for many years. Indeed her dissertation is scheduled for this semester . . . In fact, she is on the faculty of the College of the Holy Names in Oakland."

"Then they both have green cards," I said. "I'm delighted to hear that. We need those kinds of people in America."

No one from Immigration would ever say that.

"Up Kerry!" I shouted after I had hung up. Half the men in Kerry are called Sean O'Shea.

I called the public relations office at the College of the Holy Names.

"I'm Cronin O'Malley, a freelance journalist. I'm writing a piece about an article your Kathleen Houlihan has written. Is her proper title 'instructor'?"

"Actually she usually goes by her married name—Kathleen O'Shea. She's an associate professor."

"Thank you!"

Doing well in her academic career. When her dissertation is approved she'll become a tenured full professor. She must be good. A long way from Ballinasloe.

Did her Kerry husband realize that her name was a pseudonym she used when she wrote an article in Galway? He didn't need to know.

"She's still alive then! . . . Are you going to talk to her?"

"I don't think so. The poor woman is still alive, thanks be to God. Her existence is a card to be played with our friends on Mass. Avenue."

"Why the switch?"

"I've wondered about that . . . Probably they wanted an actual background for their agent in case anyone would be looking for her. They made a deal with the real Bride Mary. They would give her a new identity and a green card. Maybe they picked her up for some kind of disorderly conduct and threatened to send her back to Ballinasloe."

"The caper sounds like fun. Another Crazy O'Malley trick."

It was, I reflected, a little more dangerous than driving downtown of a Friday evening on the Congress Expressway, though perhaps a little less dangerous than the same ride with me at the wheel. So I would tell Vince tonight. He would suggest that someday my luck would run out.

"I believe, young woman," I said to my wife, "that you have removed your swimsuit."

"You have a very dirty mind . . . Any civilized person would do that before gamboling around my office."

I touched the knot on her robe. She stiffened, as she always does at the beginning of our romps.

"Don't you ever have enough of me?" she protested.

"Nope!" I loosened the knot.

"I suppose you think that you can pull off this caper and still play around with me on every possible occasion."

"Yep."

"I really don't know what we can do about you. You're impossible."

"I know."

CHAPTER TWENTY-TWO

Mary Margaret

I don't know why people create problems for themselves. I don't know either why they have to turn these phony problems into challenges for me. Poor Erin has dug in her heels on the subject of Sean Seamus.

"The poor boy," she says, "has been dumped by that terrible Oriental person . . ."

"Asian," I said, "or East Asian to be precise."

"He's innocent and vulnerable. I don't want to seduce him, which is exactly what you're trying to make me do."

"You don't like him?" I said.

"He's very sweet. I don't want to take advantage of him. And I won't."

"That's how women speak when they're afraid—afraid of a man, afraid of marriage, afraid of a decision that could shape the rest of their lives. I know the feeling from experience, but at least I acknowledge it."

"Well, I'm not going to tell him to buzz off."

"I can take care of it myself!"

"Are you sure?"

She breaks into tears and cries on my shoulder.

Then last night, Joe Moran takes me to the Lake to see *Kramer vs. Kramer.* We hold hands as we usually do. I thought it was a stupid movie about stupid people. Joey said that they were about to get together at the end and would eventually. I said they deserved each other.

When he kisses me good night it's like the last time because

I can't resist the temptation to be passionate, even when I'm sober. I don't protest, though I know I should.

At our age in life we will get more serious. Our bloodstreams are drenched with hormones. Joe Moran and I are drifting down the path, without giving much thought to it. Either we stop now, put a lid on our passions, or we'll both be in trouble, serious trouble. Which might not be all that bad.

I visited Grams in the hospital after my last class. She seems only pretty good. Insists that she simply has to go home and clean up the mess because she's sure Madge and Theresa will have made a mess of things. The two of them are dust chasers, much more obsessed with neatness than poor Grams.

I don't know what Chuck and Rosie are up to either. They're scheming on one of their plots and loving it. I am offended that they didn't invite me in and also happy because I have enough things on my mind. They also are very satisfied with themselves, which means they're fucking a lot. I don't suppose there's anything wrong with that. I wonder how often a week is healthy at their age.

And I wonder whether I'll be doing the same thing thirty years from now.

I don't know. I kind of hope so.

Joey Moran is a lot better kisser than I thought he'd be.

The next morning I ask Rosie a question I've wanted to ask her for a long time.

"Were you an alcoholic once, Rosie?"

"I still am, hon," she says calmly. "Once an alcoholic always an alcoholic. I'm a recovering alcoholic. I haven't had a drink since before you were conceived."

"Why?"

"Why did I stop drinking or why did I become one?"

"Both."

"My mom drank herself into an early death. I would go along for months, even years as a very moderate social drinker, never more than one martini or one glass of wine. Then I'd become very angry and disgusted with myself and do a binge thing."

"You were *that* angry at yourself? You aren't disgusted with yourself anymore, are you?"

"Only occasionally and, thanks to my sessions with Maggie Ward, I know how to handle it."

"Bitchin' . . . Why did you stop?"

"Your father said he'd dump me if I didn't stop."

"NO WAY!"

"So I stopped, of course . . . He should have given the order years before, but it saved my life and our marriage."

"Cool," I said for want of something else to say.

"I don't think I'm an addictive personality. I don't overeat. I don't gamble. I'm not a pathological shopper. The only addiction I have is to your father.

"Father Packy says a marriage only really becomes a sacrament when it survives a big crisis. Our marriage was a sacrament after that and you, young woman, were the first fruit of that sacrament."

We hugged each other and cried a little.

She didn't ask why I wondered about it. Maybe she figured I was really wondering about marriage. Which I was.

Chapter Twenty-Three

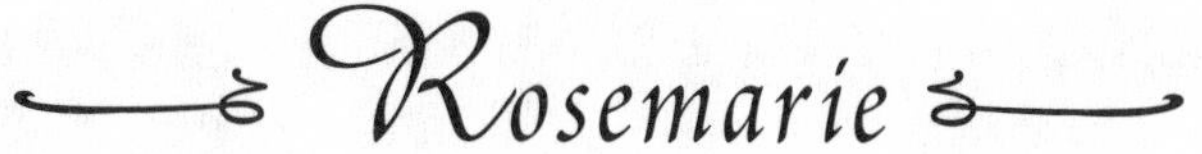

Rosemarie

Vince and Chuck and I went through the plans for our coup against the government of the United States of America. We had made our appointment to see our "friend" Colonel Chandler on Mass. Avenue and I Street on Monday morning at 9:30. If we ran into trouble, the press releases would be sent to the *Globe*, the *Times*, the *Post*, the *Trib*, and the *Sun-Times* and all the networks that night at 7:00 so as to make the next morning paper. There would be two versions of it. The second would say, "Ambassador and Mrs. O'Malley have disappeared and are believed to be in the custody of the government, if they are still alive."

"This is a crazy project, Chuck," Vince said. "Off the wall. But those guys aren't dumb enough to take you two into custody, much less try to get rid of you."

"The threat of this extra sentence will give them pause," Chuck agreed. "But we're taking no chances."

"You're taking a lot of chances," Vince replied. "I'm simply saying they're too smart to do anything to you."

"The plane we've borrowed is lined up at Palwaukee. Gulfstream III. It can cross the country in five and a half hours, maybe six against the wind. You get out of DC before noon and you'll be in the Bay Area by 3:00 in the afternoon their time. Is it absolutely necessary that you be there?"

"If we can," I said. "We want to make sure that the deliverables are safe. If you don't hear from us by 8:00, let the faxes roll."

"Both of you love this, you're like a pair of crazy kids . . . I don't get it."

"Crazy O'Malleys . . . speaking of which," Chucky said, "you don't tell anything to your wife. No point in her worrying."

"She'll be furious when she finds out."

"She doesn't have to find out. No one does," I said. "She'll only worry that we'll do it again. Besides, if the Feds want to grant our demands, we must for our part honor the bargain."

"And the deliverables?"

"You forget that she's an American patriot," I said.

"Was," Vince argued.

"They're all alike," Chuck replied. "I've seen the embedded agents in Germany and 'Nam. Not merely good citizens but almost fanatics . . . anyway, all we can promise the Feds is that we'll urge them to keep the bargain. I wouldn't blame them if they don't."

"And the real Bride Mary O'Brien?"

"As far as I'm concerned," Chuck said, "she will continue to be Ms. Kathleen N. Houlihan O'Shea. It is to no one's interest that she be troubled."

"Nice touch to choose that name," I observed. "The Feds would be too dumb to catch it . . . I'd like to meet her someday."

"And you're not going to inquire into Rosetta House?" he asked Chuck.

"No point in it. Maybe Bride Mary isn't there. That we know about the place will be enough to give the creeps the creeps . . . You have all the safe-deposit boxes lined up for our articles?"

"They'll be filled with all your material on Monday morning by law firms whom I don't know and who don't know who's behind the drop. It won't work for long, but it will last a few days, which is all you'll need."

"And the fail-safe mechanisms?"

"All in place. The most important one is the one you report from the plane."

"After I get the message from the answering machine in my

basement—which we'll make sure is working before we leave."

"What if we don't hear from you or about you from our observers?"

"Give it an hour, then act."

I shivered.

"Okay. I'll check in on Sunday evening and will expect to hear from you at Palwaukee on Monday morning."

"And we'll call you again that evening when we're back here," I said.

"Please God." Vince sighed loudly just like his wonderful Sicilian mother.

I shivered again.

Why was I doing this? Why was I permitting my crazy husband to do it?

The Good April came home from the hospital on Sunday afternoon. She seemed in good health and good spirits, though still quite frail. Home was home, but only half home without her husband.

We had a quiet little party, only ten or twelve of us; but we drank tea, ate scones, and quickly left. I noted with some interest that Sean brought Erin along. She seemed reluctant at first, but joined in the laughter and singing. Nice little voice. She'd fit in all right. But look, kid, if you're scared—and there's reason to be scared—quit now. If you become the third one to break his heart, I'll claw your eyes out.

Well, I wouldn't really.

Vince came over in the evening for a last briefing. He was somber, we were lighthearted. The Light Brigade, maybe?

We made sweet and tender love, then slept till the alarm went off at 5:00. Rather I woke at 5:00. I had to haul poor Chucky out of bed.

We were barely dressed when the limo showed up at 5:30 to take us to Palwaukee. Rain pounded on the car windows and the wind buffeted the car itself. At Palwaukee we found our (borrowed) Gulfstream III waiting for us in the dark, one engine running and its navigation lights spinning. The limo drove us right up to the boarding ramp. A cabin attendant held an umbrella over us as we were hustled into the plane. The copilot loaded our luggage in the hold. We both carried briefcases with our arguments.

The pilot spoke to us with the genial confident smile that pilots always maintain, no matter what the weather.

"The conditions are acceptable for takeoff," he said, "though just barely. We'll have no trouble getting above the weather, then ahead of it. It will be a smooth ride to DC. So relax and enjoy the flight. Janet will bring you breakfast as soon as she can . . . Incidentally, the weather will have passed through by the time we return to Chicago tonight. Please fasten your seat belts now. We expect to be in the DC area in an hour and a half, maybe a little less."

"What did he say?" Chucky stared at the luxurious comfort of the interior of the Gulfstream.

"He said fasten your seat belt."

He was so sleepy that I had to do it for him.

"This isn't the whole plane, is it?"

"It's a Gulfstream III. It has intercontinental capabilities. We could fly to Paris in it."

"Good idea."

The pilot taxied to the end of the runway. The rain pounded the windows. The plane rocked in the wind. Suddenly we were racing down the runway and off into the dark. Chicago had vanished almost immediately after we left the ground. My husband was clutching the armrests tightly.

Takeoff at 6:00. Into the general aviation airport in Maryland a little before 8:30 local time. Our appointment was at 9:30. Tight squeeze?

"Where is Mary Margaret when we need someone to say the Rosary?"

I can never tell whether my husband is joking about airplanes or whether they really frighten him. He is, however, a very poor traveler. If we staggered into the Fed's office and he vomited on them, it would be most unfortunate.

Then we shoot through the clouds and climb into the pink sky of sunrise. Old Sol himself suddenly shoots above the horizon turning our cabin red and gold.

"Who turned on that bright light?" Chuck demands.

Janet brings us a great breakfast, complete with English muffins, omelets, bacon, orange juice, grapefruit slices, toast, and jam. I prepare Chuck's muffins for him.

"That's strawberry jam," he protests.

"Eat it anyway."

He eats all of his breakfast and half of mine. Then he leans back contentedly and sleeps all the way to Maryland. Sometimes I think he enjoys consuming breakfast as much as he enjoys consuming me.

Since mothers worry, I spend some of my time worrying, not so much about our caper since I know we'll pull that off, but about my kids. We told them at home that we'd be away all day and back in the late evening. No details. Miss Nosey Parker lifts her red eyebrows in suspicion. She knows we're up to something that we probably shouldn't be, but since we're adults, she doesn't ask any questions. She and Erin will feed themselves and Shovie in our absence. Erin will try to take charge because she's the employee. Mary Margaret, shrewd little precinct captain that she is, won't resist that decision but will help her in such a way that she does half the work.

Erin is reluctant to respond to Seano's interest. It's a class thing. She's a domestic servant and he the scion of the family. She's read too many English novels. The Crazy O'Malleys don't care about such things. Our eldest son is married to a Mexican-American woman who gives her children Latino names that refer to us—Juan Carlos and Maria Rosa. Chuck insists she call him Don Carlos, which she laughingly does, and I become Donna Rosa. Erin doesn't draw any conclusions from that, poor kid. Hopefully she will.

As the Good April often says, "Everyone can't be Irish, but they're just as good as we are anyway." Except that Erin is Irish.

One time at the country club, an obnoxious commodity trader made a crack about "that little spic's tits" when he was standing behind Chucky. My husband floored him with one quick punch. The guy threatened to have us thrown out of the club, but ended up quitting himself.

I don't know where my husband, sleeping peacefully next to

me and looking like the adorable little boy that he usually is, ever learned that punch. Mary Margaret has offered to teach him the black belt stuff, but Chucky says he doesn't need it.

I also worried a little about Mary Margaret. She had caught me off guard in her question about whether I was an alcoholic. The other kids had asked less direct questions like, "Mom, why don't you drink." And I would reply with limited truth, "I had trouble with it when I was younger and just gave it up." That was all they needed to hear and all they wanted to hear. But Mary Margaret was more probing. I gave her a more detailed answer, which satisfied her for the moment. She might come back later for more details, some of which she wouldn't want to hear, especially about her half brother Karl, who was a pilot for Lufthansa. Or maybe she would want to hear it. Could she imagine what it would be like to be a few months out of Fenwick and a member of an Army of Occupation? Could she picture the loneliness? And the astonishing stories of Chucky's capers in Bamberg—all the lives he had touched? Maybe she could. I'd have to play that by ear. I would be rigorous with myself about telling her the truth, but only as much truth as she demanded.

I glance over the outline of our "presentation" to the Feds. Chuck had outlined our respected arguments. He's the bad cop, I'm the good cop, which I think is a mistake in casting, but what do I know? If the Feds are guilty about what they've done to Bride Mary O'Brien or if they are sufficiently afraid of Chucky, we'll do okay.

The plane begins to descend. Janet clears away breakfast. The pilot says we will land in Maryland on time. We circle over Chesapeake Bay, a splash of blue under the Indian summer sun, and slip into the airport at Simpsonville. We tell the crew we'll be back about 11:30. They promise lunch and an ETA Santa Rosa at about 3:00 Santa Rosa time.

A limo is waiting for us on the runway. Two local security people, both very dignified Nigerian students at George Washington University bow us into the car. They are to drive us to Dupont Circle and wait in Chevy Chase till we return.

At Dupont Circle, there is a Benz with two Reliable Security people from Chicago who will drive us the few blocks to our destination and drive us away afterward. They phone a confirmation to Mike Casey in Chicago. Chuck and I are astonishingly relaxed.

"I hope the lunch is as good as the breakfast," he says as we pull up to the obscure and worn little office building on Massachusetts Avenue just off I Street. Now I begin to worry. Will we ever get back to the plane?

The handsome man at the security desk looked at us suspiciously.

"Ambassador O'Malley and Ms. Clancy to see Colonel Chandler."

He pondered Chuck's passport very carefully.

"Where are you ambassador to?" he demanded, his accent pure hill country.

"Currently without a post. You'll see my name on your list."

The White House barrier all over again?

"What's on the list is my business, sir."

"Not when my name is on it."

"You don't look like an ambassador to me."

Chuck sighed loudly.

"Neither did Adlai Stevenson."

"Who are you, ma'am?" He glanced at my driver's license with contempt.

I almost said that I was the woman who slept with the ambassador. But we didn't have time to waste with this jerk.

"It says who I am—Rosemarie Helen Clancy."

"Yes, ma'am . . . I can read even if I am a redneck. What is your relationship to the ambassador."

Again I curtailed my wit.

"His wife, sir, of almost thirty years."

He seemed skeptical.

"Tell you what, Officer. Either you call the colonel's office and tell him we're here or I'll knock out a few of your front teeth. That will create a crisis and you'll lose your job."

He picked up the phone and punched in three numbers.

"There's a man down here who claims to be an ambassador and a woman he claims is his wife . . . O'Malley, that's the name all right . . . He don't look like any fucking ambassador . . . All right, I'll send him up."

"Third floor," he said ominously.

"I know where it is . . . You may lose your job anyway."

There was no sign naming the offices on the third floor. An officious woman met us at the elevator and said that Colonel Chandler would be right with us.

Chuck glanced at his watch.

"Our appointment was at 9:30."

"It's 9:35."

"We would have been punctual if it weren't for that fucking asshole downstairs. Tell the colonel I expect to see him immediately."

Chuck was putting on one of his acts. I had almost never heard him use that language, much less to a woman. She scurried back down a corridor and came back.

"Come with me, please," she said reproachfully.

The offices along the corridor were occupied by men and women, busily shuffling through papers.

William Chandler had put on a little weight and lost a little hair since Bonn. However, he still radiated genial, aromatic charm.

"Chuck, Rosie, great to see you again," he said, leaping up from his steel, government-issue desk. "It's been a long time."

He extended a hand which Chucky didn't take.

"What the fuck kind of asshole operation you running around here, Bill? Your security guard downstairs tries to keep us from getting up here and insults my wife. Your secretary gives me the Colonel-Chandler-is-busy stall. Is this how efficient our intelligence community is these days?"

He sank back into his chair like someone whose balloon had been pierced by a pin.

"I'm sorry, Chuck. Because we're so secret we don't exercise too much clout on picking our support staff. We pretty much take what the government gives us. I really am sorry. I've wanted an excuse to get rid of that guy downstairs. Now I have it . . . Would you like a cup of coffee?"

"Tea for both of us, please, Bill. . . . Simmer down, Chucky. It wasn't Bill's fault."

"Same fucking idiocy over at the White House."

Chandler left the room. He was one of the top intelligence people in DC but he had to make his own tea. A penalty for not being out at Langley or over at the FBI. There were costs one had to pay for top secrecy.

He came back shortly with a teapot which was probably a family antique and two elaborate china cups. As he poured the tea, he said to me, "How are all your wonderful children, Rosie, especially that little redhead who was so fluent in German?"

I was now to be the good cop.

"They're fine. The little redhead is still fluent in German and graduates from college this spring. There's an even smaller redhead who is going off to grammar school. The oldest two are married, both with two children and expecting a third. Kevin Patrick is finishing his dissertation at the University of Chicago in musicology. Jimmy will be ordained in the spring. Seano is, I think, in love with an Irish immigrant. We can't complain."

"The little redhead still knows everything?"

"And everything else besides . . . Actually, she's a dear."

"Glad to hear it . . . Chucky, congratulations on your photo of the president. Has him just right. I hear you provided him with some interesting insights."

Chuck pretended to relax.

"He didn't seem to take what I said very seriously."

"Most of our people in the various agencies wouldn't buy it either. But some of us think you may just be right."

"I am," Chuck said, "just you wait and see."

"Ten bucks on it?"

"Agreed. 1991 a cutoff date?"

"Fair enough . . . Now what can we do for you this morning?"

Chuck pretended to hesitate.

"First thing. If you or your friends have any inclination to sanction us for what I'm going to say, I warn you that all our information is hidden in several secret places you'll never find and that we have already prepared a press release."

He looked startled. He remembered the dictum from the Bonn days—never fuck around with Chuck O'Malley. He can be real mean.

"Chuck, I don't know what you're talking about . . . We wouldn't dream of sanctioning you, no matter what you said or did. You're too well known."

"So was Jack Kennedy."

"You know we didn't do that."

"I've never been sure about that . . . You certainly tried to get Fidel Castro."

"I give you that, but it was because Bob Kennedy forced us to. You're safe no matter what you want . . . But what do you want?"

"I want you to deliver Bride Mary O'Brien and her daughter to her husband by 5:00 P.M. local time today. Otherwise, all hell will break loose."

"Who?" he said as his facial expression took on an image of a man utterly flabbergasted. Unfortunately, the brief quirk of fear came first. A vein in his neck was twitching.

"You know who I mean. She's probably up in your safe house in Rosetta. It should not be hard to drive her down to the wine country this afternoon."

"I've never heard of Bride Mary O'Brien."

"That wasn't the name with which she was born. When she came in out of the cold you gave her that identity, which you lifted from an Irish immigrant in exchange for a green card. She's called Kathleen N. Houlihan now and also Ms. Sean O'Shea. Her husband is a Kerryman. Your cowboys were too dumb to get the allusion. Don't worry. We didn't talk to her. So you don't have to worry about sanctioning her."

"We wouldn't do that . . ."

"And you better not think of sanctioning the second Bride Mary either, though some of your cowboys might want to do that now that Bill Casey is the head of the CIA."

"You have murder on the brain, Chucky. We don't do that anymore, at least not very often."

"I want to establish that, if your guys didn't learn it in Bonn or Saigon, it is not wise to fuck around with me."

"I think we did learn it, but I don't know what you're talking about."

The pallor that had crept over his face revealed that Chuck had terrified him.

"Let me clarify the story for you, Colonel. The woman whom you are holding in durance vile up at Rosetta House—is the head man there Mr. Jackson still or is that a name for whoever is in charge?—and who is known now as Bride Mary O'Brien is an American, probably born in Ireland, who did something very brave as a young woman for you and your playmates. I don't care what it was or what her name was. At some point you pulled her in out of the cold, perhaps as a reward for her bravery or, more likely, because you weren't sure she would be able to withstand torture if the other side lifted her . . ."

"Nobody holds up under torture these days," he said quietly.

"Regardless. You gave her a new name, probably did some cosmetic surgery, and set her free—as free as anyone can be with you spooks watching her every move. The cowboys who supervised her were scared. She had done too much. She knew too much. What if she decided to write a memoir? What if someone turned her? They didn't want to let her go. They wanted a tragic accident to occur. The rules said that could not be done and a lot of you thought that if she died there might be an investigation of what had happened. So you called the cowboys off and warned them of ultimate sanction if they harmed her."

"This is all fiction, Chuck," he said sadly. "None of it's true."

"Then a couple of years ago, with Stan Turner out of the show and Bill Casey to take over if Reagan was elected, the cowboys came back. She was a walking time bomb. All right we can't kill her. But let's lift her for a while, at least until some of the danger goes away. They figured that eventually they could squeeze authorization for termination with extreme prejudice. Dope her and the little girl up, take them a hundred miles over the ocean in a helicopter, and dump them, just like the cowboys did in 'Nam."

"We'd never do that!"

"The hell you wouldn't! You lifted them from their home. Your guys came over the hills behind the house. Drugged the two of them and took them to Rosetta in a copter. Do you still paint them black . . . ?"

"You can't prove any of this!"

"I don't have to prove it, Colonel. I just have to say it."

"What do you want?"

"Ah, now we get down to business . . . I want the two prisoners returned to their home by end of business California time today—5:00. I want a signed promise that she will be left alone by you spooks permanently. I want a signed statement admitting what happened. And I want a check to her for a million dollars in reparation for the harm of incarceration."

"Her husband is rich. They don't need the money."

Confession!

"And they very likely won't want it and won't take it. But you'd better offer it to them . . . I want a confirmation call by three o'clock Chicago time to this Chicago number . . . Rosemarie . . ."

I gave him a sheet of notepaper with the number of an answering machine in the locked darkroom at our house and a message "The deliverables will be delivered on time."

"If it's not there by 3:05, we give a preliminary signal that the press releases should go out. They will go to the various media outlets at 9:00 DC time unless we tell our people to stop, 6:00 local time if you're having trouble with some of your people. That will give you a one-hour period of grace."

"What press release?"

"Would you read it to him, Rosemarie?"

Washington

An American hero of the Cold War has been held prisoner in a CIA safe house in northern California for more than two years, according to Charles Cronin O'Malley, former ambassador of the United States to Bonn and one of the "wise men" who counseled President Johnson about the Vietnam War. The woman, known now as Bride Mary O'Brien was "brought in from the cold," according to Ambassador O'Malley, because it was feared that her capture by the enemies of the United States would reveal many

Cold War secrets. The government gave the young woman a new name, plastic surgery, and a real estate business in California. Subsequently she married and bore a child. She and her husband owned a vineyard in the Napa Valley of California.

At the time of her rescue, Ambassador O'Malley said, some elements of the intelligence community disagreed with the policy. They argued that her work was so sensitive and that her secrets were so dangerous to the security of the United States that she should be eliminated—terminated with extreme prejudice, in the terms of the trade. This plan was rejected because the American intelligence community, the ambassador said, takes care of its own, especially when their own have been heroes who have served their country at enormous personal risk.

Then on April 15, 1970, Ms. O'Brien and her three-year-old child Samantha were "lifted" from her vineyard. The two seemed to have disappeared from the face of the earth. However, according to Ambassador O'Malley, they were taken to a "safe house," a well-known intelligence community prison in California called Rosetta House.

The little girl was held hostage, as was Ms. O'Brien's husband, whom Ms. O'Brien's captors threatened to eliminate if she made any attempts to escape.

Probably, O'Malley said, the change in policy was the result of a turnover in intelligence leadership and the anticipation of a new administration in Washington which would be more concerned about Cold War security.

"In a couple of months," he said "they will take her and her daughter Samantha on a flight out over the Pacific Ocean and push them off the helicopter as they did many Viet Cong prisoners during the Vietnam War. It will be a terrible death for an American patriot who was willing to give her life in the service of her country."

"You're bluffing, Chucky," Colonel Chandler said through clenched teeth. "You have no evidence."

He leaned forward over his desk, tense, pale, and angry.

"Once this story hits the papers," Chuck said, "it doesn't matter whether I have evidence or not. However, a persuasive dossier will follow the release of this document to all the major news sources in the country. Would you read them the last paragraph of the second release, Rosemarie."

"Sure," I said calmly.

> Ambassador and Mrs. O'Malley disappeared late Monday. Friends expressed fear that they had been taken prisoner or perhaps shot by government agents.

Colonel Chandler exploded from his desk, his face red with fury.

"You fucking cocksucker. You can't say that."

"If any of our fail-safe contacts are not made, then that goes out too. You'd better pray hard, Billy Boy, that our guardian angels protect us from your cowboys!"

He sank back into his chair, a man defeated. It was time for the good cop to make her pitch.

"I'm surprised, Colonel Chandler, that you don't seem to grasp that we're on your side. We could just as easily have called a press conference and told them this story . . . Maybe in front of your Rosetta House jail. We could have spread all your dirty linen out for the whole world to see. This way we free Bride Mary O'Brien without any publicity and protect you folks while you put your house in order. Instead of getting into a macho argument with my husband, you ought to be grateful for the deal we're offering you. If you free that poor woman today before anyone can harm her, there's no publicity and a lot less chance that you and the boys over at the Bureau or out at Langley will end up with egg on your faces."

"You haven't figured out what she did for us?"

"We don't need to know and we don't want to know. You can count on it; however, if we let this story out, someone will find out and there'll be even more scandal that she's been held in prison for two years because she loves her country. Mr. Casey will be out of the CIA immediately and the rest of you will be looking for jobs."

I make a very good *good* cop.

"I figure she was in Indonesia," Chuck said—another one of his uncanny psychic guesses.

"Don't guess any further," the colonel snapped.

"We don't have to," I said pleasantly. "We know all we need to know."

Chandler pulled off his tie and took a deep breath.

"Chuck, why couldn't you have just come in here and talked to us like we all were civilized human beings? Why all the aggressive threats?"

"Surely you know the answer to that, Billy Boy. Long ago I learned that one does not deal with your kind without credible threat. I don't trust you or the FBI or the CIA or any other spooks. You would be reluctant to let your cowboys throw a national hero in the Pacific from two thousand feet. And her little daughter. But you'd let it happen for the good of the country or for the good of the intelligence community or whatever. You'd put us on the same helicopter with many tears and much guilt, but you'd still do it. I make no mistake that I'm dealing with a civilized human being . . . We have one more document that we need. Again it is for insurance—for us and for Ms. O'Brien and her husband. Would you read it please, Ms. Clancy?"

"I hereby acknowledge that certain elements in the intelligence community kidnapped a hero agent Ms. Bride Mary O'Brien and her daughter and held them as prisoners for two years. We profoundly regret this criminal behavior and promise that it will never happen again and that we will provide permanent protection for Ms. O'Brien and her family."

Chandler closed his eyes, rubbed the sweat off his forehead, and swallowed.

"I can't sign off on any of this. We'll have to go upstairs and talk to the director."

"I assumed we would."

He picked up the phone.

"Ambassador O'Malley is here, sir, with a very interesting proposition. I think you'd better speak to him."

"NOW!" Chucky insisted.

"He says now, sir, I think we'd better do it now."

We rode up the creaky elevator and walked down a corridor just like the one on the previous floor. The door of the office at the end of the corridor was wide-open. Colonel Chandler knocked tentatively.

"Come in, Bill," said a man with a hearty voice. "And you too, Ambassador O'Malley. I've been looking forward to meeting you. And you too, Ms. Clancy. I love your stories in *The New Yorker.* They're classic Irish tales."

He was a tall slender man with curly black hair shading toward white at the earlobes and a brilliant smile. His accent was New England and Harvard. Totally secure and in command of himself. We shook hands. Fifth-generation WASP aristocrat.

"I must tell you, Ambassador, that your picture of Ronnie was perfect. I also heard, though not from the White House exactly, your advice to him. I've been awake the last couple of nights wondering if you perhaps are right."

"I must warn you, sir, that my wife and I have taken precautions that our lives will not be at risk. We have a number of contact points along the way. If we do not leave this building in twenty minutes, for example, an alarm will immediately be sounded somewhere and you and the intelligence community will be in deep trouble."

He dismissed the prospect with a wave of his hand.

"Ambassador, I am not a cowboy. Even if I were, I have enough sense not to mess around with you. Your reputation comes before you . . . What do these people want, Billy?"

"Bride Mary O'Brien by 5:00 this afternoon, local time."

He raised a carefully shaped eyebrow.

"My hat's off to you, Ambassador. I don't know how you know this story, but I'm impressed that you do."

"He knows it all, sir, except what she did for us and her real name."

"And we don't need to know either," I said, "and don't want to know. All we want is that she be freed. Today."

He sighed.

"That is a perfectly reasonable request, Ms. Clancy. I trust you will not be writing this story for *The New Yorker.*"

"Can't tell," I said, smiling sweetly. "It would make an excellent story. Here are two press releases which, in the absence of freedom for Ms. O'Brien and her daughter by 5:00 local time, will be faxed to the major media outlets of the country."

He read the two of them quickly.

"The president would have been much better advised to make you head of CIA than that old warhorse that's up there now . . . What else do you want, Ms. Clancy?"

Chucky was perfectly happy to let me take the lead.

"We want this letter signed." I handed the letter over to him.

He glanced at it, read it a second time, and shrugged.

"Reparations to Ms. O'Brien and her family?"

"They'll want a million dollars."

"Could probably hold us up for more . . . That's all?"

"If you sign it, it will be your promise that henceforth your cowboys will not threaten Bride Mary O'Brien and her family."

"You might have added to your press release that she was awarded secretly the Medal of Honor for her work . . . Billy, I told you I don't like this sort of thing. Why didn't we leave them alone?"

"I recommended against it sir. You were not sitting in that chair then."

"You said local time, Billy. Ms. Clancy, you mean DC time?"

"California time."

"That's eight hours from now, isn't it, Bill?"

"Yes, sir."

"Plenty of time to get some of our people up there from LA?"

"Yes, sir."

"Okay, let's get it rolling."

He signed the letter with a flourish and gave it back to me. "Adam Cain." Never trust anyone named Cain?

"When you can confirm that everything is in proper motion," Chuck interrupts my little conversation with Mr. Cain, "please call this number and leave the following message on the answering machine: 'the deliverables are being delivered.' Say by 4:00 DC time. Otherwise, we will go into our faxing mode. Don't try to trace the number because you won't be able to do it."

"Always prudent, Ambassador . . . We should certainly have our own resources in place by then . . . Now do you want us to defray your expenses in this matter?"

Chucky stood up, extended his hand, and said, "Always a pleasure to do business with you, sir."

Cain laughed. He really had not expected us to want a bribe.

"I hope our mutual friends will take care to be discreet."

"We can't guarantee anything." I regained my proper role in this conversation. "We will counsel them to discretion, however. Besides, as you well know, the so-called Bride Mary O'Brien is a great American patriot. That's usually an incurable disease."

He smiled wryly, shook hands with me, and we left his office.

The flow of adrenaline through my veins turned off and I just wanted to lie down.

Chapter Twenty-Four

Chuck

"Two good cops wrapping up a deal," I said to my gorgeous wife, as we rode down the creaky elevator. "You make a great good cop. You'd be an earthquake as a bad cop. Eight points on the Richter scale."

"Do you trust him?"

"No, do you?"

"Too smooth, Chuck, too smooth. On the other hand he may realize that either we hold all the cards—which we do—or that it's not worth the effort to fight us."

We emerged into the warmth of DC Indian summer, which is more humid than our Chicago version. Our limo pulled up. I looked carefully at the man who got out and opened the door for us. Same fellow. The driver was the same too. Two white Chicago cops to be replaced at Chevy Chase Circle by two Nigerian security guards, probably Nigerian army officers on the run.

"Send the signal to Mr. Casey, sir?"

"By all means."

The signal would tell Mike Casey that we had escaped the building. We'd send another signal from the airport.

"Let me know if anyone is chasing us."

"Yes, sir. No one now."

Rosemarie and I were exhausted and the day had only begun. I glanced at my watch: 10:55. Our confrontation with the Feds had taken an hour and twenty minutes, not counting the disagreement with the cop at the door. Maybe it was his job to be rude, another spook trick. We should be airborne by 11:30. A six-and-a-half-hour flight would put us into the Santa Rosa Airport before 3:00 local time. Half hour to get to the Valley. Plenty of time.

This was the most potentially dangerous part of the trip. I didn't really believe that the Feds would try to kill us in the District. We didn't have to be present for the return of Bride Mary and Samantha. If the cowboys brought them back only to kill the whole family, there wasn't much we could do except witness it. They might want to kill us too. Abel Cain, as I persisted in thinking of him, knew that if our fail-safe message did not come through, the faxes would begin to roll and his career would be finished. Did he really control the cowboys?

Did he suspect that we would be present at the exchange? If he were as smart as I thought he was, he would certainly suspect it. Did he want the cowboys to gun us down?

Maybe Abel Cain was himself a cowboy.

Probably not. But who could say for sure? Me and my big ideas.

We were at Chevy Chase Circle. The exchange went smoothly. Our first drivers would send a second signal to Mike Casey.

"Weather will be good for another hour or so," the new driver said in a clipped British accent. "You should get out before the front comes through."

I looked up. Since we'd left I Street, a cloud cover had seeped over DC. We had better not be delayed.

"Should I call ahead and tell your pilot you will be there by 11:30?"

"Fine idea."

"No one following us?"

"No, sir."

"Did we really do that act, Chucky dear?"

My wife was slumped in the seat next to me, looking worn and tasty.

"No, it was all a bad dream."

I put my arm around her shoulders. She snuggled against me. Dear God, how could I possibly deserve such a woman?

"No shooting yet . . ."

"No way there's going to be shooting."

I had been tempted to bring along a gun of some sort, just in case. There were two reasons for not doing so: I didn't own a gun. I wouldn't know what to do with one if I did own it. In my inglorious years in the First Constabulary I was a notoriously poor shot.

"You were wonderful," I said to Rosemarie. "I couldn't have asked for a better Dr. Watson."

She thought that was very funny. I held her more closely.

At the airport I found a public phone and made another call to the answering machine. "Redeploying" was the code message this time.

We climbed into the Gulfstream. The pilot greeted us with his big pilot smile.

"We'll climb over the front quickly. Some strong headwinds as far as the Mississippi, then smooth sailing. Estimate Santa Rosa at 2:45 local time."

"Grand!" I said, helping Rosemarie to her seat.

The takeoff was smooth. These little jets did not need much runway to get in the air. It would be nice to have one . . . No, it wouldn't. You could get sick in one of them just as easily. Besides, the Great Depression might come back . . .

"Buy me one of these, Rosemarie," I said.

"Stick with Shovie's little model trains."

A man gets no respect.

Janet asked us if we wanted a drink. Rosemarie wanted a glass of iced tea. I ordered a Bushmill's Green straight up.

"Would Jameson's do just as well, Mr. O'Malley?"

"It would do just fine."

"Remember what Irish whiskey does to your daughter."

"I didn't order a double."

"Where did we find her, Chucky Ducky?"

"I'm not sure. She's trying to elbow you out of your senior matriarch role."

"I was never that . . . that vigorous when I was her age . . . except when I was drinking."

"The kid is really something. Poor Joe Moran doesn't know what he's courting."

"Oh, I think he does . . . She's a real prize, Chucky. She'll drive her husband crazy, but he'll adore her."

"Just like her mother."

Sometimes I think that Mary Margaret is what Rosemarie would have been if she had grown up in a reasonably normal family.

Janet brought the most astonishing steak sandwich I had ever seen, along with my Jameson's.

"Would you like some wine with lunch, Mr. O'Malley?"

Rosemarie cocked an eye at me.

"Maybe with dinner," I said. "On the way back to Chicago."

My wife giggled.

"You have to be alert if we're going to finish this caper."

I am a notorious short hitter. On my wedding day I drank far too much champagne, a failing she does not permit me to forget. I sipped my Jameson's very carefully. I didn't think it was as strong as Green Bush. But what did I know?

I polished off my sandwich and half of Rosemarie's.

"You're going to take a nap and leave me with the draft of my *New Yorker* article," she said with a tone of reproach.

"Yep. The warrior routs the bad guys. Eats and drinks, has a good nap, then goes out looking for captive matrons to ravish."

"No captive matrons on this flight."

"Not yet. Later maybe. Wake me at 4:00 DC time."

"Yes, master."

I don't know whether the Jameson's or the exertions of battle were responsible for the depth of my sleep, but I plunged into the inner reaches of my soul. It was not a restful sleep. I think a lot of matrons were chasing me around with knives, but I don't remember exactly what they were planning. I managed to keep ahead of them.

I woke up once and looked around desperately for my Rosemarie. She too was napping, notes and glasses on her lap. She looked peaceful and happy. Where were we anyway? How had I got on this tiny plane? Why? Then I remembered and realized that I was a fool to involve us at our age in life in this crazy adventure. I wanted to be home with my wife and children, sipping iced tea.

I looked at my watch. Three o'clock Chicago time. One o'clock San Francisco time. There was something I should do . . . Oh yes, call our answering machine. I pushed the call button and asked Janet for the telephone. I called the number of my line in the darkroom. I was informed that no such number existed. Frantically, I redialed and got the same reaction.

Then I looked at my pocket notebook and realized that I had juxtaposed two numbers. Brilliant special-op. Carefully I tried a third time and heard Shovie's voice with the message. Then I keyed in a number to hear incoming messages. There was only one.

"Adam Cain here, Ambassador. The deliverables are being delivered."

Either they were cooperating or they were sustaining the lie.

The cobwebs continued to block my brain. Too much Jameson's. I was supposed to do something. Oh, yes. Call Vince's answering machine. This time Rita's silky voice gave the message.

"The deliverables are being delivered. Next check in from Santa Rosa Airport."

Vince was probably waiting for the message. He'd wait another hour, call Joe Raftery, and tell him that we were in the Bay Area and would visit him about three, just to say hello. No hint about the game we were playing. I'd check on our answering machine in hope of a confirmation. I did not want to have to deal directly with the cowboys from Rosetta.

I went to the bathroom in the rear of the plane, small but efficient. I splashed my face with water, swilled my mouth with Scope, and opened the door of the room with some difficulty.

Rosemarie was waiting in line at the door.

"I had visions of you locked in there forever," she said with notable lack of sympathy.

I turned to my proof sheets while my wife worked again on her notes. We were both in a surly mood from our interrupted naps.

An hour after my message to Vince. I called our answering machine again. Abel Cain's voice was on the machine, but not Vince. I tried at fifteen-minute intervals and there was still no confirmation.

"There's some buildup over the ocean. Fog drifting into San Francisco. Santa Rosa not threatened. But headwinds are stronger than expected. ETA now 3:05."

I adjusted my watch to Pacific Coast Time. Rosemarie did the same without my telling her. But I had scored points because she didn't have to remind me.

We circled interminably in the clouds above Santa Rosa. Finally, at 3:15, I found Vince on the answering machine.

"Confirm Friar awaits visitors."

"Friar" was the name of the Fenwick football team, a product placement for the Dominican Friars who teach at Fenwick.

"He's home waiting for us," I told Rosemarie. "I'll be glad when this is over."

"I think the real fun is just beginning."

I asked Janet to arrange for a cab to take us down California 21 to the St. Brigid's winery. She confirmed the cab a few moments later. It would be waiting for us. As we broke through the clouds and saw the valleys and the hills of the wine country spread out beneath us, I called Vince for the final time.

"Eagle is landing at Santa Rosa. Eagle is landing at Santa Rosa."

We landed at 3:35.

The pilot apologized for the delay. Traffic and weather. The flight back to Chicago would be an easy one. They'd nap in the plane and be ready for us at 7:00. Back in Chicago a little after midnight.

The cab driver said he would have us at Brigid by 4:20. We were cutting it awfully close. What if the cowboys arrived before 5:00. Not very likely.

Still . . .

Chapter Twenty-Five

Chuck

Joe Raftery watched the two black cars pull up in front of his house and onto his gravel driveway, a trail of dust settling behind them. His heart was pounding. They had roared down the dirt road, coming out of the setting October sun. Three men got out of the first car. They were wearing black suits and black hats. One of them opened the left front door. A man in a black hat and sunglasses emerged, looking very tough.

Joe walked out of the door, pondered the situation from his wide porch, waited a few moments, then slowly ambled down the steps. He must not be frightened. He must not lose his temper. He must not fight them. In fact, he must not say a word. He walked up to the man in the sunglasses. They stared at each other.

"Mr. Joseph Raftery?"

Joe nodded.

"I'm Mr. Jackson. I work for the government."

Joe nodded again.

The other three men gathered behind Jackson, like ushers at a wedding party. Their jackets bulged with weapons.

Joe wanted to kill everyone of them.

Someone opened the back door of the other car. A little girl, surely his daughter, pushed her way out and shouted, "Daddy!"

A woman, also in black, held the child so that she could not run.

"The government found it necessary to hold your wife in protective custody. It was for her protection and yours. We are directed to release her to you this afternoon."

He offered Joe an envelope. Joe stared at it but did not accept it. Jackson dropped it on the ground.

"You will read and sign this document."

Joe continued to stare at him. Jackson dropped the document. It fell on the gravel next to the check.

A blond woman climbed out of the second car and pushed the woman who was holding the child. Samantha rushed across the gravel and clung to his leg.

"Daddy! Daddy! We're home!"

Bride Mary, thin and weary, but still herself, strode briskly toward them.

"Don't let them trick you into doing anything, Joe. That will give them the excuse to kill us all."

When she was only a yard or two away, one of the men in black grabbed her. Mr. Jackson slapped her face. Bride Mary twisted away from the man and embraced her husband.

"Not a word, darling! Not a word!"

"I leave you with a warning," Mr. Jackson said. "There are many people in the government who think this is a mistake. We will continue to watch you closely, not to protect you. We don't give a damn whether you three live or die. If we see any sign that you are preparing to betray us, we will eliminate you . . . Is that clear?"

Bride Mary spit in his face.

Jackson's body swelled with rage.

"It would be a great pleasure to eliminate you, bitch."

"Get out of here, you focking shite head. You're the one that's finished."

He turned to the car, waited for one of his thugs to open the door for him, and entered the car. Doors slammed and the little cavalcade backed out of the gravel driveway and sped off into the rapidly setting sun.

"Got it all, Rosemarie?" I said to my wife, who was presiding over a cassette tape recorder with earphones.

"Of course I do," she snapped.

How dare I question her skills as an antispook.

"Let's hear the end."

She reversed it, then pushed the PLAY button.

"It would be a great pleasure to eliminate you, bitch."

"Nicely done."

"And you?"

"Two and a half roles of Minox film, including the slap."

We shook hands, left Samantha's nursery, and walked down the stairs. The Raftery family was locked in one intense embrace.

Joe looked up.

"Bride Mary, this is my fellow fighting Friar, Chuck O'Malley, and his wife Rosemarie, a woman who is much too good for him. Somehow or the other they engineered this!"

Bride Mary embraced both of us. Sam climbed into Rosemarie's arms.

"You beat the cowboys!"

I picked up the phone and called Vince's answering machine.

"Friars beat Carmel!" I said.

"Did you get the whole thing?" he asked us.

"Every word is on the tape."

"Two and a half rolls of Minox film," I said, putting the three rolls into a camera bag and entrusting it to Special Agent Rosemarie Helen Clancy. "We used your room, Sam, to take pictures of those bad men. They won't bother you again."

"What's in this envelope?" Joe asked.

"Probably a check for a million dollars, a settlement so you won't sue. The other paper, the one you didn't sign, is likely a waiver excusing the government from more suits."

He opened the envelope.

"It is really a million dollars . . . Is it tax free, Chucky?"

"I doubt it."

He tore the check in two pieces and gave it to me. "When you send your pictures and your recording include this."

Joe and Bride Mary wanted to make us supper, but we told them that we had to return to Chicago. Joe insisted that he open a bottle of their best vintage.

My wife said she'd settle for a cup of tea. We toasted one another.

"Great wine!" I said.

"We'll send you a case!"

"I won't refuse."

"Take this bottle along." He gave us a second bottle.

"He won't refuse that either. The only problem, Bride Mary, is that me husband is a short hitter, if you take me meaning."

The phone rang. Joe answered it.

"A man named Adam Cain wants to speak to Ambassador O'Malley if he's here."

"I'm not here."

He chuckled.

"The delivery was without incident?"

"We're all sitting around the table celebrating so it went well, but there were some awkward moments. Your man Jackson threatened to eliminate the whole family if there was any sign of betrayal. I believed he called Ms. O'Brien a bitch, but the latter with typical Irish feistiness called him a focking shite head."

"Mommy never talks like that," Sam insisted.

"Too bad you don't have any pictures of the exchange."

"We've not known each other very long, Adam, but you certainly know me better than that."

"Tape recording?" he asked as if he didn't believe that would be possible.

"Perfect, the good wife got every word in moderately high fidelity. We'll send it to you by courier tomorrow morning."

"I said earlier today that Ronnie ought to have sent you to Langley instead of the old OSS warhorse cowboy who's sitting out there now. I can only repeat that comment."

"I think Rosemarie would probably be better at it than I am, sir. Stronger stomach."

We both laughed.

"We must have dinner next time you're in the District."

He gave me his phone numbers.

"Do you think Bride Mary would speak with me?"

"I'm sure she would."

"Mr. Cain would like to speak to you, Bride Mary. He is the one that pulled this off."

"Helped to pull it off," my wife corrected me.

"Certainly . . . Yes sir . . ."

She stood at attention, a subaltern talking to her commanding officer.

"Thank you, sir. That's very kind of you . . . I'll keep the secret until I hear from your office that it is no longer a secret . . . Yes, we appreciate that promise very much . . . It's nice to be in out of the cold again . . . I agree, sir, Ambassador O'Malley is a remarkable person . . . I'll be looking forward to that . . . Good-bye."

"We have to catch an airplane," I said. "Would you call us a cab?"

"Better than that, We'll give you a ride."

I took a second bottle of wine off the rack.

"For Vince . . . he operated our home base."

"Then two extra for you and one for him."

He drove their old Buick around the house and we piled in.

"Three more bottles for your aircrew."

"Do you have the bag with the film and the recorder, Chuck?" my wife asked.

"Why should I have it" I replied "when I was after seeing you pick it up?"

"Will someone please explain to me what this is all about?"

"When your wife was a very young woman, probably just out of college, she had a different name and did incredibly brave work for the United States. Chuck and I don't know her real name or what she did and we don't want to know. The government was worried about her and brought her in from the cold and gave her a new identity and set her up in life, as a woman of property as the Irish call it and like most of us she was very good at it. Some of the people she had worked for were worried that she might go public with her story. So they lifted her, probably without the permission of her superiors. They probably intended to kill her, but the superiors forbade that. So she was kept in limbo for the last couple of years. I think eventually the cowboys would have disposed of her when no one was looking . . . Is that a good summary, Bride Mary?"

" 'Tis . . . I'm sorry I couldn't be telling you, me darling, but I couldn't. I thought it was all over. I guess it wasn't."

"One thing we can tell you," I said, "is that they awarded her the Medal of Honor, which they don't usually give to spooks."

"I'm proud of you, Bride," her husband said. "My head is whirling, but I'm proud of you."

"I would never be a spook again," Bride Mary said. "Wasn't I young and foolish in them days?"

"Mr. Cain promised you that he'd protect you in the future, didn't he?" I asked.

"I don't think I'd believe any of those bastards."

"Oh you can believe him all right," Rosemarie said. "Chucky has enough documentation to put the story on the front page of every newspaper in the country and on all the networks . . . Including the material we collected tonight . . . Did I tell you, Sam, that I have a daughter about your age?"

"What's her name?"

"Siobhan Marie and we call her Shovie."

"That's a nice name."

"She's a lot like you. She's very pretty and she's very smart and she's very good."

"Always?"

"Well, practically always!"

So we chatted about other things on the way to the airport.

"What happened to the real Bride Mary?"

"All I know is that she's alive and married and is finishing her dissertation."

"Maybe we'll bump into each other someday."

We hugged at the airport. I promised that I would call in the morning and passed on all the relevant phone numbers. Rosemarie said we'd have to visit often in the years ahead.

I gave the wine bottles to the crew and we settled in for the night flight home.

"I remember what my dream was about this afternoon," I said to my wife.

"You were ravishing captive matrons."

"Yeah, but at the side of a swimming pool."

"That's what they're for, aren't they? . . . How many?"

"Pools?"

"No, how many captive matrons?"

"A lot, fifteen or twenty maybe!"

"You have a hard enough time with one, Chucky Ducky."

Janet served a splendid Dover sole. The faithless Rosemarie consumed every last piece of her dinner.

We arrived at Palwaukee at 1:30 and at our house on Euclid a little after 2:00. We still had to develop the films, make prints, and produce copies of Rosemarie's tapes.

Chapter Twenty-Six

Rosemarie

The light was on in my office.

"I must have left it on this morning," I said.

"Impossible," Chucky responded.

We were both tired and irritable and we had several hours of work ahead of us. I resolved that I would keep my bitchy mouth shut.

We peeked into the office.

Mary Margaret was curled up on my couch wearing a black-and-white "Rosary" sleep tee shirt and wrapped in an Irish throw. She looked like she was fourteen.

She opened her eyes and stared balefully at us.

"What time is it? Where you guys been? Why do you keep me up all night waiting for you and worrying about you?"

Chuck answered the questions in order.

"It's two o'clock in the morning, we've been around the country, so to speak, and we told you we'd be home late."

"Oh, yeah, now I remember. One of your mysterious projects . . . Uncle Vince said you should call him no matter how late you get in . . . Oh, gosh, I was so sleepy I forgot the bad news . . ."

"Which is . . . ?" I asked.

"Poor Aunt Jane is dead! I'm so sorry, so sorry!" she cuddled up in the couch next to me. We embraced one another and cried together.

Chuck collapsed into his "official" chair and buried his face in his hands.

"What happened?"

"I don't know for sure. I think she may have killed herself . . . They're all very angry."

"You went up there?"

"My friend Ted Junior called this afternoon in tears. He wanted us to know. Aunt Peg and Rita and Father Ed and I drove up together. It was horrible. Chris and Madeleine—she's the bitch he's going to marry and, Chucky, they deserve each other—were all over poor Uncle Ted. Chris said like someone ought to sue him for malpractice on this case. She didn't belong in that nuthouse. Jenny and Micky are screaming back at them and defending their father. They're like she was out of her mind. Where else could Dad put her? Uncle Ted just sits there like a truck ran over him. He keeps asking what he did wrong. Father Ed tells him he didn't do anything wrong. And he says he should never have brought her up to this neighborhood . . . I loved her so much, and Maddy says you had a hell of a way of showing it. Then they turn on poor Aunt Peg. It's all her fault. She drove their mom out of the family when she brought that bitch into the house . . . That's you, Mom."

"I imagine it is."

"It's not true . . . Don't pay any attention to them . . . She did try to kill me after all."

"We all must be forgiving, Mary Margaret," Chuck says.

"Father Ed finally calmed them all down. Gosh, he is truly a spectacular priest, isn't he?"

"Yes, he is," I said.

"Anyway before that happens Rita goes after Maddie and Chris. No one's going to attack her mom when she's around. She tells them they're spoiled brats who were never nice to their own mother and they better shut up about Aunt Peg or she'll scratch their eyes out . . . Poor Aunt Peg looks so sad. She remembers the good old days on Menard Avenue . . ."

I couldn't think straight. I never sensed that Jane resented me on Menard Avenue. She and Peg fought a little, but no more than other sisters their age. I never participated in the fights. I guess my problem was that I was there. I couldn't believe she was dead.

"What are the arrangements?" Chuck asked in a hushed voice.

"Wake tomorrow night—private, which doesn't mean anything at all. Every snob from the North Shore will be up there crowing over her."

"Mary Margaret," I said sternly.

"Sorry, Mom, but you know it's true. There's a 'small' funeral Wednesday morning. The girls want Father Ed to say it, he's her brother after all. Nutty Chris goes ballistic. Father Delahaye was her confessor, her spiritual director. He took better care of her than Uncle Ted does. It's settled that Father Ed will say the Mass, Father Delahaye will preach, and Chris will give the eulogy. He also makes it clear that he doesn't want any family music, which he says is blasphemous. None of us are to sing either—that means you, Mom."

My daughter hugs me and breaks down.

"It was one of the ugliest things I've ever seen, even worse than when poor Aunt Jane attacked Grams's house."

"Does Grams know?" I asked.

"Not yet; Aunt Peg is going to tell her in the morning. It's going to be a real nuthouse up there. I don't think she should go to the wake. Neither does Rita."

"It's her firstborn child, hon, she'll have to go."

"I guess you're right . . . You guys better get some sleep. It will be two more days from hell."

"We have work to do, hon!"

"You know what you'd say if I said that to you."

"Age has some privilege, Mary Margaret," says her father. "We have the right to act like idiots. But thanks for worrying about us."

She hugs us both and goes upstairs.

We go down to the darkroom and I remind Chucky to call Vince.

"Yes, Mother," he says with a giddy laugh.

"Hi, Vince. All went well. They don't know it yet but Joe and his wife and daughter are coming here for Thanksgiving . . . Yeah it was crazy, but we had to do it . . . I heard about it. Mary Margaret stayed up to tell us about the scene up there in Kenilworth in all its horrible details . . . Does Peg agree with me that

Mother has to go to the wake and the funeral? Poor Jane was her firstborn . . . Yeah, both our daughters disagree . . . They think they know everything . . . Remind you of any twosome we might know!"

"We were not that bossy, Charles Cronin O'Malley!"

"Yes, you were."

We go into the darkroom to develop the negatives.

"You did remember to take the lens caps off those things?"

"Yes, ma'am."

We worked silently and efficiently, a veteran team that is very effective as long as I keep my big mouth shut.

"We saved that marriage, didn't we, Rosemarie my darling? Or to put it more precisely you did when you talked Ted into resisting Doctor's pressure."

"That's true. That was one of our first capers. I persuaded Ted that he should marry the woman he loved whether Doctor approved or not. I wonder what he thinks about me now."

"He did love her and still loves her. They had good years together."

"Yes, Chuck. He'll always mourn her, not only what she was back when he came home from the war, but what she became when she moved up there . . . I shouldn't blame it on the neighborhood. She might have gone the same way if she'd stayed here on the West Side . . . Who knows? . . . It's over now anyway."

"She's home with Dad," he says, his voice choking.

The three rolls of film had turned out fine.

"You do the proof sheets. I'll copy the tape. How many should I make?"

"One to send to Abel Cain . . ."

"Adam, Chucky Ducky."

"Right. One for our archive here. One to go into the vault where we're going to put all this stuff in a couple of days. One for Vince. Four altogether We keep the master tape. Don't wreck it."

"Bastard." I kiss him as I leave the darkroom.

I was so tired I almost did ruin the master. I wrote "master—

Brigid Winery" on its label and instead of putting it in the deck which would be copied, I put it in the deck to write on. Some kindly angel stopped me before it was too late. We needed only three. Chucky has counted the master and the archive twice when they were the same tape. Yet I made four. I tested each one of them to make sure we had not lost anything in the copying. Our audiovisual stuff is pretty good, too good to let my husband near it.

I put each of the copies in envelopes and marked them—in my own flowing hand, as different from Chuck's small, precise script as it could possibly be. "It's good you're so beautiful," he said to me once. "Otherwise, I couldn't stay married to you with that kind of handwriting."

"Yours is that of an anal-retentive male."

I knocked on the door.

"Can I come in?"

"You can always come, Rosemarie my darling."

"You never turned the red light on."

He ignored me and showed me six proof sheets, two for each of the films. Our system was that each of us would mark the best shots as we saw them, then compare our choices. The correlation, Chucky once said, showing off his knowledge of statistics, was in excess of point nine.

I marked eight shots, the witch lady grabbing poor Sam, Jackson slapping Bride Mary, her spitting in his face, his expression of rage, little Sam running to her father, Jackson announcing who he was and what he wanted, the crowd of thugs closing around him, the hate on Jackson's face as he warned Bride Mary and Joe that they would never be safe.

"Let me see yours first," Chucky ordered.

"No way, you know the rules."

"You made the rule, I didn't."

We had marked exactly the same shots.

"Eight by ten, do you think?"

"Right, and, Chucky darling, crop them so we get the horror of their facial expressions."

"Two copies?"

"Maybe three would be better, Cain, our archives, and the vault. No four, one to send to the Rafterys."

"Okay. I'll print them and you might prepare the packages and call the courier service. We want them to pick up these two packages at seven-thirty in the morning."

The couriers had a twenty-four-hour service. Expensive, Chucky had argued once. It's a tax deduction, I told him.

I made another tape and put it in an envelope, which I labeled.

Then I called the courier phone and told the sleepy Hispanic woman who answered that I needed a pickup at seven-thirty. Documents and photographs. Yes, someone would be at the door. Which meant me.

I addressed the courier envelopes, slipped the envelopes with the tape into each of them, and put them on the table right next to each of the courier packs, a firm envelope for the photos.

Chuck yelled from the darkroom.

"Come on in."

"I want your judgment on my cropping, boss lady. This is the first set."

"You seemed to have done them well enough," I said. After a quick glance. "Not perfect but your work is never quite perfect."

I needled him often on this subject, because he thinks everything he does has to be perfect.

"Go with them?"

"Certainly . . . Chucky these pictures are frightening."

"It was a terrifying scene. I was afraid when Jackson hit Bride Mary that he wanted bloodshed. Then I would have to emerge on the front door with the pair of sawed-off shotguns Joe had left downstairs. I think we could have knocked off all four almost at once."

"Enough of this Rambo talk, Charles Cronin O'Malley . . . There weren't really shotguns downstairs, were there?"

"There were indeed. We would have had surprise on our side. I learned in the military that he who shoots first usually wins. They wouldn't have a chance to draw their guns."

I shivered.

"You never fired a gun at anyone when you were in the service."

"It doesn't take much training to hit someone in the belly with a shotgun."

He wasn't kidding. I was glad he wasn't kidding. They had to be ready.

"What if the people in the car emerged shooting after you had wiped out their leaders?"

"They probably would get the hell out of there as soon as they could. We each had a charge left in our gun. We could have reloaded."

"Nightmare material."

"I'm glad it never came to that. We would have had a lot of explaining to the local sheriff. Here's the first set, Rosemarie. Put them in the courier packs and put the packs at the front door. I'll go down when the bell rings."

"You will not! I have to get up at seven anyway to feed the kids breakfast."

"They can get their own breakfast."

"Sure they can, but I'm their mother . . . You need your sleep. I'll crawl back in after the kids leave for school."

He didn't argue. I have a much greater store of energy than my husband does. I can go much longer than he can before I drop. Eventually, however, I drop too.

"Hey," he said, just remembering something. "Here's the torn check."

He reached into his pocket and produced a check which was not only torn but crumpled, a bad show from a neatness freak.

"I'll put it in the pack for I Street," I said. It was too late to score points about his not being all that neat.

I checked and rechecked the courier packs—tape, photos ready to go to the District and to the St. Brigid's Winery. I sealed that courier pack.

Chucky came out of the darkroom with a second set of pictures.

"Put them at the door and then go to bed, Rosemarie my darling."

We kissed each other gently.

"You can do the other two sets in the morning."

"Three, one for Vince too. And no, I want to get this project cleared away before we have to face the North Shore crowd.

"Oh, dear God, poor Jane."

"She's free now, Rosemarie. Life would not have become any better for her."

I carried the two packs to the doorway. Not much weight to either of them, but perhaps the difference between life and death for the Raftery family.

I staggered up to the master bedroom and jumped back into bed. The alarm rang at 7:00. Where's my Chucky?

He was sitting at the worktable, sound asleep. I roused him and sent him up to bed. Worn-out little boy, he did what he was told. At seven-thirty the rest of the family appeared, just as I sent the courier away with the packages and fifty dollars for himself.

"Where's Daddy?" Shovie demanded.

"Upstairs. He fell asleep in the darkroom."

Peg called around ten.

"How you guys doing?"

"Chuck fell asleep in the darkroom, so he's up in bed finally. I had to get the kids off to school. Physically I'm okay."

"Ed and I visited April this morning. She didn't seem surprised. Poor Jane was going to do something like that, she said. Now at least she'll have some peace. She wouldn't consider staying home. April Rosemary and Jamie will bring her up there. He's a good doctor even if he's a shrink."

We agreed that we would meet in the parking lot of the funeral home and go in en masse. Peg and I would stand on either side of Mom at the far end of the receiving line.

Chapter Twenty-Seven

Chuck

A buzz on the phone. Someone wanted me. I picked up the phone.

"Chuck, I just got your materials, for which many thanks."

"That was fast."

"It's two in the afternoon . . . It's all I need to roll up that whole operation and get rid of some people whom we should have tossed out long ago. Many thanks."

"We're putting copies away in several unbreakable vaults."

"I take that for granted . . . It was good of the Rafterys, if I may call them that, to reject our check. It will make my case stronger, though it is strong enough."

"I'm delighted to hear that."

"It was an ugly and dangerous few moments. What would have happened if Jackson lost his mind completely?"

"I would have walked out with Joe's two loaded sawed-off shotguns and we would have terminated your cowboys."

"That would have been very dangerous."

"The four of them would be dead before they could draw their guns."

"Well, no one has ever questioned either your bravery or your intelligence. I'll look forward to seeing you the next time you're in the District."

Big deal warrior, striding out into the OK Corral to wipe out the Clantons. I probably would have frozen and sat down and cried my eyes out.

My wife bustled into the room. She was wearing her swimsuit and a terry-cloth robe.

"I have a big dish of spaghetti Bolognese down by poolside. Want to join me? You need a good swim to get the kinks out before we drive up to Kenilworth."

"I assume you listened to Cain?"

"I did. He is clearly one of the good guys."

"To the extent that is possible in the spook world."

So we went down to the pool and swam and ate pasta and, under an emerging sun, felt a little better.

The plan at the funeral home was that we would walk in as a body. Rosemarie and I would lead because we are, Mary Margaret told us, "intimidation resistant." Vince and Peg would follow with Mom. Then the rest of the clan, all very solemn and proper. We would find a chair for Mom on the far side of the casket from the McCormacks. Peg and Rosie would stand behind the chair. Father Ed would hover around them. Jamie and April Rosemary Nettleton would sit in the front row of chairs in case Mom needed some medical care. We would depart after an hour or so.

There was no special assignment either for me or my intermediate daughter. We had decided, however, that we would sit right behind Jamie and April Rosemary just in case there was need for dramatic intervention. I doubted that there would be. This was Faith, Hope, and Cadillac parish. The nastiness, such as it might be, would be verbal and indirect.

"Would you rather have me or Mom as your resistance colleague?" Mary Margaret had asked.

"Well, you're better at black belt than she is, but she's meaner than you are."

My wife demonstrated this skill when we entered the mostly empty funeral parlor. A tall, blond frenetic woman descended upon us, a Valkyrie without the music.

"It has been decided," she told us loudly, "that you may pay your respects, but you may not stand by the casket."

"Maddy," Rosemarie said calmly, "why don't you crawl back into the nest of the she-coyote that whelped you?"

Poor Maddy recoiled against the wall like she had been slapped.

I tried to choke back my laugh. Don't fool around with a *New Yorker* writer.

Chris disappeared before we arrived at the line of mourners. Between the rest of them and us there was only sympathy and love. Jenny and Micky had grown up, perhaps overnight, into mature and poised young women. Ted Junior smiled sadly at us. His distraught father repeated the words, "I loved her, I still love her, I'll always love her."

"What did I do wrong, Chuck?" he pleaded with me.

"Another psychiatrist would tell you that you did nothing wrong."

"That's too easy . . . Still, I hope that's how God sees it."

Mom knelt at the casket, Peg and Rosemarie on either side. This bloated, ugly corpse had once been the beautiful, bouncy baby daughter she and her husband had brought home from the hospital before the Great Depression. Jane, bright, cheerful, enthusiastic, had been the center of their lives and love.

Then an unattractive boy child with kinky red hair arrived on the scene, an enigmatic little punk. No threat to his big sister, who could simply ignore him. But then, in 1931 at the depth of the Great Depression, Margaret Mary, forever "Peg," appeared—radiant, gorgeous, irresistible. Jane had to learn then at five years old that a love which is shared is not diminished. Apparently she never learned it. It had not seemed so in our impoverished but happy lives on Menard Avenue. Perhaps it only became so when she moved away from the neighborhood and an errant gene had kicked off a manic-depressive syndrome.

But who could say? Must someone be responsible for every tragedy? Would God have to sort it out? Or was His love like that of April Mae Cronin, the love of a mother who doesn't have to sort things out.

Father Ed told us that the pastor would lead the wake services. We would say a few prayers for Jane. Three Our Fathers and three Hail Marys—standard penance in the church in which Jane Curtin O'Malley McCormack had been raised.

After the prayers, the O'Malley clan arranged itself in the first few rows of seats. She was ours, damn it, and we were not about to let her go without insisting on that. The Good April sat in the comfortable chair with her Amazonian guard. She was dry-eyed. Perhaps all cried out.

"You're right," my intermediate daughter nudged me, "Rosie is meaner than I am."

"Yes, but she has had thirty years to practice."

"There's that."

The local pastor led a wake service in which he preached about God's implacable love.

Then Father Delahaye arrived, a thin, loose, and untidy man, with a clerical vest and the old-fashioned high Roman collar, a figure from a fundamentalist television revival.

He swept to the front of the room and, without any words to the family, turned to the assembly.

"We will now pray, pray, pray for this holy and innocent woman who died an untimely death because of the paganism, materialism, consumerism, and secularism of modern American society. We also pray for the conversion of the hearts of all those here present who are responsible for her death. We'll pray for God's mercy on all of them. We will now say the Rosary, *the entire Rosary*, that Mother Mary will intercede for all the sinners present in this room."

He flopped to his knees in front of the casket and began the prayers in a singsong voice loaded with piety and monotony. It was worse than Father McNally's performance at Dad's wake. Why do these conservative clerics use the Rosary as an instrument with which to punish the laity?

I let him say the first decade, then gave the signal to my wife and my sister that it was time to leave. They nodded.

I would like to say we left quietly. But the assembled O'Malley clan can never do anything quietly.

The Good April went home with Peg, Vince, and Rita. Rosemarie drove us back to Euclid Avenue.

"Not bad all things considered," my wife observed.

"Until that terrible priest came," Mary Margaret said. "Why do they let men like that out of the nuthouse?"

"He will be preaching tomorrow and Chris will give the eulogy," I added.

"Vomit city," Mary Margaret said.

"We must do our best to act with dignity and respect to the Jane who was and who is now again and to the pain of the woman she was for a little while."

There was silence for a moment.

"You know, Chucky," my daughter broke the silence, "you might not make a half-bad priest."

The jazz group had wanted to play their horns at Calvary Cemetery just as they had at Queen of Heaven. I had vetoed the idea. It was the McCormack family's funeral. O'Malley craziness would only make the pain worse for Dr. Ted. They had agreed to my wisdom, reluctantly.

"Surrealistic" is the only word to describe the funeral mass. Well maybe you could also use the word "macabre." Ed said the words and presided over the prayers with his usual post counciliar grace. John Raven and Packy Keenan and the pastor of the parish, all in their monsignoral robes, lent dignity to the sanctuary.

Father Delahaye's homily, however, paid little attention to the deceased or her family. It was rather a thirty-five-minute jeremiad against the modern world and modern America and its obsession with sex, laced with quotations (many of them I'm sure apocryphal) from "Our Most Holy Father" which seemed to imply that he agreed with everything Fr. D had said.

Our friends in the sanctuary looked sick.

Chris McCormack outdid him. He vented all his feelings of hatred for the rest of the family, not by naming them exactly, but by describing the cold, harsh, punitive attitudes and behavior of those "closest to poor Mom." It was the obvious lack of love which had driven her to an early death. Their own lives would be punished because "what goes around comes around" in life. They too would die in an icy, loveless place.

"The young man has a genius for cliché, doesn't he?" Rosemarie whispered to me.

I noted with some interest that Joey Moran had appeared to squire my intermediate daughter, whether by previous agreement or not. She certainly did not dismiss him.

At the graveside, the burial service returned to the calm, restrained, but joyous liturgy. Father Ed recited the prayers with his usual grace and said a few words about God's maternal love. Across Sheridan Road, a solemn and peaceful Lake Michigan seemed to be watching with calm sympathy.

Peg and Vince were to drive Mom home and stay with her for a while. Rosemarie and I were to go to the dinner at their local club to sustain support for the McCormacks.

"Do you want to come with us?" I asked Mary Margaret.

"I have class this afternoon."

"What about a ride home?"

She glanced at Joey Moran who stood next to her, ye parfait knight.

"I guess I can find one."

"I think her eyes actually twinkled when she said she could find a ride home," Rosemarie said when we entered our old Benz. "She's revealing a little emotion about poor Joey."

"Matchmaker," I said with a disapproving sniff.

"Chucky darling, that match was made long ago."

The lunch at the local club was relaxed, mostly because Chris and Maddy had absented themselves. The Lord made them and the divil matched them. By the time we left new bonds had been fashioned between our family and the McCormacks. Crooked lines of God, maybe.

We picked our way back across the North Side of Chicago in search of Oak Park. I argued that we should take the Drive down to the Congress, but my wife insisted on driving to Harlem Avenue on Touhy, patently a mistake.

"How did you think April was?" she asked me as we waited at one of the many stoplights that would slow our trip home.

"Deep, deep inside herself. Not the flapper at all, nor Panglossa either."

"And maybe just clinging to her own life?"

"I sure hope not."

"I forgot all about Joe Raftery's dreams!" she exclaimed suddenly.

"I didn't."

"Bride Mary couldn't have known about the pictures."

"I don't see how."

"Then how could she send messages to her husband to talk to you?"

"I don't know."

"You've got to know . . . I got it! Joe knew in his preconscious or unconscious or something that you're good at lost causes."

"What lost causes?"

"Like Fenwick against Carmel . . . Like me . . ."

"You were never a lost cause, Rosemarie."

"Heck if I wasn't . . . Well that's what it had to be."

"I suppose so . . . Maybe some seraph invaded his dreams."

I didn't add that said seraph might have pushed my books off his shelf.

"Chucky Ducky," she changed the subject, "are you planning on love when we get home?"

"Yes, if we ever do get home. I was preoccupied with lascivious thoughts all through Mass about the woman next to me in the black dress."

"I was the woman next to you."

"Come to think of it you were."

So we went home for our nap and a celebration of the fundamental Catholic truth that life is stronger than death.

Conclusion

Mary Margaret

Well, I graduated from Rosary College finally. *Summa cum laude*, which I dismiss as irrelevant. No one will cut me any slack at Loyola Law School because of it. However, in my heart I am extremely proud, for which I hope God is not too angry.

The cycles of life seem to change each spring. New babies everywhere—Vangelisto O'Malley, to be called "Van"; Marianne Nettleton, to be called "Polly" after her grandmother; Charley's Patricia McGrath because as her cute husband Clete McGrath says it's both an Italian and an Irish name. She's likely to be Patty or maybe Patty Anne The first two, as might be expected seem to be redheads. I could write a version of the Sherlock Holmes story and call it "The League of Redheaded Women."

Both of Aunt Peg's sons are engaged, Gianni to an Armenian and Vinny to an Irishwoman. More grandchildren soon for Aunt Peg and Uncle Vince.

Chuck and Rosie are still obviously dizzy over each other. Her article in *The New Yorker* and their book about Russia stirred up a storm. Many of the critics said that he is a better photographer than he is a political analyst. He laughs and says, "Just wait!" He's busy collecting pictures of our various redheads. If I ever have any kids, they'll probably all be black Irish like my brothers.

Erin and Sean are edging close to engagement, maybe by Christmas, though maybe before so that, as Rosie says, we'll have another Christmas wedding.

The Joey Moran person graduated from Loyola, also *summa*

cum laude, much to everyone's surprise except me. He's going to Loyola Law School too, but that's not the way to put it. I gave up on sociology at THE University because I didn't need that place. Looking around for something else to do, I decided why not law and why not at Loyola—where Joey will be. Convenient, Chuck says. Rosie just laughs.

We have not discussed our future. However, we will ride to school together on the Lake Street L and the State Street Subway and study together. If we don't fight too much, our relationship will certainly grow and I might find myself expecting a ring the Christmas of our second year of law school.

I become very frightened as I think of that.

Yet Joey is a lot like Chucky—funny and tender, though not quite as crazy as Chuck is sometimes. However, maybe he's that way too and I'll discover it. Rosie says she realizes more each year who Chucky really is.

A couple from California came to visit us during the winter. Joe Raftery and his wife, along with their daughter Samantha, who's about Shovie's age. Nice people. Chuck and Rosie apparently did something wonderful for them.

Shovie is growing up too fast. She makes me feel ancient.

Father Jimmy said his first Mass and everyone was extremely happy. He'll make a fine priest.

The bad news is that Grams died.

She lived to see all the new great-grandchildren and for Father Jimmy's first Mass. Then one night she slipped away into paradise.

I was the one who found her, which was probably best. I visited her several times a week when I run. She always laughed at how I was all sweaty but didn't smell. This one morning I show up and Madge tells me that she's still asleep. Right away I run upstairs and open the door to her room. She looks so peaceful. I feel her forehead and know she's dead. I kiss her cold lips and say through my tears, "Good-bye, Grams. I'll see you again someday and I know you will always be with us." I kneel down and say a decade of the Rosary. Then I call Father Packy at St. Agedius. He says he'll be right over. Don't worry about Ed, he tells me. I'll bring him. Father Ed lives at St. Agedius.

Then comes the hardest call. I punch in our own number.

"Rosemarie Clancy," Rosie says, cool like always.

I don't know what to say, so I say it outright.

"Rosie, I'm here at Grams's. She woke up this morning in heaven."

She breaks down and so do I.

Among the sobs, I manage to say, "Father Packy is on the way over. I'll call Aunt Peg."

I get my act together and call Aunt Peg. Same exchange.

I call Madge and Theresa upstairs and continue the Rosary. I imagine that Grams is smiling at me. The last of the flappers. We're saying the Rosary when the rest of them arrive. They join in, I pass my rosary to Monsignor Packy. He smiles and shakes his head.

The family is completely devastated. Too much death in too short a time.

Rosie says to me, "I feel like my family doesn't exist anymore."

"You have six kids and six grandkids, what do you mean you don't have a family anymore?" I say, though I know exactly what she means. "Families change."

She looks at me in surprise, then smiles kind of wanly.

"The world of Menard Avenue is all gone."

"No it's not. It will always live in the memories of those who were there and in the stories that they have told to us who weren't there. Just like the first Rosemarie still lives."

She cries but she still smiles.

"I forgot I had a daughter who reads Proust."

This time I have to be the total Ms. Take Charge. Everyone else is too wiped out to do anything. Fortunately, I suspend my Miss Know It All mask and ask Rita Antonelli to help me. She's a feisty little Sicilian with wonderful eyes and a great smile. We've always been friendly, but never exactly close, which is probably my fault because some people say that I come on strong. Maybe there's a little rivalry there too because we're exactly the same age. Also she went to Notre Dame, which is probably only a venial sin. So we work out the details for the funeral, just like Aunt Peg and Rosie would if they were functioning.

"We're the new high command," she says as we prepare our lists.

"Time they had a rest," I agree.

We bond totally, which is a very good thing. She tells me that she's thinking of going back to her real name which is Margaret Mary, Aunt Peg's real name. I tell her I think it's a bitchin' idea.

I also receive emotional support from Joe Moran. I'm surprised at how good he is at it, but then I never gave him the opportunity before.

Rosie and Chuck, Aunt Peg and Uncle Vince, are destroyed altogether as Erin says. They cry all through the wake and funeral. Dr. Ted comes with my old friend Ted Junior and Jennifer and Michele, who are very sweet. They join the crying scene.

We have the Mass at St. Agedius. Father Ed and Father Jimmy concelebrate and Father Packy preaches. Aunt Peg gives the eulogy with her violin (which I suggested). She creates a musical portrait of Grams which is like off-the-wall sensational. We sing the *Ave Maria* and do "The Saints Go Marching In" at the cemetery.

Rosie and Aunt Peg cling to each other at the burial. THE woman in their life is gone. While neither of them is much like Grams in her personalities, deep down they're mirrors of her. It will be hard for them without her example of wifely and motherly love. Now they have to do that for the rest of us.

I'm pretty much in control of myself by then, though I break down during Aunt Peg's eulogy. Like Rosie says, all Grams wanted at the end of her life was to be with Gramps again. I can understand that. Someday, if my husband, whoever he may be, dies before me I'll probably feel the same way.

"WELL," I say to Rosie, "you're like the total family matriarch now."

She hugs me and says, "And I know who the number two is."

Which is kind of cool.

I look forward to going over to the Lake in a few days before I leave for Appalachia to help build homes. At the Lake this time of the year the promise of resurrection is everywhere.

Chicago
Indian Summer 2003

Note

The story of Bride Mary O'Brien is obviously fictional. But people who know tell me that stories not unlike hers are true.